"What if I want you to stay?" His
usky tone played havoc with her
enses.

he took a fortifying breath. "Forgive me for
eing blunt, but I can't afford to stay." *I'm far too
ttracted to you.*

low could she feel this strongly about him when
. hadn't been that long ago Ferrante had died? She
lidn't want to know the pain of loving someone
.gain, and was shocked at the strength of her
eelings for him already. A prominent man like
Stavros Konstantinos could have his pick of any
voman, but he could never be serious about *her.*
t wasn't worth risking her heart to stay around
.ny longer—especially when she'd be leaving
he country with her father in the not too distant
uture.

THE RENEGADE BILLIONAIRE

BY
REBECCA WINTERS

Published in Great Britain 2015
by Mills & Boon, an imprint of Harlequin (UK) Limited,
Eton House, 18-24 Paradise Road, Richmond, Surrey, TW9 1SR

© 2015 Rebecca Winters

ISBN: 978-0-263-25116-6

23-0315

Harlequin (UK) Limited's policy is to use papers that are natural, renewable and recyclable products and made from wood grown in sustainable forests. The logging and manufacturing processes conform to the legal environmental regulations of the country of origin.

Printed and bound in Spain
by CPI, Barcelona

Rebecca Winters lives in Salt Lake City, Utah. With canyons and high alpine meadows full of wildflowers, she never runs out of places to explore. They, plus her favourite vacation spots in Europe, often end up as backgrounds for her romance novels, because writing is her passion, along with her family and church.

Rebecca loves to hear from readers. If you wish to e-mail her, please visit her website at: cleanromances.com.

To my wonderful children, who put up with me while I write books of the heart. They know I love them, but they also know my mind is often somewhere deep into a love story of my own concoction.

CHAPTER ONE

AFTER WASHING THE sweat from his body, Stavros Konstantinos wrapped a towel around his hips and walked out on his terrace. The view of the blue Aegean from his private villa atop pine-covered Mount Ypsarion always renewed him.

Because of another of many such impasses, today's board meeting in Thessaloniki on the Greek mainland had ended early for him. His proposal for a new product to be manufactured and marketed by the Konstantinos Marble Corporation had met with total defeat.

At that point a blackness had swept through him. The sickness that had been coming on for the past year had finally caught up to him. Depression was a feeling he'd never known before, but he couldn't label it as anything else.

Knowing that his family members who made up the majority of the board still lived and operated as if it were 1950, he hadn't expected any other result. With the exception of his elder brother, Leon, everyone else down to the last cousin was against any new innovations and refused to hear him out. They were afraid of change.

That was fine with him. In his free time he'd had a new plant built on his own land. Now that the family had refused to listen to him and wanted no part of it, he and his two partners, Theo and Zander, would be starting production on Monday.

Since he'd gotten nowhere with the members of the board, he'd told them he was resigning from his position as managing director of the corporation immediately. As of now, all ties were severed, including his position on the board. He suggested they should start looking for a replacement ASAP.

Just saying those words helped to drive some of the blackness away. He'd been in a cage, but no longer.

While every member sat there in utter shock at his announcement, he excused himself from the meeting in Thessaloniki and took the helicopter back to his villa on Thassos Island. En route, he checked his phone messages and discovered another text message waiting for him from Tina Nasso, the woman he'd stopped seeing three months ago.

Since he'd never responded to any of her messages, why would she text him again? Was she so desperate?

This separation from u can't go on, Stavros. You've been so cruel. I haven't seen u or even heard your voice in three months! You haven't texted me back once. I have to talk to you! This is important. Tina.

This text meant she was still pressing for him to change his mind. His black brows came together. Christina Nasso, the woman his parents had expected him to marry, didn't know how to let something go that could never have worked out. With no intention of answering this text either, he deleted it.

Parental pressure had driven him to spend some time with her, but there was no attraction on his part. He had the gut feeling her parents were still pressuring her because they'd wanted an alliance between both families. Just as his parents had planned on him marrying her, it was no secret the prominent Nasso shipping family from Kavala wanted Stavros for their son-in-law. Both family businesses were closely connected.

But when she'd wanted a deeper intimacy with him, he couldn't pretend feelings he didn't have. Though he hadn't wanted to hurt her, he'd had to tell her the truth. He wasn't in love with her and they both needed to be free.

Stavros had told his parents the same thing after they'd demanded an explanation. His great mistake was humoring them from the beginning. Never again. They could wait, but a marriage with Tina wouldn't happen.

Today he'd felt the consequences of his actions. His refusal to go on seeing her had caused a serious rift, one he'd felt at the board meeting when his father had influenced his uncles and cousins to close ranks against his new business venture instead of embracing it.

As for Tina, his hope was that one day she'd meet someone her family would approve of. She was an attractive woman with much to offer a man who wanted to marry her. But Stavros wasn't that man. One day, Tina would realize it and move on. Like salt that had lost its savor, every relationship he'd had with a woman had been missing the essential ingredient for happiness.

The only thing that brought him any pleasure right now was spending every bit of time on his new business. Stavros's company wouldn't be in competition with his family's, but there would be fireworks when they found out he'd gone ahead with production. One of theirs was doing something on his own and they couldn't tolerate it. But it shouldn't be a surprise to them. He rarely bowed to the dictates of his autocratic father or his great-uncles.

For his mother's sake, he'd tried where Tina was concerned. But once she'd learned that her younger son wasn't enamored of the Nasso girl, he'd found disfavor in her eyes too. He took a deep breath. Today had turned out to be a day like no other. From here on out, his life was going to go in directions no one would be happy about except him.

So be it!

On his way to the kitchen to quench his thirst, his cell phone rang. If it was Tina calling because he hadn't answered her text, she would find out exactly how he felt when she realized he intended to go on ignoring any and all phone calls or texts from her.

But when he looked at the caller ID, he saw it was the manager of quarry three on Thassos Island phoning on his private line. He clicked on. "What's up, Gus?"

"*Kyrie* Konstantinos?" *Kyrie* being the Greek version of Mr. "A situation with one of the student-teacher groups from PanHellenic Tours has arisen. A teenager is missing. Now the police are involved."

This was all Stavros needed to hear, especially

since he'd been the only one on the board in favor of allowing tour groups to visit the quarry. The program had been working well since March with no incidents, until today...

Stavros gripped the phone tighter. "Have the police started a search?"

When he heard the particulars, he grimaced. A helicopter would have an almost impossible struggle to see any movement beneath the dense green canopy of the forest.

"What do you advise, Kyrie?"

"I'll be there ASAP."

He returned to the bedroom and dressed quickly before he dashed out the door to his car.

It had been his hope the quarry experience would broaden the students' education and spread the word about job opportunities.

Forty percent of the marble in Greece came from an almost inexhaustible supply in the Thassos region, much of it being shipped to China, Asia and Europe. Because of this abundant natural resource, more jobs were available, which would improve the Grecian economy, a major aim of his.

With that argument, his grandfather, who'd recently passed away, had been persuaded that the free publicity generated by various tour groups from foreign climes might be a good idea. At that point the rest of the board offered their reluctant acceptance on the condition that it would be for a trial basis only. One problem with the tours and they'd be given no more access.

This particular quarry—one of many owned by the family throughout northern Greece—was on the other side of the summit, just ten minutes away. He knew the police lieutenant well and would ask his cooperation in keeping the press at bay for as long as possible.

The crisis needed to be averted before the media got hold of it. Once they turned it into an international circus, the island would be crawling with unwanted spectators. Though the staff at the quarry wasn't responsible for what had happened, the public wouldn't see it that way. Publicity of this kind was never good.

To his mind, the teacher was ultimately responsible for this type of situation and could be facing charges. Six high school groups of six on the bus with their individual teachers? How hard was it to keep track of half a dozen students?

Gus had said the teen's teacher was a younger, nice-looking American woman. Maybe too young to handle a bunch of teens? Stavros pressed on the gas as he rounded a curve in the road. He was in a mood.

Once the family found out about this crisis, they'd put a stop to the tour groups. Since he'd announced his resignation from the corporation and the board, he would no longer have a say. But for the time being he felt the responsibility heavily. Someone's teenage son was missing in a foreign land and needed to be found.

Panagia was Andrea Linford's favorite village on the Greek island of Thassos. After flying from Thessaloniki to the nearby airport of Keramoti on the mainland, she'd come the rest of the way on the ferry to Thassos, the capital city many referred to as Limenas. From the water, the island looked like a floating forest because of the pines and olive groves covering it.

She'd rented a car and driven to Panagia, ten kilometers away. Named after the Virgin Mary, it was built on the side of the mountain. From the wooden terraces of the villas with their painted ceilings and schist roofs, one had a fantastic view of the bay and the sea beyond, where other emerald-green mountains rose to fill the eye. The sight of clear, ice-cold water bubbling up from the natural springs to run down alongside the narrow streets delighted her.

Andrea had spent time in its church of the Virgin Mary, which had been built in 1831. She loved its impressive baronial style, constructed by stones from the ruins of ancient temples. The exterior and cupola were a pale blue and white, absolutely exquisite.

She'd been in a lot of churches around the world, but the interior of this particular church was like a fabulous treasure. It contained a banneret dating from the time of the Crusades. She felt there was a spiritual essence she hadn't found in other churches. If she were ever to get married, this would be the spot she would choose, but of course that was a fantasy, just like the village spread out before her.

Today she didn't have time to linger.

For the past year and a half, Andrea had worked for PanHellenic Tours, in their main office located in Thessaloniki. They were one of the biggest tour operators in Greece. Having obtained her humanities degree from the university there, she had been hired to do translations and help develop tour itineraries by researching everything thoroughly.

Andrea was the person who'd first suggested the company include a tour of the quarry she found fascinating. Her boss, Sakis, was so taken with her idea, he'd made it part of their latest itineraries for this year. But word had gotten back to him that there'd been an incident involving an American student visiting the marble quarry on Thassos. The boy had gone missing and the police had been called in.

Because Andrea was fluent in English and Greek, and because she'd been the one to make the initial arrangements with the quarry manager, Sakis had sent her to do the troubleshooting, then report back her findings.

Before leaving the office in the cotton skirt and blouse she'd worn to work, she downloaded the student's file, including a picture, and itinerary on her phone.

Knowing the way to the quarry, which was famous for its pure white marble, she left the charming island village shaded by huge oak and walnut trees—a village that maintained some of the old traditions and ways of life. She followed the road up the mountain.

Thassos was truly an emerald island, almost round in shape. Some of the locals called it a giant lump of marble. She smiled as she wound around until she came to the quarry.

Many of the stone mines scattered all over the island were open pits. A tourist who didn't know better would think they'd come across an enormous, surreal graveyard of huge, pure white marble slabs and blocks surrounded by dark green pines. They glistened in the hot late-afternoon August sun.

She made her way to the quarry office of the Konstantinos Corporation, a world leader in the production of marble from their many quarries in northern Greece. Thanks to large investments in technology, the company processed marble and granite for internal and international markets.

At the east end of the quarry, she saw the tour bus and half a dozen police cars parked by the employees' cars. The officers were obviously vetting the group of students and teachers standing outside it.

She parked her car on the end of the row and got out. Georgios, the seasoned Greek tour guide, was a harmless flirt who always made her smile when he came to the head office, but today he looked grim, with good reason.

No sooner had she gotten out of the rental car to talk to him than the police lieutenant approached her. "Sorry, but no visitors are allowed here today."

"I've come from PanHellenic Tours," Andrea said in Greek. She introduced herself as a representative of the tour company and showed him her credentials. Normally she wore the blue jacket with the PanHellenic insignia, but it was too hot out.

"My mistake."

"No problem. Our office received word that one of the American students, a seventeen-year-old named Darren Lewis, disappeared during the tour of the quarry and hasn't been found. I'm here to help if I can. Any news yet?"

The mustached lieutenant frowned. "A helicopter has been making a sweep of the mountains. Some of the officers are out searching the area for him, but so far there's been no word."

"How long has he been missing?"

"Almost three hours. All the quarry employees have been accounted for. None could shed any light and were told to keep this quiet. We're about finished getting statements from the students and teachers. Then they're free to go on to their next stop in Thassos."

Three hours… It had taken her too long to get here. By now the dark blond boy could be hiding anywhere in these mountains. Thankfully, with the eighty-degree temperature, it wouldn't get too cold tonight, if he wasn't found by dark.

"Before they leave, I need to talk to the tour guide."

"Of course."

"Excuse me."

She hurried over to Georgios, the short, wiry Greek who knew this business backward and forward. "This is a ghastly thing to happen. How are you holding up?"

He shook his head. "I've been with the company for fifteen years and never lost anyone before. After the tour had finished, the quarry manager said the group could look around. You know the routine. I told them to be back at the bus in a half hour. Darren told his teacher, Mrs. Shapiro, that he needed to visit the restroom before heading for the bus."

"That's when he gave her the slip?"

"So it seems."

"She must be as devastated as you are."

He nodded. "We did a head count when everyone got on the bus, but he was missing. One of the students who had sat by him remembered he was wearing his backpack while they toured the quarry."

"In this heat you wouldn't want to be hampered by a backpack without good reason. It sounds like he might have had a plan before he ever arrived here," she theorized.

"That's what the police think too. I'm inclined to agree with them. The group knows to leave their belongings on the bus during an excursion, but it wasn't a hard, fast rule. After this experience, I'm going to insist on it. That is, if I don't get fired."

Andrea shook her head. "Sakis knows this isn't anyone's fault but Darren's," she assured him. But she knew how the public would react. Anyone and everyone would be blamed. "According to the file, he isn't on any medications, but that doesn't rule out the possibility of his taking recreational drugs. What's he been like?"

"Throughout the tour, his behavior didn't stand out one way or the other. His teacher says he's an honor student, somewhat on the quiet side." He scratched his head. "His parents have to be notified."

"I'll report back to Sakis and he'll take care of it if he hasn't already. Right now you've got a group of hungry, thirsty students and teachers who need attention. Go ahead and get them on board. I'll catch up with you later and help you any way I can."

"Thanks, Andrea."

She turned away just as a black Mercedes sedan suddenly appeared out of nowhere and drove right up, blocking her path. A tall, dark-haired male with a powerful build alighted from the front seat with an aura of authority that couldn't be denied. The man, maybe in his early thirties, was so ruggedly Greek and gorgeous, her mind went blank for a minute.

Before she averted her eyes to keep from staring at him, her gaze took in the lime polo shirt and light khaki gabardine pants. His clothes only emphasized his hard-muscled body. He wore a gold watch, but no wedding band and looked as expensively turned out as the gleaming black car he drove. Andrea had no idea such a man existed. Where had *he* come from?

"Kyrie Konstantinos!"

The lieutenant's exclamation, plus his show of deference, answered her question. This stranger with black hair swept back from a visible widow's peak had to be one of the men whose family owned and ran the internationally renowned corporation.

He shook the lieutenant's hand. "After the plant manager told me the news, I got here as soon as I could. Tell me what happened." The two men discussed the situation and talked about keeping this incident from the press while the search was ongoing.

Between impossibly black lashes, his dark gray gaze swerved to Andrea. For a heart-stopping moment, she was subjected to a thorough, faintly accusing male scrutiny of her face and body that made her go hot and cold at the same time. To have such a visceral reaction to a man she'd never met stunned her.

He broke off talking to the lieutenant and moved toward her. Switching to English, he said, "I take it *you're* the American teacher who was in charge of the runaway teen? How was it possible he disappeared on your watch?"

He'd fired the question with only a trace of accent. That didn't surprise her given his affluent background and education. What did surprise her was the fact that he'd correctly assumed she was American. Something about her had given her away. Furthermore, it seemed he'd decided that she was the teacher in question, the one whom he'd already tried, judged and convicted as the guilty party without knowing all the facts.

Andrea expected the lieutenant to step in at this point and explain, but his attention had been diverted by one of the officers. It was up to her to clarify the situation before he made any more erroneous assumptions.

"I believe introductions are in order first," she answered in Greek. "My name is Andrea Linford. I'm a representative of PanHellenic Tours in Thessaloniki. My boss sent me out to be of help to the tour guide, Georgios Debakis, and offer any assistance before I return to the office with my report."

She held out her hand, which he was forced to shake. His firm grip tightened a little before he released her, but she felt the imprint of his hand travel through her whole body and stay there. There it went again. That shocking sensation from just being in his presence. To fill the disturbing silence since he hadn't spoken yet, she said, "Which Konstantinos are you in the hierarchy? Leon, Stavros, Alexios or Charis?"

More silence ensued before he muttered, "Stavros." She'd studied the facts of the company on the way here and remembered that Stavros was managing director of the Konstantinos Corporation. "You've done your homework, Kyria Linford."

"Despinis," she corrected him. She wasn't married.

"My apology for misreading the situation."

His apology had been difficult for him to verbalize, but she would cut him some slack. "You were half-right. For all my sins, I am American. But I'm not poor Mrs. Shapiro, who no doubt you assumed didn't have the maturity to handle a group of teenage students away from their parents. If I'm wrong in that assumption, then *my* apology."

His intelligent eyes flickered with some unnamed emotion. "You weren't wrong," he admitted in his deep voice.

"Thank you for your honesty. I think we can both agree this is an ugly situation all the way around and no one is at his or her best. My boss is beside himself. He has to make the call to the teen's family and explain that their son is missing. Hopefully they'll supply him with a reason why he might have run off midtour."

"Let's hope he's found within the hour."

She nodded her blond head. "We all want that. Unfortunately, his disappearance happened on your company property and will put the Konstantinos name in the spotlight, bringing you adverse publicity. As for poor Mrs. Shapiro and Georgios, they'll be in agony until Darren's found."

He raked a bronzed hand through his gleaming black hair. "I asked the lieutenant to keep this quiet for as long as possible."

"I heard you. Let's hope one of the officers doesn't leak it for a while. That boy has got to be found!"

Her voice shook because she was remembering the long ten-day wait before her fiancé's dead body had been spotted on the mountain ledge, dashing her dreams for their marriage. The thought of Darren's parents having to wait that long for any news made her shudder, a reaction Kyrie Konstantinos observed while he studied her.

She tore her eyes from his in time to see the tour bus drive out of the parking area to the road. Her heart was heavy for the teacher and Georgios, who had to keep doing their jobs while they were dying inside. Andrea felt anxious over the situation too. Where *was* Darren?

"With only a three-and-a-half-hour head start, he can't get too far." The incredibly handsome Greek read her mind aloud.

Andrea folded her arms to her waist. "Did you know he has his backpack with him? I wonder if he'd been planning his escape long before today in order to survive while he was on the run."

"If so, he picked the right spot. It's true these mountains will give him cover and the forest is dense, but I've lived here all my life and know every inch of ground. If the search and rescue teams don't find him, *I* will."

Stavros Konstantinos instilled such confidence in her, Andrea had no doubts he could do anything. She was alarmed by her thoughts about him—considering he was a stranger, she shouldn't have been thinking about him at all. "You'll need his description and a picture. I can email the information in his file to your phone right now."

He pulled out his cell and gave her his number. Within a minute, he'd received it. She watched him study the dark blond boy's passport photo. "He's nice looking with that Marine cut. It says he's five-eleven with brown eyes. He'll be easy enough to recognize."

"Unless he was carrying a disguise in his pack. Maybe turn himself into a woman?"

He flicked her another searching glance that sent a curl of physical awareness through her. "That would definitely throw anyone looking for him off the scent. I'll pass your idea on to the lieutenant in case he hadn't thought of it. You never know.

"Perhaps you noticed Darren's birth date on the passport. He turned eighteen yesterday, which makes him an adult."

"I didn't catch that." This man's mind was a steel trap.

"What else do I need to know about him?"

She sucked in her breath. "My boss found out Darren comes from a well-to-do Connecticut family, so he probably has enough money on him to last for a while. Maybe he planned this before leaving the States, possibly with someone else who's waiting for him at another destination."

"Anything's possible."

"My guess is he'll try to leave the island by boat rather than ferry. I've been studying my map of Thassos. There are dozens of harbors. How hard would it be for him to pay a fisherman to take him somewhere else and escape under the radar, so to speak?"

His eyes narrowed on her features. "It sounds like you've had experience with this kind of thing before."

"Some," she admitted. But not while she'd been working for the tour company.

"If he tries to get away in a boat, the harbor police will be onto him. In the meantime, I'll head back to my house to change and go after him. As I recall, your tour brochure mentioned the Dragon Cave near Panagia."

"Yes. They would have toured it this morning."

"Then he might have decided to go there to hide for the night."

"You're right." She hadn't thought of that. "You'd make an excellent detective if you hadn't been born a Konstantinos." The comment had slipped out of her mouth before she could stop it. What in heaven's name was wrong with her?

After a pause his lips twitched. "There's a thought." His amused tone played havoc with her breathing.

Andrea had visited the Dragon Cave months ago. It contained amazing stalactites and stalagmites. She'd seen the stalactite shaped like a dragon. "The literature says the cave hasn't been fully explored." Fear clutched her heart to think Darren might be foolish enough to penetrate a danger zone.

"I'll check there first. There's no time to waste."

"Kyrie Konstantinos—" She thought he was about to walk away and wanted to stop him. He eyed her with such a penetrating gray gaze, she felt he could see right through her. This important man was ready to drop everything to look for a boy he didn't know. With the police already doing a search, he didn't have to do it and no one would expect it of him.

On top of his overwhelming male attributes, there was a goodness in him she could feel. The combination startled Andrea. She felt drawn to him in ways she couldn't explain and would have to analyze later. "I'd like to go with you and help."

He looked stunned. "Why would you want to get involved?"

"Because in a sense this is my fault. I'm the one who asked the quarry manager if we could bring our tours here. These quarries have been worked for a thousand years, yet many tourists still aren't aware of their existence. I find them fascinating and convinced my boss to agree to the idea of a tour here in the first place."

His head reared back in surprise. "*Your* idea?"

"Yes. I can only imagine how much you wish your quarry manager had said no to me. I realize everything is a risk, but you could have no idea how responsible I feel now that this has happened on your company's property. And to be honest, there's another reason..."

She felt his gaze travel over her. "What would that be?"

"Eighteen months ago I lost my fiancé. He was a mountain-climbing guide who'd gone up on Mont Blanc with some other climbers. They were caught in a terrible storm. When it was discovered he was missing, I was told I couldn't assist in the search because it would be too dangerous."

"I'm sorry," he whispered. Immediately, his eyes softened with compassion. She could feel it.

"I had to wait ten agonizing days until they found his body on a ledge. When I think of this boy's parents hearing the news that their son is missing, I can't stand by and do nothing." Her eyes smarted with unshed tears. "Even if I'm not able to do any good, I want to help in the search for him."

She heard him inhale sharply. "You can add me to that list of people who feel responsible because *I'm* the person Gus appealed to for permission to allow tours here."

A small cry escaped her lips. "I knew he would have to go through channels. What a surprise to find out it was *you*." Incredible.

"I'd say today has brought several surprises. But I don't regret giving permission, not even under these circumstances."

She took an unsteady breath. "Neither do I. Hundreds of students and teachers have benefited from what they've learned here."

"That's been my hope too."

His words warmed her. She sensed he was a man she could trust. It was her own unexpected attraction to him she didn't trust. "Whatever the outcome, please don't worry that you'll be liable. The tour company will take full responsibility."

In the silence that followed, she took it to mean he *was* thinking about a possible lawsuit from the boy's family once their attorney found out the Konstantinos family's worth was in the millions. She wouldn't blame this man for having no use for today's litigious society. It was also apparent he wasn't keen on her help.

Disappointed that she couldn't be of help, she started to walk around his car to get to hers.

"Despinis Linford?"

Andrea whirled around.

"You're welcome to come with me. But we could be out all night."

All night alone with him? Her heart thudded for no good reason—except that wasn't true. She knew exactly why it was thudding. She wanted to be with him. "I don't care about that. If we can find Darren, that's all I ask."

"Then we'll have to go back to my house for a few provisions."

"Thank you. I'll follow you."

She got back in the rental car. En route, she called her boss and told him what was going on. Then she phoned Georgios and explained that she was going to help in the search for Darren and would keep in close touch. He thanked her in a shaken voice before they hung up.

The fact that Darren was now eighteen meant he was no longer a minor. Maybe his parents had given him this tour for a birthday present. To Andrea, his disappearance was more troubling than ever. As an adult, he could do what he wanted.

Andrea didn't think she could handle it if anything happened to him before he was reunited with his parents. It hadn't been that long since Ferrante's death. Being hired by PanHellenic Tours had saved her life and she was doing better these days. But Darren's disappearance triggered remembered pain from that terrible ten days when she'd waited for word.

CHAPTER TWO

THROUGH THE REARVIEW MIRROR, Stavros watched the rental car following him to the house. Andrea Linford had come as a complete surprise in so many ways; he was still in mild shock. Her Greek was amazing, but there was a lot more to her than her linguistic ability.

When he'd first laid eyes on her, he'd jumped to the wrong conclusion. To his chagrin, the first words to come out of his mouth had been accusatory. But she'd turned the tables on him with that very maturity he'd thought had been lacking. Over the course of a few minutes, he'd found himself utterly overwhelmed by the unexpected strength of his feelings for her.

The fact that she wanted to help find a boy she'd never met revealed a depth of character that appealed to him. For her to confide her agonized feelings to Stavros over the death of her fiancé—to have felt so helpless while she'd waited for word of him—it had torn him up inside.

The shocks kept coming. Since she'd been the one to plan an itinerary that included a tour of the quarry, she must be a person who thought outside the box. He found that intriguing.

As for her physical attributes, those long legs and

the way she moved her shapely body had branded her an American. She was a natural, honey-blonde beauty with deep, sky-blue eyes who needed no makeup to be attractive.

No wonder Gus hadn't been able to turn her down when she'd approached him on behalf of PanHellenic Tours. She'd probably had that same effect on her boss, who couldn't help but hire her.

Hell. She'd had that effect on *him* or he wouldn't have agreed to let her come along to search for the boy. Talk about a day like no other!

When he reached the house, he pulled around the back next to his Jeep. She parked on the other side of him. He tried not to stare, but he couldn't help glancing sideways when she got out of her car. In an odd way, her sensible walking shoes only drew more attention to those beautiful legs of hers.

"Come in the house and freshen up in the guest bathroom while I gather a few items. I'll pack some food and drinks so we can eat along the way."

"Let me help."

Once inside the rear entrance, he showed her where to go before he loaded up a food hamper in the kitchen. With that done, he walked through the house to the bedroom to change into jeans and a crew-neck shirt.

After checking with the police lieutenant, who had no good news to report yet, Stavros pulled on his hiking boots, then drew some parkas and sweaters from his closet. On the way back to the kitchen, he stopped in the storage room for his large flashlight and extra batteries. A smaller flashlight was in the Jeep.

His soft top was loaded with everything else they

might need: blankets, a small tent, a bedroll, a couple of fold-up camp chairs and extra petrol. He was always prepared in these mountains. Whether they found Darren tonight or not, they'd be comfortable.

Stavros had never taken a woman camping with him. It was going to be a novel experience. He realized he was looking forward to being with her. When he'd walked out of the board meeting for the last time earlier in the day, little had he dreamed that by nightfall he'd be searching for a runaway teen with this lovely woman.

When Andrea saw him coming, she relieved him of the coats and sweaters so he could carry everything else. They left the house and hurried out to the Jeep. By the time they were packed up and ready to go, twilight had fallen over the lush landscape.

He started down the road toward another one that would lead to the Dragon Cave. "Did you talk to your boss?"

"Yes. He's already informed Darren's parents. They'll be on the next plane to Thessaloniki."

"Could they shed any light concerning their son?"

"No. He's a scholar who'll be attending Yale in the fall. They're baffled and in agony.

"Sakis told me not to come back to work without the boy. That's how anxious he is."

"We'll find him."

"Since this is your backyard, I believe you."

Her faith in him was humbling. "How about digging in that hamper for a couple of sandwiches. My housekeeper makes them up for me."

"Sure."

She turned around on her knees and reached in the

hamper behind his seat. Her movement sent a faint flowery scent wafting past his nostrils, igniting his senses, which had been in a deep sleep for longer than he cared to remember. After handing him one and taking one for herself, she pulled out two ice-cold bottles of water.

They rode for a few more minutes before she asked, "How high up are we?"

"About four thousand feet."

"That's high for an island. Have you climbed to the top of Mount Ypsarion?"

"Many times." He darted her a glance. "Have you ever climbed a mountain?"

"Yes. Mount Kilimanjaro."

At her unexpected answer, Stavros let out a whistle. "That's over nineteen thousand feet high."

"I found that out when I needed to stay on the oxygen above fourteen thousand feet. My dad took me up while he was working in Tanzania."

Fascinated, he said, "Does he still work there?"

"No. From there he was sent to French Guiana for two years, then India for three. Later he spent two years in Paraguay and another two in Venezuela. From there he was sent to the Brusson area of northwestern Italy for three years. Then he came to northern Greece. We live in Thessaloniki, where I got my degree in history and archaeology from Aristotle University."

Stavros marveled. "What does your father do?"

"He works for W.B. Smythe, an American engineering company in Denver, Colorado, where I was born. Gold practically built the state. His company designs and fabricates modular plants and equipment for the extraction of gold and silver. As of this year, they've established a global presence in twenty-four countries. From the time I was born, I've lived with my father wherever he was sent." He'd be going to Indonesia next.

"How many languages do you speak?"

She let out a sigh. "Besides the obvious, I'm fluent in Italian and French, and speak some Hindi, Afrikaans, Swahili, Spanish and Guarani. It's no great thing. You have to learn a country's language while you're there if you hope to survive. Lucky for Darren, a lot of your countrymen speak English."

"Amen." He cleared his throat. "What about your mother?"

"She died giving birth to me."

He smothered a moan. *No mother*...

"Dad and I have been nomads, traveling the globe. He was the one who taught me about the white marble quarries here."

The feminine fountain of knowledge sitting next to him was blowing him away. Everything about her had already gotten under his skin. "What exactly did he tell you?"

"Besides the fact that the quartz crystalline structure resembles freshly fallen snow and is only quarried on this island?"

"Besides that."

"He passed on a piece of trivia I found interesting. The visual effects team working on the American films of the *Twilight* saga used very fine pure white Thassos marble dust, which they added to the face paint. That's why there's this incredible sparkling effect when sunlight touches the vampires' skin! Trust my dad to know details like that. He's the smartest man I ever met."

Stavros filed the information away. "Have you told him that lately?"

"All the time."

"Lucky man." Since Stavros's father already believed he was the smartest man living, Stavros had never paid him such a compliment.

"I'm the lucky one to have a father like him."

"You know what I think?"

She flicked him a curious glance.

"Despinis Linford is the smartest woman *I* ever met."

"Hardly." Another troubled sigh passed her lips. "Please. Call me Andrea."

"Then I insist you call me Stavros."

"The sign of the cross. A holy name."

"My parents regret giving it to me. I'm afraid I'm the *apololos provato* of their brood."

She turned her head to look at him. "You? The black sheep of the Konstantinos family? Why would you say such a thing?"

"Maybe because I choose to do things other than live up to my father's dreams for me."

"It sounds like you have dreams of your own and think for yourself. There's nothing wrong with that. You ought to wear it as a badge of courage rather than a curse."

A curse. That was exactly what it had been like, but she made it sound like something to be proud of. A different way to look at himself? How did she manage to do that without even being aware of her power? The thought was daunting because he realized he could really care about her. That was a complication he didn't need right now.

"You're fortunate to have a father who approves of you."

"You mean yours really doesn't?"

"Afraid not." His voice grated. "Your incredulity tells me how different our fathers are. In my whole life, we've rarely seen eye to eye on anything. Unless it's his way, it isn't right."

"But you're obviously successful!"

"Not in his eyes."

"That's horrible." Her voice shook. "How painful for you."

"I'm used to it."

"Even so, I can hear the hurt in your voice deep down." Her keen perception astounded him. She studied him for a minute. "For what it's worth, I approve of you."

"Why?"

"When we first met, you were ready to give me a full interrogation at the quarry. But after I introduced myself, you listened, and in your unique way, you apologized and let me look for Darren with you. I find that admirable and think I like you much better now."

Andrea Linford, where did you come from?

Little did she know he already liked her to the point he was ready to carry her off to an unknown location where they could get to know each other for as long as they wanted, undisturbed by anything or one. It shocked him that he would entertain such a thought when he'd only just met her.

They'd neared the trail that led to the cave. It was

getting too dark for tourists to be out. Stavros had been watching for anyone walking along the winding stone road bordered by heavy underbrush.

He pulled to a stop. "We'll have to go on foot from here. Grab one of the parkas. I know it'll drown you, but it will also keep you warm. The temperature inside the cave is always cooler, especially at night. Darren might not be here. If he isn't, then let's whisper once we get inside while we wait and turn off the flashlights. In case he does show up, we don't want our voices and lights to scare him off before we approach him."

"Understood."

Andrea understood about a lot more things than he could have imagined.

They both got out and put on a coat. She reached for two bottles of water she could carry in the pockets of her parka.

He handed her the smaller flashlight, making sure it worked, then turned on the big one. After throwing a blanket over his shoulder, he locked the Jeep. Before he knew it, she'd gone down the path ahead of him. Because of the overgrowth of mountain foliage, it grew so narrow in spots that they had to proceed single file. So far, they hadn't seen anyone.

Soon, they came to the large mouth of the cave. It looked like a dark hole. He moved past her, flashing his light around the interior for any sign of the teen. They went deeper, until the shaft of light lit up the dragon-like stalactite. Though it was always dark in the cave, the night gave it added menace.

If Darren intended to hide in here, Stavros doubted he'd go much farther for fear of getting lost. He turned to Andrea and put his lips close to her ear. Again, he was assailed by the delicious scent of her. Maybe it was the shampoo from her wavy dark blond hair, which fell loose to her neck. "Let's sit here awhile and see if he comes."

Andrea nodded and edged away in order to counter-act the feel of his warm breath against her skin. He hadn't touched her, but he didn't have to for her to be intensely aware of him. After he spread out the blanket, she sat down cross-legged. In the next moment he'd taken the same position facing her.

The last thing she saw before they turned off their lights was the bone structure of his striking eastern Macedonian features. He was fiercely male, *all* of him.

Just thinking about all of him made her swallow hard. She felt the cool darkness enshroud them. If she was nervous and disturbed, it wasn't because they were in a cave that was black as pitch. Something had happened to her from the moment Stavros Konstantinos had alighted from his car looking like a Greek statue come to life. It was so strange because she hadn't been interested in any man since Ferrante.

"Do you know what a rare creature you are?" His whisper came out of the darkness.

Her body trembled in reaction. "Why do you say that?" she whispered back.

"Because your behavior is so perfect, you've forced me to break the silence in order to tell you so."

Andrea couldn't help but smile. "I learned early in life that most men don't like chatter. Of course, my father isn't like most men. I loved him and always wanted to go with him wherever he was sent."

"Is he waiting for you in Thessaloniki?"

"No. He stays in a village near the Skouries mine for three weeks at a time. Then he comes to our furnished apartment in the city to see me for a week. While I'm at the office, he cooks up a storm for us. I take time off when he arrives so we can explore the sites together."

"Your father never married again?"

"I once asked him that question because he's had his share of girlfriends. He told me that because he has to move around the globe every so often, he decided it would be too difficult to be married. Plus, he said, I was the only child he wanted."

"I can understand that. Both his reasons make perfect sense. Would you have liked a stepmother?"

No one had ever asked her that question. "I don't know, since I never grew up with my own mother. To be honest, I didn't care for some of his girlfriends and they didn't care for me, so I'm glad he didn't marry one of them."

She could hear a change in his breathing. "How old are you, Andrea?"

"Twenty-six. And you?" she fired back, growing more curious to know everything about him.

"Thirty-two. Tell me about the man you were going to marry."

He'd changed the subject fast.

"Ferrante was Italian-Swiss from Ticino. He came from a large family with five brothers and sisters of whom he was the eldest. I've never met anyone so happy and friendly. Some people have a sunny spirit. He was one of them."

In the silence that followed, a warm hand reached

out and found one of hers to squeeze. "I'm sorry you lost him."

His sincerity reached the deepest part inside her, but Andrea wished he hadn't touched her. Still, she didn't pull away because she didn't want to offend him when he was trying to give her comfort.

"I'm much better these days. What about you? Do you have a girlfriend?"

He removed the hand that had spread warmth through her body. "Like your father, I've had my share."

"But so far you've stopped short of marriage."

"Yes."

"That *yes* sounded emphatic," she observed. "With a last name like yours, I guess you can't be too careful."

"Your perceptiveness must be a gift you were born with."

"I think it's the influence of my rather cynical father."

"So he *does* have one flaw..." His response sounded almost playful. "I was beginning to worry."

"Why?"

"A perfect father is hard to live up to."

"Are we talking about mine?"

She was waiting for his answer when she heard a faint noise. Andrea supposed it could be a rodent running around, but she hoped it was Darren and jumped to her feet. In the process, her body collided with Stavros, who was also standing, and he wrapped her in his strong arms.

"Don't make a sound." This time his lips brushed

her cheek while he whispered. Instantly rivulets of desire coursed through her bloodstream.

While she stood there locked against his well-honed frame, there was more noise, a little louder than before. Whatever made the sound was getting closer to them. Stavros must have been holding his flashlight because he turned it on in time to see a ferret scurry away.

Andrea relaxed against him, but Stavros still held on to her. No longer whispering, he said, "It's past eleven o'clock. If Darren had planned to come here tonight, he would have arrived by now, don't you think?"

She eased out of his arms and turned on her flashlight so he couldn't tell how much his nearness had turned her body to mush.

"I do." Until she got herself under control, Andrea wasn't capable of saying anything else.

"Since the lieutenant hasn't phoned me with news yet, that means Darren's still out there, but I doubt he'll do any more hiking before first light." He scooped up the blanket and folded it. "Since he's not here, it's possible he took the trail leading away from the quarry that eventually goes down the mountain. There are firebreaks that crisscross it. We'll take one, then another. Hopefully we'll locate him."

"That sounds like a good plan." Together they left and made their way back to the Jeep. The slightly warmer air outside the dank cave felt good, but she kept the parka on. Once they'd climbed inside, he started it up and they took off at a clip. He turned on his brights to help them in their search. Andrea drank some of her water, thankful he knew where to drive.

"Are you hungry, Stavros?"

"Another gyro sounds good."

She turned around and got another one out of the hamper and handed it to him. He'd also packed some plums, so she took one for herself and settled back to eat. "Seeing Thassos Island in the dazzling light of day isn't anything like driving through this forest at night."

"Not so benign, is it?"

A shiver passed through her. "No. Wherever our runaway is, he couldn't be feeling as comfortable about his plan right now. My boss checked with the American consulate. Darren has never been issued a passport before. Since this is his first trip to Europe, it's amazing he'd be willing to run away from the tour in a place so foreign to him. He has to be desperate."

"Or adventurous and headstrong," Stavros suggested, "and too spoiled to realize how hard this has to be on his parents or anyone who cares about him."

She had a hunch he was talking about his younger self. "We have to find him before the press turns his disappearance into an international incident."

"You took the words out of my mouth." His voice sounded an octave lower and resonated to the marrow of her bones.

At the first crossroads they came to, he braked and turned right. "While I drive slowly, shine the big flashlight into the trees. We'll take turns calling out his name. If he's hurt and needs help, he might show himself."

"That's a good idea, but if he wants to stay hidden—"

"Then the sound of our voices will make him nervous that people are looking for him," Stavros supplied. "Hopefully he'll try to run and in the process give himself away."

For the next half hour, he drove them over one rough firebreak, then another. "There doesn't seem to be any sign of him, Stavros. Do you think it's possible he hid himself in one of the employees' vehicles while no one was paying attention? Maybe the back of a truck or the trunk of a car?"

Andrea noted the grim expression marring his arresting features. "Those are the first places I assumed the police had looked before I got there. But if they weren't thorough enough…" His voice drifted off.

"Do all the workers live nearby?"

"Their homes are in or around Panagia. If that's what Darren did, then he could lose himself among the tourists in the morning."

Andrea nodded. "With enough money, he could buy a bike or steal one. Once in Thassos, he could take the ferry to the mainland."

For the second time that night, Stavros clasped the hand nearest him. "Who should have been the detective now?" Heat passed through her system in waves before he let it go. "I'll find us a place to camp on the outskirts of Panagia."

The gorgeous man at the wheel had no idea that the thought of spending the rest of the night with him sent her pulse ripping off the charts.

"We can try to get some sleep for what's left of the rest of this night. In the morning, we'll make early rounds of the bike shops."

"We might actually bump into him."

"Or her," he added. "If he's wearing a disguise."

He hadn't forgotten what she'd said. "If not there, maybe at the ferry landing."

"I want to believe that." She was worried sick about Darren of course. Stavros couldn't help but hear the tremor in her voice.

"That makes two of us."

Before too long, he found them a secluded spot. "Do you mind if we don't set up the tent?" His question prompted her to lift her gaze to him, noticing the shadow on his firm jaw. If anything, he was more attractive when he needed a shave.

"No. It's a beautiful night. I've slept out with my father like this hundreds of times. A tent is too confining and we could miss spotting Darren if he were to come this way."

"You're too good to be true. I think I must be dreaming."

"You'll know this is for real if I scream out loud because another ferret the size of the one in the cave creeps onto me."

With a low resonant chuckle he unraveled the bedroll for her to sleep in and made himself a bed on a couple of blankets. They both ate and drank from the contents of the hamper. Then she snuggled into the bedroll and turned on her side toward him.

"Stavros? Thank you for letting me search for Darren with you. I appreciate everything you've done, not only for me, but for him. You're a remarkable man." He was a lot more than that. She needed to turn off her feelings for him. They were spinning out of control.

"Don't give me any credit," he said. "I have just as much at stake here as you. And how long it's taking to find him is convincing me he's more clever than I realized." His hand went to his watch. "I'm setting my alarm so we'll have time to grab some breakfast at one of the cafés first thing in the morning." Andrea watched him pull out his phone. "I'm going to leave a message for the lieutenant about our plans for tomorrow. Then it's lights out."

She turned off her flashlight while she listened. In a minute, he shut the big light off and stretched out on his back with only one blanket pulled over him. He put his hands behind his dark head. "You're a very trusting woman to be out in the forest with me."

"I know the important things," she came back readily. "I did my research and learned that the Konstantinos Corporation enjoys an excellent reputation far and wide for the quality of their products and their fair dealings. The fact that you cared enough to look for Darren on your own time when you didn't have to says a lot about your character."

His compassion and understanding of her loss had really been the things that told her he could be trusted. But she refrained from sharing that with him.

"I'd rather talk about your character, Andrea. No one would expect you to have joined in the search. I'm touched that you would tell me about your harrowing experience waiting to hear news of your fiancé."

She stirred restlessly. "I couldn't just stand by this time. You'd be surprised how many searches I've gone on in the past."

"What do you mean?"

"Living in some of the third-world areas meant helping out in a crisis at a moment's notice. In some ways, it was easier to find someone's lost son or daughter from a remote village than to track down a teen like Darren who wants to be lost in a country as modern and sophisticated as Greece. With money he could be anywhere doing anything. His poor parents must be frantic."

Stavros turned on his side. "Has this happened before on one of the tours?"

"There've been a few serious health issues, but no one ever left in the middle of a tour before. Georgios has been with PanHellenic fifteen years and said he's never had someone disappear on him."

"It's a bizarre situation, one we can't solve tonight."

"You're right. Good night, Stavros." She rolled onto her side away from him.

"Kalinychta, despinis."

His silky voice permeated her body, as if it had found a home. The sensation shocked her before oblivion took over.

The alarm awakened Stavros at six thirty. He hadn't wanted the night to end and was surprised he'd slept. Probably knowing he'd be with her first thing in the morning was the reason he'd fallen off fast. For the first time since he could remember, a woman had come into his life who excited him in inexplicable ways.

Andrea was still asleep, her shiny blond hair splayed around her. He could still feel her wrapped in his arms in the cave. Between that memory and the intensity of those blue eyes fastened on him last night, it was all he could do not to move closer and draw her into his body. But until the boy was found, he needed to focus on matters that could have an adverse impact on everyone involved.

He packed up and started putting everything in the Jeep. When he went back for the hamper, he discovered Andrea had awakened and was rolling up the bedroll.

"Good morning, Stavros." Her smile filled his body with warmth. "How long have you been up?"

"A few minutes."

"Don't tell me if I snore. Some things are better not to know."

She looked so beautiful with her hair in attractive disarray it took all his self-control not to kiss her voluptuous mouth. "You were quiet as a mouse."

"So were you. I think." Despite the seriousness of their situation, she didn't take herself seriously, a trait that appealed to him. They both chuckled.

He took the bedroll from her and put it in the back of the Jeep. She joined him a few minutes later. He noticed she'd brushed her hair and put on a frosted pink lipstick he'd love to taste before he started on her.

Stavros was thunderstruck by his strong physical attraction to her. But right now he needed to concentrate. "Let's go find Darren."

Once they got in the Jeep, he drove back out to the road that led into Panagia. He stopped in front of a cafeteria, where they went in for rolls and coffee. The proprietress recognized him and hurried over to their table.

He questioned her about Darren and showed her his picture from the cell phone. She said she hadn't seen the American teenager in her café, but she'd call the police if he came in.

For the next half hour, they made the rounds of the bike shops. No one had seen the missing teen. When they went back to the Jeep, Andrea turned to him. "I think we should drive to Thassos and watch for him at the marina. He may have stolen someone's bike in order to get there."

"Or maybe he hitched a ride with some local."

"Let's check out all the bars and *tavernas* at the docks. He could be hanging out near the ferry landing stage."

"The police will be searching everywhere, but we'll add our eyes."

For the next two hours, they covered the waterfront, but didn't see anyone who resembled Darren. "Stavros? Let's go on board the ferry that's loading and take a look inside the vehicles. I know the police will have already done that, but maybe they missed something. What do you think?"

He saw the pleading in her eyes. It tugged at him. Neither of them wanted to give up the search, even if the police had already looked here.

"You're reading my mind again."

This was the first ferry of the day leaving for Keramoti. If Darren wanted to get off the island as fast as possible, this would be the one to take.

After parking the Jeep, he paid the fee and they walked on board, following the line of passengers. Since it was a Saturday of full-on summer, crowds of tourists slowed the lines down. He saw two police officers working the line.

Those people with cars had parked them end to end along the sides of the open air hold.

While everyone else went up on the deck to watch

their departure, Stavros and Andrea inspected the interiors of each vehicle. All were empty. There were several small trucks. They eyed each other before he looked in the back of the first one. It was filled with lawn mower equipment.

Andrea moved forward to look inside the back of the next truck parked farther down. Stavros knew she'd found something when she came running toward him. "Quick," she whispered. "There's a tarp covering something. I thought I saw movement and I don't dare lift it off without you."

He grasped her upper arms. Their mouths were only centimeters apart. It was a miracle he restrained himself from kissing her senseless. "You stay here."

Her breathing sounded shallow. "I won't let you do this alone."

Stavros inhaled sharply. "Then stay behind me." After letting her go with reluctance, he walked to the pickup truck in question and took a look for himself. In the next instant, he climbed over the tailgate. Reaching down, he removed the tarp. Sure enough, a body dressed in jeans and tennis shoes was wedged between several packing boxes. A pair of brown eyes stared up at him in shock. His head was resting on his backpack.

"Darren Lewis." Stavros spoke in English, standing over him. "Stay where you are." He pulled out his cell phone and called the police lieutenant.

After a moment the other man answered. "Kyrie Konstantinos? I wish I had better news for you."

"Our worries are over. We've found the missing teenager on board the ferry in Thassos town. He's hiding in the back of a white pickup truck."

"My men said they searched every car."

"This teen has been elusive. Contact the ferry captain and tell him not to leave shore yet. Despinis Linford and I will detain the Lewis boy until you arrive."

"I'll be there in ten minutes."

Stavros helped Andrea up over the tailgate. She thanked him and sat down on one of the packing boxes. By this time, the teen was sitting up, but he didn't try to get away.

"Darren? I'm Andrea Linford from PanHellenic Tours. This is Mr. Konstantinos, the managing director of the Konstantinos Marble Corporation." Not anymore. "We've been looking for you since you disappeared yesterday."

He averted his eyes.

"Your tour director, Georgios, and your teacher, Mrs. Shapiro, have been frantic. Your parents were notified of your disappearance and are on their way here."

The boy went a sickly ashen color. "My mom and dad are coming?"

She nodded. "That's right. The police will take you to them in Thessaloniki."

"I'm eighteen and don't have to see them if I don't want to."

So *that* was what this was about. "Nevertheless, they want to see you," Stavros stated. "Whatever is wrong, nothing can be resolved by running away."

"I hate my father. I never want to see him again."

The pain in his declaration wasn't lost on Stavros or Andrea. "Then you have the legal right to be on your own," he said. "But you're in a foreign country and have broken the law by stowing away in a truck that isn't yours. You have some explaining to do to the police and they'll insist on speaking to you and your parents."

Darren was fighting tears. "I don't want to talk to them."

"I'm afraid you don't have a choice while you're still on Greek soil."

Andrea got on the phone to her boss to tell him the good news. Before long, everyone, including the tour bus group, would know that the crisis had been averted. But the boy's nightmare was just beginning. From past experience, Stavros knew what it was like to be at loggerheads with his own father and had some compassion for Darren, whatever the problem.

"If you're hungry or thirsty, I'll get you something," Andrea volunteered after hanging up. She had a sweetness in her that wasn't lost on Stavros.

"I don't want anything."

"You must have had a bad night. Tell us how you got away from the quarry, Darren."

"I hid underneath someone's truck. When the police walked off, I got inside the back." Andrea and Stavros exchanged glances. "After it stopped at a village, I jumped out and walked down here during the night. While the cars were lined up to board the ferry, I got underneath another truck."

"Even wearing your backpack?" Andrea marveled aloud.

"Yeah. People do it all the time in the movies. When the man parked his truck and left, I climbed in the back and hid under the tarp."

"You were very resourceful." Stavros would give

him that. Six miles wasn't so great a distance. Obviously the boy had handled it without problem.

"Thanks."

Thanks? Even though he was caught? Stavros saw a little of himself in the boy, who was hungry for approbation. Maybe even from his father? He sat down on one of the other packing boxes. "While we're waiting for the lieutenant to come, why don't you tell us why you hate your father so much?"

"He's got my whole life planned out—what he wants me to be, where he wants me to go to college."

Stavros understood Darren better than the teen knew. "What does he want you to be?"

"An attorney like he is and go into politics."

Stavros bowed his head. "And what do you want to be?"

"I don't know yet! One day I'll figure it out."

"Do you have siblings?"

"No. I'm the golden child."

That made the boy's journey much harder. "Now that you're eighteen, you can choose the life you want to live."

Darren looked up at him, imploring him to understand. "Dad just doesn't get it, so I ran away. I wasn't going to stay away a long time."

"You were hoping he'd suffer enough to see the light." Stavros got it. "I have an idea. Go with the police and meet with your parents. Tell them the honest truth. If your father still can't be persuaded, then you'll have to decide whether you can stand to alienate him and go your own way."

Darren nodded. "I can stand it. I don't want to be an attorney."

"But you still love him, right?"

"Yeah."

"Then stick to your guns, but don't shut him out. In time I'm sure things will work out."

"You think?"

"I do."

Tears filled the boy's eyes.

"Here comes the lieutenant. I'll talk to him."

"You will?"

"Of course."

"Thanks for listening." He looked at Andrea. "Thanks for being so nice."

"You're welcome, Darren. Remember how lucky you are to have two parents who care so much. My dad had to raise me because my mom died when I was born. He loved me to death the way I'm sure your parents love you. Try to remain calm when you talk to them. When they see how rational you are, they'll be more receptive."

"I doubt it," he muttered.

Stavros jumped out, then helped Andrea down. "Come on." He turned to Darren, who got to his feet and climbed down the tailgate with his backpack.

While two officers started talking to him, Stavros took the lieutenant aside and told him about the boy's fears. "He's having problems with his father about what he wants to do with his life."

"I had the same problem with my father at that age."

Yup. "I know he's not violent or dangerous. Just unhappy. We've talked and he's promised to go willingly to Thessaloniki and have a talk with his parents. Let me know what happens."

"Of course. Congratulations on finding him so quickly. This is a great relief for everyone."

"He might not have been caught without the help of Despinis Linford."

The lieutenant turned to shake her hand before following his officers, who escorted Darren off the ferry to the police van. The teen waved to them. They waved back.

Stavros looked at Andrea and glimpsed tears in her fabulous blue eyes. She was equally anxious for Darren to reconcile with his father. "Let's go home, Andrea."

They left the ferry and hurried to the Jeep. When they got inside, she buried her face in her hands. It took all his control not to pull her into his arms. "I'm so thankful we found him."

He turned on the engine and drove out of the parking area. "You're not alone."

She finally lifted her head. "Because of the problems you've had with your father, you were wonderful with him. It touched my heart. You gave him hope and the direction he needed. I'm in awe of the way you handled a very difficult situation."

Moved by her words, he glanced at her. "The lieutenant will fill me in after they release him to his parents. In the meantime, all we can do is hope this means the beginning of some kind of reconciliation, but it's not our problem."

She wiped her eyes. "No. Thank heaven he's no longer missing. That's because of you. I couldn't have done the search for him I wanted without your help."

Satisfied he could concentrate on her from now on, he lounged back in the seat. "We worked well together. After our fine piece of detective work, we deserve the best lunch I can make for us after we reach the house."

"Only if you let me help."

"Do you like to cook?"

"If I have the time."

He liked the sound of that since he had plans for them for the rest of the weekend. When they reached the villa, he walked her to the guest room. "I'm sure you'd prefer a shower before we eat. I need one myself and a shave. There's a robe and toiletries in the en suite bathroom for the use of guests. Bring your clothes to the kitchen and we'll get them washed while we eat."

She looked away, but he caught the flush on her cheeks. "I couldn't impose on you."

Stavros had been waiting for that response. "I'm afraid you don't have any say in the matter. We camped out in the forest all night. You helped a teacher and tour guide hold on to their jobs and saved your company and mine from notoriety we don't need. When you get to know me better, you'll find out I'm prepared to indulge you endlessly."

Before she had time to argue, he walked away from her.

CHAPTER THREE

ANDREA HUNG ON to the handle after she'd shut the door to the bedroom. Had he said *endlessly*?

She knew he was grateful that both their companies had been spared making headlines in the media. But his comment had indicated something more personal. For a man like Stavros Konstantinos to be interested in a foreigner working for a tour company when he could have any woman he wanted didn't make sense.

After removing her clothes, she went into the bathroom and stood under the shower, but she couldn't get him off her mind. While they'd been talking last night, she'd inferred he was allergic to marriage, but he'd admitted to having girlfriends. Naturally he did. With his kind of potent male charisma, what woman in her right mind would resist him?

Her thoughts flicked to Ferrante, who had attracted her for other reasons, particularly his happy nature. You couldn't compare him to Stavros, who was more brooding. They were in different leagues. Andrea couldn't think of another man who measured up to the dynamic member of the Konstantinos family. Though she knew he was powerful when necessary, she admired the kind way he'd handled Darren when he'd found him.

Intuition told her he was the real force behind the corporation's success. He was a man who lit his own fires in spite of his father's heavy hand. Who wouldn't admire him for the courage of his beliefs? Last night he'd told her they'd find Darren and she'd believed him.

In the light of day she realized it was amazing she'd trusted him enough to spend the night alone with him. He'd had that effect on her. Such a complete effect, in fact, she was taking a shower in his villa before joining him for lunch.

Andrea shut off the water and stepped out on the bath mat surrounded by a floor of gleaming white Thassos marble. A white toweling robe hung on a hook on the back of the door, but she stopped short of walking around his home in it.

Just remembering that moment on the ferry when he'd grasped her arms to keep her from danger made her breath catch. His lips had come too close to hers. Here they'd been looking for Darren, yet she'd wanted him to kiss her.

You need to go home, Andrea.

When she got back to her apartment she would wash her clothes.

After reaching for a towel to dry off, she brushed her teeth and then went back to the bedroom to put on her blouse and skirt. A thorough brushing of her hair, a coat of lipstick, and she was ready to face her host for a meal before she left for Thessaloniki.

Her stomach growled as she walked on stunning stone-and-marble floors on her way to the kitchen.

Everywhere she looked she saw the ancient blue-and-white Greek pattern, whether it was on the tufted cushion of a couch or a vase of flowers. During her rare shopping jaunts, she'd learned its geometric elegance was thought to resemble the waves of the sea and shapes of labyrinths, a symbol for infinity.

When she reached the kitchen, she found Stavros putting a salad together and hoped he hadn't heard her hunger pains. While they'd been apart, he'd showered and shaved. Andrea could smell the soap he'd used. It was impossible not to stare at the way the white collared polo and khaki trousers fit his incredible physique.

His gaze played over her, but he made no comment that she wasn't wearing the robe. "Except for a dip in the ocean, there's nothing as refreshing as a shower. I've got lunch ready and thought we'd eat out on the patio."

"What can I do to help?"

His black brows lifted. "Not a thing except to join me."

"Do you know I'm getting more indebted to you by the minute?"

"What if I told you I like the odds?"

Avoiding those penetrating gray eyes, she said, "Well, as you can see, I'm not complaining."

She followed him through an alcove to the patio with a lattice covering and was greeted with a breathtaking view of the Aegean. They sat down to a glass-topped round table. He'd provided iced tea and rolls, along with a salad of olives, feta cheese, tomatoes and chunks of succulent chicken.

They both ate with a healthy appetite. "This is delicious."

"Again, I can't take the credit."

Andrea put down her fork. "You're talking about your housekeeper."

He nodded. "Raisa."

"Does she live with you?"

"No. She and her husband live in Panagia. She comes twice a week to clean the house and keep my fridge stocked."

"You're an interesting man, Stavros. Every time I want to talk about you, you somehow change the subject, but this time it won't work. There *is* something for which you can take full credit."

His eyes swerved to hers. "What's that?"

"When you discovered Darren lying there between the boxes, you could have come down hard on him with every right, yet the opposite happened. Maybe if his own father treated him the gentle, reasonable way you did, the two of them wouldn't have a problem. One day, you're going to make a terrific father."

Something seemed to flicker in those pewter depths. "I was just about to pay you a similar compliment. Instead of berating him, you asked if he needed food or water. Under the circumstances, your compassion was refreshing."

"Surely not. Anyone could see he was just a teenager, even if he'd just turned eighteen. You could tell he was frightened."

"Not everyone would have responded the way you did."

Her mouth curved into an impish smile. "Then that must make both of us exceptional human beings."

Except for his smiling eyes, she didn't know how Stavros would have reacted because a female voice had called out from the interior of the villa. In the next instant, he got to his feet in time for an attractive woman with silver in her cap of black hair to appear at the patio entrance. She looked maybe early sixties and was stylishly dressed in a summer suit.

"*Mama*—I didn't hear the helicopter." He walked over and gave her a kiss on both cheeks. "Why didn't you call to tell me you were coming?"

"I didn't want you to know, *o gios mou*. When I heard the news yesterday that you've left the company, my heart failed me."

Andrea was stunned. Stavros had left the Konstantinos Corporation?

"I've been planning it for a long time. You know that."

"I never believed it would really happen." She shook her head. "When I couldn't find you at your condo, I decided to pay an unannounced visit to the island to find out what has possessed you to do this. You've caused an explosion in the family that has shaken it to the very foundation."

"It'll run smoothly without me."

That was Stavros's modesty talking. Andrea was still trying to comprehend it.

"Why have you done this?" his mother cried. "I don't understand. Neither does your father. He's livid that you chose the board meeting to make an announcement that has hurt him to the core."

"He'll live."

At his response, Andrea's hand gripped her glass tighter.

"How can you be so cold?"

"I've always gone my own way. This is nothing new."

"When you talk like this, I can't believe you're our son. What has happ—?" His mother suddenly stopped midsentence because she'd just spotted Andrea seated at the table. Her cool brown gaze took swift inventory as she moved toward her. "But I'm interrupting and can see you have a guest. No wonder you didn't hear the helicopter arriving."

"I'd like you to meet Despinis Linford."

Andrea stood up and shook the older woman's hand. She admired Stavros's aplomb in handling what had turned into a painful confrontation. A lesser man wouldn't be able to brush his mother's concerns aside with such diplomacy. But it was obvious Stavros had the strength to swim against the tide when necessary.

She hadn't truly understood some of the dynamics of his family until this moment. More than ever, she knew the Konstantinos Corporation would suffer with him gone. But she sensed there was something that went even deeper for his mother to show up like this.

"It's a pleasure to meet you, Kyria Konstantinos."

"Would you like some iced tea, Mama?"

"Please." She sat down on one of the chairs near the railing. He poured a glass and walked it over to her. His mother took a sip before she regarded Andrea. "I had no idea my son wasn't alone." She looked at him. "Are you going to enlighten me?"

Stavros lounged against the railing, the urbane host. "Andrea works at the headquarters of PanHellenic Tours in Thessaloniki. An incident at the quarry

developed yesterday, and she came to investigate."
Without hesitation he explained what had happened,
but left out certain details his mother didn't need to
know. "The teen was found today and returned to
his parents. We've been having a celebratory lunch."

She frowned. "Maybe now you'll understand why
allowing tour groups at the quarry isn't a good idea.
You should have listened to your father."

His mouth tightened into a white line. "Careful,
Mama, or you'll hurt Andrea's feelings. She's the
one who approached our corporation in order to add
it to the student itineraries. Like me, she's anxious
to increase the public's education concerning one of
Greece's greatest resources. I'm glad my grandfather
thought it would be beneficial and backed me before
he passed away."

Andrea was subjected to another taste of his mother's disapproving scrutiny. "Where are you from?"

"I was born in Denver, Colorado, but I've lived in
many places around the world with my father."

"She's fluent in many languages besides English
and Greek," Stavros interjected. "It might interest
you to know she received her degree from Aristotle
University."

Needing to stop the inquisition in the most polite
way she knew how, Andrea got up from the table.
"Stavros fixed our lunch, Kyria Konstantinos, so the
least I can do is clear up. Since you came to talk with
your son, I'll give you some privacy and do the dishes
before I leave. Please excuse me."

Whatever his reaction, Andrea avoided looking at
him. After gathering up their plates and glasses, she
headed for the kitchen. When she went back to get

the salad bowl, she discovered the two of them had disappeared, which was a relief.

Once she'd restored the kitchen to order, she reached for her purse and went out to the patio to wait for him. The view was so heavenly, it almost didn't seem real. A few minutes later, he made an appearance alone and stood in front of her with his hands on his hips in a forbidding male stance. His fierce expression was so different from that of the relaxed host who'd made their lunch earlier. She could hardly believe she was looking at the same man.

"I apologize for my mother, Andrea."

She shook her head. "Why? Among other things, I now know where you get your good looks."

"Because she walked in on me when she knew better." Andrea decided he hadn't even heard the compliment she'd paid him.

"She's your mom, and she was obviously so upset about the news she'd heard and was afraid you would remain unreachable."

"That's no excuse for rude behavior. To be honest, she has never burst in on me before in my own home." Andrea believed him. "She's normally quite gracious. I can promise you that my resignation from the company had little to do with her springing herself on me the way she did."

Andrea didn't know the exact reason for his mother's reaction, but the sight of a strange woman with her son had set her off even more. There was more to that story, as he'd said, but it was none of her business.

"You don't owe me any explanation, Stavros. I need to get the car back to Thassos and catch the

next ferry, but I waited so I could thank you for everything."

His black brows furrowed. "Your boss won't be
expecting you before Monday. Why are you in such
a rush?"

Her heart pounded too hard in her chest. "I have
work waiting at the office that must be done before
next week."

He cocked his handsome head. "I think you're trying to get away from me."

The best way to handle this was to agree with him.
She smiled. "I admit it. But if you remember, I asked
if you would let me come with you to look for Darren. Since the crisis is over, it's time for me to get
back to Thessaloniki."

After a short silence, "What if I want you to stay?"
His husky tone played havoc with her senses.

She took a fortifying breath. "Forgive me for being
blunt, but I can't afford to stay." *I'm far too attracted
to you.*

How could she feel this strongly about him when
Ferrante hadn't died that long ago? She didn't want
to know the pain of loving someone again and was
shocked at the strength of her feelings for him already. A prominent man like Stavros Konstantinos
could have his pick of any woman, but he could never
be serious about her. It wasn't worth risking her heart
to stay around any longer, especially when she'd be
leaving the country with her father in the not-too-
distant future.

"Thank you again for letting me play detective
with you. I won't forget your generosity."

Andrea walked past him and out the rear door of

the house to her car. It was the longest walk of her life. Getting away from him now meant she'd escaped before it was too late. To remain here another minute would be putting herself in emotional jeopardy.

She'd had enough time to think about his mother's shock at finding her son with Andrea. Stavros had admitted this had nothing to do with his recent business decision, but it was all too much of a mystery for Andrea. She pressed on the gas as she made her way down the mountain.

As Andrea was finding out, Stavros was more complicated than she'd first realized. Not so Ferrante, who'd been open with her from the start. No mystery, no secrets. He'd asked Andrea to marry him. He'd wanted a life with her. Marriage, children. The whole thing. Why that fierce mountain blizzard had to come along and destroy their dream, she didn't know.

The first set of tears she'd shed for him in a long time made her vision blurry. She needed to slow down or she'd get in an accident. Maybe it would be years before an uncomplicated man like Ferrante came along again. Maybe never.

Forget Stavros Konstantinos!

"Andrea? I know it's time for you to go home, but would you step into my office for a minute, please?"

She couldn't say no to Sakis, but it *was* Friday night. Her single friend Dorcas worked in the accounts department for the tour company on the next floor up. Maybe she'd want to get some dinner and go to a film later with Andrea. After she talked to Sakis, she'd give her a call.

"I'll be right there."

The mock-up for the latest itinerary just needed a few finishing touches, but it could wait until Monday. She closed the file, backed it up on the computer and reached for her purse in the bottom drawer of her desk. A little lipstick and a quick brush of her hair would have to do to make herself presentable.

Andrea said good-night to a couple of coworkers as she walked past their desks to reach Sakis's office. The door was closed, so she knocked.

"Come in!"

Sakis, in shirtsleeves, reminded Andrea of an overweight newspaper editor who smoked, drank tons of coffee and talked with ten situations going on at the same time. He loved to tell crass jokes to provoke a reaction. But for once she didn't even notice him because there was another man in the office, seated across from his desk. A striking, dark-haired male dressed in a gray business suit and tie. The sight of him robbed her of breath.

Stavros.

No, no, no. A week had gone by since she'd left his villa. It wasn't enough time...

He got to his feet, making her more aware of his virility than ever. Stavros didn't have to try to knock a woman dead. It just happened automatically in his presence.

"Andrea," he murmured in that deep voice. "How are you?"

How am I? She was reeling. "Fine, thank you. And you?"

"I wasn't fine until now."

Warmth spread up her neck and face.

"Sit down, my dear." Sakis indicated the chair

next to Stavros, unaware of her shock. "I've wanted to speak to both of you since the incident with the Lewis boy. But Kyrie Konstantinos couldn't break away from business matters until now."

Sakis had phoned Stavros?

"Words can't express my gratitude to both of you for finding the teen in such a short period of time. An international incident was avoided, sparing both our companies adverse publicity and possible litigation."

Andrea sat forward. "We're all happy about that. Do you have any news of how he is now?"

"I understand he's back in Connecticut with his parents."

"He told us he was upset with his father. That's why he tried to run away."

Sakis spread his hands apart. "It happens. My son has threatened to kill me several times." But he laughed when he said it. In that moment, Stavros's eyes sent her a silent message, as if to say the two of them knew the teen's situation hadn't been a laughing matter.

Her boss sat back in his swivel chair. "Kyrie Konstantinos? The police lieutenant told me you influenced him not to bring charges against the teen." Andrea hadn't known that. "Such a gesture on your part is amazing."

"Nonsense. Except to worry everyone, the teen did no harm."

"Not everyone is as forgiving as you."

As Andrea had already come to find out, Stavros was no ordinary man.

"I've brought you two together to get your opinion about continuing the tours to the quarry. Another incident like this one might not turn out so well next time." He eyed Stavros. "Would you prefer we cancel future tours? It's up to you."

"I'm afraid it won't be up to me any longer," Stavros stated. "I've resigned from the Konstantinos Marble Corporation. I suggest you phone the company immediately and ask for Dimitri."

Sakis's eyes rounded. "You resigned?"

"That's right. Life is full of surprises and difficulties. Hopefully the new CEO won't stop these tours because of one troubled teenager."

Sakis looked genuinely upset. "We're very sorry to hear this, aren't we, Andrea?"

"Yes," she said, aware of Stavros's gaze. "To see the resources of the earth up close gives you a new reverence for the whole plan of creation. Mounds and mounds of marble here from the beginning of time for men to use."

"I believe you're wasted in this office," Sakis said. "You should be a publicist out selling Greece to the world."

"You're full of it," she teased, but was pleased by the rare compliment, especially in front of Stavros.

He extinguished the last of his cigarette. "All right. I'll make the call. In light of this information, thank you for coming in person, Kyrie Konstantinos. Nothing would have been possible without your generosity." Stavros *was* a generous man. Andrea had firsthand knowledge. "We're honored that you would allow our tours to come on your property."

"It has been my pleasure."

Sakis stood and shook his hand. "The arrangement worked well for everyone."

"Perhaps it will still work. Good luck."

But Stavros's father hadn't approved, not according to his mother. With Andrea's heart racing now that this meeting was over, she got to her feet. It was imperative she get away from Stavros. "Have a good weekend, Sakis."

"You too. See you on Monday."

"I'll be here."

She left the office first, hoping to lose Stavros by going down in the elevator. But when she found she had to wait for it, she opted for the stairs.

Stavros caught up to her at the landing, not the least winded. "Where's the fire, *despinis*?"

Andrea darted him a glance. "I have a bus to catch." She knew she was behaving like an idiot, but she was afraid of her feelings for him.

"You don't own a car?"

"I don't need one in town. When Dad comes home, I use his." She kept going until she came out into the foyer.

"I'll drive you home."

"I appreciate the offer, but it isn't necessary."

"I'm afraid it's of vital importance to me."

Something in his tone made her realize he wasn't toying with her. She stopped walking and looked at him. "That sounded serious."

"At last I've gotten through to you. Do you have plans for this evening?"

Andrea could lie, but was resigned that he would see through it. "No."

"You do now. The limo is waiting out in front. I'll run you home so you can change into something comfortable and pack an overnight bag. Bring a bathing suit. I want to spend the weekend with you. Surely that couldn't come as a surprise—or am I wrong and you have no interest in me?"

That meant two nights alone with him. Her body started to tremble. "I think you're an exceptional man."

He studied her through veiled eyes. "Yet you don't trust me?"

"That's not the point." *I'm the one I don't trust.*

"Then there's no problem, is there?"

She lifted her head. "If Sakis hadn't asked you to come to his office, this wouldn't be happening."

"Contrary to what you believe, I would have gotten hold of you earlier in the week. But certain business matters prevented me from doing what I wanted to do. I purposely arranged this meeting with your boss at the end of your work week so we could be together."

Oh, Stavros, she moaned inwardly. "I'm not sure this is a good idea."

"My mother's interruption upset you, but she won't do it again."

"This doesn't have anything to do with your mother. I'm just not ready to get involved with another man."

"You're still mourning Ferrante, aren't you?"

"Yes. I may not be actively grieving for him, but I have a full plate with my work and can't handle anything else."

"Up until today you've been honest with me. Why can't you be truthful now?"

"Because I don't want to get hurt again!" she blurted in exasperation.

"I don't plan to hurt you," he said in that velvety voice she couldn't ignore.

"Mother died. Ferrante died."

"I don't plan on doing that anytime soon," came the wry reply. "What happened to the girl who takes risks traveling around to third-world countries and was willing to spend the night in a forest with a near stranger? Where did that girl go?"

"You know what I meant," she murmured.

"No. I don't. Do you think I'm some kind of womanizer?"

Andrea couldn't look at him. "I have no way of knowing, do I?"

"Did you give Ferrante this much trouble when he showed interest in you?"

"Let's not bring him into this." To care about Stavros meant going through more heartache again. After Ferrante, she couldn't handle it.

"Why not? Afraid to give me an answer?"

"No."

"He was a mountain-climbing guide and would have been around beautiful women all the time. Did you accuse him of using them?"

"Of course not."

"So how come you're having trust issues with me when you don't really know me yet? I thought you liked me a little."

"You know I do," she whispered fiercely.

"Then spend the weekend with me. If you discover I'm not worth knowing, then so be it."

Andrea couldn't find fault with his logic. It was her heart she was worried about. He might decide she wasn't worth knowing.

"We're wasting time. What's your address?"

He'd broken her down so fast she couldn't think. When she answered him, he cupped her elbow and walked her out to the limo. "Let's hurry. We'll take the helicopter from the airport and eat dinner on Thassos."

That meant they were going back to his fabulous villa. Andrea hadn't thought to ever see him again, let alone stay in that heavenly place. She closed her eyes, full of questions and incredulous this was happening.

She still had time to tell him no, but her self-control had deserted her. Throughout the week she'd done everything possible to put him out of her mind. But her heart had leaped the second she'd seen him sitting in Sakis's office. It was still leaping. Andrea was terrified it might always remain in that state.

CHAPTER FOUR

STAVROS SAT IN the copilot's seat, but looked over his shoulder at Andrea, who, from her seat behind the pilot, was devouring the lush scenery of Thassos Island. This was the first time he'd seen her wearing jeans. An ivory linen jersey top with sleeves pushed up to the elbow covered her womanly figure. Between that and her honey-blond coloring, he had trouble not devouring her.

A trip like this would never be wasted on her because she was a female of exceptional intelligence and she had an interest in everything. "Is this the first time you've seen Thassos from the air?"

Andrea nodded. "I'm glad it's not too dark yet. The green of it is almost unreal."

His gaze locked with her azure-blue eyes. "It has different looks, but twilight is the most beautiful time to see it."

"Were you born on the island?"

"No. Thessaloniki. All my family lives there, but I fell in love with Thassos the first time my father brought me to one of the quarries. When I climbed to the top of Mount Ypsarion for the first time, I knew

I wanted to live here and planned exactly where I would build my house one day."

"You're very fortunate to have realized your dream. Not all of us can do that."

"It was only one of them, Andrea. Since then I've had more. What was yours?"

"That's easy to answer. When I was little, I used to play dolls with my friend and pretend my mommy was alive. I would dream that she came back to life and lived with me and Daddy. By the age of six, I realized that dream would never be realized in this life. I haven't dreamed since."

The pathos of the moment produced a lump in his throat. "Do you have a picture of her with you?"

She blinked. "A couple."

"When we reach the house, I'd like to see them. Are you hungry?"

"Starving."

"My housekeeper has our dinner waiting for us."

"Oh, good. I'm thankful we don't have to cook anything. I don't think I could wait that long."

He laughed. Her honesty was one of the many traits he admired about her. "We'll be at the villa within a few minutes."

His gaze traveled to her practical duffel bag stowed on the other seat. No designer luggage for her. She'd traipsed around the world with her father and had discovered that less was always better than more.

The pilot dipped them down to the landing pad. It had been built on the west side of the villa with steps leading up and around the foliage to the front entrance. Stavros had planned it that way so it would be out of sight.

When he was in the house, he could usually hear the rotors. But last week he'd been so enthralled with Andrea, he hadn't realized his mother had arrived in his father's helicopter until she'd walked out on the patio.

So much had happened in a week. Through Leon, he'd found out their older cousin Dimitri had been promoted to CEO. Dimitri had wanted to be in charge for a long time. As for the state of affairs between Stavros and his parents, they couldn't be worse. There'd been only one brief phone call from his mother since she'd left the villa.

He'd known how disappointed she was that he'd stopped seeing Tina, but he'd never dreamed she'd show rudeness in front of Andrea. Tonight he wanted to make it up to Andrea and planned to concentrate on the two of them.

Once they were on the ground, he thanked the pilot and helped Andrea down from the helicopter. After grabbing her duffel bag, he climbed out and ushered her up the steps to the front door of the house. To his surprise, Raisa opened it before he could use his remote. He'd thought she would have gone home by now.

"Kyrie..." she said in a hushed voice. "You have a visitor. Despinis Nasso arrived an hour ago by car and insisted on staying until you returned. I showed her into the living room."

He couldn't believe this had happened right after the conversation with Andrea about other women. Stavros decided he *was* cursed and ground his teeth.

Tina must have parked around the back. With the exception of Andrea, he'd never brought another woman to his house. The only way Tina could have found out where to come was through his mother.

When she had finally called earlier that day, his mother had begged him to come to dinner at the house with her and his father. No doubt she'd been contriving a small party that included Tina. He'd told her he would have to miss it because he had important business back on Thassos.

For Tina to show up here meant his family had declared war on him and wouldn't hesitate to use Tina to achieve their objective.

"Thank you, Raisa."

He turned to Andrea. "I apologize for another unexpected interruption. Please make yourself at home in the guest bedroom while I deal with this. I'll only be a minute."

But the second the words left his mouth, Tina appeared in the front hallway. She looked fashionably turned out in a pale pink suit that highlighted her long black hair. "I'm sorry, Stavros. I heard the helicopter, but I had no idea you'd be coming home with company. You didn't answer my phone calls or my texts. I need to talk to you privately."

Even if she had his mother's permission, her effrontery appalled him. "I'm afraid that's not possible. We said our goodbyes over three months ago. You weren't invited here. Please have the courtesy to leave."

With a sangfroid that chilled him, her gaze swerved to Andrea and the duffel bag. "You must be the American woman who works for PanHellenic Tours. Stavros forgot to introduce us. I'm Tina Lasso."

Ice filled his veins. He opened the door for her. "Goodbye, Tina."

She walked toward him. "I've just come from your parents and thought you'd want to know I'm pregnant with your child."

The oldest lie in the world. Tina had sunk to an all-time low.

"I never slept with you, Tina." The words came out like a quiet hiss. "If you *are* pregnant, it isn't mine."

"Oh, darling," she said after stepping outside. " Do you really expect Despinis Linford to believe that?"

"I have no expectations, Tina, only sadness that you've let our parents' wishes rule your life. Once you start thinking for yourself, you'll never have to be desperate again."

Spots of red filled her cheeks. "How dare you—"

He closed the door in her face, attempting to gain control of his anger. Not so much at her. She was a puppet. This kind of behavior happened to the inse-cure offspring of parents who didn't know what life was all about, yet were determined to impose their will at any cost.

Out of the stillness came a voice. "If she *is* preg-nant with your baby, then you should run after her. Don't let my being here stop you."

Stavros wheeled around. "It couldn't be my baby."

Andrea's solemn eyes stared straight into his. "The same thing happened to Dad one time in Venezuela after he'd decided not to see this one woman anymore. As it turned out, she wasn't pregnant, but she'd hoped he would believe the lie and marry her. Is this Tina that kind of woman? Or could she be telling the truth?"

He sucked in his breath. "Tina comes from a good family and is the woman my parents have expected me to marry. We spent some time together, but I couldn't love her. Once again, I've disappointed them by preferring to choose my own wife when the time comes.

"I haven't seen her for over three months. She could be pregnant, but not with my baby. We were never intimate. Naturally you have no way of knowing if I'm telling the truth or not. If you want to leave now, I'll ask the pilot to fly you back to Thessaloniki."

Her answer was a long time in coming. "My father never lied to me, so I had no reason not to believe him. So far, I don't believe you've lied to me about anything either. Under the circumstances, I prefer to reserve judgment. On that note, do you think we can eat now?"

"Andrea—"

Without conscious thought he crushed her against his chest. Holding her was all he'd been able to think about since the moment they'd met. Losing track of time, he rocked her in his arms while he clung to her. As he started kissing her hair and cheek, her stomach rumbled. He not only heard it, he felt it, and they both broke into laughter.

"You probably think *I've* got a baby inside *me*."

Drowning in her smile, he was on the verge of covering her mouth with his own when he heard, *"Kyrie?"*

His housekeeper's voice had sounded on cue.

"Your dinner is on the table in the dining room. I'm leaving now."

Andrea eased herself away.

"Thank you, Raisa." He grasped Andrea's hand and drew her toward the dining room off the other end of the kitchen. For the time being, she was willing to trust him. It was a gift beyond price. He felt as if he'd been let out of a dark prison where he'd been chained for years and years and had suddenly emerged into blinding sunlight that filled his whole being.

His housekeeper had prepared oven-baked lamb and crab salad. For dessert, she'd fixed his favorite grape must pudding. Between him and Andrea they made short work of it.

When they'd finished, she let out a deep sigh of contentment. "That has to be the best meal I've ever eaten. How did you find her? She's worth her weight in gold."

"Her husband worked at the quarry until retirement. He became ill last year and I often dropped by to visit him."

"What a kind thing to do."

"I had an agenda. Raisa always forced food on me. One day, I told her I'd pay a king's ransom if she'd be my cook. They needed the money, so she took me up on it."

"Is he still sick?"

"He gets bouts of pneumonia, but so far he's managing."

While he sat there drinking his coffee, she got up to clear the table and clean up the kitchen. She'd probably been in the habit of waiting on her father. As Stavros was discovering, old habits died hard.

"Andrea? Come back in the dining room and bring your purse so I can see those pictures of your family."

"I only have three in my wallet."

She returned and pulled them out so he could picture her parents. One of the photos showed her mother pregnant. She'd been a lovely blonde woman. "You strongly resemble her."

"Dad says the same thing."

Andrea's lean, chemical engineer father had rugged features with light brown hair and blue eyes. "To a Greek like me, your parents represent the handsome American couple."

She smiled and sat down to drink the rest of her coffee. "Why do we look American?"

"I don't know. Your mannerisms maybe. The way you hold yourself. I really can't explain it."

"You Greeks give off your own vibes too. At first, Sakis didn't want to hire me because it would give a non-Greek a job." She put the photos away.

"But he was already smitten," Stavros murmured, unable to prevent himself from eating her up with his eyes. "I saw it at his office. Combined with your résumé, he was hooked. That was a lucky day for him and my family's corporation, even if my grandfather was the only one who had vision."

A gentle laugh escaped. "Do you miss him?"

"Very much. Just once, he admitted that my father was a harsh taskmaster. He said it surprised him. That was my grandfather's way of telling me he approved of me."

Her eyes misted over. "How difficult for you. I'm sorry."

"Don't be. I've grown a second skin. I'd rather talk about you. Are you planning to stay with PanHellenic Tours as a career?"

"Oh, no. Only until my father leaves for his new assignment in Indonesia."

Stavros felt as though he'd just been punched in the gut. That was one answer he hadn't expected. "How soon will he be leaving Greece?"

"Mid-October."

Less than two months?

His stomach muscles tightened in reaction. "That country has seen a lot of turmoil."

"Not where Dad and I will be living."

Stavros stifled a groan. "Does your boss know yet?"

"Yes. Why do you ask?"

"The way he talked with you today, I got the feeling he won't want to let you go."

"We've had a good relationship, but he always knew I'd leave when my father had to relocate."

He rubbed the back of his neck. "Is that what you want to do?"

A haunted look crossed over her classic features. "Dad and I have never been separated. If Ferrante hadn't died, we were going to live with my father wherever his work took him. Ferrante planned to give up his job. He was a linguist and would have found work with me so we could be together. The climb up Mont Blanc was going to be his last. As it turned out, it was his final climb." Her voice shook.

Stavros reached out to squeeze her hand before releasing it. "How old was he?"

"Twenty-seven."

Ferrante had been young and so much in love with Andrea, he was willing to give up his interests to be with her. He didn't know any man willing to do that. But to live with her father? Why? That question was on the tip of his tongue, but he didn't feel now was the time to broach the subject.

Her father couldn't be an invalid—otherwise he wouldn't be working at a mine site. Stavros didn't understand. "What about his family?"

"We planned to fly to Ticino for vacations to be with his parents." Her soulful eyes searched his. "What's wrong, Stavros?"

What *wasn't*!

"Nothing important." This new information had knocked him sideways. "Do you know your eyelids are drooping? It's getting late and I must confess I'm tired too. Why don't we put off more talk until tomorrow?" He needed time to think.

"You're a master at hiding your feelings, but I happen to know the incident in the foyer a little while ago has upset you. If you want to talk about it, I'm a good listener."

Stavros had already forgotten about it, but it was just as well she didn't know what was really bothering him. "I've already learned that about you and will take you up on your offer in the morning."

"Then I'll say good-night."

She shot out of the chair with her purse and disappeared from the dining room before he realized her intentions. He could have called her to come back, but then he'd have to admit he couldn't comprehend his life without her in it. *That* was what was bothering him.

He'd never wanted a woman so much in his life. But if he told her this soon, she'd never believe him. Stavros hardly believed it himself. What had it been? Only a week since they'd met each other? It was asking too much of her when she'd just been witness to Tina's lie, a lie Stavros couldn't rule out definitively without proof.

On top of that nightmare was the news she'd be leaving with her father in October. Stavros was staggered by tonight's events. He might as well have been smashed by one of those enormous marble slabs being loaded on one of the flatbed trucks. Heaven knew there'd be no sleep for him tonight. As for all the other nights to come, it didn't bear thinking about.

After Andrea reached the guest bedroom, she shut the door and rummaged for the cell phone in her purse. Maybe her dad was already asleep, but she needed to hear his voice. Her call went through to his voice mail. She left a message for him to call her back when he could.

Once she'd taken a quick shower and brushed her teeth, she climbed into bed with a bestselling Jean Sasson novel. She needed to keep her mind occupied so she wouldn't think about a troubled Stavros somewhere in the villa. If Tina had lied, then he had to be enraged.

When he'd locked Andrea in his arms a little while ago, it had felt so right she'd never wanted to leave them. Her heart had steamed into his. He was beyond wonderful. No man could compare to him.

Andrea couldn't imagine what it was like for Stavros to live with that kind of pressure to marry a woman his family had picked out for him. How sad his grandfather wasn't still alive.

But what if Stavros had lied to Andrea...?

She barely knew him, yet until Tina had appeared, Andrea had felt she knew all the important things about the core of him. In her heart, she didn't believe he would lie to her. *Because you don't want to?*

Her thoughts went back to Tina Nasso. Maybe she *was* pregnant, just not with Stavros's baby. If that was true, then to confront him with Andrea standing there was a desperate act. Wretched and unconscionable, if Stavros wasn't the father. What a nightmare for Stavros, who, through it all, had shown remarkable restraint.

She'd never known pressure from her father. With him for a role model, she knew the kind of man she wanted to marry. One who had her dad's goodness and gentleness. When she'd told her father she loved Ferrante and planned to get married, he'd been totally accepting because he'd liked him from the beginning.

Maybe it was different between fathers and sons. Stavros's mother had come right out, in front of Andrea, about her husband's disapproval of the quarry tours Stavros had sanctioned. Those outspoken words—meant to chastise Stavros—had hurt Andrea for him.

Her thoughts jumped to Sakis, who had admitted

to problems with his son. Though he'd made light of it, Andrea suspected his son probably wouldn't laugh.

She decided she was the luckiest daughter in the world to have such a fantastic father. After showing Stavros her pictures, she was feeling exceptionally emotional. When the phone rang and she saw the caller ID, she picked up and blurted, "Dad? Do you have any idea how much I love you?"

He laughed for a long time. "I love you too, honey. What has brought all this on?"

"Things. Life." Her voice wobbled. "Every day I appreciate you more and more. A lot has happened since we last talked."

"For me too. If you hadn't phoned, *I* would have. You need to give your boss notice in the morning."

How strange he would mention her boss when Stavros had just questioned her about her job earlier. Alert to a serious tone in his voice, she sat up in bed. "What's wrong?"

"Nothing to do with me personally, honey. It looks like there's too much political unrest at the mine in Papua. Remember my telling you about the Free Papua Movement?"

"Vaguely."

"They've turned into a revolutionary organization whose purpose is to overthrow the government in Papua and West Papua. It has been blamed for a lot of attacks happening near the mine."

Stavros had mentioned the turmoil there. The Konstantinos Corporation did business all over the world. That was why he knew everything.

"My company doesn't want me taking any chances, so I won't be going there after all."

That meant they wouldn't be leaving Greece for a long time! *Thank you, thank you,* her heart whispered.

"The good news is, they're sending me to Brazil for a short-term assignment. I have to be there in ten days. At this point, I'm finishing up my work here as fast as I can."

Andrea reeled. Wait a minute—in ten days she'd never see Stavros again? How was she going to handle that?

"Think you can be ready by then?"

She slid out of bed, too upset by his news to lie there. "O-of course I can." Her voice faltered. "But the lease on the apartment isn't up until the middle of October. We'll have to pay for the time we won't be living in it."

"No problem. I'll take care of it. Honey, this short-term assignment in Brazil will be my last one. While we're there, you don't need to get a job. It might be fun for you to work on the language and add Portuguese to your long list."

Andrea held the phone tighter. She'd been listening, but one comment stood out. "What do you mean your last one?"

"I'm finally tired of moving around. I miss Denver, and the main office wants me there. By Thanksgiving we'll be home for good."

Home? For good? She'd never heard him sound so happy. His excitement rang in her ears.

"We'll buy a house and I'll get all the furniture and possessions out of storage."

She had to sink down on the side of the bed or she would have fainted on the spot. Her father sounded so ecstatic about his future plans, she didn't want to say anything to change that excitement. Denver was a long way away from Thassos Island. She couldn't believe it, but her father sounded homesick.

"Now tell me what's been going on with you, honey."

Tears trickled down her cheeks. "Nothing as important as your news. I'll fill you in later. Get a good sleep. I'll call you soon. Love you, Dad." She clicked off.

For his whole life, he'd taken perfect care of her. He'd taken her everywhere with him so they'd never be apart. Now he wanted to go home and assumed she'd be going home with him.

Up until a week ago, she would have been happy with his plans. But something earthshaking had happened to her.

Never being with Stavros again was anathema to her.

If only Sakis hadn't asked him to come to his office—if only her boss hadn't called her in at the same time—then Andrea wouldn't have wound up at Stavros's villa. But she *had* come. There was only one explanation. She'd fallen madly in love with him. It was as simple and painful as that.

She knew Stavros was attracted to her, but she had no idea how deep his feelings ran. He'd just come out of another relationship. Had his mother sent Tina to Stavros's villa because she believed Tina and was upset he hadn't answered Tina's calls or texts?

Had his mother suspected Andrea would be here? Did she hope Andrea would stay away from Stavros when she heard the news about the pregnancy? Would a mother do that? Andrea didn't know, but she didn't want to believe his mother would be that calculating.

As for Tina, Andrea had seen for herself that the Grecian beauty would do anything for Stavros's affection. Was she so in love with him, she'd come to the villa on her own because she couldn't help herself? Had this kind of thing happened to Stavros in the past with other women?

If so, it could explain why he was still a bachelor. Maybe her father's bad experience in Venezuela was the reason he hadn't remarried. When there was no truth in it, how could any man ever trust in love, let alone marriage, after an exhibition like Ms. Nasso had put on tonight?

But what if Stavros was lying? She'd told him she'd withhold judgment, but that took a lot of faith.

Confused, bewildered, she got back in bed with an aching heart and pulled the covers over her shoulders, not knowing what to think. Ten more days would fly by, then no more Stavros. Maybe it was just as well. Just leave Greece before she got in too far over her head. But that was a joke.

She turned on her stomach and buried her wet face in the pillow.

The next thing she knew, it was morning. Crying herself to sleep had been one way of bringing on oblivion. But she'd awakened with the same pain, knowing her time with Stavros was growing shorter by the minute. She checked her watch. It was ten after nine.

One look in the bathroom mirror and she did what she could to repair the damage before getting dressed. After brushing her hair, she slipped into white denims and a short-sleeved powder blue T-shirt. She'd just finished tying her white sneakers when Stavros rapped on her bedroom door.

"Andrea? Are you up?"

Ridiculous how the sound of his voice thrilled her. She reached for her purse and opened the door to the exciting man dressed in a black polo and jeans. Anything she might have said got blocked in her throat because of the way he was looking at her.

"You look beautiful."

Heart attack. He was the one who was beautiful in that male way. "I don't think you're awake yet, but thank you."

His eyes narrowed on her mouth. "I've been wide awake for quite a while waiting for you. If you think I'm paying lip service, then take another look in the mirror. The color of your top has enhanced the blue of your eyes."

She got this suffocating feeling in her chest. "I can smell coffee."

"I'm good at coffee and toast. It's waiting for us out on the patio."

"Admit you're afraid I'm going to have another hunger attack. I've had several embarrassing moments in my life because of my stomach."

A chuckle followed her through the hallway and alcove to the patio, where they were treated to another glorious day of sunshine. He'd prepared eggs and fruit too. A feast. When they sat down to eat, she decided there wasn't anything he couldn't do.

Andrea ate a second helping of eggs. "You're such a great cook, I'd hire you to be mine if I could afford you."

"Let's talk about that after we go for a Jeep ride. I want to show you something."

She'd only been teasing, but his unexpected remark sounded serious and sent a curious shiver down her spine. "I'm ready to leave whenever you are." But first she got up and took their dishes to the kitchen.

"Leave them. I spoke to Raisa. She'll be in later."

"It will only take a minute."

"But *I* can't wait that long."

She flicked him a glance, thinking he was being playful, but the hard set of his jaw wiped away that notion. Without saying anything to him, she went back to the patio for her purse, then followed him out the rear entrance of the house to his Jeep.

He'd left the bedroll and blankets in the backseat. The sight of them brought back haunting memories of that first night with him. With that inscrutable expression on his face, Andrea couldn't tell if he was remembering or not. Aware of her accelerated pulse, she climbed in the front seat and attached the lap belt.

Stavros's near sleepless night had put him in a dark place. The idea that Andrea would be leaving Greece in two months had changed the timing on the playing field. He drove them out to the main road, heading in the opposite direction from the quarry.

"Where are we going?"

The breeze teased her hair. Each golden strand caught the light. "To the other side of my property."

"You mean we're still on it?"

"The villa and the swath of woods on your right are mine. Beyond them lies my future."

She shifted in her seat toward him. "That sounded cryptic."

He studied her profile. "Do you remember us talking about our dreams?"

"How could I forget?"

"I'm going to show you another one of mine, although it's in its embryo stage. Every bit of money I earned growing up, I invested so that one day I could be independent. You'd have to belong to a family like mine to understand where I'm coming from."

"It doesn't take a lot of imagination to realize you want to be your own man."

He breathed in deeply. "As you heard from my mother, last week I claimed my independence when I resigned at the board meeting. The Konstantinos family doesn't own me anymore. Best of all, I don't owe them."

He felt her speculative gaze on him while he made a turn to the right and followed the mountain road to an area of cleared land. It housed a cluster of new buildings, flatbed trucks and other machinery.

Stavros brought the Jeep to a halt at the front entrance of the office building. "Welcome to Mount Ypsarion Enterprises."

She looked all around. "This isn't a quarry."

"No. That's my family's business."

Her eyes flew to his. "What's *your* business?"

"That six-thousand-square-meter plant you see is putting out forty-five tons per hour of a new product I call Marma-Kon. It's made from those mounds of marble waste dumps behind the buildings."

"Waste?"

"Refuse from the cutting of the marble blocks. The

idea came to me years ago when I visited the different quarries and saw the wasted marble. I began talking to a group of independent chemical engineers like myself from Kavala."

"I didn't know you were an engineer like my dad."

Everything got down to her dad. Her hero worship of him meant they had a very strong bond. Ferrante had wanted her enough that he was willing to give up his own career to be with Andrea and her father. Had Andrea pressured him? Or had Ferrante loved her beyond reason and known it was the only way he could have a life with her?

"It was necessary if I hoped to build a business. Together, my engineering friends and I brainstormed about what could be done with the residue because no one was interested in the waste. In time, we came up with various products used to make dry mortars, glues and tile adhesives that are superior to those on the market because of their marble base. They're ideal for every application.

"After successfully testing the products with building contractors and architects, we saw the great potential and formed Mount Ypsarion Enterprises. From that moment on, I began negotiating with quarries all over northern Greece to buy their waste for a nominal fee and bring it here by the truckload to be processed. We house the finished products in bags and place them in those warehouses, ready for delivery by truck, train or ship."

She shook her head. "That's incredible, Stavros. Utterly incredible and it's all brand-new. Can I see inside your office first?"

"You want to?"

"Of course."

They both got out of the Jeep. Using the remote, Stavros let them inside the one-story office building. He walked her past the front desk of the main foyer to his own suite. "This is my secretary's office. Further down the hall my colleagues, Theo and Zander, have their suites with their own secretaries. If my projections are correct, this will be the first of other plants we plan to build in Penteli, near Athens, and in the Cyclades."

She swung around and smiled at him. "You planned all this."

"Along with my partners."

"But you thought of it first. You're brilliant."

He was touched by her earnestness, but he flashed her a dry smile. "A brilliant financial disaster, you mean, if my marketing projections for thirty thousand tons a year of product aren't met. Only time will tell. I and the two-hundred-plus workers we've hired could lose everything. I won't have anyone to blame but myself."

"You won't fail. You *couldn't*."

He'd needed Andrea in his life for a long time. Years, in fact...

"Such faith deserves a reward. I asked Raisa to have the hamper packed by the time we return. We'll go back to the house for it and our bathing suits. Then we'll drive to Thassos and take my speedboat. There's a secluded beach close by I know you'll love."

"I can't wait, but could I see inside the plant first? My dad was pleased when I told him your company had given permission for the tours to visit your quarry. But he'll be more than impressed when I tell him about your brainchild. It's hard to impress him."

With a work ethic like her father's, Stavros could believe it. But he was troubled by their conversation because her dad figured in it more and more. Stavros led her back outside and used the remote to activate the electronic lock. They walked to the plant in the distance and he let her inside.

One would have thought Andrea was a child on Christmas morning. But instead of exclaiming about the presents, she marveled over the up-to-date technology installed. "Would you mind if I took a few pictures with my phone to send to my father? Or would you think I'm an industrial spy?"

"I'll give you the benefit of the doubt like you gave me last night."

He noticed she let that remark go. "Dad would enjoy seeing them."

"You think?"

"I promise. He's taken me to gold mining refineries all over the world, many of them old and needing a lot of work. Trust me. This is the most elegant plant I've ever seen in my life." She lifted a beaming face to him. "You must be ecstatic. I want a couple of pictures of you too. Smile."

He did her bidding, but his patience had worn thin. "I think that's enough photos for now. Put your phone away." Stavros had only one thing on his mind. Unable to resist, he cupped her flushed cheeks in his hands and kissed her warmly on that enticing mouth of hers. "Seeing this place through your eyes is my reward," he whispered, then kissed her again, deeply this time.

A tiny moan escaped her throat as he pulled her into his body. She fit in his arms so perfectly, it was as if she were made for him. One kiss grew into more until he lost count. When he finally lifted his head so she could breathe, they were swaying together. "You have no idea how much I've wanted to do this. From the first moment we met, it's all I've been able to think about."

"Don't say anything more." He saw a tortured look enter those blue eyes as she eased out of his arms. "I was afraid this would happen if I flew to Thassos with you."

"But you came with me anyway because you couldn't help yourself, so don't bother to deny it."

She averted her eyes. "I'm not. But it scares me to have feelings like this so soon after meeting you. You're the first man since Ferrante. Our relationship took time to grow. Where you're concerned, I don't know if I can trust what's happening to me. I feel out of control."

Andrea must have been reading his mind, but he could see it had cost her a lot to admit that. "I'm not going to apologize for kissing you. If you're afraid of being with me, then I'll ask my pilot to fly you back to Thessaloniki once we reach the house. I can't blame you after what happened last night with Tina. Are you ready to go?"

Without looking at him, she nodded and started for the entrance. He let them out, then set the lock and they walked back to the Jeep. A few minutes ago he'd had a little taste of heaven, but only a taste before everything had changed. Stavros couldn't put time back to the way it was before he'd given in to his desire and kissed her. Her passionate response had set him on fire. He was still burning. *Out of control* didn't cover it.

They rode back to the villa in silence. Before he got out of the Jeep, he reached for his cell phone. She turned toward him with an anxious expression. "Who are you calling?"

"My pilot."

"Please don't, Stavros. I'm not afraid of you. You *know* I'm not."

"Maybe you should be," he bit out. "I can't give you proof that I never made love to Tina."

"I've chosen to believe you. What I think we should do is go to the beach for a good swim. I could use the exercise."

Relief swept through him that she didn't want to run away yet. "Then let's hurry. Last one to make it back to the Jeep has to pay a penalty."

"It won't be me!" Stavros could almost hear a giggle as she darted toward the house in search of her swimsuit. He used his remote to unlock the door for her, then called out, "Want to make a bet?"

He'd come prepared and was already wearing his suit under his jeans. After bounding up the steps, he hurried into the kitchen and carried the hamper down to the Jeep. To his surprise, she wasn't far behind.

After he put the hamper in the backseat, he caught her in his arms so she couldn't climb in front. "I'm afraid you'll have to pay me now."

He could feel her trembling. "You don't play fair."

"I know," he whispered. "Give me your mouth, Andrea. I'm aching for you."

"Stavros—"

Her lips slowly opened to the pressure of his. In the next breath he was lost in sensation after sensation as she gave herself up to him. Never had he known hunger like this. She couldn't seem to get enough either.

He braced his back against the door and lifted her closer so there was no air separating them. In another minute, he was going to carry her into the house and not come out again. But he had to slow down or he really would scare her away.

Forcing himself to come to his senses, he broke off kissing her and removed his hands from her arms. Like him, she fought for breath and backed away. He turned to open the front passenger door for her. "It's a good thing one of us has to drive." His voice sounded thick, even to him.

Andrea moved past him and climbed inside without saying anything. She didn't have to. Her eyes had glazed over and he could see the pulse throbbing at the base of her throat. If he put his lips to it, he wouldn't be able to stop. Summoning his willpower, he closed the door and walked around to his side of the Jeep.

"I'm glad it's you at the wheel, Stavros." Her tremulous voice gave her away even more. "I couldn't possibly function the way I'm feeling."

"I'm not sure *I* can." He locked the house with his remote, then turned on the ignition and they were off. "You realize we have Darren Lewis to thank for our condition."

"I was thinking the very same thing while we were inside your plant."

He inhaled sharply. "When I got the call from Gus, I'd just come from the board meeting. His news was the last thing I needed to hear. If you want to know the truth, before I knew your identity, I was jealous of Georgios, who'd been traveling around on the tour bus with the gorgeous American schoolteacher."

She stirred restlessly in the seat. "Georgios is happily married with a grown family."

"When you introduced yourself, I was thankful that I was happily *unmarried* and could pursue you. After you asked to come with me, I took advantage of your gift. Otherwise I would have shown up at your tour company with an excuse that I needed to talk to you."

She flicked him a glance. "It shocked me when I saw you in Sakis's office yesterday."

"After what we shared, did you really think I would let you get away from me?"

Andrea lowered her head. "I didn't know."

"Something extraordinary is happening to us. I know you feel it."

"That's the problem. In ten days I'll be leaving for Brazil with Dad."

Brazil? He almost went off the road. "What do you mean? You said you were leaving for Indonesia in two months!"

"Dad's plans were changed. You were right about the unrest there. After this weekend, I don't plan to spend any more time with you. So if you'd rather I went back to Thessaloniki tonight, I would understand."

He'd been ready for that. "I have a much better idea. Why don't we enjoy the rest of this day and forget everything else, including deadlines. I haven't had a true vacation in ages and would like to celebrate the end of my career at the Konstantinos Corporation with you. Is that too much to ask?"

His question was met with silence.

He realized she was trying to stop things before they went any further, but it was too late. It had been too late from the moment they'd met. The thought of her leaving Greece, leaving him, was too horrendous to imagine.

CHAPTER FIVE

"WE'RE IN LUCK, ANDREA. The tourists haven't come to this secluded stretch of beach yet. Those with boats will arrive later in the day in droves, but for now they prefer umbrellas and drinks available on the other side of that headland."

Andrea was delighted. A quick five-minute ride from the marina in Thassos and they had this island paradise to themselves with its backdrop of lush vegetation. Once he cut the engine, the blue-and-white boat drifted onto fine white sand.

After peeling off her clothes to reveal a two-piece white bathing suit, she jumped off the rear of the boat into aqua-blue water. Eighty-degree weather had warmed it close to bathtub temperature.

"This is heavenly, Stavros!"

While treading water, she tried not to be obvious as she watched him strip down to his black suit. It rode low on his hips. Without clothes, he could be Adonis come to life, perfect in coloring and form.

Like lightning he entered the water and reached her in seconds. A brilliant white smile was the first thing she noticed when he lifted his head close to her.

With his black hair slicked back, he was so danger-ously appealing, her breath caught.

Beguiled by the sight of him, she ducked beneath the water and started swimming away from him. But when she came up for air, he was right there in front of her. From then on began an hour game of hide-and-seek with him the hunter and her the prey.

"Stop!" she begged, laughing, every time she sur-faced to find him blocking her way. "It's my turn to chase you."

"Come right ahead," he challenged, but stayed where he was.

"You have to try to get away."

"What if I don't want to?" He was waiting for her to swim right into him.

"You're impossible." Exhausted by so much ex-ertion, she did an about-face and started to head for shore when she saw a roundish shape moving beneath the water. "Stavros!" she cried. "I think a stingray is out here!"

Somehow, she didn't know how, he was right there beside her, putting himself between her and the men-ace. "Keep swimming like hell for the beach and shuffle your legs hard." *His* legs moved like pistons, churning the water.

They hadn't been swimming that far out. But it felt like an eternity before her feet touched sand and she collapsed on the beach out of breath. Stavros knelt down next to her and turned her over. "Are you all right?" His voice sounded unsteady.

Andrea would never forget the anxiety in his eyes. "I'm fine. What about you?"

"We got out of the way in time. Thank God you

spotted it and are an excellent swimmer, or you'd be on your way to the hospital. I haven't seen a stingray in these parts for at least four years. Their sting isn't fatal, but it can make you sick."

"I know. My dad got stung in the foot by one—years ago at Kourou beach in French Guiana. He was in bed for several days. I was so worried about him, I stayed home from school so I could take care of him."

He traced the shape of her mouth with his finger. "I'm sure that helped him get well in a hurry. Now that you've brought his name up, I'm curious to know something. Why did you and Ferrante plan to live with your father once you were married?"

"Because he's alone and doesn't have anyone else. Ferrante came from a big family and understood why I felt the way I did. Dad and I had never been separated. Stavros, I'll never be able to repay him for everything he's done for me throughout my entire life. But let's not talk about me.

"You put yourself in danger by shielding me just now." Her heart was in her throat. "How am I ever going to thank you?" She sat up and kissed his strong jaw. But what started out to be an outpouring of her gratitude turned into something else as he lowered her to the sand. Once he'd found her mouth, he began kissing her in earnest.

Those powerful legs of his entwined with hers. She clung to his hard, muscled body, craving the contact of skin against skin. One long kiss grew into another. His lips roved over her face and throat, filling her with rapture she'd never known before.

"Do you have any idea how much I want you?" He kissed her again with almost primitive force. It unleashed passion in her she didn't know herself capable of. Andrea felt on fire and kissed him back just as hungrily. He was fast becoming her addiction.

Before she lost complete control, she buried her face in his neck. "We need to slow down, Stavros. It frightens me because I've never felt this way before, not even with Ferrante."

He was a beautiful specimen of manhood, but there was so much more to him than the physical. For Stavros to find her attractive enough to want a relationship with her constituted something of a miracle. She was no femme fatale, yet he'd kissed her as if she was the most important thing in his life.

But the truth had to be faced. There was no good time for them. He'd launched a new multimillion-dollar business here on the island. She'd be leaving Greece shortly. The situation with Tina wasn't going to go away. Besides a ton of work at the office in Thessaloniki, she had packing to do and still needed to talk to her landlord and Sakis.

To go on trying to work things out with Stavros when they could find the time to fit it in made absolutely no sense. All it would do was prolong the agony. After losing Ferrante, she couldn't go through that kind of pain again. Better to cut things off now before they became any more involved. Soon they'd be on opposite sides of the world.

It was a long time before Stavros spoke. "Fear is the last emotion I want you to feel." She felt energy shoot through him before he rolled away from her and got to his feet. "What we need is to enjoy the lunch Raisa packed for us."

The moment was bittersweet because she didn't

want him to stop kissing her. At the same time, she marveled over his self-control because she didn't have any. Slowly, she sat up, but it was difficult because the desire she felt for him had dazed her. "We look like we've been bathing in sand."

"We'll wash off next to the boat. Come on." He reached for her hand and helped her all the way up. Together, they walked across the sand into the shallows. The next thing she knew, he'd swung her up in his arms as if she were a bride.

"No—Stavros!" Her protest came out on a nervous laugh as he waded deeper. "What are you going to do?"

"Give us a proper bath."

"No—" she squealed again, but by then they were both immersed.

"There." He smiled broadly after bringing them back up. "That wasn't so bad. Now our sandwiches won't taste of grit. Let's see if we've gotten all of it off your lips." Once again, Stavros started kissing her as if his life depended on it and carried her to the boat. She moaned when he finally relinquished her mouth and lowered her onto a banquette.

"I don't know about you, but that swim for our lives gave me an appetite. Kissing you has made me even more ravenous." In one deft masculine move, he levered himself inside the boat. "We're safe here, Andrea. The only thing that's going to take a bite out of you now is me."

After kissing her thoroughly once more, she felt exposed with his all-seeing eyes roving over her figure. Better put on her T-shirt. It wouldn't hurt to fix her hair either. She reached in her purse for a comb while he opened the hamper. Soon, they dug in to tasty finger food and fruit.

When Andrea had eaten all she could, she sat back and lifted her face to the sun. "This is one of those moments I'll treasure forever. Out of all the islands I've visited in the Aegean, Thassos is my favorite. Think of all the conquerors and invaders who have left their mark here. I can see why you wanted to make your home here. You have it all. Mountains, beaches, the sun, the perfect climate. It's like your own fairyland nestled in the greenery." After a pause, she said, "I have a confession to make."

He darted her a curious glance. "What's that?"

"One of the commandments says, 'Thou shalt not covet.' As I was standing on your patio, looking out over this glorious spot of earth, I understood its meaning for the first time. When you climbed the mountain, no wonder you claimed this place for your own. To live where you live really is paradise on earth. Your mythical Greek gods must be jealous of you."

Stavros stared out at the water. "I haven't needed the gods to cause me trouble. The family I was born into has made enough mischief."

"At one time or other I think most people have said that about their families."

"But there are degrees of mischief."

"Stavros? Was it always hard for you?"

He nodded. "Pretty much from day one. I didn't want to do things the way my father did. He wanted me in private school. I wanted to go to public school. He didn't like my close friends who weren't good enough for him. He didn't like me dating a lot of girls. I went through them like water."

"Was there one you fell hard for?"

"All of them."

"Be serious."

"I am. I never went with someone I wasn't crazy about."

"For a time, you mean."

He grinned.

"How long did the attraction last?" she asked.

"Maybe two dates."

"I was the same way," Andrea confessed. "I never had myriads of boyfriends, but I liked guys a lot better than girls."

"Your only problem was that none of them measured up to your dad except Ferrante."

"It wasn't like that, Stavros. I never compared him to Dad. What I loved about Ferrante was his gentle nature, and that's one of Dad's best qualities. But in other ways they were completely different."

Stavros made an odd sound in his throat. "My father has never kept his opinions to himself. He didn't like my doing jobs for anyone but him. I was happy for any job that would help me save money and get away from him micromanaging me. He had his mind made up I would go to college in London for a business degree. I decided I wanted to be an engineer and went to MIT. He wanted me to live in Thessaloniki with the rest of the family. I wanted to live here on Thassos.

"We disagreed on every issue. He let me know when he thought it was time for me to get married. I told him I wasn't sure that day would ever come. He'd picked out Tina to be the woman I should marry. The

Nassos came from the right bloodline with all the important connections and affluence."

"Does your mother have no say in how you conduct your life?"

"She mostly goes along with my father, especially where Tina is concerned. But I think that of all my decisions, choosing to live on Thassos has caused her the most grief. Mother sees us like a clan, all closely knit. I'm afraid I'm a person who needs more breathing room."

Andrea pondered everything, almost afraid to ask her next question. "Has there ever been a time when you and your father agreed on something important?"

"Yes. He supported me when I played soccer. When the board proposed new names for vice president of the corporation, we both felt that my brother, Leon, had the stability and wisdom to be the best choice over my two cousins."

"That's it?"

"I'm sure there were a few other times, but not many. That's something you can't comprehend, can you?"

"No...but then I'm not a man."

His smile was devilish. "I'm happy to say you're the personification of femininity."

"Be serious for a minute."

"I'm trying, but it's hard when I'm looking at you."

It was hard on her when his eyes seemed to devour her. "Did your brother pick his own wife?"

"Yes, but she had the right breeding and family history to satisfy my parents. Leon gets along without making waves. He's a terrific father to their children. I manage to do things that get under my father's skin.

It's not on purpose. I love my father because he's my father. But I don't like him very much. Can you understand that?"

"I guess I can, but it makes me sad. Dad and I just click."

Stavros nodded. "Otherwise you wouldn't be leaving Greece with him."

She averted her eyes. "How does your father treat Leon's children?"

"He's still dictatorial, but a little nicer."

"Then there's hope. I've told you before that I think you'll make a wonderful father, Stavros. Maybe it'll take giving your dad some grandchildren to soften him."

In the midst of their conversation Andrea heard music. She turned her head and saw that a cabin cruiser had discovered their special spot. People were on board playing loud music, disturbing the tranquillity. In the far distance, she saw a sailboat coming closer.

She and Stavros hadn't come back to the boat any too soon. A little earlier and the sight of the two of them wrapped in each other's arms on the sand would have provided unexpected entertainment for anyone watching. Heat swept through her body as she remembered how expertly Stavros had brought her alive. Andrea still felt alive and he wasn't even touching her.

"Our paradise has been invaded," Stavros murmured. "No more isolation for us." All of a sudden, he closed the hamper and got up, unaware of her private thoughts. He stood there shirtless in the hot sun while the breeze blew his black hair away from his fore-head. There couldn't be a more fabulous man alive.

"It's time to leave. Besides the overcrowding, you've gotten enough sun. Put your life jacket back on, Andrea." She'd forgotten, but he never forgot anything to make her comfortable or safe. "I'll jump out and push us off."

Something was bothering him, but she couldn't read his mind. Already she regretted he was bringing this glorious outing to a close. With what looked like effortless male agility, Stavros got out to move the boat into deeper water. It took a lot of strength, though he made it look like child's play. In a minute, he came around the driver's side to climb back on.

But as he started to get in, she heard a groan. He managed to make it inside the boat, but he sank to the floor, grabbing his lower leg. His features contorted in pain.

"Turn over on your stomach, Stavros."

Groaning again, he made a great effort to do as she'd asked. Andrea hunkered down and noticed immediately the small cut just above his ankle. The bleeding was minimal. "I don't believe it. That sting-ray got you. This looks like the cut on Dad's foot. Don't move. I'm phoning for help."

She lunged for her purse and pulled out her cell phone to call emergency services. Stavros was already losing color.

The second the dispatcher answered, she said, "This is Despinis Linford. Send an ambulance to the private boat dock at Thassos marina ASAP. Kyrie Stavros Konstantinos has been stung by a stingray above the back of the ankle. He'll be in a blue-and-white speedboat. I'll blast the horn to help you spot him. Hurry!"

"Andrea," he muttered when she clicked off. "You shouldn't have told them my name." She could tell he was barely holding on because of the pain.

She got behind the wheel of the boat and turned on the engine. "Everyone knows who you are. I did it to get you the best care immediately." She backed the boat around, then put the gear in forward and they shot away from the beach. The marina was just around the headland.

"Hang on, Stavros. You'll be out of your pain soon." Andrea thanked providence that they hadn't gone to some beach farther away where help wouldn't be available as fast.

Once she'd rounded the point, she headed straight for the boat dock. To her joy, she saw an ambulance drawing near. She pressed on the horn and kept pressing. After lowering her speed, she cut the engine and allowed the boat to slide into its private berth. The ambulance attendants came running with a gurney. A crowd of people had assembled, wanting to know what was going on.

"Take good care of him," she begged as they lifted him out of the boat.

"I'll be fine, Andrea." His voice sounded weak.

"I know you will. I'll come to the medical center in a few minutes."

She watched him being put in the ambulance. After it drove off, she slipped on her denims. Then she gathered up his clothes. The keys to the house and Jeep were in his pocket. She pulled them out and put them in her purse along with the boat key. Andrea would have to leave the hamper for now.

One of the bystanders tied up the boat for her. She thanked him before heading for the Jeep in the parking area.

There were signs leading to the medical center, but she knew where it was because she'd checked it out as part of her job, in case of emergencies on the tour here. She found a parking space near the ER entrance and rushed inside. The staff person in triage needed information. Andrea told her what she could.

"Are you a relative?"

"No. A friend. How soon can I go in to see him?"

"Let me call the desk."

Andrea waited ten minutes in agony before she was allowed through the doors to his curtained cubicle. Stavros, dressed in a hospital gown, lay there with his eyes closed. The middle-aged ER doctor smiled at her. "Despinis Linford?" She nodded. "I'm Dr. Goulas. Come in. I understand you're the heroine who got our island's most famous resident here in record time."

Andrea knew Stavros was revered. "I tried. How is he?"

"We're already giving him pain medication through the drip. He's drifting in and out of sleep. The pain from that sting has traveled up his limb and could last forty-eight hours. I've checked his vital signs. Kyrie Konstantinos is doing well. I've given him a tetanus shot to be on the safe side.

"What we're going to do now is soak his lower leg in hot water for about an hour. That reduces a lot of the pain. Then I'll inject more painkiller around the cut and take a look to see if there's any foreign matter before I sew it up."

She took a shaky breath. "Can I stay in here with him?"

"I'd like you to. When he was brought in, his greatest concern was you. It will ease his mind to know he can see and talk to you. Why don't you sit down? This has been an ordeal for you too."

Andrea nodded and took a seat in one of the chairs. "We'd seen the stingray earlier, but it was out in deeper water. I couldn't believe it had come in right by his boat."

"They hide in the shallows under the sand."

"Stavros must have stepped on it while he was pushing the boat off the sand. I heard him groan and then he paled so fast."

"It's the shock. But the cut doesn't appear to be deep and I doubt it will become infected."

"Can I take him home tonight?"

"If his blood pressure is good and he doesn't have any trouble breathing, then I would say that's a real possibility. He'll have to stay on oral antibiotics for a while." Her father had been given antibiotics too.

While she sat there waiting for Stavros to wake up, she could tell he was getting his color back, thank heaven. In a minute, a technician wheeled in a cart holding a rectangular basin of hot water. The doctor lifted Stavros's left leg. Once the basin was in place, he lowered the bottom half and foot into the water.

Stavros was such a striking man. To see him incapacitated…to see one of those long, strong legs injured…it just killed her.

"There's a lounge on the other side of the clinic with food and drinks."

"Thank you, but I'm not hungry. We'd just eaten a big meal before this happened."

"Very good. I'll be back."

"Thank you for everything, Doctor."

"It's a privilege."

That was the sentiment Andrea saw in the people who interacted with Stavros. She loved him so much and pulled the chair closer to his side where she wouldn't disturb the drip in his hand. Her mind played over the events of the past ten days. It was pure chance that they'd met at all.

If Sakis hadn't sent her to investigate Darren's disappearance—if the teen had decided to run away at another stop on the tour—if Stavros hadn't been available. So many ifs that had to occur with split-second timing for them to have been brought together in the cosmos.

And now this injury.

It could have been fatal if he'd been stung in the heart or abdomen. A shudder ran through her body. While she sat there trying not to think about his close call, the doctor came in again, followed by the technician, who wheeled in another basin of hot water. They repeated the process.

"His vital signs are holding," the doctor informed her. "This sleep is doing him good. I'll give this another twenty minutes, then take a look at the cut."

Ten more minutes and she heard him say her name. "I'm here, Stavros."

"I need to feel you." He moved his hand toward

her. When she grasped it, his heavily lashed eyelids opened.

Andrea leaned closer. "How's the pain now?"

"What pain?"

She squeezed his hand. "You don't have to act brave around me."

"Whatever they gave me knocked me out. I don't feel a thing."

"That's good."

"Have I told you you're the most amazing woman I've ever known?"

"It takes an amazing man to recognize one."

"I'm serious."

"So am I." She smiled. "Your doctor says it's an honor to be taking care of you. I agree. Is there anyone who ought to know what's happened to you?"

"The only person of importance is you. With you watching over me, I don't want anyone else."

"That's the painkiller talking."

"Andrea—" He tugged on her hand. "You're not really going to Brazil with your father, are you?"

Her breath caught. "Let's not talk about that right now. You need to rest and let the medication work."

"You can't go. We've only started getting to know each other."

If only he knew the pain she was in just thinking about it. "Right now, you need to concentrate on getting better."

"Don't change the subject." His grip on her hand was surprisingly strong. He would have said more, but the doctor and the technician walked in, interrupting him.

"Let's take a look at the cut." He eyed Andrea.

"We have to turn him over. If you'll step out, this won't take long."

"I want her to come right back," Stavros stated in what she considered had to be his boardroom voice.

Dr. Goulas smiled at her. "Is that your wish too?"

"Yes. Please."

"Then stay outside the curtain. I'll tell you when you can come in again."

Stavros's grip on her hand tightened before he released her. She welcomed the pressure. They had a connection that was growing stronger every minute.

When she'd asked him if she could call someone in his family to let them know he was in the clinic, he'd said no. His history with his father haunted her. When she thought of her own relationship with her dad, her heart bled for Stavros because he hadn't had a loving experience.

Ten minutes passed before she was called back in.

"Come over here, Andrea." Stavros reached for her hand.

"Good news," the doctor said. "I've cleaned the wound and put in some stitches. This should heal nicely."

"How soon can I be released?" Stavros wanted to know.

"Let's finish out the drip. Then I'll want to check your blood pressure. If you remain stabilized, you'll be able to go home this evening, but it will be bed rest until Monday. I'll send an antibiotic with you, and I'll want to see you again on Friday to check the wound."

Andrea sensed the doctor was about to leave and eased her hand from Stavros's grip.

"Where do you think you're going?" he demanded.

How she loved him! "I'll be right back." She hurried to catch up with the doctor outside the curtain. "Dr. Goulas? Thank you more than I can say."

He nodded. "Kyrie Konstantinos is a very important man, but his type makes the worst kind of patient. See that he stays down and follows directions. If you can stop him from going to work on Monday, that would be best. Between you and me, he's not out of the woods yet. Follow-up care with this kind of wound is critical to make certain there's no recurring infection."

"I know. My father received a similar sting on his foot years ago and was absolutely impossible."

"I take it he's an important man too."

"Very, especially to me."

He patted her arm. "The more sleep our patient gets right now, the better. I'll be around again later."

When Andrea peeked inside the curtain, Stavros's eyes were closed. Taking the doctor's advice to heart, she walked through to the other side of the clinic for some coffee. Today's experience had taken a toll. Some caffeine would give her energy for what lay ahead.

Taking advantage of the time, she phoned her boss. It went through to his voice mail. Andrea left the message about Stavros's ordeal and explained she needed to nurse him for a little while. Would it be all right if she didn't come in to work until Tuesday? If the answer was yes, then Sakis didn't need to call her back.

Next, she phoned her landlord and left the message that she'd be vacating the apartment within ten days to travel with her father to Brazil. But she would pay the money still owed to honor the lease.

Thinking of her father, she sent him the photos she'd taken of Stavros's new plant. She texted an explanation so he'd understand what he was looking at, but she stopped short of sending him pictures of Stavros. She explained about the missing teen and the opportunity to see the plant before she returned to Thessaloniki.

On her way back to the ER, she went to the restroom and was horrified to see how bad she looked. She needed to shower and wash the sand out of her hair. But all that would have to come later after she'd driven him home.

She freshened up the best she could and went back to look in on Stavros, pleased to see he was no longer hooked up to the drip. To her surprise, he was awake. One of the staff must have helped him to dress in his jeans and polo shirt. His penetrating gray eyes centered on her.

"I wondered when you were going to come back. I'm good to go home. They're bringing a wheelchair."

"In that case, I'll go out to the Jeep and pull it around."

"If you want to know the truth, I'm glad this happened."

Andrea sucked in her breath. "How can you say that after being in a life-and-death situation?"

"Because before I got stung, I knew you were going to ask me to send for the helicopter so you could leave for Thessaloniki tonight."

She looked away. He knew her better than she knew herself. "I'll see you out in front."

Her heart was at war between the two most wonderful men in the world. She loved both of them, but owed her dad everything. Her desire to be with Stavros for as long as he still desired her was self-ish. When her dad had worked so hard for them all his life, how could she say goodbye to him and stay in Greece knowing he was facing the future alone? He had no one else.

Andrea walked out of the clinic to the Jeep, oblivi-ous to her surroundings because a sadness had taken hold of her, one she couldn't throw off. It wasn't like the pain after Ferrante's death. That had been final. She'd finally gotten over it because she knew he'd never come back.

But Stavros was vibrantly alive despite that awful stingray's sting.

No matter how many thousands of miles separated them, she'd be tormented by the knowledge that he was here and she'd walked away from him. Not be-cause she'd wanted to.

But because she had to.

A few minutes later she saw a male staff member wheeling him out of the ER exit in a wheelchair. After the vision she'd had of him lying in the bottom of the boat writhing in pain, to see him looking this good caused her heart to skip a beat. You'd never know his jeans covered a potentially serious wound.

After helping him climb in the Jeep, the orderly came around and handed her a plastic bag. In a whis-per, he said, "He's a little dizzy." She nodded. Inside the bag was a packet of dressings and two kinds of pills. She thanked the orderly and put it on the back-seat.

Turning to the man she adored, she said, "Ready to go home?"

"As long as you come with me."

Now her pulse was racing. "I won't abandon you. I promise." She pulled out of the ER driveway, onto the road, and headed for the road that would take them past Panagia to his villa.

"I'm going to hold you to that." His vaguely fierce tone sent a shiver through her.

"Try to relax against the seat and sleep until we get there."

"I've been sleeping on and off for hours. Tell me how you learned to do everything so well."

"What do you mean?"

"You drove us away from that beach without a hitch and you handle this Jeep like you've been driving one all your life."

"My father's work meant he lived in some pretty remote, out-of-the-way places. He needed a four-wheel drive to get anywhere on unpaved roads. I had to learn fast. When we took little vacations, we usually headed for water anywhere we could find it. Dad loves to fish. We rented a lot of different kinds of boats. I drove while he looked for the best spots."

His hand squeezed her shoulder. "Because of your expertise at everything, you saved me from going into irreversible shock. I don't know another woman who would have your quick thinking in a crisis and sense instinctively what to do."

"Sure you do, but you've never given them a chance. You're so self-sufficient, you're not the kind of man who gets himself into trouble he can't get out of. I just happened to be there at the exact moment you actually needed help, not that you'd ever ask for it."

"Am I that bad?" he teased.

"Worse! I guess that stingray got so mad at being foiled the first time, he came after you out of revenge."

Laughter broke from Stavros, the deep male kind that thrilled her. "How do you know it was a he?"

"I don't. It was a figure of speech, but men do love a challenge, don't they."

He laughed again. "It sounds like you've been around a lot of them."

"Living with my dad, my life's been filled with men. Mine workers, plant workers, chemists, engineers. Thousands of them," she volunteered. "Maybe even a million."

She could feel him staring at her profile. "So how on earth did you meet Ferrante?"

"My dad and I took a ski holiday in Cortina. Ferrante and I shared a chair lift. He was on vacation too. We got talking, and then he followed me down the mountain, and then followed me to the hotel where he met Dad. Before lon—"

"You were in love." Stavros filled in the rest.

"Not right away. Let's just say he was a better skier than Dad. I loved it because my dad does everything well. He'd also climbed more mountains than my father, leaving Dad and me totally impressed."

"So my little jaunt up Mount Ypsarion wouldn't make a dent in your father's estimation."

"A dent is a dent." Her reply produced a smile from him. "But I sent him the photos of your plant along with an explanation. It'll blow his mind knowing you've created a product no one else has. You have genius in you, Stavros."

"That's nice to know," came the mocking comment.

"I wasn't patronizing you." She made a turn into his private road. "We're almost to the house. I can tell you're going to need another pain pill right away. I'll pull up in front where you won't have to negotiate so many steps."

Thankful they were home, she jumped out and ran around to help him. "Put your arm around my shoulders and let me take some of your weight. You need to get off your leg as soon as possible."

He not only slid his arm around her, he pulled her against him and kissed her hungrily on the mouth. "I love my life being in your hands."

His words shook her to the foundation.

"Come on, Achilles. Let's get you into bed."

He let out a bark of laughter. "I need a shower first," he said.

"Not tonight, Stavros. The doctor said you can do it in the morning."

They made it inside and down the hall to his bedroom. She hadn't been in it before and tried not to think about it as they moved inside. "What can I do to help?"

"Take me to the bathroom."

She did his bidding and waited outside until he appeared in the doorway. Once again, she lent him her strength until they reached the bed. He let go of her long enough to unfasten his jeans. "I'll need you to pull them over my leg."

Andrea knelt down.

"I can see you're blushing. Don't worry. The hospital dried my swimming trunks before I put them back on."

"I wasn't worried."

"Liar," he whispered in a silky voice.

As soon as that was accomplished, he stood up so she could draw back the covers. Without any urging, he removed his polo shirt, then lay down on his side. She helped ease his bad leg onto the mattress. The other followed. Earlier in the day she'd been caught by those legs, loving every second of her entrapment.

By the sound of his sigh, she knew bed felt heavenly to him. "I'm going out to the Jeep to bring in the rest of our things. Be right back."

In another five minutes she'd given him two pills and tucked him in. "Here's your phone, wallet and keys. I'll put them on this side table with your water. If you need me in the night, phone me."

"It's only eight thirty. I'm not ready to go to sleep yet."

"You will be once those pills take effect. Good night."

He called to her, but she ignored him and headed for the guest bedroom. She needed a shower in the worst way. After working up a lather of shampoo, she rinsed off and emerged feeling sparkling clean.

With a towel wrapped around her hair, she went back in the bedroom and pulled a nightgown and robe from her duffel bag. It was nice feeling normal again. She padded through the house to the kitchen to get a bottle of water. As she took it out of the fridge, she heard a loud couple of knocks. The sound was coming from the back door.

Had Stavros's mother or ex-girlfriend heard about his injury? Or maybe it was Raisa.

She cinched the belt tighter on her pink-striped robe and hurried through the rear hallway to the door.

She jumped when she saw a man on the other side. He bore a superficial resemblance to Stavros. This had to be his brother. Maybe someone at the hospital had called him. She hadn't heard the helicopter because she'd been in the shower.

Andrea undid the lock. He came inside and shut the door. The way he looked at her, it was apparent he was equally shocked to see a strange woman answering the door.

"I'm Leon, Stavros's brother. And you are…?"

"No one important. It's nice to meet you."

"Likewise," he murmured. "Where's Stavros? He hasn't answered his phone all day."

"You'll find him in the bedroom, where all will be explained. If you'll excuse me, I'm going to bed myself. Be sure to lock up when you let yourself out again. He's in no condition to do it."

CHAPTER SIX

"WHAT THE HELL is going on?"

At the sound of his brother's voice, Stavros lifted his head off the pillow. Something had to be wrong for his forty-year-old brother to fly all the way from Thessaloniki at this hour.

"Leon? What are you doing here?"

"You haven't answered my phone calls all day," he accused without preamble. "I got worried and flew here because it isn't like you not to respond."

"Take a breath and I'll explain. Sit down, bro. How's your family?"

"They're fine." Leon picked up the chair and put it at the side of the bed. They were alike in coloring, but his married brother was an inch taller and carried about thirty more pounds. He grinned. "Who's the beautiful blue-eyed woman who opened the door wearing a pink-and-white-striped robe and a towel covering her hair?"

Well, well. That was a sight Stavros had yet to behold. "You mean she didn't tell you?"

"No. She said she wasn't anyone important and told me she was going to bed, would I lock up on my way out."

Stavros let go with another burst of laughter.

"What's so funny? Why *are* you in bed?"

He was glad Leon had come. The medicine had knocked him out earlier. Now he was awake and going crazy without Andrea's company. "Why don't you grab a beer from the fridge and then we'll talk."

"You don't want one?"

"I can't."

"You're not making sense."

"The doctor told me no alcohol for a while."

Leon's brows met in a frown. He leaned closer to him. "I knew something had happened to you."

"Would you believe I got stung by a stingray today? The pain was unreal. That unimportant person who answered the door saved my life."

"Is she a nurse from the clinic? Is that why she's here?"

"It's a long story."

"I've got the time."

For the next little while, Stavros explained everything. But at the mention of PanHellenic Tours, Leon made a strange sound in his throat. "Wait just a minute. This Andrea is the blonde American woman who has Mother and Tina Lasso in fits? She speaks Greek like a native. I would never have guessed."

"Try a dozen languages she's mastered. Brains and beauty."

"Despinis Linford is a knockout, all right. But she's also one of the reasons I flew here to see you tonight."

"I figured you had some bad news for me or you wouldn't have come."

"It's serious, I'm afraid. Dad's in a rage."

"That's old news. He knew I was forming my own

company. My resignation was inevitable. My company is already a week into production."

"I know, but it's not just that, Stav. He expects you to do the right thing for Tina now that she's pregnant."

"If I'd ever loved Tina, I would have married her long ago. She's bluffing, Leon. But in any case, I never slept with her, so it couldn't be mine."

"You and I both know that, but our father is beyond listening to reason. I came here to warn you. I overheard him tell Mother that if you don't marry Tina, he's going to prevent any more sales of the marble waste from our quarries to be sold to you."

"He *what*?" A pain stabbed him to the depths. His own father would really do that?

"Are you serious?"

"I'm afraid so. He'll try to shut you down in order to get his own way."

"Leon—what kind of man does such a thing to his son?"

"I'm sorry, Stav."

Tears filled Stavros's eyes, unbidden. "Father really hates me to consider betraying me like this. It's one blow I could never have anticipated." He thought back to his earlier conversation with Andrea about his father. If his father was willing to go that far, it could impact Stavros's relationship with her. Stavros didn't want this touching Andrea and would go to any lengths to keep her in his life.

Leon put a hand on his shoulder. "He doesn't hate you, Stav. If you want to know my opinion, Tina's father has put the squeeze on our father. He may even have threatened to take away the shipping services he has provided all these years."

"So I'm supposed to do the right thing by Tina?"

"It's the only way to solve the problem."

He looked in Leon's eyes. "Are *you* asking me to do it?"

"Hell, no. I couldn't marry a woman I didn't love. I wouldn't! To my way of thinking, this is pure sabotage on Nasso's part and he's railroading our father. You need to confirm the facts of Tina's so-called pregnancy first."

"She might be pregnant, Leon, but doing a DNA before the baby is born could prove dangerous to the fetus. I'd have to wait until after it's delivered before the test could be done to prove it's not mine."

His brother frowned. "That could mean six months or longer. Can you keep your new business afloat that long without suffering?"

Stavros nodded. "There are other quarries, but I'll be forced to do some fast negotiating to provide backup when the need comes. Orders are pouring in."

"Then get better and do it! I'd help you if I could."

"You already have by giving me a heads-up. I owe you. Anyway, I know your hands are tied. Tell you what, Leon. Tina's father can plot till doomsday, but he and Father aren't going to put me out of business," Stavros said icily.

"There's more."

He stared at his brother. "How could there be more?"

"Mother believes you're involved with—"

"Andrea?" Stavros supplied the name. "She'd be dead-on right."

Leon blinked. "You mean…?"

"Yes."

"But—"

"There's no but. Only *if*."

"What are you saying?"

"If Andrea doesn't love me enough, then my life will have to go on without her. But for the life of me, I can't figure out how I'll be able to live without her."

Leon looked shocked. "I thought she saved your life."

"She did. However, there's someone else more important to her."

"More important than you?"

Stavros loved his brother for being there for him. "You have no idea."

"Who is it?"

"Picture a single father who's been all things to his motherless daughter from the day she was born. They've traveled the world and have been inseparable. At the end of this month, he's leaving for Brazil and she'll be going with him. He's got an unbreakable hold on her. It's called love."

"Then you'll just have to find a way to make her love you more. You have the power."

"Not if she fears Tina really is pregnant with my child."

"I think if she thought that, she wouldn't be here waiting on you hand and foot." He got to his feet. Stavros prayed his brother was right. "Your eyelids are drooping. I'm going to leave. The pilot's waiting for me. Take care of that wound. Don't be surprised if Tina's father has more surprises in store to hurt you."

"I'll consider myself warned."

Leon leaned down and they hugged. "Do me a

favor. Answer my phone calls from now on and keep me up to date. I'll help any way I can."

"Will do. Thanks for coming. I owe you, bro."

Stavros listened until he heard the helicopter lift off. His brother had left him with one salient thought. *You have the power.* Without hesitation, he phoned Andrea. He wasn't going to let his father drive her away. She answered on the second ring.

"I just heard your brother leave. Are you all right?"

"No. Would you mind coming to my room?"

"I'll be right there."

To his delight, she appeared in the pink-and-white-striped robe, but was minus the towel. While his brother had been here, she'd blow-dried her hair. The silky texture had natural curl and waved around her neck. She was like a delicious confection.

"Can I get you something?"

"I don't need anything, but I'd like to ask a favor of you if you're willing, and provided you can even do it. This can't wait."

"Hmm…you've got me curious." She walked over to the bed and sat on the chair Leon had placed there.

"My brother brought me unsettling news." After he'd finished telling her about his father's plan to sabotage his business, and what part Tina's father played in the whole scenario, her eyes filled with tears.

"Your own father would do that so you'll marry Tina Nasso?" Her voice shook.

"He's afraid of the consequences if I don't. He and her father have business connections in common, so he's hoping I'll cave before he has to carry out that threat. Leon came to warn me."

She shook her head. "But you're his flesh and blood."

"With a father like yours, I realize you can't comprehend it. Unfortunately, the time has come where I have to be a step ahead of mine because I've worked years to see the fruition of my business plans. As I told you earlier, if I fail, it'll be letting down my colleagues, not to mention hundreds of employees with families. I can't risk that." *Or you...*

She drew in a deep breath. "What favor do you want from me?"

"In the next few days I have to visit some quarries in Thassos not owned by my family in order to negotiate contracts for their marble refuse."

"But you're supposed to be resting your leg or it might not heal."

"That's why I need someone to drive me around and be my mouthpiece. I can't expect my colleagues to do this. I've let them know I'm laid up for a few days. In that amount of time, I can get this other work done. Is it possible your boss would give you the time off? I'll pay you for your time."

She bit her lip. "I don't want your money. You saved me from the stingray. That's payment enough. Since I'm leaving Greece so soon, I think Sakis has kind of given up on me doing much work. He would probably okay me for one more day off. I already asked him if I didn't have to come in until Tuesday."

His heart did a swift kick. "You did?"

"Yes. The doctor told me you shouldn't try to go to work before then, and he wants to see you back on Friday. But, Stavros—riding around in the Jeep would never do."

"We'll go in the Mercedes. I'll rest my leg across the backseat. By Tuesday we should have covered four or five quarries. Hopefully I'll come home with enough contracts to keep the plant running in case my father carries out his plan."

Andrea got up from the chair. "I'll phone Sakis first thing in the morning. If he's in agreement, then I'll be happy to drive you around. But tomorrow's Sunday, and you *have* to stay down."

"I'll be good."

"Ha! The doctor and I had a discussion about you."

He smiled. "What did he say?"

"It's a secret. Now, is there anything I can do for you?"

"One thing."

She shook her head. "Just not that one."

"You're still afraid of the way you feel about me." He loved it because it meant her feelings for him ran so deep.

"Good night."

When she'd gone, he turned off his lamp. At least she hadn't left him yet.

Andrea got up early and dressed in jeans and a short-sleeved, botanical-printed blouse. She hadn't heard a peep out of Stavros. After fixing him a breakfast tray, she took it through to his bedroom and discovered he wasn't in bed.

She put the tray on the dresser and waited for him to come out of the bathroom. In a few minutes, he emerged shaved and wearing a navy toweling robe. His hair was still damp from his shower. She could smell the soap.

It wasn't fair that one man should be endowed with the kind of male attributes that made a woman breathless at the very sight of him. The fact that he was limping did nothing to take away the sheer vital essence of him.

"Good morning, Stavros."

His gaze zeroed in on her. Maybe it was the color of his robe that made his gray eyes look almost black. "How long have you been waiting?"

"For just a minute. I brought breakfast for both of us. Though I'm sure that shower felt good, you need to get right back in bed. I'd like to take a look at that wound. You probably need a fresh dressing. If you'll lie facedown, this will only take a moment."

He limped to the bed and stretched out. She pulled one clean dressing from the box and leaned over to undo the old one. "There's been a little drainage, but that's to be expected. Everything looks good."

Andrea applied the new one and discarded the other one. "If you'll turn over while I wash my hands, then we'll eat." Satisfied he was able to get on his back with less difficulty than last night, she hurried into his bathroom and came right back. "If you'll make some room, I'll put the tray on the side of the bed and we'll eat."

She brought their food over. "As you see, I can make toast and coffee, just like you. I also brought you some fresh water to take your pills."

He took them first, then lay propped on his side while they ate. She'd peeled an orange and pulled the wedges apart for them. "How's the pain?"

"It's sore, but the intensity of it has gone."

"When you climbed into the boat yesterday, I could

see the pain in your face. I'm so thankful you're feeling better."

"Me too, and we both know who deserves the credit for getting me immediate help."

"Except that, in my haste, I'm afraid the hamper is still in the boat."

"No problem. I'll get it later in the week. Did you phone your boss?"

"I left him a message to call me."

"Good." When he'd finished eating, he said, "Okay. Now that we've gotten all the small talk out of the way, let's get rid of the tray."

Adrenaline filled her bloodstream. "I'll take it out. Is there anything you want me to bring you?"

"If you'd bring my laptop from the den."

"Coming right up." She hurried to the kitchen, darted to his den and returned. "Here you go." As she handed the computer to him, he pulled her down on the side of the bed where the tray had been. "Stavros—" Her heart pounded outrageously.

"What's the matter? I only want to thank you properly. Come here, Andrea."

He'd put one arm around her neck, forcing her down until their mouths fused. The unexpectedness of his action had caught her off guard. She half lay against his chest, unable to fight those seductive forces taking over her body. Her hands had a will of their own and slid into his hair. She loved its vibrancy.

"I could eat you alive," he cried softly, treating her to every kind of kiss imaginable until she was losing awareness of the surroundings. Her longing for him had reached a dangerous level of intensity. She had to fight not to go under.

"Your leg—we have to stop." She found the strength to tear her lips from his and pulled away so she could stand up. Weaving on her feet, she drank in gulps of air. "This isn't the kind of bed rest Dr. Goulas had in mind."

"Not even if it's the best medicine for me?"

She let out a laugh bordering on hysteria. "Only you would say that. You're impossible, *Kyrie* Konstantinos, so I have an idea. While you do some work, I'll drive down to the marina in the Jeep and bring the hamper back. I might as well fill the gas tank and buy a newspaper for you at the same time. You can phone if you need me. I promise to be quick."

"As long as you're going, buy me a pasteli."

"I'll get one for me too." She reached for the car keys on the nightstand. "Those sesame seed candy bars are yummy."

"So are you, Andrea. Hurry back."

Two hours later she returned, having done all her errands. She emptied the hamper, then did the few dishes and cleaned up the kitchen. With that accomplished, she hurried through the house to Stavros's bedroom with goodies. He'd propped himself on his side to work on the computer.

She put the newspaper and candy bars down next to him. His piercing gaze found hers. "You were gone so long, I was starting to worry."

Andrea laughed. "Sure you were." She sat down on the chair next to him. "What have you been working on?"

"Our trip. Did you hear from your boss yet?"

"Yes. He's rough around the edges, but has a kind heart. When he heard about your encounter with the stingray, he told me to take care of you and not worry about things at the office. Dorcas is going to fill in for me."

"I haven't heard that name before."

"She's a friend of mine who works in Accounts. Already I can tell Sakis is thinking ahead."

One side of his mouth turned up at the corner. "You have him wrapped around your little finger. Even though you haven't left him yet, inside I wager he's been mourning his loss."

She let out a sigh. "You always manage to say the right thing."

"Do I?"

"Yes. For being so nice, I've brought you another present." She pulled a packet of playing cards out of her jeans pocket. "How about a game of diloti?"

"You know how to play that?"

"Casino is the game of choice in every country where I've lived. Diloti is the Greek version of virtually the same thing. Are you up for a few rounds?"

"Watch me," he said with a satisfied gleam in his eyes.

"But we won't play for money."

"I'm way ahead of you."

Her adrenaline surged. "I bet you are, but since I intend to win, I'm not going to worry about it. We'll play until one o'clock."

"What happens then?"

"Lunch. I bought some fresh spanakopitas." She loved cheese pies more than about anything.

"I'll set my watch alarm so we have to quit at the same time."

"That's fair."

"So be it." She glimpsed fire in his eyes. "You're on!"

The race was all about winning the most points. She got lucky and made a sweep early. Then luck was on his side and he made one. As the pressure began to build, Andrea started to eat her candy. Stavros had already devoured his.

Cards had always been serious business for her. Naturally he was good. What Greek man worth his salt wasn't! So good, in fact, she feared she might lose. Andrea kept looking at her watch. Time was almost up. "I can hear your awesome brain doing calculations, Stavros. You're making me nervous."

That deep chuckle of his permeated her bones just as the alarm sounded. He checked her last play. "You can't build upon a four-join with an ace on the board and a five in your hand. I win!"

"You don't have to sound so gleeful about it." She gathered up the cards and put them back in the pack. "It's time for your pills." She handed him the water.

His smile taunted her before he swallowed his medicine. "What's the matter? You have nothing to fear from me. I'm pretty much incapacitated."

Stavros wasn't the problem. *She* was. "Come on. I'll help you to the bathroom on the condition that you behave."

A glimmer of a smile hovered on his lips. "I don't know how to do that."

Her temper flared. "Do you want help or not?"

"I do, but then I want to eat on the patio. The lounger out there is as good as this bed."

She knew he was going stir-crazy. "You're right."

Andrea offered her support and in a few minutes they reached the patio. She fixed the lounger so it lay flat. That way he could stretch out on his side. "Don't get any ideas about pulling me down with you or we'll both end up with a broken back."

His chuckle followed her as she left for the kitchen. Before long, she brought out the pies and iced tea he'd liked before. After she put his drink on the stone flooring and handed him a couple of pies, she pulled one of the chairs over and sat by him to eat.

"Uh-oh. You're facing the wrong way and can't see the coast."

"I'll be looking at it for the rest of my life, but you won't be here after a few more days, so I'd rather look at you." Stavros knew how to press on a sore wound.

"If the heat gets too much for you, tell me and I'll help you back in the house."

"Why is it you always change the subject when I mention your leaving?"

Because I'm in pain and don't want to be separated from you. "I didn't realize I did that."

He eyed her over his glass. "Where will you be living in Brazil?"

"The Serra do Ouro gold mine is near a town called Itapetim in the northeastern area. Dad says it's mostly agrarian."

"What kind of work do you think you'll do there?"

She took a long drink first. "I'll find something. We won't be there very long."

A stillness seemed to come over Stavros. "Why not?"

"Dad's tired of traveling the world. He wants to

go back to his roots in Denver and work in the home office."

At this point, Stavros sat up, propping himself with his arm. "You mean for good?"

"Yes. When we left Denver, he had everything put in storage. Furniture, photographs, albums, so many things I've never seen. Things I've forgotten that are mine. He plans to buy a house for us."

Stavros lay back on the lounger. "I wonder if a man can return home after so many years away and find the happiness he's looking for."

Andrea jumped out of the chair. Thoughts of that future without Stavros sounded so bleak, she could hardly stand it. "I've been haunted by the same question. Now you know why I don't like talking about it."

"I'm sorry, Andrea. It was insensitive of me."

"Not at all. I'm going to run inside and bring you the laptop. I plan itineraries for tours and am interested to see what you have mapped out for us."

When she came back to the patio, she found Stavros on the phone. She heard the name Theo and knew he was talking about business. How much he would divulge to his colleagues about his father's ploy, she didn't know. He hid his heartache well, but deep down she knew he had to be devastated.

After handing him the computer, she slipped inside the house for her novel, imagining he'd be on the phone for quite a while. She couldn't conceive of her father doing something so cruel. And even though Stavros's father might not carry through with his scheme, it didn't take away the hurt of betrayal.

When she came back out on the patio, she found he'd finished his conversation. His eyes were closed.

There were shadows and lines on his arresting face that hadn't been there before his brother had shown up last night. Alarmed, she cried, "Is your pain worse again?"

He turned his head toward her and opened his eyes. Through the black lashes they looked like a dark cloud before a storm. "It's not my leg."

"Then it's this threat your father poses."

"Afraid so. Theo and Zander will be arriving at the house within the hour so we can talk strategy."

"I'll make more iced tea and fix some sandwiches."

"Andrea Linford, do you know you're the best thing that ever happened to me?"

Stavros, Stavros. Don't say things like that. Don't you know I'm dying inside at the thought of leaving you?

CHAPTER SEVEN

MONDAY MORNING, STAVROS was able to walk out to
the car on his own. Yesterday's rest had made all the
difference. He stretched out in the backseat with his
laptop and waited for Andrea to come. She was so
practical she packed everything they'd both need in
her duffel bag for their overnight trip. He loved it. His
and her things all thrown together. A precursor of a
future with her. He refused to think any other way.

Stavros watched her walk toward him dressed in
a wraparound khaki skirt and a cream-colored knit
top. Her shapely figure did wonders for anything she
wore. The guys had done triple takes when he'd introduced them to Andrea yesterday. Theo was married, but Zander was still a bachelor and had had a
hard time keeping his eyes to himself.

She'd brought them a never-ending supply of food
and drinks. Stavros could tell how impressed they
were that she knew so much about their line of work
and had been inside the plant.

He'd asked her to stay with him while they discussed the threat facing them. His partners hadn't left
until much later that evening because Andrea had en-
tertained them with a few hair-raising stories of her

adventures in the Gran Chaco of Paraguay. Close calls with a poison dart and a feeding frenzy of piranha fish in an area inhabited by natives who spoke Guarani had had them glued to every word. She'd fit in like a guy, but retained a beguiling femininity.

He heard her close the trunk, and then she came around and slid behind the wheel. She looked over her shoulder. "Have we remembered everything? Did you talk to Raisa?"

"I told her we wouldn't be back until Tuesday night."

"Then we're good to go." She started the engine and backed the car around. "I used to think it might be kind of fun being a driver for some top-brass military general. But driving the legendary Kyrie Konstantinos around is much better."

He never knew what was going to come out of her luscious mouth next. Their eyes met through the rearview mirror. Hers were a vibrant blue this morning.

"Why's that?"

"Because you're in a different kind of war—one I believe in—and I want you to win."

Sometimes the things Andrea said and the way she said them…

"Maybe my father won't fire the first shot after all."

"Maybe not. One lives in hope."

Yes, one does.

"Stavros? Why do you think he's the way he is? You know what I mean."

"Leon and I have asked each other that question dozens of times. Our grandfather, his own father, didn't understand him either. He always has to be right. I don't know where that comes from."

"Do your parents go to church?"

Her question made him want to laugh and cry at the same time, because she was trying to understand the complex relationship he had with his parents, which not even he could fix.

"On the important holidays. How about your father?"

"The same."

Stavros was curious. "Does he expect you to go?"

"Not anymore."

"What does that mean?"

"When we were living in Venezuela, I went to a Catholic school and a couple of nuns befriended me. For a while I thought I might like to be one when I grew older. When I told my dad, he had a fit."

"I'll bet."

"That was one of the few times I'd ever seen him really upset. He said he loved me so much he never wanted me to go away from him. At the time I believed him and gave up on the idea. But as I matured, I realized he really wanted me to grow up with the opportunity to be married and have children. He said children are a parent's greatest blessing."

"I know *you* are," Stavros said moodily.

"I've tried to be."

The trend in their conversation had become painful for him. Her father wanted his daughter to be married, but only on *his* terms? Father, daughter and son-in-law all under the same roof in Denver, Colorado?

"We've arrived at the first quarry on the list." She got out and came around to open his door. "I'll go inside and see if the manager will come out to talk to you. Wish me luck."

"There isn't enough money to pay what I owe you, Andrea."

"Don't be silly." She headed for the quarry office. He experienced pure pleasure just watching the womanly way she moved. Her hair shimmered in the sun.

He'd wanted to get a head start finding new sources of marble material, but feared this wouldn't work if he didn't make the initial introduction. The doctor had told him not to walk around on his bad leg until tomorrow. His wound was feeling better, so he'd be a fool not to follow his advice.

Soon, he saw Andrea accompanied by an older man. Stavros lowered his legs to the floor and got out so at least he was standing. They both joined him. She'd given the manager one of his business cards.

"When your beautiful assistant said Kyrie Stavros Konstantinos himself was outside waiting with a proposition for us, I couldn't believe it. You were stung by a stingray?"

"That's right. I still have trouble walking."

"You're lucky to still be alive. I could tell you stories."

Out of the corner of his eye, he could see Andrea smiling.

"Thankfully my story has a happy ending, otherwise I wouldn't be standing here, but it's all I can manage."

The quarry manager scratched his head. "This is a very unusual way to do business. You were very smart to send her first." His mouth widened into a grin. "So you are now in business for yourself. No more papa?"

Stavros had to smother a groan. "I still have a papa, but no more ties to the Konstantinos Corporation. My partners and I are in business producing a new product called Marma-Kon." He took advantage of the moment to explain why he wanted to buy their marble waste.

"I'll email you the contract today so you can read it over. It should answer all your questions. If you are in agreement to do business, contact Theo Troikas, whose name is on the card. He's the contracts manager."

"I tell you what. I have to talk to the owner. He owns two quarries. I think he will say yes, but I'll get back to you. Thank you, and get well." He shook Stavros's hand.

After he'd walked away, Stavros climbed in the backseat once more and Andrea closed the door for him. Then she got back in the driver's seat and turned around. "What do you think?"

Stavros stretched out to rest his leg. "Do you even have to ask? With you as my ambassador, it was like taking candy from a baby. The hitch will come when he talks to the owner."

"Why wouldn't he agree? They'll be making money off you."

"You never know. Prejudice maybe, because I'm the son who's no longer working for his father. The owner's a proud Greek, remember? We're a pretty patriarchal bunch."

She nodded. "With the god Zeus serving as the role model, you are. His autocratic handling of his son Arcas was a great example of fatherly love. That poor boy was so upset he said, 'If you think you're so clever, Father, make me whole and unharmed.' That relationship got nowhere in a hurry."

That was a little-known part of the myth. The fact that she could pull such information out of her head at a moment's notice astounded him.

"Stavros—" Her eyes clouded over. "I'm trying to get you to ease up on yourself. You're not actually buying into your own pathetic fiction about not living up to your father's expectations? As far as I'm concerned, you've exceeded any dreams a father might have for his son. The respect everyone has for you should warm your heart."

"Does it warm yours?" He couldn't see her face.

"I told you the other night that I've chosen to believe in you."

Stavros put his head back. "If only I'd heard that kind of faith come from my father, even one time…"

"Please don't torture yourself." She had tears in her voice. "You need to stop! Your brother, Leon, is your champion or he wouldn't have come to the house the other night to warn you. Even if you didn't notice it, I saw the manager's eyes gleam while you told him about your product. He stood there wishing he'd thought of it first and probably wished he had a son like you.

"You're really onto something big, Stavros. As long as you're searching for new sources, why not buy some quarries no longer being used? You know the old saying about one man's trash being another man's treasure."

"They cost money, but I hear what you're saying, Andrea." Every single brilliant word.

"Good. Then let's drive on to the next target."

Andrea marveled at the scenery after they reached the place where they were spending the night. Outside the door of her hotel room, which adjoined Stavros's, she looked south and east to the pine trees and sweet chestnut forests. They surrounded the village sitting at the foot of Mount Ypsarion. Its charm lay in the old houses with their stone walls and wooden roofs.

While he got ready for bed, she went to a local *taverna* for oven-baked pizza that was chewy like focaccia bread and topped with gyro meat in a sauce tasting strongly of basil. After she returned, they drank fruit juice in lieu of wine with their meal. Knowing Stavros had a sweet tooth, she'd picked up some baklava.

Before she got ready for bed, she went back to his room to make sure he'd taken his pills and was settled. She knew he was tired, but he seemed in better spirits than when they'd stopped at the first quarry.

She felt his eyes on her the second she entered his room. "How do you feel after meeting with managers from three different quarries?"

"I'll know better when contracts come in, but I'm satisfied we've made a dent."

"Do you think you're up to more visits tomorrow?"

"Are you?" he questioned right back. "You must be exhausted after all you've done today."

"I'm not the one with the wound. If you don't mind, I'd like to check it before you go to sleep, just to be on the safe side." She pulled a clean dressing from the box.

He threw the covers aside. For his convenience, obviously, he'd put on a pair of shorts for bed. Nothing else. The dusting of black hair on his well-defined chest reminded her of those hours on the beach when they'd gotten tangled in each other's arms. As if reading her mind, he turned over. She sucked in her breath and leaned down to make an inspection.

Relief swept through her. "It's healing, Stavros. There's almost no drainage."

"That means I can do my own walking tomorrow."

"Within reason," she reminded him. After discarding the old dressing, she washed her hands and came out of the bathroom to affix a new one. "Is there anything else I can do for you?"

"Stay with me tonight, Andrea," he asked in a compelling voice. "Lie by me."

"Stavros—"

"I swear I won't do anything you don't want me to do. We don't have a lot of time left before you're gone for good."

She knew that a lot better than he did. She'd had nightmares about never seeing him again. But what he was asking would be a mistake for both of them, a voice inside warned. Stavros had no idea how much she'd come to love him. To spend more time with him was only going to make it harder to leave. After losing Ferrante, she was terrified of loving another man again.

"Can't we at least have this night together like we had out in the woods when we were looking for Darren? I don't know about you, but I remember every moment of it lying next to you. I remember your fragrance. You always smell divine, did you know that?"

Andrea could hardly breathe. "Let me think about it." She darted toward the door that separated their two rooms. Once inside hers, she reached in the duffel bag for her nightgown and robe. During her shower, her brain screamed at her to remain in her room until morning. But by the time she'd brushed her teeth and was ready for bed, her heart had won out. Stavros was right. This would be their last night together before she had to fly back to Thessaloniki.

On legs that trembled, she turned off the light and went into his bedroom. His light was off too. She drifted through the semidarkness to the bed. Without removing her robe, she got in on the other side. No sooner had she rested her head on the pillow than she felt his arm snake around her waist and roll her into his strong body.

"Finally," he said in an unsteady voice and buried his face in her hair. "I've been willing you to come to me. I love you, *agape mou*." His hand roved over her arm and back possessively. "I fell in love with you that day on the mountain. I'm a different man because of it. Don't tell me it's too soon to say those words to you."

Tears trickled out of her eyes. "I won't. I love you too. But you already know that, in the same way you know everything else," she murmured against his lips. "I adore you." She kissed him over and over again. "I knew it when you got out of your car to castigate me for losing one of my students."

"Forgive me, darling."

"There's nothing to forgive. I didn't think a man like you existed, yet there you were, bigger than life and so handsome I didn't think my heart could take it.

When I thought I might never see you again, I asked if I could look for Darren with you. It was so bold of me I should be ashamed, but I couldn't help myself."

"Do you think a lesser woman could ever hold me?" Stavros kissed her long and hard before he lifted his head. She moaned in protest. "We need to talk, my love. About us."

"Let's not ruin tonight with talk," she begged.

"There are other ways of communicating." He covered her face with kisses. "It's all I can do to keep myself from making love to you, but I made you a promise."

She loved him more fiercely for honoring it. Once again, she was the one spinning out of control. This wasn't fair to him.

"If I stay in this bed any longer, then I'll pay a price for giving in to my desire. It'll be too heavy a price considering I'll be gone soon. It's already tearing me apart to imagine leaving you. But my agony will never end if I sleep with you tonight. After knowing your possession, nothing will ever be the same for me again. I know myself too well."

Stavros propped his head on his hand to look at her. "You're talking about Ferrante."

"No. When Ferrante found out I'd never been intimate with a man, he said he wanted me to be his wife before he took me to bed. I loved him for loving me that much. For several months after his death, I was angry because I felt I'd been cheated and it was my own fault.

"But because I didn't have that memory, I'm convinced it helped me to heal. Otherwise, how can I explain falling in love with *you* so fast? After meeting you, I can't imagine loving another man again whether we sleep together or not."

He smoothed some hair off her forehead. "So what are we going to do about us? Does your father expect you to stay with him for always?"

"It isn't a case of expect, Stavros. I'm the one who doesn't want him to be alone."

"Why? It's normal for a grown woman to fall in love with a man and set up her own household."

She buried her face in his neck. "I know, but— Oh, you just don't understand."

"Try me. Please."

"He's so selfless and has never asked for anything for himself. I can't bear to think of him alone to live out the rest of his life. His parents were killed in a train accident when he was young. He had to live with an aunt, but she died before he met Mom. Then she died giving birth to me. I'm all he has left in this world."

The words came out in heavy sobs. Stavros held her closer, kissing her hair and cheek. Ferrante had loved her enough to know what he had to do to keep her. Maybe there was another way around what seemed to be an insoluble problem, because Stavros flat-out refused to lose her.

When the sobs subsided, Andrea rolled away from him and stood up, realizing she'd taken him by surprise. "I've given you all the honesty I have in me, but now I know what I have to do. I'd only be torturing myself to stay the rest of the night with you. Our meeting at the quarry was accidental. We've had some very precious moments together, but we need to get on with our lives since they're going in different directions. Try to get some sleep. We have two more quarries to visit tomorrow."

Andrea hurried to bed. She tossed and turned most of the night. After awakening early, she dressed and slipped out to bring breakfast back. She avoided Stavros's eyes as she put their food on the table in his room and reached for a roll. He'd dressed in white lightweight trousers and a collared tan shirt. He looked terrific and could walk a lot better this morning.

After eating, she packed up the duffel bag and turned to him. "Have you taken your medicine?"

He reached for his coffee. "I took it when I got out of bed. Thank you for the reminder and the food."

"You're welcome. I'll just take this bag out to the car and wait for you."

"I'll be right there."

In another few minutes, he climbed into the passenger seat next to her and they drove away.

"Are you sure you wouldn't be more comfortable in back?" After driving around in the Jeep with him, it was a strange experience with him sitting next to her in his elegant car. She was so aware of him, it was hard to concentrate.

"I'm fine. But after we've stopped at the next quarry, I want to go back to the house. I've decided I can accomplish much the same thing by making phone calls from home."

She frowned. "Do you wish you hadn't come?"

"No. It was necessary for me to see if my physical presence has made a difference. But in every case, the person I really need to convince isn't on the premises.

Part of the reason I wanted to do things this way was so I could spend more time alone with you."

She'd loved this time with him more than he would ever know.

"However, since I don't need any more help, and because being together has put an unbearable strain on both of us, I'll let you get back to your office. The helicopter will be waiting to take you. I daresay your boss will be thrilled to see you walk in."

Andrea's heart plunged to her feet. Stavros admitted he'd fallen in love with her, but sometime between last night and this morning, he'd had some sort of epiphany. She knew what he was like. Once he'd made up his mind, that was it. He'd made a decision about the two of them, the only one that made sense.

There was no going back to the way they had been before last night and they both knew it. But she was so devastated it took all her strength to focus while negotiating the mountain roads. Stavros worked on his laptop, not interested in talking to her. They'd run out of words. He was able to freeze her out, an ability she'd give anything to possess.

By noon they'd visited the quarry before heading back toward Panagia. She had no idea if he'd felt it was a successful morning or not. En route, they stopped for food, which they ate in the car. He turned on some typical soft rock music, his way of letting her know the music wouldn't bother him while he did work on his computer.

They arrived at his villa just after two o'clock. His fabulous house felt more like home to her than any furnished apartment she and her dad had ever lived in over the years. Her heart was in so much pain, she wondered if it could literally break.

Andrea let Stavros off in front. Even if he was walking better, he shouldn't have to climb a lot of steps yet. After he shut the door, she drove around to the back and parked the car next to the Jeep. His posh Mercedes had been a sheer pleasure to drive. When she let herself in the back door, she found he'd gone straight to his den.

Taking advantage of the time, she went to his bedroom and unpacked the duffel bag. Toiletries in the bathroom, medicine on his side table. As for her own packing, there was very little to do. In ten minutes, she was ready to go. The sooner, the better, because she was on the verge of breaking down.

On her way to the kitchen with her bag, the front doorbell rang. Maybe Raisa had come to the house for some reason, but didn't want to just walk in on them. Since Stavros was still in the den, she walked through the alcove to the door and opened it.

A stern-faced man in some kind of uniform handed her an express mail envelope. "Are you Andrea Linford?"

"Yes?"

"This is for you and Kyrie Konstantinos. See that he gets it."

What on earth? She watched him go down the steps before she shut the door.

Stavros was right behind her as she turned around. He caught her in his arms. For a moment, she saw the torment in his eyes. It matched her own.

His fingers kneaded her skin before he released her with seeming reluctance. "Who was that?"

"A—a courier," she stammered and handed him the envelope.

He ripped it open and pulled out an official-looking document. She watched him as he read it and saw lines of anger mar his striking features. For the first time since she'd known him, she heard him let go a curse.

Andrea got a sick feeling in the pit of her stomach. "Stavros? What is it?"

His eyes went hard as flint when he looked at her. "Draco Nasso is suing me for breach of promise to his pregnant daughter Christina and naming *you* co-respondent. We're both to appear before the judge day after tomorrow in Kavala."

She shook her blond head. "You didn't promise her anything! He has no just cause!"

"That doesn't matter to him," he said in a gravelly voice. "He most likely owns the judge in question. Come in the den with me while we get my attorney on the phone. Everything's coming into play even faster than I had thought." His gaze shot to hers. "With Draco on the warpath, my father's threat will be realized. Thank providence you were here to help me get around to those quarries."

This couldn't be happening, but it was. "While you do that, I'll be happy to call the quarries we didn't get to visit on the mainland and set up conferences on Skype for you."

She heard him inhale sharply. "How did I ever function without you?"

How am I going to live without you, Stavros?

They walked to the den. "Go ahead and sit at my

desk. The file is open with all the phone numbers. Call the ones that don't have a check by them."

Andrea was thankful to be able to help and got busy making the calls. Stavros sat in one of the chairs near his bookcase and got on the phone with his attorney. He was still on the phone when she'd finished lining up appointments.

"Andrea?" He covered the mouthpiece of his phone. "Since you're sitting in front of the screen, would you be willing to speak with my attorney over Skype now? He can take your deposition this way and present it in court without you having to be present."

"I'll do anything you ask."

His eyes thanked her before he spoke to his attorney once more. In another minute, they rang off. Stavros walked over and set everything up. His hands slid to her shoulders from behind. He squeezed them gently.

"I know how horrendous this is for you," he said in a low voice near her ear.

"It's you I'm worried about," she murmured shakily.

"It's another form of harassment to wear me down, but it'll be over soon. My attorney's name is Myron Karras."

Within seconds, Mr. Karras appeared before her. "I can see you just fine, Despinis Linford."

"I can see you too, Kyrie Karras."

"Fine. We'll do this in a question-and-answer format. If you're ready, we'll start now."

She eyed Stavros. "I'm ready."

"Please state your full name, nationality, age, marital status, address and occupation please."

Andrea complied.

"When was the first time you met Stavros Konstantinos."

"At quarry three on Thassos Island." She named the date and time.

"Why did *you* specifically come to the quarry?" After she'd explained, he said, "When the teen wasn't found, what did you do?"

Her cheeks went hot. Stavros had sat down on another chair, studying her through veiled eyes.

"Though the police had started a search for him, Kyrie Konstantinos said he was going to go look for Darren because he knew the mountain well and felt somewhat responsible."

"Why would he say that?"

"Because he was the one who gave permission through the quarry manager to let our tour groups come to the quarry. I asked if I could go with him because I'm the one who planned the student-teacher tour to the quarry in the first place and also felt partially responsible."

"Did you two go alone?"

She shivered. "Yes. I followed him to his villa, where I left my rental car. He packed a hamper of food and we left in his Jeep. We were out all night looking for him and eventually found Darren hiding in a truck on the morning ferry ready to leave Thassos for Keramoti. The police lieutenant in charge of the case took Darren into custody."

"What did you do then?"

"Kyrie Konstantinos drove us back to his villa, where I got into my rental car and left for Thessaloniki."

"Why did you arrange for tours to go to that particular quarry?"

"My father, Paul Linford, took me to quarry three when we first arrived in Greece. He said it produced the whitest marble of all. I thought it should be added to the tour agenda and made arrangements through the quarry manager, Gus…"

"Patras," Stavros whispered.

"Gus Patras. He got permission from the Konstantinos Corporation to allow tour groups to visit."

"Before you were hired by PanHellenic Tours, where did you live?"

"Italy."

"Before that?"

"Venezuela, and before that French Guiana, Paraguay and India." She rattled it all off to get it over with.

The attorney's brows lifted at that bit of information, producing a half smile from Stavros.

"So you'd never been in Greece before."

She and Stavros exchanged a silent glance. They both knew where these questions were leading. "Never. Because of my father's work, we were sent to Greece and got an apartment in Thessaloniki. I went to the university there, then was hired by PanHellenic Tours."

"Who hired you?"

"Sakis Manos, the owner."

"How did you happen to go to Thassos Island at all?"

"My father is a chemical engineer, interested in the history and geology of Greece. Thassos fascinated him because he said it was a big lump of marble."

"What else can you tell me about him?"

"He works for W.B. Smythe, an American engineering company based in Denver, Colorado, where I was born." After explaining his job, she said, "We traveled around when he had time off. He told me the marble quarries had existed anciently and I should visit them. Since he's the smartest man I've ever known, I was eager to see them."

Stavros's attorney smiled. "To your knowledge, did your father ever meet Kyrie Konstantinos or talk to him?"

"No."

"Tell me the date, time and circumstances involving you and Kyrie Konstantinos that prompted the 911 call."

No wonder Stavros had told her she shouldn't have mentioned his name to the dispatcher. The news traveled so fast, it had reached the ears of Tina's father in no time. She explained everything the best she could.

"So you were there to take him home and nurse him."

"Yes. His stingray wound needed watching."

"When did you first meet Christina Nasso?"

Oh, no. Andrea mentioned the date and time.

"What were the circumstances?"

"I was in his house when she came to visit him unexpectedly."

"Did you see her?"

"Yes. In the front hall."

"Did you hear anything?"

She darted Stavros a nervous glance. "Yes. She came to talk to him about her pregnancy. He denied being the father and asked her to leave."

"Are you involved with him?"

Blood hammered in her ears. "We've spent a little time together, but I'll be in Brazil in a few more days with my father, where he has work."

"You're resigning your job with PanHellenic Tours?"

"Yes."

"Are you leaving because you believe Kyrie Konstantinos is the father of the baby and you have no hope of marrying him for his money?"

"No!" Enraged by the question, she shot out of the chair, then realized where she was and sat down again. "I have no hope of anything!" Not without Stavros.

"I'm leaving because my father loves and needs me. As for Kyrie Konstantinos, he told me he has never loved her and ended their brief relationship over three months ago. I believe him. Besides my father, he's the most honorable man I've ever known."

"Is there anything else you'd like to add or change to your testimony?"

"No."

"Thank you."

The screen went blank, but Andrea didn't notice because she'd already hidden her wet face in her hands.

CHAPTER EIGHT

I HAVE NO hope of anything!

Andrea's plaintive cry resounded in Stavros's heart. He turned off the computer before pulling her into his arms. For a long time, he simply rocked her back and forth in an effort to give her comfort while he drew some solace from simply holding her. Those quiet little sobs shook him to the deepest recesses of his soul.

He kissed her forehead. "You didn't deserve any of this. I know that deposition was brutal, but Myron had to learn everything he could so he'll be prepared when he and I go before the judge. If Tina is pregnant, it's not mine. When a DNA test is done, then she'll have to come clean. If she isn't pregnant, she'll be cited for contempt.

"At that point my attorney will bring a lawsuit for perjury. In the end, her father will be the all-time loser, but I know that doesn't repair the damage this has done to you." He kissed her eyes and cheeks. "There's no way to make this up to you, Andrea. Ask me for anything. If it's within my power to give, I'll do it."

She sniffed and lifted her head. She looked at him

through glazed eyes. "I know you would. What I need is to get back to Thessaloniki. Is your pilot down on the pad?"

His pain was worse than any the stingray had inflicted. "Yes."

"Then I'd like to leave now."

A great shudder racked his body before he released her and reached for his phone on the computer desk. He called the pilot and told him to get ready for take-off. After he hung up, his gaze darted to hers. "Do you have everything packed?"

"Yes."

With a sense of inevitability, Stavros picked up the duffel bag against her protest. Her nursing days were over. They walked through the house and down the back steps to the pad. When they reached it, he cupped her face in his hands and kissed her precious mouth one more time before helping her into the helicopter. Anything more and he wouldn't have been able to let her go.

"You'll be home before dark. There'll be a limo at the heliport waiting to drive you to your apartment."

She wore a pained expression. "You don't have to do that."

"After what you've lived through and sacrificed for me, you can say that? I want to give you everything. I'm the one who absconded with you on Friday after work and brought you into this hornet's nest. The least I can do is make certain you get home safely."

He could tell she was struggling to swallow. "Thank you for everything, Stavros. I'll never forget." Her voice trembled.

No. Stavros wouldn't forget either.

He shut the door and stepped away. The rotors started up and began to whine. He waved to her as the helicopter lifted off and swung in a northwesterly direction toward Thessaloniki.

Last night, their passion for each other had driven them over a threshold to a more precarious place. He knew it had shaken her. Though she'd professed her love for him, they were in an impossible situation because the bond with her father went fathoms deep.

Without a mother all her life, Andrea revered the man who'd raised her. She was so attached to her father, she wouldn't allow another man to come between them if it meant a separation.

I'm leaving because my father loves and needs me.

That said it all. Stavros didn't blame Andrea for anything, but he refused to pressure her. His parents had done that to him his whole life and it had caused a rift he doubted could ever be mended. Look what pressure had done to Tina.

Andrea would have to come to terms with her emotions on her own. Ferrante had recognized he wanted her enough to accommodate her. But Stavros didn't have that luxury. He'd started a new business. Hundreds of plant workers and truck drivers depended on him. If he wanted her with him, he would have to find a way, but there were certain things he needed to clear up first.

Stavros had achieved two of his lifelong dreams, but the third one still eluded him. To find the right woman was difficult enough, but to make a relationship work meant sacrifice on both parts to achieve real happiness.

When he couldn't see the helicopter any longer, he walked back in the house and headed for his den. His work was never ending. That was good because he doubted he'd be able to sleep. For the time being, Andrea was only as far away as Thessaloniki, but she might as well be on another planet.

After his flight to Kavala on Thursday for the hearing generated by evil design, he'd fly to Thessaloniki and see her one last time. He couldn't leave her hanging about the results of the hearing. She deserved to know the outcome from him in person. If he went to her office before she left work, she couldn't refuse to see him.

Once seated at his desk, he opened the accounts file. The difference between profit and loss was in the numbers, which he constantly scrutinized for errors. While he was deep in calculations, his cell phone rang. It couldn't be Andrea. She was still in the air, but just the thought of her caused his pulse to speed up.

He checked the caller ID and clicked on. "Leon?"

"Hey, bro. I heard old man Nasso served you with a breach of promise notice."

"He did more than that. He named Andrea codefendant."

"He's a sick man. Does Andrea know?"

"She was the one served when she answered my door."

"Hell, Stav."

"There's more. Myron deposed her on a Skype conference call so she won't have to appear at the hearing. The questions tore her apart. Right now she's flying home in the helicopter. In another few days, she'll be going to Brazil with her father."

"I thought you loved her."

His eyes closed tightly. "With every fiber of my being."

"Then how come she's leaving?" When Stavros didn't answer, his brother called, "Stav?"

"I'm still here."

"Does she know you love her?"

"Yes."

"Does she love you?"

"Yes."

"Then what in the hell is the problem?"

"Because she's leaving with her father, and my life is here."

"You're serious."

"Afraid so." Stavros told his brother about Ferrante. "He gave up everything for her. It was the only way he could have her."

Leon was quiet for a long time. "That's a tough one. I don't envy what you're going through. I wish there was something I could do to help."

"Just be in my corner like you've always been."

"Stav—I don't like the idea of you being in your hideaway all alone. Why don't you come to my house and stay with us and the kids. I'll go with you when it's time to see the judge."

"Thanks for the offer, but I'm not fit company for anyone."

"If you need me, call anytime, day or night. I mean that."

"I know. Talk to you soon."

The depression he'd lived with before Andrea had come into his life had descended on him like a paralyzing, impenetrable darkness.

Andrea had been home from work for only a few minutes on Wednesday evening when she heard a knock on the apartment door.

"Andrea?" a familiar voice called out.

"Dad!" She couldn't believe he was here.

He opened the door with his own key. "Hi, honey. I decided to surprise you."

She flew into his arms and hugged him so hard, he laughed. "What's going on?" When she lifted her tearstained face, he frowned. "I thought you were happy to see me, but you look like the Wreck of the Hesperus."

That was a playful expression of her father's he often used to make her laugh when she was upset. But she was in too much pain since leaving Stavros to respond.

He wiped the moisture from her cheeks. "Hey— this *is* serious. It's a good thing I was able to finish up my work early and get home to you."

"Do you mean you're through at the mine? Literally?"

"Yes, honey. I told my superior I needed to help my daughter get ready for our move to Brazil." There was more gray in his dark blond hair, but she hadn't noticed until he cocked his head. "How come I've walked in to find you in tears? Is this still about Ferrante?"

She shook her head.

"Do you enjoy your job so much it's going to be hard to leave?"

"That's not it, Dad, although I'll miss Sakis."

"Okay. I'll stop playing twenty questions. For you to be in this kind of shape, your problem has to do with a man."

"Yes."

"He wouldn't by any chance be the mastermind behind that plant, would he?"

"Yes."

Her father was so smart he could always divine what was wrong with her. "Those pictures you sent were pretty impressive. Come on. Out with it." He put his arm around her shoulders and walked her over to the couch. Then he sat down in the chair near the coffee table.

"I don't know where to start."

He leaned forward. "The beginning is always a good place. What's his name?"

"Stavros Konstantinos."

"You're talking the Konstantinos Marble Corporation, of course."

"That's the one, except that he no longer works for the family. He has started his own company." Her father had opened the floodgate and it all came spilling out. Everything about the time she'd spent with him, the search for Darren, the problems with his parents, the hearing before the judge because she had been named codefendant.

"Unfortunately, having a name like Konstantinos and all the money that goes with it makes him a living target. Has he asked you to marry him, honey?"

"No." Her voice shook. "He knows I'm leaving Greece with you." She got up from the couch, unable to sit still.

"Does he know about Ferrante?"

"Everything."

"Have you told Stavros you're dying of love for him?"

"Yes."

"Then why are you going to Brazil with me?"

She wheeled around to stare at her father. "Because I love you and don't want you to be alone."

He got a troubled look on his face. "Did you tell *him* that?"

"Yes. What's wrong?"

Her father stood up. "Honey—I hope you're not sacrificing your own happiness because you're worried about me."

"Of course I'm worried about you. We've never been apart."

"I'm afraid that's my fault. I think I've done a terrible thing to you without realizing it."

"What do you mean?"

"Somewhere along the way you've decided you have to be my caretaker."

"No, Dad. It's not like that."

"It's exactly like that," he countered. "So *that's* why Ferrante was willing to move around with us. I thought it odd, but you seemed so happy about it, I never questioned it."

She was shocked. "Dad—"

"Honey, this is the last thing I ever wanted to happen. I raised you hoping that one day you'd get married. It broke my heart when Ferrante was killed. Now that you've met another wonderful man, I don't want to be the reason why you don't stay here and really get to know Stavros. You've known each other, what? All of two weeks? You need more time to-gether."

She couldn't believe he was saying these things. "But what will you do?"

"Without you?" He laughed. "I have my own life to lead, but we'll always have each other. If you love this man heart and soul, then you need to stay here and give it a chance. I'd give anything if your mother were here right now. If she were alive, she'd give you the same advice. Honey—you and I will get together whenever possible, right? But you need to pursue your own life."

Andrea had never loved her father more than at this moment. "Yes! Oh, yes!"

He held out his arms and she ran into them. The tears kept coming. Just a different kind. "I want you to meet him. He's so wonderful, you can't imagine."

"I think I got a clue when you sent me those pictures. Now how about showing me a picture of him?"

"I will, but first you need to know he's in trouble and I've been named codefendant because of that woman."

"They mean business, don't they?"

"I'm afraid so." For the next little while, she told him everything. "His father has never shown him love."

"Some people don't know how, but he had to have loved him all these years, otherwise why would he let his son be the managing director of the corporation?"

She blinked. "You're right!" Her dad could always make her feel better. "But I can hardly stand how much he's been hurt. When you meet Stavros, you just won't believe how fantastic he is. For this woman's father to put pressure on Stavros's father and take him to court just tears me apart."

"Sounds like this woman's father would do anything to have Stavros for a son-in-law."

"He tried because Stavros is a breed apart from other men. But Stavros doesn't see himself as exceptional."

"Maybe it'll be up to you to help him take off the blinders. Anyway, nothing at this hearing is going to stick. He says it's not his baby, so at some point it's all going to come out in the wash one way or another. I've been there and know it for a fact."

She smiled up at him. "Your facts outweigh everyone else's. You've always been the smartest man I've ever known."

"You mean until you collided with Stavros Konstantinos."

"If you hadn't taken me to Thassos to visit the marble quarry, we would never have met."

Elek Cadmus, the attorney for Draco Nasso, was known for his cutthroat tactics. Stavros didn't put anything past him. There were five of them in the judge's courtroom for the closed hearing Myron had insisted upon. But he couldn't prevent Tina from being present.

When Stavros saw her and her father sitting by the attorney, he thought she looked pale. Maybe she *was* pregnant and had morning sickness.

They'd already heard the recording of Andrea's deposition. Now the judge addressed Myron. "We want to hear about the events of the evening when your client and Despinis Linford began their search for the missing teen known as Darren Lewis."

Myron stood up. "The court has heard her deposition. My client has nothing more to add."

"I'd like more details, Your Honor," Elek demanded.

The judge nodded to Stavros. There was no question the judge was in Draco's pocket to allow this farce to continue.

"We left in my Jeep for the Dragon Cave near Panagia, thinking we might find the teen hiding there. After staying inside for a half hour without seeing him, we left and drove through the forest looking for him. Finally we stopped and camped out, sleeping separately—she in a bedroll, I on some blankets."

"Did you and Despinis Linford have physical contact? Remember, you're under oath."

"No, we did not. At dawn, we went into Panagia for breakfast and asked salespeople in several bike shops if they'd seen the young American. When nothing panned out, we drove down to the ferry landing and went aboard thinking he might be hiding in one of the cars or trucks. We found him hiding under the tarp of a truck. After the police came for him, I drove us back to my home. She left in the helicopter."

"I've already listened to your mother's deposition. In it, she states that when she arrived at your villa, she discovered you and Despinis Linford were having lunch on your patio after having spent the night together."

"That's correct, but my guest slept in the guest bedroom."

"Why did you invite her?"

"Because I was attracted to her and wanted to spend more time with her."

"You were taken to a clinic by ambulance due to a sting from a stingray. It was Despinis Linford who called 911. By this time, were the two of you lovers?"

His hands tightened into fists. "No."

"Do you deny she stayed overnight after you came home from the hospital?"

"No. She nursed me while I was confined to my bed. She saved my life and I'll always be in her debt."

"Do you still deny you're the father of Christina Nasso's baby?"

"Yes." For the second time during the hearing, Stavros looked at Tina and her glowering father. "We were never lovers and I never made a promise to marry her. A DNA test will be the proof."

Elek looked at the judge. "I have no more questions, Your Honor."

"Very well. I've heard all the testimony I need. This case will stay open until a DNA test can be made after the baby is born to determine paternity. At that time, I'll deliver a verdict."

He addressed Myron. "Neither of your clients is free to leave the country until my verdict is rendered. This hearing is adjourned until further notice."

Andrea couldn't leave?

Stavros was too jubilant to sit still. After the judge vacated the room, he turned to Myron. "Thank you for all you've done."

"You're welcome, but it was a waste of time."

"No, it wasn't." The judge's ruling would keep Andrea close to him.

"What do you mean?"

"I'll explain later. It's clear Draco wanted to punish me. Now that he's had the chance, I want to forget about it."

"If you get any more harassment, call me immediately."

"Of course."

"Can I give you a lift to Thessaloniki in my car?"

"No, thanks. My driver is waiting outside to take me to the heliport. First though, I need to phone Andrea. She needs to know today's outcome." *I have to tell her she must stay in Greece under a court order.*

They shook hands and Myron left, leaving Stavros alone in the courtroom. No sooner had he pulled out his cell phone than he thought he heard the door open. He turned his head to discover Tina hurrying toward him. Her father was nowhere in sight. As she drew closer, he could see she'd been crying.

She put out a hand. "Please, Stavros. I'm not here to cause you more trouble. My father thinks I'm in the restroom and he's waiting for me in the limo. I don't blame you if you hate me forever.

"The truth is, I'm not pregnant, but my parents think I am. When I get home I'm going to tell them I made it up because I didn't want to lose you. If my father doesn't tell your parents the truth and call off this lawsuit, then I will. That's all I have to say except I'm sorry I put you and Despinis Linford through this. What you told me at your house brought me to my senses. You were right. I can't let my parents' expectations drive my life anymore."

Stavros got out of the chair and hugged her. "We've both had to learn that lesson the hard way. Your truth has set both of us free. Good luck to you, Tina."

"You too, Stavros."

He phoned Myron immediately and told him what had just transpired. Myron said he'd get in touch with the other attorney to put a stop to the case. He doubted Tina would suffer from contempt of court since it was her father who'd engineered it.

Two hours later, Stavros rushed inside the building in Thessaloniki where Andrea worked. He wanted to deliver this news in person. But when he approached the receptionist at PanHellenic Tours, she told him Andrea had quit her job and wouldn't be coming back. He asked to speak to Sakis but learned the owner of the company was out of the office on business.

Something twisted in his gut. Was she still at her apartment packing, or had she gone without saying a final goodbye to him? She wouldn't do that to him, would she? He had to find out and took a taxi to her address.

No one answered the door. At this point, he tried her phone again, but all his calls went to her voice mail. Wherever she'd gone, she didn't want to be found. That was obvious. He didn't know where to turn. Frantic at this point, he left for the heliport to take the helicopter back to Thassos.

Once he reached the house, the emptiness of his life loomed so large it was unbearable. He couldn't stay there. As soon as he changed into jeans and a sport shirt, he got in the Jeep and drove to his office. There was a ton of work for him to catch up on while he waited for her to return his phone call.

Theo's car was still out in front. Another car was parked next to it. He didn't recognize it, but it didn't matter. After unlocking the main door with the remote, he headed for Theo's office, but as he passed his own, he noticed the door was open. He always kept it locked. Who'd been in there? And why?

"Stavros?"

He'd know that feminine voice anywhere and spun around in shock. There was Andrea, sitting in his desk chair looking sensational in a yellow sundress he'd never seen. She had an uncertain expression on her beautiful face, as if she didn't know what to expect from him.

"I've been waiting several hours for you. When you weren't at the villa, I didn't know what to do but come here. I hoped one of your partners could tell me where you were."

Stavros was afraid he was hallucinating. "How did you get here?"

"My dad's car. Theo let me in." She got to her feet. "Was the hearing ghastly?"

The hearing…he'd already forgotten about it. "Draco's attorney managed to make it as hideous as possible. When he'd finished my interrogation, the judge said he'd give his verdict after Tina's baby was born and the DNA results were in."

"Was she there?"

"Yes."

She bit her lip. "How horrible for you. I should have been there to support you."

"Andrea—Tina approached me after it was over. She admitted that she'd lied about the baby in order to hold on to me."

"Oh, Stavros—" The happiness in her voice was something he'd never forget.

"You believed in me. That was the support I

needed to get me through. She's going to tell both sets of parents. The lawsuit will be dropped. We made our peace."

Her eyes shimmered with tears. "How's your leg?"

"It's fine."

"That's good."

He couldn't take much more of this. "When are you and your father leaving?"

"Dad's already gone."

His heart lurched. "I don't understand."

"He finished up at the mine and now he's on his way to Brazil."

"But when I stopped by your office earlier, the receptionist told me you'd resigned and wouldn't be coming back. Why didn't you leave with your father?"

"I decided I'd rather stay here."

The blood pounded in his ears. "Why?"

"I'm tired of the tour business and would love to get a job working in an office or in a plant. You wouldn't happen to have a job opening for me, would you? Maybe a chauffeur? I'm not particular. I thought I'd rent an apartment in Panagia. It's my favorite village. Since Dad left the car with me, I have transportation now."

Stavros didn't know her in this mood. "Andrea—enough of your teasing. Why are you here?"

She moved closer to him. "You mean you really don't know?"

"If I did, I wouldn't be asking."

"I want to be near you. I love you until it hurts, but you already know that."

He did know. "But your father—you idolize him."

"That will never change, but another great love

has come into my life. There's room for both." She smiled that beautiful smile.

Stavros couldn't swallow. "I want you more than anything else in my life."

"But in what capacity?"

"In all the ways you can think of," he exploded.

"You mean like employee, friend, girlfriend, lover, confidante, nurse, cook, housekeeper? What?"

"I mean *wife*." The beautiful word reverberated against the walls of his office.

"I'd give anything to be your wife. Are you asking me?"

"Andrea—" His voice shook. "You've worked this out with him?"

She lounged against the edge of his desk. "We had a heart-to-heart the other day. He says he's lived the life he wants. Now he wants me to live the life I want. He says if I'm happy, then he won't worry about me and we'll always work things out to be together when we can. And in between times, we'll talk over Skype."

Stavros was incredulous.

"I think he feels like Tevye from *Fiddler on the Roof*, who wanted peace in his life, but in order to achieve it, he had to marry off his daughters first. Dad will go on leading his own life and wants me to lead mine. I believe him. He's going to be back in a month to see how I'm doing before he flies to Denver. Naturally he's anxious to meet you. I told him you're the smartest man I know next to him. That really got him going."

"You're being serious now."

Andrea could see her darling Stavros still needed

confirmation. She walked up to him and put her arms around his neck. "Life-and-death serious." Her voice throbbed. "After everything we've been through, do you really think I could leave you? Dad saw what a wreck I was the minute he walked in our apartment. He knew his daughter had lost her heart to another man. A great man. That's you."

Stavros could feel himself coming back to life.

"He was so sweet about it, Stavros. He said that two weeks wasn't nearly long enough for two people who've fallen madly in love to be torn apart. We need time to find out all the wonderful things that are still waiting for us. So I have an idea. Why don't we take a moonlight ride in the Jeep? There's this beautiful church in Panagia I want to show you."

"I'm way ahead of you, but before we do anything else, I want to do *this*." He wrapped her in his powerful arms and covered her mouth with his own. The urgency of his possessive kiss sent thrill after thrill through her body.

"I love you, Andrea. I love you. Don't ever leave me." He covered her face and throat with kisses.

"Stavros—don't you know by now I worship the ground you walk on."

"Knock, knock," sounded a male voice. "If this is a private party, I don't apologize because I'm too happy for you."

Stavros lifted his head, smiling broadly. "Theo—you're the first person to know Andrea and I are going to be married in a month." He sounded exultant, just the way she felt.

"Congratulations! Zander and I have had a bet on to see how long it would take you to propose.

He thought it might be another week, but I figured sooner. I won, but then I'm a married man and know the look of a man under the spell of woman magic."

"My wife-to-be has it in spades."

CHAPTER NINE

"Ready, honey?"

"I've been ready for this a long time." Andrea stood there outfitted in white silk, carrying gardenias. A lace mantilla covered her hair.

"You look like your mom did on our wedding day. Absolutely gorgeous."

"You're going to make me cry, Dad."

"We can't have that. Stavros is waiting for you at the front of the church. I like him, honey."

"I love him so much."

She put her hand on his arm, proud of her attractive father as they walked down the aisle of the Virgin Mary Church in Panagia. Her eyes fastened on Stavros. He looked so dark and splendid in his black dress suit, she couldn't see anyone else. But she knew the whole Konstantinos family and all of their close friends were there, with the exception of Stavros's father. Stavros didn't have hope that he'd come, but Andrea prayed he would.

Stavros had talked to the priest, expressing his desire that they have a simple ceremony. Over the past month Andrea had come to know him better and rec-

ognized his need for understatement, even in his re-
ligious vows. He truly was a modest man.

Her father led her to the front of the church and
took her bouquet. Stavros reached for her hand and
squeezed it. His gray eyes had a glow she'd never seen
before. It ignited the flame that burned inside her.
This was no longer a fairy tale, but blissful reality.

The priest nodded to them. "Andrea and Stavros,
let us pray."

Their ceremony didn't take long. Rings were exchanged. She was so excited to be married to him,
she could hardly wait for the part to come where the
priest pronounced them husband and wife.

The second the words were spoken, Stavros drew
her into his arms. "You could have no idea how long
I've dreamed of this moment," he whispered against
her lips before kissing her. For a little while, she forgot the world and kissed him back, unable to believe
he was now her husband.

"Come on, you two," Leon murmured. "You're
taking forever. Dad wants to be the first to congrat-
ulate you. He and Mom are waiting."

They both heard what Leon said. Andrea stopped
kissing her husband. "Your father came," she whispered against his lips. Joy filled her heart. "Oh,
darling—"

Stavros lifted his head. In that instant, she saw a
light in those beautiful gray eyes she'd never seen
before.

"I can see him. Except for silver in his hair, he's a
cross between you and Leon."

Her husband crushed her to him. She knew what
this moment meant to him. When he'd gotten hold

of his emotions, he grasped her hand and walked her down the aisle to the vestibule to greet the two people who'd brought her beloved Stavros into the world.

While Stavros's father reached for him, his mother hugged Andrea. "You've made my son very happy," she said in a voice filled with tears. "I saw it in his face at the villa."

Andrea was so thrilled, she hugged her harder. "I'm going to try to make him happy forever. My mother died when I was born. I want us to be friends." By now, both of them were crying.

Stavros pulled her away. "Andrea? This is my father, Charis. I've wanted to introduce you for a long time."

The older man's eyes were a lighter gray than Stavros's, and they were moist with emotion. He had to clear his throat before he spoke. "It's an honor for me to meet the woman my son has chosen. He tells me you've saved his life and the company's reputation. I can't ask for more than that from a daughter-in-law. Welcome to the family."

Andrea smiled up at him. "I love him to the last breath in me. And I love you because you and your wife have raised the most marvelous son on earth."

Stavros put his arm around her waist and pressed her to his side. "There are no words to express how I really feel about you, Andrea," he whispered. "All I can do is show you." She didn't know how long they clung to each other before Leon reminded them other people were waiting.

They moved on to sign the wedding documents. Once that was done, Stavros walked her out into the hot noonday sun for pictures and congratulations.

Andrea's dad was the next person to hug her. His blue eyes twinkled. "You're Kyria Konstantinos now."

"I know. Can you believe it?"

"Stavros is getting the jewel in the crown, but I think he knows it by now."

"Dad—" She hugged him harder.

Leon butted in. "Save me some room. My brother is a lucky man." He kissed her on the cheek.

"Thank you, Leon. You don't know how much that means to me."

Then came his wife and children. They were followed by Theo and his family and Zander. Soon there was a crush of Stavros's relatives and friends, Raisa and her husband among them.

Suddenly she felt Stavros grab her around the waist. "Let's get back to the house. The sooner we feed our guests, the sooner we can leave on our honeymoon."

Leon drove them in a limo to the villa. A procession followed behind them, but Andrea was oblivious because Stavros was kissing the life out of her. She loved him so terribly and knew that his father's appearance had taken away the crushing pain of the past.

The first person Andrea hugged when they reached the house was Raisa. The housekeeper had spent several days preparing the wedding feast. Andrea had helped her with some of it.

A florist had come to fill the house with flowers. The villa was a showplace. Everyone marveled. Andrea was so proud of Stavros she could burst. He'd done all this and had accomplished so much in his life.

After many toasts and a lot of laughter, the wedding guests began to leave. While Stavros walked his parents out to Leon's limo, Andrea said goodbye to her father at the helicopter pad. He was flying to Thessaloniki, where he'd board a jet headed for the States.

Andrea was thankful for the privacy because she'd burst into tears with joy over Stavros's reconciliation with his father. "I'm so thankful he came, Dad."

"I am too, but don't forget that Stavros is going to need you more than ever."

"Thank heaven I have you. Thank you for my life, Dad. Thank you for everything you've done for me, everything that you are and stand for. Take care of yourself. Stavros says we'll fly to Denver next month to see you. I can't wait."

"Neither can I, honey. Love you." He gave her one more kiss before climbing into the helicopter.

She backed away to watch it take off and felt Stavros's arms encircle her waist. He waved to her father, then turned her around. "Guess what? Everyone's gone. Now it's just you and me. Let's hurry inside and change."

"You haven't told me where we're going tonight." Their bags were packed for a trip to Paris tomorrow.

A smile broke one corner of his compelling mouth. "You'll find out in a few minutes. I've been dreaming about it since the night we went searching for Darren."

He wanted to camp out with her! How did he know that was one of her secret desires?

They climbed the steps together. "I've been wait-

ing to do this," he said and picked her up to carry
her over the threshold. She didn't know how he did it
while she was still in her wedding finery. He kissed
her as he walked her through the house to the guest
bedroom she'd been using. After he put her down, he
undid the buttons on the back of her dress.

She felt him kiss the nape of her neck. His touch
melted her.

"Hurry." He didn't have to tell her that. "Last person to the Jeep pays the penalty."

Andrea trembled with excitement as she stepped
out of her dress. After laying it on the bed, she pulled
a pair of shorts and a T-shirt out of the drawer and
dressed in record time. After stepping into leather
sandals, she raced through the house. But no matter
how fast she'd been, Stavros had beaten her outside
and was waiting in the Jeep wearing a crew-neck shirt
and jeans.

"You cheated," she accused him.

He laughed hard and leaned across to give her a
kiss. "I admit I changed out here."

"Where's your suit?"

"In the car."

"I hope you're not going to take a long time to find
the right spot."

"Is my gorgeous wife nagging already?" he teased.
Stavros started the engine and they were off down
the road.

"Well, it *is* our honeymoon and I've never been
on one before."

"Neither have I."

"I'm nervous."

"So am I."

"No, you're not."

"I've never been a husband before. I want everything to be perfect for us, Andrea."

"It already is because your father came and he loves you."

"Agreed."

"I have hopes of his coming to our first baby's christening."

"First?"

"Yes. I want your babies, darling. I told your mother I want us to be friends. She'll make the most wonderful grandmother. Honestly, Stavros, she's such a beauty it's no wonder you turned out like a Greek god."

He grinned. "I did?"

"My friendship with her is important to me."

"When she gets to know you better, she'll come to realize that the daughter she always wished she could have is my angel wife."

Tears trembled on her lashes. "Dad is crazy about you."

"I like him."

"He said those exact words to me about you before he walked me down the aisle. The ceremony was perfect."

"Short."

She chuckled. "I know traditional Greek weddings take hours. Thank you for sparing us that in this heat."

"The black sheep strikes again."

"Now that we're partners in crime we'll be known as Mr. and Mrs. Black Sheep."

He threw back his head in laughter.

It thrilled her that he sounded so happy.

"Did you know you looked like a vision coming down that aisle? I was so mesmerized I couldn't think."

"You weren't the only one in that condition. But I feel that way whenever I see you or sense your presence."

The night was exquisite as they drove through the scented pines. When he slowed down outside the village, it wasn't long before he found them the secluded spot where they'd spent another memorable night. He stopped the Jeep and turned off the engine.

"Would you believe me if I told you that the night we spent here the first time, I wanted it to be our wedding night."

"So did I," she whispered.

They climbed out of the Jeep and set up their little camp with the aid of the big flashlight.

"Oh—you bought a new sleeping bag!" Already her heart was pounding outrageously.

"Tonight we're doing this Italian-style. I measured this spot for our marriage bed to make sure it would hold two."

"You've outdone yourself, Figaro."

"So you like our bedroom."

"I adore it." She took off her sandals and climbed inside the bag. He could probably hear her heart thudding.

"Well, aren't you a brazen little hussy."

Andrea pulled the bag's edge up to her chin and looked out at him. "You already knew that about me when I asked if I could come with you to look for Darren. I figured that since you're going to wield a heavy penalty tonight, we might as well hurry and get this over with."

"Get what over with?" His voice sounded like silk as he turned off the flashlight and climbed in next to her.

"The thing the nuns talked to me about back in Venezuela."

"Like what?" He chuckled and pulled her into him to nuzzle her neck.

"Oh…just things."

"I'm not sure I know where to start."

"Don't drive me crazy, Stavros! I've been waiting for this all my life."

He started kissing her. "You mean this?"

"Yes."

"And this?"

"Y-yes."

"How about this?"

"Stavros!"

Andrea woke up several times during the night tangled in her husband's arms. Ecstasy like she'd never known had caused her to cling to him. He'd taught her a new language to speak. Eager for more, she started kissing him to wake him up so she could show him how fluent she was becoming. He responded with a husband's kiss, hot and consuming.

Oh, yes… Out of all the languages she'd learned, she liked this one best and intended to become an expert at it.

* * * * *

Oh, man, he'd pegged her so completely wrong.

Her tough, big-city woman persona was nothing but a shield for a vulnerable girl, and Gunnar's desire to protect and serve had never been stronger.

"I'm sorry. I'm so, so sorry." He hugged her tight, wishing he could take back the last hour, trying desperately to make things better. Hell-bent on being the opposite of his father, he'd acted nothing short of a bully tonight, apparently just like Lilly's father. It would never happen again. Ever. "I'm sorry, Chitcha, please forgive me."

The soldier-like tension in her body relaxed. She leaned into his chest and rested her head on his shoulder. "I shouldn't have been following you. I wasn't even that interested."

He kissed the top of her head. "Agreed. You absolutely shouldn't have been following me. So no more games, okay?"

"No more games." She looked up.

"No more snooping?"

"No more secrets?"

"Touché," he said, just before capturing her mouth for a long and tender kiss as they stood under the light of the perfect half-moon. He was in a sticky situation, being on a committee that Lilly was dying to find out about, and just now promising not to keep secrets. How was he supposed to juggle that double-edged sword and not get injured?

HER PERFECT PROPOSAL

BY
LYNNE MARSHALL

Published in Great Britain 2015
by Mills & Boon, an imprint of Harlequin (UK) Limited,
Eton House, 18-24 Paradise Road, Richmond, Surrey, TW9 1SR

© 2015 Janet Maarschalk

ISBN: 978-0-263-25116-6

23-0315

Harlequin (UK) Limited's policy is to use papers that are natural, renewable and recyclable products and made from wood grown in sustainable forests. The logging and manufacturing processes conform to the legal environmental regulations of the country of origin.

Printed and bound in Spain
by CPI, Barcelona

Lynne Marshall used to worry that she had a serious problem with daydreaming—then she discovered she was supposed to write those stories! A late bloomer, Lynne came to fiction writing after her children were nearly grown. Now she battles the empty nest by writing stories that always include a romance, sometimes medicine, a dose of mirth, or both, but always stories from her heart. She is a Southern California native, a dog lover, a cat admirer, a power walker and an avid reader.

Special thanks to Flo Nicoll who always makes me dig deeper. And to Carly Silver for being a bright light and for being there whenever I need help.

Chapter One

"Is this because I'm an outsider?" said the petite, new and clearly fuming visitor in town. She'd jaywalked Main Street in broad daylight, far, far from the pedestrian crosswalk. As if it was merely a street decoration or a pair of useless lines. Did she really think Gunnar wouldn't notice?

Dressed as if she belonged in New York City, not Heartlandia, she wore some high-fashion fuchsia tunic, with a belt half the size of her torso, and slinky black leggings. Sure, she was a knockout in that getup, but the lady really needed to learn to blend in, follow the rules, or he'd be writing her citations all day long.

He took his job seriously, and was proud to be a cog in the big wheel that kept his hometown running smoothly. Truth was he'd wanted to be a guardian of Heartlandia since he was twelve years old.

"I won't dignify that slur with an answer," Gunnar said, though she *was* an outsider. He'd never seen the pretty Asian woman before, but that wasn't the point. She'd jaywalked!

With the often huge influxes of cruise-line guests all

disembarking down at the docks, and now with the occasional tour bus added to the mix, he had to keep order for the town's sake. The tourists rushed to the local stores for sweet deals and to the restaurants for authentic Scandinavian food without having to fly all the way to Sweden or Norway. If he let everyone jaywalk, it could wreak havoc in Heartlandia. The town residents had to come first, and it was up to guys like him to regulate the influx of visitors. Plus, jaywalking was a personal pet peeve. If the city put in crosswalks, people should use them. Period.

He kept writing, though snuck an occasional peek at the exotic lady. Shiny black hair with auburn highlights, which she wore short, her bangs pushed to the side, and with the pointy and wispy hair ends just covering her earlobes and the top of her neck. *Interesting.*

Most guys he knew preferred long hair on women, but he was open to all styles as long at it complemented the face. The haircut and outfit were something you might see on a runway or in a fashion magazine, but not here. And those sunglasses… She had to be kidding. Did she want to look like a bee?

Even though her eyes were shielded by high-fashion gear, he could sense she stared him down waiting for his answer to her "Is it because I'm an outsider?" question. Not wanting to be rude by ignoring her, he came up with a question of his own.

"Let me ask you this. Were you or were you not jaywalking just now?"

"I'm from San Francisco, everyone jaywalks." She leaned in to read his name tag. "Sergeant Norling."

"You with the cruise ship?" It was too early for a new batch of tourists to set foot on the docks, though there was no telling when those buses might pull up.

She huffed and folded her arms. "Nope."

"Well, you're in Heartlandia now, Ms...." He stared at his citation pad waiting for her to fill him in. She didn't. "Name please?" He glanced up.

"Matsuda. Lilly Matsuda. Can't you cut me some slack?"

"I need your license." Gunnar stared straight into where he imagined her eyes were, letting her absorb his disappointment at her obvious lack of regard for his professional honor. Something he held near and dear. Honor.

She wouldn't look away, so he motioned with his fingers for her to hand over the license and continued, "Did you jaywalk?"

She sighed, glanced upward and tapped a tiny patent-leather-ultrahigh-heeled foot.

For the record, he dug platform shoes with spiky heels, and hers looked nothing short of fantastic with the skin-tight silky legging things she wore. Didn't matter, though. She was a jaywalker.

"Yes."

His mouth twitched at the corner, rather than letting her see him smile. The way she'd said yes, turning it into two syllables, the second one all singsongy, sounded like some of the teenagers he mentored at the high school.

She lowered her sunglasses, hitting him dead-on with deliciously almond-shaped, wide-spaced, nearly black eyes. Hers was a pretty face, once he got past the Kabuki killer stare.

He tore off the paper, handed it to her and waited for her response.

Snagging the notice for jaywalking she frowned, then glanced at it, and the discontented expression broke free with a surprisingly nice smile. "Hey, it's just a warning. Thanks." She suddenly sounded like his best friend.

"Now that you know the rules, don't jaywalk again.

Ever." He turned to head back to his squad car, knowing for a fact she watched him go. He'd gotten used to ladies admiring him from all angles. Yup, there was definitely something about a man in a uniform sporting a duty belt, and he knew it. Just before he got inside he turned and flashed his best smile, but instead of saying have a nice day he said, "See you around."

She had to know exactly what he meant—if she was sticking around this small city, he'd be sure to run into her again, and he'd be watching where she walked.

"Officer Norling?"

The petite Matsuda lady stepped closer, her flashy colorful top nearly blinding him. He gave his practiced magnanimous professional cop smile, the one he hoped to perfect one day when he ran for mayor. "Yes?"

"Know any good places to eat in town? Bars for after hours?"

"Just about any place here on Main Street is good. Lincoln's Place does a great happy hour." Was she planning on sticking around? Or better yet, was she trying to pick him up?

"You go there? Eat there? Drink there?"

His bachelor radar clicked up a notch.

She dug into her shoulder bag and brought out a small notepad and pen. "I'm looking for the best local examples of everything Scandinavian."

What was she doing, writing a book? Maybe she was one of those travel journalists or something. Gunnar stopped dead, hand midway to scalp for a quick scratch. Or maybe she was one of those annoying type A tourists, who had to know it all, find the best this or that, snap a few pictures while never actually stepping inside or buying anything, just so they could impress their friends back home. She looked like the type who'd want to impress her friends.

"Yeah. My favorite lunch joint is the Hartalanda Café. And you can't beat Lincoln's Place for great dining. Got a crack new lady pianist named Desi Rask playing on the weekends, too, if you like music."

She didn't look satisfied, as if he'd failed in some way at answering her query—the question behind the question. Too bad he hadn't figured it out. Maybe she was a food reporter for some big magazine or something and wanted some input from a local. "Well, thanks, then," she said. "See you around."

See me around? That's what I said. So is she new in town, planning to stay here, or just here on assignment? His outlook took a quick turn toward optimistic without any specific reason beyond the possibility of Ms. Matsuda sticking around these parts. An exotic woman like her would be a great change from the usual scenery.

But wait. He wasn't doing that anymore—playing the field. Nope. He'd turned a new page. No more carefree playboy, dating whoever he wanted without ever getting serious. If he wanted to be mayor of Heartlandia one day, he'd need to settle down, show the traditional town he knew how to commit.

Gunnar slipped behind the steering wheel, started the engine and drove off, leaving her standing on the corner looking like a colorful decoy in a *Where's Waldo?* book.

Lilly stood at the corner of Main Street and Heritage, watching the officer drive away, having to admit the man was a knockout. Yowza, had she ever seen greener eyes? Or a police uniform with more laser-sharp ironed creases? This guy took his job seriously, which was part of the appeal, and he'd already cut her some slack on the citation.

Hmm, she wondered, slipping her sunglasses back in place. *What's his story?*

She'd been in town exactly three days, started her new job yesterday at the newspaper, and was already hatching her plan to buy out the owner, Bjork, and breathe new life into the ailing local rag. She'd taken a huge risk moving here, leaving a solid job—but one without room for advancement—back at the *San Francisco Gazette* in a last-ditch attempt to finally win her parents' respect. Somehow, despite all of her efforts to overachieve, she'd yet to live up to their expectations. Why at the age of thirty it still mattered, she hadn't quite figured out.

In her short time in Heartlandia she'd noticed things from her extended-stay apartment in the Heritage Hotel—things like a nighttime gathering at city hall of an unlikely handful of residents. Oh, she'd done her homework long before she'd moved here all right, because that was what a serious reporter and future newspaper mogul did.

She knew the newspaper was on its last breath, mostly copying and pasting national news stories from the Associated Press, instead of doing the legwork or being innovating and engaging. She recognized an opportunity to start her own kind of newspaper here, for the locals. The kind she'd want to read if she lived in a small town.

Before arriving, she'd gotten the lay of the land, or should she say *landia*? She snickered. Sometimes she cracked herself up.

She'd spent several months getting her hands on everything she could about Heartlandia. Their city website told a lovely, almost storybook history that didn't ring completely true. Could everything possibly be that ideal? Nope, she'd seen enough of life, how messy it could get, to know otherwise. Or maybe San Francisco had jaded her? She'd memorized the city council names and faces, noting they'd appointed a new mayor pro tem, one Gerda Rask. She'd also scoured old newspaper stories and dug up pictures of the locals, including police officers, firemen and businesspersons. The *Heartlandia Herald* used to focus on those kinds of stories, and there were many to choose from. Not anymore.

She knew more about this town than the average resident, she'd bet, which, if it was true, was kind of sad when she thought about it.

Turn and walk, Matsuda. Don't let on to that taller version of a Tom Hardy look-alike that you're watching him drive off. A man that size, with all those muscles, a cop, well, the last thing she wanted to do was get on his bad side.

Once the light changed, Gunnar drove on with one last glance in his rearview mirror. Lilly hadn't budged. It made him grin. That one was a firecracker, for sure.

He'd heard old man Bjork had hired a new reporter. It was to save his sorry journalistic butt since running the *Heartlandia Herald* into the ground with bad reporting and far too many opinion pages—all Bjork's opinion. He'd also heard the new hire was a big-city outsider and a she. *Could the she be her?*

Maybe the *Herald* did need a complete overhaul from an outsider since the newspaper he'd grown up reading was failing. Sales were in the Dumpster, and it bothered him. Over the past few years he'd watched his hometown paper slowly spiral into a useless rag. It just didn't seem right. A newspaper should be the center of a thriving community, but theirs wasn't.

Truth was old man Bjork needed help. Who cared what other people thought about world politics? Everyone got enough of that on cable news. *Keep it local and engag-*

ing. That's what he would have told the geezer if he'd ever bothered to ask for advice since they worked across the hall from each other, but the guy was too busy running the paper into the ground.

What with the new city college journalism department, why couldn't they save their own paper? Heartlandia had always stood on its own two metaphorical feet. Always would. Fishermen, factory workers, natives and immigrants, neighbors helping neighbors. The town had remained independent even after most of the textile and fishing plants had closed down.

Only once had the city been threatened from outsiders, smugglers posing as legitimate businessmen. His own father had fallen for it. Once the original fish factory had closed, he'd been out of a job. Gunnar had been ten at the time and had watched his mother take on two part-time jobs to help feed the family. His father's pride led him to take the job as a night watchman for the new outside company, and he'd turned his head rather than be a whistle-blower when suspicious events had taken place. The shame he'd brought on the family by going to jail was what made Gunnar go into law enforcement, as if he needed to make up for his father's mistakes.

It had taken two years before the chief of police at the time, Jon Abels, had taken back the city. Gunnar had been twelve by then, but he remembered it as if it had just happened, how the police had made a huge sweep of the warehouse down by the docks, arresting the whole lot of them and shutting down the operation. That day Chief Abels had saved the city and became Gunnar's personal hero.

He drove back to the station in time to check out, change clothes and grab a bite at his favorite diner, the Hartalanda Café—he hadn't lied to Ms. Matsuda about that—before he hit city hall for another hush-hush Thursday-night meeting of the minds. It had been an honor to be asked, and joining this committee was the first step on a journey he hoped one day to take all the way to the mayor's office.

Sleepy little Heartlandia's history lessons had recently taken a most interesting plot twist, and he was only one of eight who knew what was going on. The new information could change the face of his hometown forever, and he didn't want to see that happen. Not on his watch.

Gunnar held the door to the conference room for Mayor Gerda Rask. She was the next-door neighbor of his best friend, Kent Larson, and a town matriarch figure who'd agreed to step in temporarily when their prior mayor, Lars Larsson, had a massive heart attack. She'd also been the town piano teacher for as far back as Gunnar could remember, until recently when her granddaughter, Desi, came to town and took over her students.

The city council had assured Mayor Rask she'd just be a figurehead. Poor thing hadn't known what she was stepping into until after she'd agreed. And for that, Mayor Rask had Gunnar's deepest sympathy, support and respect. When he became mayor, he'd take over the helm and transform the current weak-mayor concept, where the city council really ran things, to a strong-mayor practice where he'd have total administrative authority. At least that's how he imagined it. Any man worth his salt needed a dream, and that was his.

The older woman nodded her appreciation, then took her seat at the head of the long dark wooden boardroom table. Next to her was Jarl Madsen, the proprietor at the Maritime Museum. Next to him sat Adamine Olsen, a local businesswoman and president of the Heartlandia Small Business Association, and next to her Leif Andersen, the contractor who'd first discovered the trunk that could change the town's reputation from ideal to tawdry.

Leif had found the ancient chest while his company was building the city college. Though he was the richest man in town, he chose to be a hands-on guy when it came to construction, continuing to run his company rather than rest on his laurels as the best builder in this part of the state of Oregon. He hadn't turned in the chest right away—instead he'd sat on the discovery for months. Once curiosity had gotten the best of him and he'd opened it, saw the contents, he knew he had to bring it to the mayor's attention. After that, Mayor Larsson had his heart attack, Gerda stepped up and this handpicked committee was formed.

Gunnar nodded to his sister, who'd beat him to the meeting. She smiled. "Gun," she said.

"Elke, what's shakin'?"

She lifted her brows and sighed, cluing him that what was shaking wasn't all good. He'd signed on to this panel, like he had to his job, to protect and serve his community. Since his family tree extended back to the very beginning of Heartlandia, and his father had slandered the Norling name, doing his part to preserve the city as it should be was Gunnar's duty.

So far the buried-chest findings had rocked the committee's sleepy little world. He'd heard how some places rewrote history, but never expected to participate in the process. He lifted his brows and gazed back at his kid sister.

As the resident historical maven and respected professor at the new city college, Elke's services had been requested. Her job was to help them decipher the journal notations from the ones dug up in the trunk during construction. Apparently, the journals belonged to a captain, a certain Nathaniel Prince, who was also known as The

Prince of Doom and who might have been a pirate. Well, probably *was* a pirate. The notations in the ship captain's journal held hints at Heartlandia's real history, but they looked like cat scratches as far as Gunnar was concerned. Good thing Elke knew her stuff when it came to restoring historical documents and deciphering Old English.

Across from Elke sat the quiet Ben Cobawa, respected for his level head and logical thinking, not to mention for being a damn great fireman. The native-born Chinook descendent balanced out the committee which otherwise consisted entirely of Scandinavians. But what could you expect from a town originally settled by Scandinavian fishermen and their families? Or so he'd always been led to believe.

Cobowa's Native American perspective would be greatly needed on the committee. They'd be dealing with potential changes to town history, and since his people had played such an important role in the creation of this little piece of heaven originally called Hartalanda back in the early 1700s, they wanted his input.

"Shall we call this meeting to order?" Mayor Rask said.

Gunnar took a slow draw on the provided water. Judging by the concerned expression on his younger sister's face he knew he should be prepared for a long night.

Lilly sidled up to the bar at Lincoln's Place. A strapping young towhead bartender took her order. But weren't most of the men in Heartlandia strapping and fair?

"I'll have an appletini." She almost jokingly added "Sven" but worried she might be right.

The pale-eyed, square-jawed man smiled and nodded. "Coming right up."

She wasn't above snooping to get her stories, and she wanted to start off with a bang when she handed in her debut news story, like her father would expect. She'd been casing city hall earlier, had hidden behind the nearby bushes, and lo and behold, there was Sergeant Gunnar Norling slipping out the back door. She'd watched him exit the building along with half a dozen other people including this new Mayor Rask.

She'd combed through old council reports on the town website and noticed a tasty morsel—"A new committee has been formed to study recently discovered historical data." What was that data, and where had it been found?

The website report went on to mention the list of names. The one thing they all had in common with the exception of one Native American, if her research had served her well, were Scandinavian names that went back all the way to the beginning of Heartlandia, back when it was founded and called Hartalanda. Of course, the Native Americans had been there long before them. Yup, her type A reporter persona had even dug into genealogy archive links proudly posted at the same website.

These people weren't the city council, but they had been handpicked, each person representing a specific slice of Heartlandia life.

She'd met the handsome and dashing Gunnar Norling today, and the idea of "getting to the bottom" of her story through him had definite appeal. Her parents had trained her well: set a goal and go after it. Don't let anything come between you and success. Growing up an only child in their multimillion-dollar Victorian home in Pacific Heights, Lilly's parents had proved through hard work and good luck in business their technique worked. As far as her father was concerned, it was bad enough she'd been born a girl, but for the past five years, since she'd left graduate journalism school, they'd looked to her to stake her claim to fame. So far she hadn't come close to making them proud, but this new venture might just be the ticket to their respect.

A half hour later, nursing her one and only cocktail, she was deep into conversation with the owner of Lincoln's Place, a middle-aged African-American man named Cliff. It seemed there was more to Heartlandia than met the eye once you scratched the Scandinavian surface.

"Looks like you get a lot of tourist trade around here," she said, having studied the bar crowd.

"Thank heaven for the cruise ship business," Cliff said, with a wide and charming smile. "If it wasn't for them, I'd never have discovered Heartlandia."

"Are you saying you cruised here or worked on a cruise ship?"

"Worked on one. Thirteen years."

"Interesting." Normally, she'd ask more about that assuming there might be a story buried in the statement, but today she had one goal in mind. She took a sip of her drink to wait the right amount of time before changing the topic. "So where do the locals go? You know, say, like the regular guys, firemen and police officers, for example." She went for coy, yeah, coy like a snake eyeing a mouse, looking straight forward, glancing to the side. "Where do they hang out after hours?"

He lifted a long, dark brow, rather than answering.

"I'll level with you, Cliff, I'm the new reporter for the *Heartlandia Herald*. I'd like to bring the focus of the newspaper back to the people. I've got a few different angles I'd like to flesh out, and I thought I'd start with talking to the local working Joes." Funny how she'd chosen "flesh out," a phrase that had certain appeal where that Gunnar guy was concerned.

He nodded, obviously still considering her story. And it was a tall tale…mostly. She did have big plans to bring the human interest side back to the paper, but first off, she wanted a knock-your-socks-off debut. Introducing big-city journalist Lilly Matsuda, ta-da!

"There's a microbrewery down by the river and the railroad tracks. To the best of my knowledge, that's where the manly types go when they want to let off steam." He tapped a finger on the bar, smiled. "Here's a tidbit for you. Rumor has it that in the old days, down by the docks in the seedy side of town, right where that bar is today, an occasional sailor got shanghaied."

"Really." The tasty morsel sent a chill up her spine. She had a nose for news, and that bit about shanghaied sailors had definitely grabbed her interest. Though it was an underhanded and vile business, many captains had employed the nasty trick. The practice had been an old technique by nefarious sea captains. First they'd get a man sloppy drunk. Then, once he'd passed out, his men would kidnap the sailor onto the ship and the unsuspecting drunk would be far out at sea when he came to and sobered up. Voilá! They had an extra pair of hands on deck with no ticket home, and they didn't even have to pay him. With Heartlandia being on the banks of the gorgeous Columbia River, a major water route to the Pacific Ocean, the story could definitely be true.

Wait a second, old Cliffy here was probably just playing her, telling her one of the yarns they told tourists to give them some stories to swap when they got back on ship.

"Yes indeed," Cliff said, touching the tips of his fingers together and tapping. "Of course, a lot of the stories we share with our tourists have—" he pressed his lips together "—for lack of a better word, let's say been *embellished* a bit. No city wants to come off as boring when you're courting the tourist trade, right? So we throw in those old sailor stories to spice things up."

She appreciated his coming clean about pirates shang-haiing locals. "I hear you. So you're saying the shanghaied stuff may or may not be true?"

He tilted his head to the side, not a yes or no. She'd let it lie, take that as a yes and try a different angle.

"Hey, have you noticed any after-hour meetings going on at city hall? Or am I imagining things?"

He cast a you-sure-are-a-nosey-one glance. "Could be. Maybe they're planning some big tercentennial event. I think the town was established around 1715."

"Tercentennial?"

"Three hundredth birthday."

"Ah, makes sense. But why would they keep something like that a big secret?"

"Don't have a clue, Ms.…." He had the look of a man who'd had enough of her nonstop questions—a look she'd often seen on her father's face when she was a child. Cliff suddenly had other patrons to tend to. Yeah, she knew she occasionally pushed too far. *Thanks, Mom and Dad.*

"Matsuda. I'm Lilly Matsuda."

He shook her hand. "Well, it was a pleasure meeting you. I hope to see you around my establishment often, and I think you've got what it takes to make a good reporter. Good luck."

"Thanks. Nice to meet you, too."

After Cliff moseyed off, attending to a large table ob-viously filled with cruise-ship guests on the prowl, she scribbled down: "Microbrewery down by the river near railroad." She'd look it up later.

She'd been a reporter for eight years, since she was twenty-two and fresh out of college, and had continued part-time while attending grad school. Had worked her way up to her own weekly local scene column in the *San Francisco Gazette*, but could never make it past the velvet ceiling. She wanted to be the old-school-style reporter following leads, fingers on the pulse of the city, always seeking the unusual stories, and realized she'd never achieve her goal back home, much to her parents' chagrin.

When the chance to work in Oregon came up, after doing her research and seeing a potential buyout opportunity, she'd grabbed it. Statistics showed that something happened to women around the ages of twenty-eight to thirty. They often reevaluated their lives and made major changes. Some decided to get married, others to have a baby, neither of which appealed to her, and right now, since she was all about change, moving to a small town and buying her own paper had definite appeal.

Lilly finished her drink and prepared for the short walk—no jaywalking, thank you very much, Sergeant Norling—back to her hotel.

Once she bought out Bjork, she could finally develop a reputation as the kind of reporter she'd always dreamed of becoming—the kind that sniffed out stories and made breaking headlines. If all went the way she planned, maybe her dad would smile for once when he told people she was a journalist and not a famous thoracic surgeon like he'd always wanted her to become.

Her gut told her to stick with those discreet meetings going on at city hall, and to seek out a certain fine-looking police officer partaking in them. He may have almost written her a citation, but he might also be her ticket to journalistic stardom.

Tomorrow was Friday night, and she planned to be dressed down and ready for action at that microbrewery. If she got lucky and played things right, she might get the decidedly zip-lipped Gunnar Norling, with those amazingly cut arms and tight buns, to spill the proverbial beans to the town's newest reporter.

Chapter Two

After a long week of rowdy tourists, teens in need of mentoring, plus last night's special council meeting, Gunnar needed to blow off some steam. He got off work on Friday, went home and changed into jeans and a T-shirt then headed out for the night. After downing a burger at Olaf's Microbrewery and Gastro Pub, he ordered a beer, and while he waited he thought about last night's meeting. Again.

Elke had uncovered a portion of the journals suggesting there might be buried treasure somewhere in the vicinity of Heartlandia, and until she could get through all of the entries, while carrying a full teaching load at the college, they wouldn't know where to look.

First pirates. Now buried treasure. What next? Was this for real or had they been set up for some kind of reality gotcha show?

"Thanks," he said to the short and wide Olaf, turning in his empty burger plate in exchange for that brew. The historic old warehouse by the docks had been transformed into a down-to-earth bar, no frills, just a wide-open place guys like Gunnar could go to let off steam, have a decent meal and be themselves. A workingman's bar, it had mismatched tables and chairs, open rafters with silver airvent tubing, good speakers that played solid rock music, an assortment of flashing neon signs, posters of beer and burgers, and a few sassy photos of women. Nothing lewd, Olaf's wife wouldn't allow that, but definitely provocative shots of ladies, that and work-boot ads galore.

Olaf kept a huge chalkboard he'd snagged from a school auction and filled it with all of his latest microbrews. Tonight Gunnar was sticking with dark beer, the darker, toastier and mellower the malt, the better. He glanced around at the pool tables, card tables and dartboards there for everyone's entertainment, when they weren't drinking and talking sports or cars, that is. Very few women ventured into the place. The ones who did usually had one thing on their minds. Most times Gunnar avoided them and other times, well, he didn't.

Not anymore, though. That was all behind him since he planned to change his bachelor reputation.

He picked up the Dark Roast Special, first on the list on Olaf's blackboard, and headed back to the dart game where he was currently ruling the day. But not before hearing a lady's voice carry over the loud music and louder guy conversations in the bar. Somehow that high-toned voice managed to transcend all of the noise and stand out.

"Word has it there're some secret meetings going on at city hall," she said. "You know anything about that?"

"Do I look like a politician?" Jarl Madsen, Clayton County's Maritime Museum manager and fellow member on the hush-hush committee, said to the woman, doing a great job of playing dumb.

Gunnar cocked his head and took a peek to see who was being so nosey. Well, what do you know, if it wasn't Lilly the jaywalker with the sexy shoes, elbows up to the bar chatting up Jarl. He looked her over. She knew how to dress down, too, wearing tight black, low cut jeans and a black patterned girly top with sparkles and blingy doodads embedded in the material. In that getup she blended right in.

Right.

At least she'd traded her sexy heels for ankle boots, killer boots, too, he had to admit, and from this angle her backside fit the bar stool to perfection. Yeah, he knew it wasn't polite to stare, so after a few moments, and he'd memorized the view, he looked away. He glanced around the room. Only a handful of other ladies in pairs were in attendance, and this one appeared to be flying solo.

Gutsy.

Or dumb.

But dumb didn't come to mind when he thought about Lilly Matsuda. She seemed sharp and intelligent, and if he trusted his gut, her being here meant she was on task, not here for a simple night out. The task seemed to be related to the committee meetings.

If he were a nosey guy himself, it would be really easy to wander over to Jarl and insinuate himself into the conversation. But that could be considered horning in on another guy's territory, even though in his opinion Jarl and Lilly were completely mismatched. His honorable side won out over the curious cop dude within, mainly because he was off duty and loving it. So back to darts he went, ready to win the high score of the night, trying to forget about outlander Lilly at the bar.

A few minutes later he put his heart and soul into the second game with his latest victim, Jake Bager, a paramedic who was seriously low on bull's-eyes. All three of Jake's darts had made it into the inner circle, but were an inch or more away from the center.

On his next turn, solely concentrating on the game, Gunnar stepped up and threw one, two and three darts dead into the center of the board, the last one so close it nearly knocked the second one out.

Jake groaned. A person behind him clapped.

"Bravo," she said.

Gunnar turned to find Lilly with the fashion-model hair smiling, applauding his efforts.

"Well, if it isn't little miss jaywalker." Damn, she filled out those jeans in a slim-hipped petite kind of way he rarely saw. He knew that shouldn't be the first thing he noticed, but as sure as Mother Nature made little green apples, he had. Her mostly bare arms showed the results of gym workouts, not overly done, just nice and tight, and her nearly makeup-less face was as pretty as an ink-wash painting. He knew because he happened to like that Japanese art technique and had several posters in his home to prove it.

"Thanks," he said, thanking her more for looking nice than for her paying him a compliment. "And what are you doing here?"

She gave a coy smile, even though nothing about her personality that afternoon hinted at coy, lifted her shoulders and dug her hands into her back pockets. He had to admit the move put her perky chest on much better display. He knew he shouldn't focus on that, either, and tried not to notice for too long, but he was a guy and those dang blingy things on the shirt caught the light just right. He lingered a beat longer than he'd meant to, which seemed to be a pattern where Lilly was concerned.

If she'd noticed, she didn't let on. Or seem to mind. That was more like the lady he'd met yesterday afternoon.

"Since you went the touristy route when I asked for the bars where locals hang out," she said, "I had to find out where the action really was from Cliff over at Lincoln's Place."

He nodded. Solid fact-checking. She knew how to gather her information. He hoped she was a travel writer and not the new journalist, since that might complicate his resolution to quit playing the field. "You play?" He offered her the three darts he held.

She left her hands in her back pockets. "Not much. I'm better at pool."

He nodded. "Okay, well, if you'll excuse me, then," he said, deciding to stay put and let Lilly explore the joint on her own, "I've got to teach my man here, Jake, another lesson on darts."

Ten minutes later, Lilly was back at the bar chatting up Kirby, the local pet controller and town grump. Her nonstop questions, and choice of conversation partners, both well past middle age, made it obvious she wasn't here to get picked up. Which, surprisingly, relieved Gunnar.

"And what makes you outsiders think you can just walk into our bar like you belong here?" hairy-eared Kirby said, his voice loud and territorial, carrying all the way to the dartboards.

"The bar sign said Open, nothing about members only." She didn't sound the least bit fazed. Yeah, that was more like the lady he'd met yesterday than little miss coy snooping around a few minutes ago.

Even though she seemed to have things under control, Gunnar knew Kirby's sour attitude mixed with a few beers could sometimes take a turn for ugly and, never really off duty, he hightailed it over to them to keep the peace.

"Kirby, my friend, have a bad day?"

The man with iron-colored hair, in bad need of a barber, grumbled to his beer. "I liked it better when we only let locals in here."

Olaf noticed the scene and was quick to deliver a new beer to Lilly. "This one's on the house, miss. I hope you'll come here often." He smiled at Lilly first, then passed a dark look toward Kirby, who didn't even notice. Or, it seemed, care.

Lilly nodded graciously. "Thank you." She glanced at Gunnar, an appreciative glint in her eyes.

Gunnar turned back to Kirby, patted his back. "Cheer up. Why don't you try enjoying yourself for a change?"

The codger went back to mumbling into his beer, "If you had to deal with what I do every day…"

Gunnar was about to remind the old fart that he was a cop and had to deal with the tough stuff every day, too, but he cut him some slack. Being a cat lover, he understood it must be hard to deal with stray and homeless pets day in and day out, but that's what Kirby got paid for. And just like Gunnar's job, someone had to do it to keep order in their hometown.

He gazed at Lilly, ready to change the subject. "You said you were better at pool than darts. Feel like playing a game?" Mostly he wanted to get her away from Kirby's constantly foul mood because he had the sneaking suspicion she'd tell him where to stick it if Kirby made one more negative remark. And who knew where that might lead, and like he'd maintained all night, he'd come here to let off steam, not be the twenty-four-hour town guardian.

Her expressive eyes lit up. "Sure."

"What do you say I put my name in for the next table, and in the meantime, I'll show you around the bar?"

She got off the bar stool, lifted the toe of her left boot, grinding the spiky heel while she thought. "Sure, why not?"

The circular tour lasted all of three minutes since there wasn't much to show. He used the time to get a feel for

Lilly, pretty sure why she'd showed up here tonight. As he spoke, she studied him and seemed to be doing her own fair share of circling him. At this rate, in a few more minutes they might be dancing. He smiled at her, she smiled back. Seeing a shyer, tongue-tied version of Lilly was surprising, and didn't ring true with how he'd sized her up yesterday. Maybe she was putting on an act.

Gunnar waved down Olaf's wife, who worked as a waitress. "We'll have a couple of beers," he said to Ingé, then turned back to Lilly. "I'll get this one, okay?"

She gave an appreciative look and after perusing the blackboard ordered pale ale named after some dog Olaf used to own. She made a dainty gesture of thanks and accompanied it with a sweet smile. Beneath her tough-girl surface, maybe she was a delicate work of art, and he kind of hoped it was true.

There was something about those small but full lips, and her straight, tiny-nostriled nose that spoke of classic Asian beauty, and Gunnar was suddenly a connoisseur. Yeah, Asian beauty, like a living work of art, or just like those ink-washed prints back at his house. He liked it.

He pulled out a chair for her to sit near the pool tables while they waited, then one for him, throwing his leg over and sitting on it backward.

"You said you were from San Francisco, right? What's it like living there?" he asked, arms stacked and resting along the back rim of the chair.

She crossed her legs and sat like she was in school instead of at a bar. "You remembered."

"Part of the job."

"Well, for starters, it was a lot busier than I'm assuming living around here is." Under different circumstances—not giving her a citation—she was friendly and fairly easy to talk to.

"We're small all right, but there's lots going on. I wouldn't jump to judgment on life being any easier or less interesting here."

"Okay." And she seemed reasonable, too.

Their drinks arrived. He took a long draw on his, enjoying the full malt flavor. She sipped the nearly white clear ale. Things went quiet between them as he searched his brain for another question. She took another drink from her mug, and he could tell her mind was working like a computer. Before she could steer the conversation back to business, he jumped in.

"You have any brothers or sisters?"

"I'm an only child."

"So you're saying you're spoiled?"

She gave a glib laugh. "Hardly. There's a lot of pressure being the only child. When it's just you and two adults, well, let's just say sometimes they forget you're a kid."

"I guess I can see your point."

"If my dad had it his way, first I'd have been a boy and then I'd be a thoracic surgeon."

"I see. So what was your major in college?"

"Liberal arts."

Gunnar barked a quick laugh. "I bet Daddy liked that."

She went quiet, stared at her boots, took a sip or two more from her beer. "To this day I hate hospitals. Can't stand the sight of blood. Probably has to do with a Christmas gift I got when I was eight." She pressed her lips together and chanced a look in his direction, then quickly away, but not before she noticed Gunnar's full attention. That must have been enough to encourage her to go on. "I got this package, all beautifully wrapped. I'd asked for a doll and it looked about the right size, so I tore it open and found the ugliest, scariest, clear plastic anatomical 'Human' toy with all the vessels showing underneath."

He smiled and shook his head, feeling a little sorry for her, but she'd chosen the entertaining route, not self-pity. It made her tale all the more bittersweet. "If you removed that layer there was another with muscles and tendons, and under that another with the organs." She glanced up and held Gunnar's gaze. He sensed honest-to-goodness remorse for an instant, but she kept on like a real trouper. "It had this scary skeleton face with ugly eye sockets."

Under other circumstances, this might be funny, but Gunnar knew Lilly, under the guise of funny stories, was bearing her soul on this one, and he had the good sense to shut up and listen.

"Anyway—" she looked resigned and took another sip of beer "—all I wanted was a doll with a pretty face and real hair I could comb." She shrugged it off and pinned him with her beautiful stare. "What about you? You have brothers or sisters?"

"One kid sister named Elke."

"You close?"

He nodded. "It's just the two of us now."

"Sorry to hear that."

"Well, that's how it goes sometimes, right?"

Lilly tipped her head in agreement. "So what made you become a cop?"

He couldn't blame her for taking her turn at asking questions. But since he was on the hot seat, he went short and to the point—*Just the facts, ma'am.*

"My dad."

"Family tradition? Was he a cop, too?"

Gunnar opened his mouth but stalled out. How should he put this? "No." She'd been flat-out honest with him so he figured he owed her the same. "I guess you could say he was a bad example. Did some time for making really poor choices. Took our good family name and stomped it into the ground."

She inhaled, widening her eyes in the process. "I see. But look at you—you're an honest, upright citizen."

"That I am."

An old Jon Bon Jovi track blasted in the background, and to change the subject, he thought about asking her to dance, nearly missing when they called out his name for pool. "Oh, hey, our table's up," he said, relieved to change the subject. "You ready?"

She passed a smile that seemed to say she was as ready as he was to drop the subject of messed-up families. There was something else in that smile, too, like she might just surprise him tonight, and to be honest, he hoped she would. After that story about her father, he'd decided to go easy on the new girl in town, since it sounded like her childhood had been as rocky as his.

Chapter Three

Lilly followed the hunk with the sympathetic green eyes to the pool table against the back bar wall, the one closest to the bathrooms. What had gotten into her, opening up like that, telling a near stranger about her messed-up family? She could blame it on the beer and his Dudley Do-Right demeanor, but knew it was more than that. It was part of that scary feeling that had started taking hold of her in the past year, that twenty-eight-to-thirty-year-old-lady life-change phenomenon—and the desire to connect with someone in a meaningful way. The thought made her shudder, so she took another sip of beer before glancing up.

Holy Adonis, that man filled out those jeans to perfection. Out of his neatly ironed uniform, he still cut an imposing figure. Extrabroad shoulders, deltoids and biceps deeply defined, enough to make him an ideal anatomy lesson with every muscle clearly on display. Far, far better than that old plastic doll. With those thighs, and upper body strength, he could probably single-handedly push an entire football blocking sled all the way down the field. Or flip a car in an emergency. The guy was scary sturdy.

He'd stepped in when things had gotten sticky with Kirby at the bar, like it was second nature. Gunnar's family had been through the wringer with his father going to prison. Apparently that had influenced his career choice.

She continued to watch him. There was something sweet and kind about his verdant eyes with crinkles at the edges. He hadn't let the tough times or stressful job turn him hard. And his friendly smile. Wow, she liked his smile with the etched parentheses around it. That folksy partial grin gave him small-town charm, and the self-deprecating, beneath-the-brow glance he occasionally gave added to that persona, though nothing else about him gave the remote impression of being "small."

She finished her ale, had really liked the crisp, almost apple taste, and chalked her cue while he racked up the balls in the triangle. She'd played her share of pool in college dorms, enough not to humiliate herself, anyway.

"Eight-ball okay with you?"

She nodded. It was the only game she knew.

"Stripes or solids?" he asked.

"Stripes."

"Want me to break?"

"Sure. Thanks."

Once Gunnar set everything up, he waved the waitress over and ordered some chips and salsa with extra cheese. She'd eaten a salad for dinner, and the beer was already going to her head, so she wouldn't sweat the extra calories.

When Ingé brought the food, he joked with her and gave an extra nice tip. Lilly liked friendly and generous guys—guys who maybe wanted to make up for their pasts. A couple of cops, probably subordinates since they referred to Gunnar as "Sergeant," lined up nearby to watch the game, looking amused. "Go easy on her," one of them said.

"Don't worry, miss," said one of the other men sitting at the bar, who looked big like a construction worker. "He's a gentleman. Right Gun-man?"

From the way people talked to Gunnar, always smiling when they did, some calling him Gun-man, others Gun, and the way everyone responded to his casual style, she could tell he was liked and respected by his peers. She'd also noticed that Kirby had taken Gunnar's firm hint, and kept quiet. Adding up all of that, plus the company of the charming police officer, helped her relax and let her usual guard down. This Gunnar was a nice guy. Gee, maybe she'd actually have a good time tonight. Come to think of it, she already was!

"Did I mention he tried to give me a ticket for jaywalking?" She joined in the fun and chided his buddies.

Gunnar laughed. "A warning."

"Yeah, he's a stickler sometimes," said the dart player named Jake.

Could she blame a guy overcompensating for his father's wrongdoings?

Lilly suddenly wanted to be treated like one of the guys, so she glanced around at the half dozen men taking special interest in her playing pool with *Gun-man*, and decided to put on a show.

"The next round is on me," she said as Gunnar stepped back to let her take her shot. The call for more drinks went over well with the small audience, according to the assorted comments.

"Great!"

"Thanks!"

"Now, that's what I'm talking about."

Gunnar had, once again, set her up with some good and easy shots, if she didn't blow it from being a bit rusty and all, and she'd gotten the distinct feeling he'd done it

on purpose. She leaned forward, and since he had an audience, she waited for him to step in and pull the oldest
come-on in the book—to show her how to hold the cue
stick and make the shot, meanwhile his hands running
over her body for a quick and sneaky feel-up.

But he didn't. He stayed right where he was and explained the technique from there. He really was Dudley
Do-Right.

"Try keeping your shoulder back and your elbow like
this." He demonstrated. "See how my fingers are? Try that.
You'll have more control."

He never got closer than two feet away.

She knew how to play well enough, but she'd let him
school her, make him think he was helping her compete.
Clicking back into her reason for being here tonight, she
decided to play along for now, forget about her news quest.
She did exactly as he'd said and made her shot. In the
pocket. Yes!

She smiled at him and he winked. Uh-oh, that wink
flew through her like a warm winged butterfly searching
for a place to light. Good thing her fresh beer was within
reach to give her an out to quickly recoup.

She smiled and made a quick curtsy, then got back to
business.

She'd come here with the plan to find Gunnar, pepper
him with drinks and get the information she wanted for
her first breakout story. But after their surprising conversation, where they'd both shown a bit of their true colors,
all she wanted to do was fit in. This was fun. To hell with
the story. She could follow up on that later.

The pool game was the center of her attention, well,
that and Gunnar and his every sexy move, and she had a
nagging desire to impress him. Just like a kid. Eesh. If she

could keep her head straight and concentrate on the game, not him, she'd do just fine.

As the game went on, he used his cue as a pointer to suggest where she should stand for which shot and she followed his every lead. As a result she had the best, most competitive game of pool in her life. Who knew how fun it was to play pool in a stinky men's bar?

Between the beer and chips breaks, and their undeniably steamy looks passing back and forth over the scraped-up, green felt-covered table, the game kept getting extended. Occasionally while changing places they'd brush shoulders, and the simple interaction made her edgy. Man, he knew how to rattle a woman with his laser-sharp gaze, too.

As she watched Gunnar make his shots, he seemed to ooze sexy. Whether it was her beer or his smoldering gaze—he was one hot guy—her knees turned to noodles. But he was also very human, just like her, with "issues" as she always jokingly referred to the pressure from her parents to be the best at everything she did.

Gathering her composure, Lilly called the pocket and sank the eight ball. More surprised than anyone, she put down the cue and jumped with hands high above her head. "Yay! I did it. I beat you."

Gunnar smiled, took a step closer and, being anything but a poor sport, patted her shoulder in congratulations. "Good job, Ms. Jaywalker."

"Thanks." Every thought flew out of her mind when he touched her. Having him close scrambled her brain, twisting her thoughts into knots. She needed a moment to recover.

"I'm going to the ladies' room," she said, edging away from his overwhelming space invasion. This seemed far more intimidating than when his easygoing charm had gotten her to let her guard down and spill about her past.

While in the bathroom she gathered her composure and remembered why she'd come to the bar tonight, then returned to the game with new intent. But the first thing she saw was Gunnar. He leaned his hips against the pool table, long legs outstretched, ankles crossed, arms folded, talking casually to Jake. Could he give a better display of his biceps? Man, it was going to take a lot of effort to concentrate on the next game. And, uh-oh, there was another beer waiting for her.

"I always buy the winner a drink," he said, seeing her surprised glance when she got closer.

"Thanks." How could she refuse? Even though she rarely exceeded her two-drink limit, she'd take a sip or two just to be nice.

He'd already set things up for the next game. She broke, and watching the balls scatter to all corners of the table, she mentally chanted her personal promise for tonight's bar visit. It was time to get back on task, if nothing more than to get her mind off Gunnar.

"So, I've heard some mumblings around town about secret meetings going on over at city hall." She stopped midplay, stood up and gave him a perfected wide-eyed, play-it-dumb glance. "You know anything about them?"

He scratched the side of his mouth. His tell? "Can't say for sure I've heard about any secret meetings on the beat. What else have you heard?"

Liar. She'd seen him with her own eyes going into that building from her room at the Heritage, and later leaving, from the bushes where she'd staked out last night. Though she supposed the officer wasn't brazenly lying, saying he couldn't say "for sure," and using a technicality, "not hearing anything *on the beat*," but he was definitely fudging. And he'd turned the tables on her asking what she'd heard. Lilly could feel in her journalistic bones there was a big story behind those meetings and her proof was his inability to admit to or deny them. Which only made her more curious about the after-hours comings and goings over at city hall.

What had she heard, he'd asked? She shook her head, again taking the dense tack. "Just that things are going on and it may be important to Heartlandia."

He touched her arm. The spot went hot. "Tell you what, if I hear anything from anyone in town about those meetings, you'll be the first to know." Again, he'd set up his phrase to keep it from being a bona fide lie.

Without warning, he leaned across the table for something that was behind her, and because she didn't budge, on his way back he brushed her cheek with his shoulder. "Chalk," he said, showing her the prize. Was this a ploy to throw her off track?

From this proximity she looked into his baby greens and, oh-baby-baby. Their eyes locked up close and personal and she thought someone had poured warm honey over her head. *Good move, Gun-man, I've forgotten my own name.* Close enough to smell his sharp lime-and-pine aftershave, she turned toward his face at the exact moment he'd shifted closer to her, and their lips nearly touched. What if she bridged the gap and snuck a quick kiss just for the heck of it? She'd bet her first paycheck there'd be a tingly spark when she made contact.

Their eyes met for an instant, and she didn't even need to make contact to get that zingy feeling again.

You're on the job, remember? She let the moment pass, but was quite sure she'd made her almost-intentions known, and there it was, she'd gotten to him. His eyes went darker, and she sensed a surge in his body heat. He probably wondered the same thing about that potential kiss.

Don't overanalyze everything.

"Okay," she said, acting as if she almost kissed guys on the run all the time, taking the proffered chalk. "Then I start." After she chalked up her cue, and before she made her shot, she sipped more beer as euphoria merged with lust and tiptoed up her spine. Wow. She rolled her shoulders and willed her concentration back, then made her next shot.

She needed to pace herself with the beer or, the way her mind was buzzing all around from the nearness of Gunnar, she might get into trouble. She glanced at her wristwatch. It was only eleven.

Midway through the game, she made a decent shot but, feeling a little tipsy, lost her balance. She leaned against Gunnar since he was close by, and since he felt so darn nice, she put her head on his chest for a second. He wrapped a hand around her waist but immediately let go once she was back on her own two feet.

Do not make a fool of yourself. It's dishonorable to act foolish. Her father's mantra drilled through her thoughts. *Concentrate on the game. Win!*

The game progressed. They spontaneously bumped hips after his next good shot and high-fived on hers, but he cheated. He pulled his arm in just enough so her chest touched his when their palms met. Dirty trick, but *zing-oh-zing!* She liked touching his chest with her breasts.

So Officer Dudley Do-Right played dirty with a few beers under his belt. But she'd also noticed he'd forgotten about his last beer. She needed to do the same, to stay on her toes, but unfortunately his sex appeal was throwing her too far off balance for that.

He won the game, and came around the table grinning to collect a winner's high five. She had an overwhelming urge to forget the victory slap and surprise him with a full-on mouth kiss, but fortunately came to her senses before she acted on it.

As their palms slapped together, and he didn't pull his dirty trick a second time, their eyes met and held for several beats, the pool game all but forgotten. After lowering their now-interlocked fingers, neither of them moved, instead they stood staring at each other.

"Come on, come on, come on, you gonna play another game or stand there drooling on each other?" One of the guys impatiently waiting for a pool table broke the magical moment, which—considering Lilly's continuous urge to kiss Gunnar—could have gotten out of hand at any given second.

Gunnar cleared his throat, gestured for her to take the first shot then racked the balls. Thank goodness he was a gentleman because right about now she couldn't begin to remember what it was like to be a lady. *Sorry, Mom.* She must be out of her mind to think about making out with a practical stranger in a bar on her first Friday night in town. Yet it was foremost in her mind and completely doable if she deemed it. *Wasn't that what Daddy had always taught her? Set a goal. Go for it. Let nothing get in the way.*

Between her and Gunnar's lips?

"Okay, okay," he said to the impatient guy, sounding diplomatic as all hell. "The last game." But he nailed her with a heated look—it melted into her center and spread like warm fingers stroking her hips.

"Let's do it," she said, breathless, thinking she could be up for almost anything tonight as long as it included Gunnar Norling. "Can we get another round here?"

Olaf's wife was passing by but Gunnar intercepted and ordered a couple of waters and coffee instead.

Okay, she got his point, but that was taking his job too far. Was the guy ever off duty?

Truth was Lilly had no intention of drinking another drop of beer anyway—she knew her boundaries—but she needed Gunnar to get a little looser-lipped. Not that his lips and everything else about him weren't doing a great job already. But maybe next time when she brought up the meetings, if he had another beer, he'd at least admit to taking part in them. That would be a start. Then she could begin to slowly and meticulously strip him down to the truth.

She leaned on her pool cue as the journalistic euphemism morphed into pure, unadulterated sex thoughts with Gunnar stripped down and standing buck naked at the center of them. Almost losing her balance and falling off the stick, she swallowed and looked at her shoes, hoping he hadn't seen it, or couldn't read her mind, or notice *her tell*—burning, red-hot ears.

He scratched the corner of his mouth.

Before the water and coffee came she reached for her beer, but soon realized Gunnar had moved hers far out of reach. Was he worried about her? Heck, she was a big girl, could handle her liquor. If his gesture hadn't seemed so darn sweet and protective, she might have flashed her feminist membership card, ripped into him about being a chauvinist and suggested he mind his own business.

Instead, she took her sexual frustration and went all competitive. In the heat of the faster-paced game, they touched a lot, whether intentional or not, she couldn't tell and definitely didn't mind, but each and every time it kept her nerve endings on alert and craving more.

In between pool shots, she tried to dial things back a notch by bringing up old family pets. She told him her favorite pet story from when she was a kid. Her favorite pet was a Chihuahua from a puppy mill store that won her over with the offering of a tiny paw. She'd named it Chitcha, then explained that was Japanese for *tiny* and her grandmother still called her Chitcha to this very day. She liked how he repeated the name, Chitcha, as if memorizing the word.

His favorite pet turned out to be a stray cat named Smelly, whom he'd found while he walked home from school one day. The homeless cat was half-dead and hosting a dozen abscesses. According to Gunnar, that red tabby lived fifteen years with his family.

Knowing he was the kind of guy to rescue a stray cat made her go all gooey inside.

They played on, and she enjoyed getting to know a bit more about this man who, despite a couple of close calls, continued to act the gentleman—except for the high-five incident, which would really be unforgivable if she hadn't enjoyed it as much as he apparently had.

Good thing he'd ordered the coffee because the drinking had definitely caught up to her. The bar had taken on the appearance of golden-warm tones, fuzzy around the edges and a little distant, and Gunnar looked like the sexiest man on earth—probably was.

Something about Gunnar made her edgy, though, like he was the kind of guy a girl could fall really hard for. Most men his age would already be married if they wanted to be. Her journalistic intuition told her he wasn't the committing kind. Nah, he was too charming and smooth around ladies, well, around this lady anyway, proving he'd had a lot of experience. Which would be par for the course in Lilly's world, since none of her boyfriends ever had the least bit of interest in commitment.

Nope. This guy could be trouble.

The best way to deal with Gunnar would be professionally, journalist to cop. She had to break him down, and after this game she'd make her move. She'd invite him somewhere closer to her hotel for coffee and quiet conversation. This time, instead of relying on a pool hall and beer, she'd use more of her hard-earned journalistic prowess and throw in a few more naturally acquired wily ways to get him to open up.

Charm didn't come second nature to her, like it did with him, but she could pull it off if she had to. For the sake of her story.

He won the game and since she was still feeling pretty darn good from her last beer, and was in close enough proximity, she decided to give him another high five. In order to do that, she had to move toward him. Shifting from where she stood to Gunnar felt the way slow-motion photography looked, with streaks of light trailing the object. Boy, she should have eaten more of the chips and salsa. She stopped, shook her head and regained her balance.

"Whoa, hold on there, Chitcha." He steadied her with hands on her shoulders. "You okay?"

Amused, she chose to think he'd called her the nickname her grandmother had given her, not her dog's name. "I think I'm a little tipsy."

She moved gingerly toward him, and he drew her close, wrapping around her like a warm rugged blanket. "I better give you a ride home. Is that okay?"

She'd never felt such strength in her life. Solid. Like a rock.

"But you've been drinking, too."

"Two beers," he said. "Didn't even finish the last one. I'm fine."

She dared to glance into his eyes again, and could tell he was perfectly okay. The biggest question was did she trust herself enough to let him take her home without falling all over him? One more glance into those dreamy green eyes and she made up her mind.

"Okay."

"I'll get my motorcycle."

She gulped as if he'd just suggested jumping off the bridge as he led her outside the bar.

The former warehouse covered in weathered wood with a rusted aluminum roof stood stark against the night sky and sat in the center of the crowded asphalt parking lot. The Columbia River rushed by behind the bar giving a calming effect after the noise from Olaf's. Lilly's car was a sporty red sedan and Gunnar's motorcycle was two aisles down. He led her to the bike.

"I can call a cab," she said, panic brewing in her dark eyes.

"I'm a safe rider. You'll be fine." He handed her his helmet.

Her decision to put it on seemed more about saving face.

Gunnar liked how Lilly threw her leg and spiky-booted foot over the pillion seat of his motorcycle. He twisted around and helped her fasten the helmet. She'd clearly never taken a ride on a bike before, so he decided to take the back route from the docks through residential streets. Whenever he leaned into turning a corner, her hands tightened around his middle, and it felt good. Beyond good. Going far slower than usual, never over thirty-five for her sake, they crossed the railroad tracks, a small houseboat cul-de-sac section of the harbor, and Fisherman's Park with its distinct fishy smell, then rode past the town library, grammar school and finally drove down Main Street to the Heritage Hotel.

Regretting the end of the ride with *Chitcha* nearly strapped to his back, he parked in front.

"Thanks," she said over his shoulder the moment he stopped.

He waited while she got off the back of the motorcycle, then shut off the engine and parked, leaning it on the kickstand.

"So, thanks for bringing me here." Again with the thanks business. "Guess I'll see you around." She seemed nervous and flighty compared to earlier, and as she headed for the rotating door he pulled her back and pointed to the helmet she'd forgotten to take off.

"Oh. Sorry," she said, flush-faced, removing it and handing it to him.

Her hair stuck out every which way, and it made her look even cuter. He didn't want to humiliate her, so he held back his grin, only letting one side of his mouth hitch upward the tiniest bit. He tried his best to make eye contact, but hers darted around as if planning a major escape.

What had happened to the bravado lady at the bar, the one who he could have sworn almost kissed him after one particularly successful shot?

Not wanting to make her uncomfortable, he backed off. He may be knocked out by the feisty Asian beauty, but the last thing he'd ever do was push himself on her. Or any lady. Hell, if history repeated itself, women always returned to Gunnar. He'd wait for her to come to her senses and make the next move, even though he wasn't supposed to be doing that anymore.

"Okay," he said. "So I'll see you around, I guess."

"Sure thing." Her expression turned all earnest and he braced for something awkward to happen, like an apology, but something much better than that came next.

Lilly went up on tiptoes, hands balanced on his shoulders, and bussed his cheek—his reward for being a gentleman. He thought he'd been kissed by a butterfly and liked the way tiny eyelash-type flutters marked the spot. It surprised him.

She must have picked up on that "something more" reflex she'd caused, because he stole a glance into her eyes and an open book of responses filled him in on the rest of the story. She was interested. Very interested.

So was he, and he was damn sure she could figure that out. For a few breathy moments they stayed staring under the light of the street lamp, trying to read each other. He could still detect her fresh and flowery perfume, and resisted taking a deep inhale.

Having spent the better part of the evening in Lilly's company, he'd already understood she liked to take the lead with questions, pool and drinking. If he read her right, and he liked to think that being a policeman had taught him how to read people, she'd prefer to make the next move. So he waited, counting out a few more breaths while taking a little excursion around her intelligent and thoughtful eyes...and getting lost. Her creamy skin contrasted the dark, straight hair and meticulously shaped eyebrows. And those eyes...

She wrapped her hands around his neck and drew him close. Her fingers cool on his skin, and with a twinkling glint in her night-like eyes, she carefully touched her mouth to his and kissed him as if she meant it. Her small but well-padded lips, soft and smooth, fit over his in petite perfection.

Beyond pleasantly surprised, he inhaled, catching that fresh scent again, found her waist and tightened his grip. The kiss felt right on-target and he liked that. Boy, oh boy, did he like it. His stout and her pale ale complimented each other perfectly as their tongues managed a quick touch here and there before going for more exploration.

Not stopping there, his hands cupped her face, his

thumbs stroking those creamy cheeks, and he kissed her lips, the delicate skin beneath her eyes, her neck, cheeks and ear. He brushed her jaw with his beard stubble, sending shock waves along his skin, driving his reaction inward and starting a slow burn. Not wanting to overpower her, since the kiss had been her idea, he let up the slightest bit, but pulled her body closer. She settled into his embrace, curled up and stayed there for several long tantalizing moments, basking as he planted more soft-lipped kisses on the top of her head, along her hair, the shell of her ear.

She let him kiss wherever he wanted, so he went back to her mouth.

It didn't feel like a first kiss. Nope. This felt more like a kiss that had been waiting a long time to be born and today was the day the right two people made it happen.

She tilted her head upward and their lips met again. Could she read his thoughts?

Things were working out just fine. He really liked his theory about the kiss taking on a life of its own, so he just went along with the sexy thrill…

Until she stopped kissing him.

"I'm sorry I got tipsy and that you had to give me a ride home."

He'd been so swept up in the moment he hadn't realized she'd been multitasking, kissing *and* thinking. And she'd finally gotten into her apology.

"You are? Because I'm really liking how things've turned out."

She gave a gentle-lipped smile, her arms edging away from his neck. "The fresh air's helped a lot. Oh, and thank you for not taking advantage of me."

"Would never do that." He wanted to make it clear he wasn't anything close to smarmy if that was what she thought. He wasn't that guy, not like his father, who'd say one thing then do another, and never would be.

Her gaze shifted from his chest to his eyes and registered some kind of sincerity. "I'm very grateful for that." They stared at each other for a couple more beats of his pulse, which was definitely thumping stronger than usual.

"I don't know what kind of guys they raise in your neck of the woods, but we're a mostly honorable bunch here."

"Good to know. Like I said, sorry for getting tipsy back there."

He liked looking at her pointy chin and long, smooth throat, and it made it hard for him to read the moment. Was she cooling off? "Don't worry about anything. You were fine."

"I don't want you to get the wrong impression about me."

"I haven't and wouldn't."

"Thanks."

"But maybe stay out of bars for a while." He thought a little teasing might loosen her up again. "Keep your nose clean. Stay under the radar." He disengaged his hands from her small hips and used one to demonstrate flying under the radar.

"Hey, I'm an adult, remember?" She'd taken it good-naturedly. "And I didn't exactly make a fool out of myself."

"In the bar or just now?"

She nailed him with a disapproving stare. "I'm an emancipated woman and I kiss whomever I want, wherever I want."

"Got it. In fact, you can do it again if you want."

He'd done his job, made her laugh against her will. "Let's make the next one a rain check, okay? I'm all kissed out for tonight."

All kissed out? They'd just gotten started. Maybe she wasn't as turned on as he'd hoped.

At least she'd said "the next one." Yeah, that was the spirit. "Definitely." He went along with the distancing process because he sensed she needed it, and underplayed his honest-to-goodness disappointment. Anything to make her comfortable with the fact she'd laid a pretty spectacular kiss on him right there in front of the Heritage Hotel entrance, yet didn't want to take things any further. "Your reputation's safe with me."

"My reputation is just fine, thank you very much."

Usually, after a kiss like that, the ladies invited him in, and even though she'd just asked for a rain check on the next one, she'd gotten her feathers ruffled over his playful comment, and it puzzled him. Maybe that's all he could expect from a lady who was supposed to be a thoracic surgeon but hated the sight of blood.

Gunnar had a strong hunch getting invited into her hotel room wasn't going to happen with Lilly the jaywalking journalist anytime soon. He wanted to let her know it was okay. He was fine with taking things slow. Especially if he could look forward to more spectacular kisses like that.

"Write some good stories for the newspaper, and no one will remember your pool-hall days." Her head shot up. "You didn't think I knew that, did you?"

Those pretty brown eyes lit up. "How did you know?"

Of course he knew she was a reporter. Hell, with all those questions about hush-hush meetings he'd have to be a damn fool not to figure it out. The lady wanted to know the secret so she could blab it all over the newspaper before the committee decided how best to handle things.

Well, she wouldn't find out from him, that was for sure, no matter how great she kissed.

"For one thing, the newspaper is right across the hall

from the police department and Bjork has a big mouth. For another, you're the nosiest lady I've ever met. I put two and two together."

As if she'd been outed, she went brazen-faced. "The thing is, I want to make a big impression with a breaking story. I feel like I'm on the scent of something."

She was, and it was his obligation to stop her.

"Stop trying so hard. Take some time to get a feel for Heartlandia first. You'll figure out some angle. It may not be a big splashy lead story, but you'll find a way to capture your audience. Maybe even the heart of the town." He could think of a few ways she'd already captured his attention, but he was starting to sound like a big boring town guardian and needed to back off.

She nodded infinitesimally. "You're probably right. I try too hard." For an instant she changed into a self-doubter, but before his eyes, she switched back to the overconfident woman from the first day he'd met her. "Well, thanks again for the ride. I'll catch a cab to my car in the morning. See you around."

All business. Any possibility of her kissing him again had been taken off the table, which probably meant there wouldn't be an offer to come inside, either. Funny how he had to keep reminding himself it wasn't going to happen.

Okay. He could deal with that. But she'd knocked him off balance enough to hesitate asking for her phone number, and he didn't want to ruin the memory of that perfect kiss if she didn't give her number to him. So, out of character, he let things lie and took a step toward the curb and his bike.

One thing he'd already learned—Lilly liked to be the leader.

Problem was so did he. But not today.

"Don't be a stranger. I work right across the hall from

you," he said, doing his best to forget the mind-boggling kiss and sound nonchalant.

She nodded. "Okay. Good night. I had fun." With that she headed for the entrance, waved goodbye and disappeared into the revolving door.

He started the bike and revved the engine. Forgetting his new resolve to quit playing the field, he'd wait for her to make the next move.

And if history repeated itself, the ladies always did.

Chapter Four

Saturday afternoon Lilly had a long talk with herself. Evidently her ethics regarding getting the story at all costs were in the tank. She never wanted to be caught in such a vulnerable position as getting tipsy in a strange bar, or having to accept a ride home on a motorcycle with a man she barely knew, again. But good thing Gunnar had been there like she'd planned.

He was a law-enforcement officer and from what she'd observed, a well-respected guy. A guy making up for the sins of his father? Maybe. Most important, he was a gentleman.

The problem was she'd lost focus on her plans drinking those beers. She'd shared far too much with Gunnar about her personal life. Did he really need to know about what a disappointment she'd been to her parents? And, as far as she was concerned—and she was sure her mother would agree with her—she'd nearly made a fool out of herself telling him the Christmas doll story, then followed that up with getting a little tipsy. What must he think?

It wouldn't happen again. Couldn't.

But she had to admit, she'd had a great time hanging out with Gunnar, and she'd surprised herself initiating the kiss, which had been more than she'd ever expected. Wow. That's why it couldn't happen again. She couldn't let Gunnar get in the way of her plans. So Sunday afternoon, when she'd absentmindedly picked up her cell phone to search for his phone number, she'd stopped. What was she thinking?

On Monday, she put her best foot forward with her new boss, Mr. Bjork. She'd come to work with a gazillion ideas, each of which he'd nixed until she'd brought up doing a human interest story about the local animal controller, Kirby Nylund. Carl Bjork's eyes lit up at the suggestion. Perhaps he had a soft spot for pets?

Bjork also put her on assignment regarding the local firemen and a slew of recent Dumpster fires around town and along the railroad tracks. Now she felt like part of the reporting team.

Unfortunately, the police department was just across the hall, and both the newspaper and PD offices were on either side of the lobby, their front walls being all glass, making it difficult to avoid Gunnar. Once or twice that morning she'd already seen him enter the building in all of that law-enforcement-officer splendor, filling out the perfectly ironed uniform, and sporting the low-slung duty belt, shiny badge and cop sunglasses. Totally out of character, after gawking at him she'd ducked down at her desk, below the chair-rail cubical partition in order not to be seen, and in the process had garnered more than a few odd looks from Bjork and his skeleton newspaper staff. What was it about Gunnar that caused her to repeatedly make a fool out of herself?

Until she figured out how best to handle the big friendly—and sexy—cop, she'd avoid him like a bad story. Since Gunnar might be the source of her future news flash,

Lilly couldn't risk getting personally involved with him, compromising the story.

But no matter how busy she'd kept herself over the past few days, bits and pieces from their fun night together—she really had to admit the bar had been the most fun she'd had in years—haunted her quiet moments. She remembered touching his face and kissing him, surprised how tender his lips were, and thinking wow, just wow, this guy was something else. He might look big and tough, but he kissed like she was the most delicate creature on earth. Then she remembered that big ol' red flag popping into her brain... *Careful, Lilly, this one could be a heart-breaker for sure.*

With all her big-city ways, she might give the impression of sophistication and world wisdom, but in reality she'd spent so much time and energy pursuing her studies and job, not to mention trying to please her parents, that she'd yet to figure out how to make time for relationships. Whatever "relationship" meant.

She'd dated a few men here and there, but nothing came close to being serious. Who had time?

Anyway, Lilly Matsuda had far more important things to do than get all infatuated with a bossy cop.

Just before lunch, grateful to hit the beat, she grabbed the strap of her purse, thrust her trusty notepad and mini recorder inside, and set out, taking the back exit to avoid the big Swedish sergeant with eyes the color of pine trees.

She'd learned well from her demanding parents that nothing must stand in the way of your goal, and Gunnar Norling was not her goal, no matter how appealing he was.

Even though Lilly lived in a hotel, it was an extended stay and she had a small kitchen with a half refrigerator, hot plate and a microwave. Just like in college. Since she'd run out of breakfast cereal and a few feminine items, Tuesday night she stopped in at the local market chain, the only place in town that didn't carry a Scandinavian name. She pushed her cart toward aisle ten. Having just grabbed the special hair gel she'd run out of that morning, she now loaded up on the items she needed for that time of the month. After that she'd buy some fruit and cereal, oh, and she couldn't forget the milk.

Just before leaving the aisle, something caught her eye. Condoms.

A certain handsome face came to mind. Gunnar.

Hmm…what if?

He's not your goal. Remember.

Another thought overrode the first.

She was a modern girl. Shouldn't she be prepared if the occasion ever arrived? Looking at the small box of extra fancy condoms, "ribbed with heating lubrication," on impulse, she picked them up, read the back cover, then tossed them into her cart and moved on.

Rounding the corner, focused on the task of groceries, she nearly ran into another shopping cart. "Oh, sorry!"

Lilly glanced up to see Gunnar holding a couple of packages of deodorant, one in each hand, as if making the biggest decision of his life, and looking as surprised as she must have running into him.

"Hey," he said. "Fancy meeting you here." He'd made his choice and put one brand back on the shelf.

"I needed a few things." She couldn't help herself, and looked into his cart loaded with food items and paper products. The guy obviously lived on his own, judging by the contents of his cart, not one feminine thing to be found.

"So how've you been?" He looked honestly interested.

"Very well, thank you. How about you?" *Hide the con-*

doms! How was she supposed to do that without being obvious?

"Not bad. Breaking into that new job?"

"Yes," she said, edging from behind the cart to alongside it, then standing in front of it altogether. Unfortunately, this put her in much closer proximity to him. Close enough to see those green, green eyes. "Bjork's teaching me the ropes and sending me out on assignments."

"Good. Good." The guy looked as if he wanted to settle in and have a real conversation, his expression inquisitive and his brows mildly furrowed, yet he held back. And she held her breath, preoccupied with the condoms and him not noticing them. Were they destined to discuss the weather?

"Anything new or exciting going on in the police department?" She broke the lingering moment of silence and as she spoke leaned against the front of the cart, surreptitiously moving her other hand behind her, searching around, hoping to make contact with the naughty little box. But the cart was too deep. The condoms were out of her reach. Whatever possessed her to buy them, anyway?

"No breaking news." He smiled, imparting the obvious— he wouldn't tell her anything if there was, and she could count on that. "How about you?"

"Nope. No breaking stories." She glanced at Gunnar, the handsome homegrown stud in fitted jeans and a blue plaid flannel shirt. Her cheeks warmed. She needed to get away from him. This was the guy she'd kissed with all of her heart the other night, and even though she'd been a little under the influence at the time, she'd really wanted to. That kiss had influenced her thoughts just moments ago. Now she'd been caught buying condoms. Wouldn't that go right to his head. Oh, not that head!

Her warming cheeks advanced into an all-out hot-from-the-neck-up affront.

Lilly shook her head, hoping to clear out all the crazy thoughts. *Get away. Go. Now!* "Well, I better get over to the produce aisle. A girl needs her five pieces of fruit a day."

"Sure thing." He glanced toward her cart, but couldn't see around her. "The apples are good this time of year. But here's a tip, they're much better at the farmer's market every Sunday afternoon. Our local growers are best."

Always up for a good story, she searched in her purse for the notepad, ready to scribble a reminder for that coming Sunday farmer's market, unmanning her cart. "Thanks, I'll do that."

He glanced into her cart and with a twinkle in his eyes nailed her when she glanced up again. Damn. He'd seen them.

He winked and scratched the corner of his mouth. She could read his face so easily it was sad—*Hmm, you planning on using those with me?*

"Well, I guess I better go check out," he said, making her squirm in her tracks.

"See you around the office building," she said. *Cringe.* Every assumption known to man must be elbowing its way into his already oversize masculine ego. She needed to stay away from him.

"Sure thing," he said, far more confident than necessary.

Just for the record, the one thing she wasn't was a *sure thing*.

So why did she have that little box with her other items?

She fumed, mostly at herself, and pushed her cart toward the back end of the aisle as he headed for the checkout clerk up front.

Ten minutes later, having calmed down and completed her shopping, distractedly putting the contents of her cart on the small conveyor belt at the checkout, she reached for the box. Lifting it, she saw the extra fancy, ribbed-with-heating-lubrication condoms and blushed again. Gunnar'd had a frisky look on his face when he'd said goodbye, and she'd put it there because of these.

"You gonna want that, miss?" the checker asked.

"Oh." Instead of letting her eyes bug out and making some excuse about having made a mistake the way she wanted to, just to spite Gunnar she handed the condoms to the clerk with her head high, looking straight into his eyes. "Yes."

She was a grown-up. If she wanted a box of condoms, she'd buy them, and it didn't matter what Gunnar thought about it. But an unwanted image planted in her mind—using one of the condoms on Gunnar—and it made the tips of her ears burn hot as she left the market, one bag of groceries in each arm.

Gunnar couldn't figure it out. It had been five days since he'd given Lilly a ride home and they'd kissed, and almost another day since she'd snuck the condoms into her grocery cart, yet she still hadn't called him. Sure she'd been embarrassed when he'd dropped her off at her hotel last Friday, but she hadn't been drunk or anything, just tipsy enough to need a ride home. No harm, no foul.

His mouth twitched into a partial grin. That kiss had been damn fantastic, and this wasn't the first time he'd thought about it since Friday night. Which was unsettling. Since when did Gunnar get all floaty-headed over the memory of a hot kiss?

When she'd opened up about her parents pressuring her into becoming a surgeon, and how instead she'd followed her heart in college, and then told the touching story about the little girl who'd only wanted a doll, not a science lesson, well, his chest had tightened with compassion. There was definitely more to Lilly than her sexy and sophisticated exterior.

Gunnar parked his unit that Wednesday midmorning and headed inside to the police department from the back parking lot. The close-to-retirement officer working the front desk waved him over.

"Got a message for you," Ed said, offering a sealed envelope to Gunnar.

"Thanks." Gunnar took it and noticed the feminine handwriting then smiled. Yeah, so he'd been right, sooner or later she'd come around.

He took the envelope back to his desk, sat and fished out his letter opener then tore that sucker open. He was a bit disappointed to see typing inside, instead of the handwritten "call me" note with a phone number and a real lipstick kiss he'd imagined.

He read on.

Hi Gunnar—I wanted to get your approval to use your heartwarming story about that stray cat you once gave shelter in a little piece I'm doing on our local pet control. It will run on Thursday. If you're okay with it, please let me know at…

She left her work phone number. That was a start. But she'd only signed off with her name. Not *look forward to hearing from you*, or *let's get together soon*, or any number of catchy coy phrases that would have made it easy for him to suggest they have dinner together that weekend. Nope, she'd gone the just-Lilly route. Very professional.

He dialed the number she'd given and it went straight to messages. *Bummer. Not even gonna get to talk to her in person.* After the beep, he used his charming voice and gave her permission to share his story and any other noble thing she'd like to share about him, but stopped short of asking her out. He'd decided to do that face-to-face the next time he saw her.

The mysterious outsider with the wide-spaced and beautifully shaped eyes, that when you looked closer were maybe a little sad from growing up with overbearing parents, wasn't making his job easy. Now he smiled full-out because, truthfully, he was looking forward to the challenge of getting Lilly Matsuda to go out with him.

Thursday morning Gunnar let his cat, Wolverine, out for his morning explorations then walked down the driveway to pick up the paper. Pulling it out of the thin plastic cover he headed back inside. Once he'd gotten his coffee together and a peanut-butter-and-banana sandwich on toast, he settled at the kitchen counter to read the news. Back on page five was an article written by Lilly featuring, of all people, Kirby Nylund, the curmudgeon himself, half smiling, half scowling for the camera.

Gunnar was impressed with Lilly's style of journalism. It included a little bit of folksy banter with Kirby, a bit of a history lesson on Heartlandia's approach to animal control, the current state of stray pets in Clayton County, and informative tips on where and when to have pets spayed and neutered at a reasonable cost. Then she did something that hit home with Gunnar, she threw the question out to the local readers: "Tell us about your personal pet-rescue story for a chance to see yours in print." After that she started things off with Gunnar's story about Smelly.

When he finished reading the article he had a big grin on his face. Yes, that's what the *Heartlandia Herald* had been missing, that personal touch, with the invitation to the locals to participate in the newspaper. If his hunch was right, there would be an avalanche of responses to her invitation.

Lilly might put up a tough facade, but beneath that stylish, modern-woman exterior she had a big heart. He'd experienced it firsthand the night she'd kissed him stupid in front of the hotel. Why she'd gone into hiding, he didn't understand.

Gunnar finished following up on the complaint about a disturbance in the city college parking lot later that night. Several such calls had come in almost simultaneously across town. Because he was closest to the college, he rolled on that one, leaving the other units to investigate the different areas.

Everything checked out fine at the college, no sign of disturbance at all, other than night students heading to their cars after class. He decided to take one more trip around the parking lot to make sure he hadn't missed anything when a call about a fire came through the radio just after 9:00 p.m. *Old warehouse. 300 block of First Street. The railroad tracks.*

Hell, it was Olaf's place.

He hit his emergency lights, sped off and, when he'd gotten onto the main road, seeing huge black clouds of smoke off in the distance, turned on the siren and raced toward the scene down by the river.

As a police officer his job at a fire was crowd-and-traffic control of the area, the biggest hazard being looky-loos swarming the scene and getting in the way. Within five minutes he arrived behind another police cruiser and jumped out.

Tactical planning was the sergeant's job, and he took it seriously.

"How many on the way?" he called to Eric, the other

police officer. Heat from the huge explosive flames at the brewery warmed his face even from this distance. Three fire trucks and dozens of men flocked to the blaze hitting the pavement at full speed toward the old warehouse.

"Six other units that I know of are on the way," Eric said.

Soon, several other blaring sirens made known their arrival and Gunnar had half a dozen units spaced evenly and parked in a line at the outskirts of the parking lot. Fortunately, the river acted as a natural boundary on the back side and was one less thing to worry about.

The police officers worked as a team, some marking boundaries with flares and bright orange cones and others taking to the streets directing and detouring what little traffic was out this time of night.

Like moths to light, employees from nearby businesses and residents from local neighborhoods poured outside to have their own up-close-and-personal view of the fire.

The crowd grew as the fire put on a diabolical performance in the night sky, and Gunnar concentrated on his immediate surroundings, the citizens, and fellow police officers, leaving the firefighting to the well-trained pros. There were more sirens, more police units to strategically place and also an ambulance, which he assisted through the crowd and police line.

Things could get out of control fast if they didn't demarcate the perimeter. "Get the traffic control unit out here and tell them to bring the sawhorse barricades," he said.

"Roger, Sarge." Eric headed for his unit to put in the request.

Gunnar got on his radio for the latest updates, wondering if his best friend, Kent, who ran the local Urgent Care, had been notified. Another ambulance arrived, and he hoped beyond hope that the injuries would be kept to a minimum, especially since the nearest hospital was the next town over thirty miles away, and there was only so much Kent and his staff could handle at his UC. As it was Kent would be inundated with smoke inhalation patients from the gathering crowd.

With his mind flitting to a hundred different thoughts, Gunnar saw a petite silhouette break from the main group of bystanders and head his way.

"Gunnar!"

It didn't take more than a second to recognize the lovely Lilly, and since it was the first face-to-face he'd had with her since that night at the market, a mixture of bad—Olaf's, the place they'd first gotten to know each other, had been decimated by the fire—and good—it was great to see her again—feelings took him by surprise. A single word popped in his head: *Chitcha.* On reflex he smiled.

She returned the smile, then flashed her reporter's ID. "Hi! This is horrible. Can you tell me what's going on?"

Gunnar gave her the general rundown of time and events while he took in her jeans, boots and half-off-the-shoulder purple sweater. "No word yet on how it started." But something had been niggling at the back of his brain ever since he'd received the call. Thinking back to the college parking lot disturbance that had been a false alarm, and which he'd rolled on, he remembered hearing several other calls, all with the same complaint, right at the exact time around 8:30 p.m. He wondered if all of those had been false alarms, too, like a widespread decoy. Putting that together with the recent onslaught of trash-can fires around the docks and train tracks the past few weeks, he also puzzled over whether there might be a connection.

"Has the fire captain issued a statement yet?" Lilly asked. "Anything I can use?"

"Not yet." Looking at Lilly, remembering how great

she'd felt Friday night in front of her hotel, wishing they'd had more time together since then, some protective instinct clicked on in his gut. "You shouldn't get so close. Who knows what toxic fumes might be spilling into the air."

"Like twenty feet will make a difference?" She had a point. "I'm here for the *Herald*, can you give me any information?"

"Nothing official. But all the alcohol in the bar and brewery is probably what made the huge blast about an hour ago. Did you hear it?"

She nodded. "I thought someone had dropped a bomb."

Gunnar glanced over his shoulder at the raging orange-and-red flames. Smoke plumes rose into the night sky like an ancient genie finally released from his bottle. "Kind of looks that way, doesn't it?"

He used his hand on her shoulder to direct her farther back and to the side of his car, thinking they may be able to hear each other better over there.

One of the rookie cops burst onto the scene, a cardboard multiple-cup holder in his hands. "The coffee shop insisted I bring some coffee. You want one?"

Gunnar looked at Lilly. "Coffee?" She nodded her thanks so he grabbed two. "Thanks, Darren."

Off the new officer went, spreading his good-coffee cheer to the other policemen working nearby. Something crackled over his radio in the car. "Excuse me," he said, handing Lilly his paper cup and hopping inside to listen. Lilly followed close behind.

"A fireman's been injured. Make space for medevac emergency landing. ETA ten minutes." Gunnar saw an upsurge in activity around one of the ambulances. His stomach cramped at the possibility of anyone getting killed tonight, and his hunch about the source of this fire plumed in his thoughts.

Getting right back on task, he gave an apologetic look to Lilly. "I've got to take care of this."

"Any word on who the fireman is?"

"Not at this time, I'll let you know as soon as I find out."

"Thanks. Hey, I was interviewing some firemen this week about the trash-can fires going on around town. Of course they said they were all intentionally set. Do you think there is any connection?"

He remembered from earlier reports how well planned all the trash-can fires that didn't pan out were. Someone had made sure to distract the police officers with bogus calls. "Don't know for sure." He looked around the scene again. "Though I've got to say—" he looked at Lilly, thinking of her as a friend "—my hunch is this fire and those trash cans might be related and this could be arson, too."

Her eyes went big enough for him to see the fire reflected inside the irises. She stepped back and he cut in front of her, heading back to the parking lot. "Cobawa. It's Ben Cobawa." The fireman's name crackled over the radio. "Looks like second-degree burns on his face and neck, which means smoke inhalation, too. Better hope that unit gets here quick."

Damn. "Ben's been injured," he said so Lilly could hear.

"Who's Ben?"

"One of our best firemen."

"I realize that, but what's he to you? You seem really upset."

He'd known Ben all his life. The gentle Native American was also on the pirate project at city hall. And sometimes, he could swear there was something going on between Elke and Ben, but he'd never had proof.

"A friend of my sister's." Gunnar sped up, leaving Lilly standing taking pictures of the fire as he threw out directions to his men left and right. He had a hell of a lot to accomplish in a short time, and from the looks of the angry fire across the way, things were going to get worse before they got better. And it would be another long, long night ahead.

He glanced over his shoulder, seeing Lilly's tiny frame in the shadows diligently scribbling notes and snapping pictures, and wished this latest meeting with her had been under completely different circumstances.

Gunnar rolled out of bed early Friday afternoon. He'd been up all night with the fire that had finally been put out around four. He'd stuck around doing his part to make the situation navigable until the morning shift, and more importantly until his lieutenant insisted he go home and take the day off.

His eyes still burned from the smoke, and even though he'd showered when he'd gotten home, the smell remained fresh in his nostrils. Wolverine snubbed him as if he were nothing more than a pile of ashes, until he got out the bag of kitty kibble. Then the cat acted as if Gunnar was the lion king himself and rolled belly-upward, allowing Gunnar to pet the softest fur. Gee, such an honor.

After he'd made his coffee and had thrown on his guy-type Japanese spa robe—otherwise he was naked—he tied the sash and went outside to get the newspaper to keep him company while he ate some cereal.

Around the fifth crunchy bite, he opened the paper and got hit with a headline that nearly had him spewing his honey and oats across the kitchen.

Arson Thought to Be at the Center of Brewery Fire. He hadn't given her the okay to print that!

He read on about how the fire captain had confirmed his hunch about arson, and lectured himself about jumping to conclusions regarding Lilly, then calmed down. She brought up the cluster of calls coming in as decoys just before the fire got set. That someone set Olaf's bar and brewery on fire on purpose, and wanted to make sure everyone was scattered around town when it happened. Then she'd covered the diligent firemen putting out the flames and the dramatic medevac of Ben Cobawa. Excellent reporting, in his opinion. Next she focused on the police force keeping order and protecting the local citizens who'd lined up for a firsthand view of the dangerous fire. His name popped up after that.

Concerned and giving orders, Sergeant Gunnar Norling put all of his efforts into manning the front line of this fire with his fellow officers. Norling, a ten-year veteran on the police force takes his job to protect and serve seriously. Giving orders and drinking donated coffee, he doesn't miss a detail. Perhaps he is driven by his own father's mistakes, occasionally overcompensating for being the son of an ex-con with his stiff, by-the-book attitude.

He blinked at the flaming wall of anger encircling him. He hadn't even known Lilly for a week and she'd already crossed into the forbidden territory of his past. In public! For the whole town to read and remember how his father was a common criminal, who'd done time...

Leaving his cereal bowl on the counter, he stomped to his bedroom, threw on some clothes and headed for the door.

He'd slipped up, made the mistake of thinking Lilly was a friend and talking honestly with her, sharing part of his painful past, and now he'd paid the price.

Well, lesson learned.

As he put on his helmet and hopped onto his motorcycle, he planned to chew Lilly out when he cornered her.

Lilly glanced up from the computer screen Friday afternoon and saw a human hurricane blowing her way. Gunnar.

She jumped up and steadied herself, meeting his glower by lifting her chin. "What's up?" she asked, bracing herself for who knew what, but from the looks of him, something unpleasant was about to go down.

He tossed the front page on her desk. "I'll tell you what's up, *this* is what's up." His usual affable masculine voice was tempered by a slow, hot simmer. He pointed to the headline. "I made the mistake of confiding in you about my father, and now you've pasted it all over the front page for the whole town to read."

His penetrating green-eyed stare could be unsettling for the average person, but she'd had to face the steely glares of her mother and father her entire life. Gunnar was no contest. "I added it to give a human interest side—hey, we can be better than our parents, look at Gunnar Norling."

"You had no business bringing that up without my permission." His voice was quiet, yet the words slashed at her confidence.

Out of habit, she donned her good-soldier attitude and stood straighter. "Do you remember the message you left me the other day?" She waited for him to remember, but he showed no sign of it. It was her turn to go on offense, and she played it to the hilt. He wasn't the only person around here who knew how to lean into an argument. "Then let me refresh your memory." She put her hands on her hips and glared at him. "'Sure—'" she tried to sound like Gunnar when he played it charming "'—you can use that information...*and any other noble thing you'd like to share about me...*'" She emphasized the last part.

He stopped briefly to digest what she'd told him. "I may have said that, but come on, you should have known better." Quiet yet cutting to the quick.

"Are you calling me dense?" Her voice rose and she failed at hiding her frustration.

"The last thing I'd call you is dense. How about insensitive." He failed at hiding his ire, too, but his tone was more of a molar-grinding growl.

She couldn't retort because it was true. She should have known his father was off-limits, and yet she'd let that part slip her mind when writing the article because it was good press—the son atoning for the father's sins. She'd been all fired up about the front-page story, and had given it her all, ignoring a couple of really important points. Never leave your source hung out to dry. Not if you hope to use them for future articles. Journalism 101.

Damn.

She blinked and took a quick breath, preparing to do something she was really lousy at. "I'm sorry." She said it quietly, biting back an ugly old feeling she used to get whenever her father called her on the carpet—shame. She cast Gunnar a contrite glance. Was she bound to spend her adult life trying to please the entire male population thanks to her father?

Gunnar went still, as if in the eye of the storm, taking time to pick up the newspaper and read the rest of the article. His jaw should have been making popping noises from all the gritting of teeth. He took in a long breath, glanced at her with less glaring eyes, then slowly let out the air. "I've got to be able to trust that when I talk to you, you won't go blabbing everything on the front page."

"I said I'm sorry. I get it. It won't ever happen again." What the heck did he want her to do, grovel?

He rolled his lips inward and rubbed his stubble-covered

jaw. His hair went every which way from wearing the motorcycle helmet, there were dark circles under his eyes from the long and stressful night and he still managed to look sexy as hell.

All she wanted to do was make him forgive her. Quick decision. Okay, so she would grovel. A little. "Let me buy you dinner tonight so I can give an official apology."

He torqued his brows and got that steely-eyed look again, then shook his head. "You don't have to do that."

"I want to. Please, Gunnar, let me buy you dinner." Against her better judgment, she'd been meaning to get in touch with him anyway. Something about a rain-check kiss she'd promised. "That is if you don't already have plans."

"No plans." He shifted his weight from one jeans-clad muscular thigh to the other, then ran his fingers through the mishmash of hair, still thinking.

"Then, let's do it." She walked closer, stood right in front of him, engaging his slow-to-trust gaze. Heck, she'd been trained by two of the toughest tiger parents on the planet. She could make him do what she wanted. "Have dinner with me. Come on."

Something twinkled way in the back of those green irises. "Okay, if you insist. I'll take you to *husmanskost* for a proper Swedish meal. I'll pick you up at eight."

She'd won the match, but was careful not to gloat, and he'd quickly taken over the plans. She needed to regain some control. "I'm paying."

One corner of his mouth twitched, the way it had the first day she'd met him when he wrote out her jaywalking warning and she knew he didn't want to smile. He scratched it, then turned to leave. "We'll discuss that later."

Chapter Five

Gunnar patted the aftershave on his cheeks and crinkled his nose over the initial potent spicy scent. Okay, so he hadn't opened it since his sister had given it to him two Christmases ago because that was the month his mother had died and Christmas hadn't seemed possible to bear that year. Had the stuff fermented or something? He fanned the air, grateful aftershave didn't last like cologne, then ran a comb through his short hair and took one appraising look in the mirror. Looked good enough for him, but would he look good enough for Lilly?

Since he was still ticked off at her for exposing something so personal about him, something he worked to make up for every single day of his life, it would take a lot of effort and charm on her part to make him forgive her. He shouldn't give a darn what she thought about how he looked.

Truth was it never took much to set off those horrible memories, to relive the mortification of a twelve-year-old kid who'd found out his father had broken the law and was going to jail. Gunnar brushed away the quick thoughts of panic and how he'd literally thought it meant the whole family would be homeless, but more importantly, how ashamed he'd been of his father, and how he wouldn't be able to hold up his head in Heartlandia ever again.

If it wasn't for a big Swedish kid two years older than him, one of the cool and popular kids named Kent Larson who, seeing how distraught, unpredictable, angry and explosive Gunnar had become, insisted on being his best friend, well, Gunnar may have very well followed in his old man's footsteps.

All he knew for sure was that not a day went by when he wasn't trying to make up for the shadow of shame on his family name and, damn it, Lilly had nailed that part, said it for everyone to read right there in the newspaper.

He took a deep breath and shook his head, walked shirtless to his closet and grabbed his favorite royal oxford shirt, fresh from the laundry and perfectly pressed, the way his mother used to do. *Gunnar, we may not have money for nice clothes like the other people around here, but we can keep what we do have clean and pressed, yes?*

The shirt was pale blue with navy pinstripes and he'd been told by a lady or two that it made his eyes look blue.

Not that he wasn't happy with his green eyes, it was just that they'd always reminded him of his father. Shifty sea green eyes. And the lies his old man had told. *I'm innocent*, he'd sworn. *Been set up.* The way he'd left his mother after she'd been so loyal to him. She'd never said a word against the man when he was in jail, while she worked two jobs to keep him and his sister fed. Her reward? The minute the man got out of the slammer he took off and was never heard from again. That was until he got sent back to jail ten years later and needed money for bail.

Some role model he'd turned out to be.

Gunnar shook his head. *Knock it off.* He was taking a

new lady out for dinner, his favorite pastime. Now was not the moment to get all morose about his father.

When he became a teenager, Gunnar had discovered that girls could take a guy's mind off his lousy family history and put it on much more entertaining things of the physical nature. Since then he was rarely without a lady. Yet these past few months, seeing Kent so happy with Desi, Gunnar had slowed down on the constant superficial dating. So why was he so hell-bent on going out with Lilly?

Because she was different? Or maybe because, since she'd let slip some pretty telling information about her own old man, Gunnar thought they might have something in common. Since when did he give a hoot if he and a lady had anything in common besides attraction?

Okay, he was starting to give himself a headache, so he looked into the mirror and said, "Dude, knock it off."

He buttoned and tucked, slipped on his best loafers. Tonight, like every other day of his life, he'd be the man he wanted his own father to be. And that was all there was to that. Gunnar grabbed a sports jacket and headed for the door. Wolverine made a disapproving meow.

He patted his head. "Oh, hush up. You'll be fine. Go take another nap or something."

But unable to get off the rough subject of his father, he admitted he had major issues with people who said one thing but did another. Lilly had run his name in the paper, said some strictly private information and made a very public connection between him and his dad without his official consent. She'd said it was an example of his honor and dedication to the job, but Gunnar wondered if it wasn't more to prove how good she was at getting a story so her own old man might cut her some slack.

For now he'd give her the benefit of the doubt, especially since she was taking him for an apology dinner. But he'd make it clear that from now on everything he said was strictly off the record and he expected to read in advance *anything* she intended to print about him. If she couldn't deal with that, then sayonara, baby.

He parked in the guest section at the Heritage and took the elevator up to the fifth floor—the top floor, because that was as high at it got in Heartlandia thanks to a hundred-year-old city building code. Truth was, he liked that there weren't any high-rises, like so many other coastal communities had, blocking the view of the water for those like him who dwelled on the hillside.

He tapped on her door and, wow, when it flew open she looked stunning. In pink. She greeted him wearing a loose-knit sweater that casually fell off one shoulder with a darker pink cami underneath, and a frilly girlie necklace. Once he pulled his gaze away from the smooth white skin of her shoulder he noticed she'd sculpted her hair in a sexy and fun way, and that her eyes were enhanced by mascara and perfectly applied three-toned eye-shadow. And those fine lips glistened, also in pink.

Which was beginning to be his favorite color.

"So how's it goin'?" he asked, sounding like a doofus even to himself.

"Pretty good. You hungry? Because I am. This is way past my dinnertime."

He'd noticed the black pencil skirt and black hose and pointy black heels, so his answer got delayed. "Oh, sorry. But the wait makes everything taste better."

"Well, I cheated and ate some cheese and crackers about an hour ago."

"Someone your size probably has a picky and fast metabolism, right?"

"I've never thought of it that way." She'd picked up her

purse from the hotel-style living room chair, leaving him waiting at the threshold rather than asking him in. The lady really was hungry.

She closed the door, which automatically locked shut, and they walked down the hall of the oldest hotel in town. With a replica of the original patterned wallpaper making the walls feel claustrophobic, and thick red carpet splattered in huge yellow-and-white hibiscus nearly lifting off the floor, he ducked on reflex thinking he might bump his head on the ceiling, then broke the silence. "The restaurant is just a couple of blocks away. It's really pretty out tonight, and I thought it would be nice to walk there. You up for that?"

She made a decisive nod.

"You going to be able to walk in those shoes?" With the sexy pointy toes…

"No problem. They're more comfortable than they look."

"Could have fooled me." He used the excuse of looking at her shoes to notice her legs and athletic calves. Okay, so he was ogling her, he admitted it, but he'd make up for it over dinner with pithy conversation, where he'd let her talk all she wanted.

Truth was, he really wanted to get to know more about Lilly.

The late-summer evening was crisp and cool, with the hint of moisture from the river, and it felt great on his skin. Others might complain about the weather in Oregon, but he loved it here. Of course, it was his home and the only place he'd ever lived.

She looked straight ahead. "So I hope you've had time to cool down." She looked up at him with earnestness in her eyes, like it was really important. "The last thing I ever wanted to do was make you upset."

"I don't want to rehash things, but when it comes to trusting, let's just say I have issues with people who aren't straightforward."

"I understand. I don't like to think of myself as not being straightforward, though. It's not a good quality."

"Is that the only reason?"

"No. Of course I don't want to be thought of as a liar."

"I didn't call you that."

"No, but that's what you implied."

"Not true. I was complaining about not being notified or giving approval."

"And so by skipping that part, I lied to you. Right?"

"Okay." They'd stopped in front of Hannah's Handmade Sweaters, and he really didn't want to get stuck in an argument with Lilly all night, because something told him she wouldn't back down. "Hey, it's a beautiful night, let's not muck it up with semantics. What do you say we call a truce?"

"Sounds good to me."

"With the promise that we can trust each other from now on."

"Okay."

He encouraged her to walk again with a gentle touch to her elbow. "And whatever I say when we're together is *always* off the record."

She paused again, but smiled. "I get it."

"And anything you print about me in the future gets my approval first."

She saluted. "Yes, sir. Tell me whatever you want. My lips are sealed."

"Well, that's a shame because I was just thinking how kissable they looked."

She nailed him with a "seriously?" kind of glance, then trudged ahead of him. Okay, unsubtle, he got it, plus he might be behaving a little chauvinistically, but he was a guy and he was allowed now and then to slip up, and man, someone needed to remember their kiss.

She didn't pursue the kissing topic, which disappointed him a little, and thankfully after a few more steps they were already outside the restaurant.

He gestured to the door of the modest white building with the blue-and-yellow canopy.

She squinted at the sign out front. "What is *husman-skost*?"

"A style of Swedish cuisine. You're gonna love it." He swung the door wide open into a darkened dining room lit only by candlelight. Bringing Lilly here made him see it from another perspective. Tables for two were selectively arranged near plants and white-lattice-panel room dividers. All the tables were round with white tablecloths, with a hint of blue-and-yellow thread woven around the edges. The overall appearance was clean and modern. He liked it and hoped she would, too.

It had been a long time since Gunnar had brought someone here as he usually came by himself when he got nostalgic for his mother's cooking. The young waitress brought the menu with the night's supper specials, then left to retrieve some water.

"So how do you say it? Hus-mans-kost?"

"That's right."

"What does it mean?"

"It's traditional Swedish countryside cuisine made with local ingredients. You don't get to pick and choose from the menu, like at other restaurants. Basically we eat what they've made today."

She glanced at the long list on the day's specials. "All of this?"

He liked how her eyes lit up with wonder. "I'll help."

"I won't be eating animal brains or pickled eyeballs or anything, will I?"

He gently laughed. "Don't worry. I guarantee you'll like the food or I'll pay for dinner. How's that for a money-back guarantee?"

"I'm so hungry it won't be a problem."

When the waitress returned he ordered some dishes from the night's menu. *"Ärtsoppa, rotmos med fläsk."* He leaned toward Lilly. "Would you prefer potato dumplings or potato pancakes?"

"Dumplings sound good."

"Okay. We'll have *palt*. Oh, and why not, we'll have some *raggmunk*, too."

The waitress nodded. He glanced at Lilly. "You've got to try *raggmunk*."

She lifted her narrow shoulders in a "whatever" gesture.

"Oh, and you can warm up the apple cake now, because we're definitely going to have that."

"Share," Lilly said. "We'll share a piece."

Lilly obviously liked to take control. Problem was, so did he.

Once the waitress walked off, Lilly tapped Gunnar's arm. "What did all that mean?"

He smiled. "Pea soup with yellow peas, boiled and mashed carrots, rutabaga and potato with free-range pork tenderloin and, since you wanted potato dumplings, that comes with ground meat, also free-range. But I decided you had to try potato pancakes, too, so I ordered *raggmunk*."

"That's a lot of potatoes. I'll explode if I eat all that."

"We'll take it slow, and you can take the leftovers home."

"Sounds like comfort food."

"It definitely is." He took a moment to study Lilly, looking so pretty in pink, appreciating her being open to food she'd probably never try otherwise. "I know after your little incident at the bar last week you probably don't want to drink, but the best way to eat this food is with vodka."

"My incident at the bar?" She immediately bristled.

He used his thumb to imitate a person drinking from a beer bottle.

"I beg your pardon, but I was fine." She pulled her sweater up over her shoulder and sat straighter. "Well, almost fine."

Continuing to tease, he shrugged his shoulders and tilted his head, giving her some slack. She went quiet, but not for long.

"Vodka? Like a martini?"

"No. Just vodka. Straight," he said.

"Well, anything would taste good after that."

"It actually enhances the flavors. That is if you sip it. No guzzling like you and beer."

She playfully slapped his arm and he realized how much he enjoyed giving her a hard time, and being around her in general.

"Let's go for it, then. I may as well experience my first *husmanskost* the authentic way. Maybe I'll even do a piece for the paper on it. That is if it's okay with you?"

Did she ever get her mind off work? But in this case he really liked that angle—a human interest story spotlighting a local business, just what they needed more of these days.

He smiled. "That would be a great idea."

He waved the waitress over and made their drink orders, then not wanting the easy flowing conversation to go dead, thought up another topic. "So what's your favorite food?"

"I'm a California girl, sushi, what else?"

"That's it?"

"Sticky rice, teriyaki chicken, seafood. Oh, and avocados."

"Can you make sushi?"

"My sobo taught me to make *makizushi*." She played with the silverware on her napkin and he detected a nostalgic gaze.

"Maki sushi?"

"Close enough. Rice-filled rolls wrapped in seaweed. Mostly vegetarian, celery, cucumber, avocado, since she didn't trust me with raw fish."

"Who is Sobo?"

"My grandmother." There it was again, endearment in her eyes. All he remembered about his grandmother was that occasionally she'd pull him by the ear when he'd acted up.

"I'd love to try some of your maki sushi."

"Once I find a place with a kitchen I'll make you some."

"You're looking for a permanent place?"

"I'm planning on sticking around and making something out of that newspaper. Maybe even asking Bjork to sell it to me."

"Really?"

"Yes, really."

"Well, in that case, I know a man who has a guesthouse sitting empty. He built it about ten years ago for his mother after his father died. But then a few years later she died, and a year after that his wife died, so it's been sitting empty for two or three years now. Maybe he'd rent it to you."

Her eyes enlarged and brightened. "Can you ask for me?"

"Sure. His name's Leif Andersen." The excitement in her gaze doubled when he mentioned the name. "The best contractor in this part of Oregon. Built the city college. Sure, I'll put in a good word for you."

* * *

Lilly couldn't believe her good fortune. Leif Andersen was on that secret committee, and maybe he'd be her ticket to Big News so she could lay off Gunnar. "The sooner I can move out of the Heritage, the happier I'll be."

"I'll talk to him tomorrow, then."

Another secret meeting? She'd have to stake herself out in the bushes again.

As they ate, she watched Gunnar relax and his face brighten. Food could do that, bring back good memories.

"Good as Momma used to make?" she asked.

He nodded. "Almost." He smiled. "I always think about picnics and camping trips from when I was really young, when I ate cold potato pancakes." He gazed at her. "They travel well."

"Did you do a lot of camping when you were a kid?"

"Doesn't everyone?"

Not her. In fact, she couldn't remember a single family vacation until she graduated from high school and her parents decided it was time to take a trip to Europe. "Actually, I went to camp a lot, but never went camping."

He screwed up his face, not figuring out what she'd meant, like it was some sort of riddle.

She nibbled on some beef. "My parents always sent me away to these themed camps in the summer. They'd ship me off to Maine or Montana or Washington. All over the country. Every summer."

"Did you like it?"

The memories were sad and lonely, but she knew how to put a carefree spin on things so as not to make Gunnar feel sorry for her. "I learned a lot."

"Did you make friends?"

The question almost threw her out of breezy mode,

but she didn't miss a beat. "A few. Mostly other nerds and castaways like me."

His head popped up. "You? A nerd? Never."

She laughed. "The thing is, when I figured out my gift was writing and I'd proved it by getting my first C ever in science, and was only mediocre in advanced math, well, let's just say it didn't go over well with good old Dad."

She didn't want to lay a sob story on him, but she certainly had his interest so she forged ahead. "That year Dad found a science camp on Catalina Island off the coast of California. Though I did enjoy the outdoor activities, hiking and kayaking and snorkeling, it didn't set a fire in my heart for science. We suffered through a few more rocky semesters in school before I admitted I wanted to major in journalism."

"And Daddy didn't like that."

She shook her head, suddenly losing her appetite even though the aroma of the apple cake was out of this world. She picked at her share, claiming to be too full to eat more. One lonely memory forced its way out of the recesses of her mind, where she'd packed it away in her busy life. She'd entered a statewide writing contest and had taken first place. The day of the awards ceremony neither of her parents could be there, both claiming they had important appointments with clients that couldn't be rescheduled. What had started out as a moment of great pride had turned into one of the loneliest mornings of her life, and in the Matsuda household, there were many to choose from.

As if reading her mind about something much deeper going on than she'd let on, Gunnar reached across the table and wrapped his big warm hand around hers. The look in his eyes was both tender and understanding, and for an instant she wanted to give him another mind-boggling kiss.

Instead she gave a weak smile, hoping her eyes weren't welling up.

The waitress appeared. Evidently while Lilly was buried in her thoughts, he'd asked for the check and a small box to take the apple cake home in. Since things had gotten a little too heavy for her liking, she was grateful for the change in venue.

After a long and incredibly delicious meal, Lilly was glad they'd walked to the restaurant, desperately needing the exercise or she'd fall asleep from the overabundance of comfort food.

Gunnar had been right, the vodka did enhance all the different flavors. She definitely planned to write a spotlight article on the place, and had gotten the owner's name and phone number on her way out. Lilly looked forward to hearing more about the free-range ranchers and the local farmers the owner used for the ingredients. The man mentioned that many of the farmers came to the weekly farmer's market held right in the center of town. She'd already gotten a huge response from her shout-out regarding stray animal stories, and wanted to keep the human interest aspect of Heartlandia rolling in the newspaper. Who knew, maybe subscriptions might go up, too.

The minute they stepped outside into the fresh night air a fire truck zoomed down Main Street...toward the Heritage.

Gunnar looked at her. "I wonder what's going on?"

"Me, too."

They walked briskly and arrived at the scene. A small but growing crowd filled the sidewalk.

Gunnar went up to one of the firefighters he knew and she stuck to his side like seaweed on rice. "What's going on?"

She fished in her purse for her notepad.

"Someone set off all of the fire alarms. We're evacuating the entire hotel until we know for certain everything is safe."

"A prank?" she asked.

"We don't know yet. Just being cautious right now."

"But I'm staying here."

"We can't let anyone in until we've checked everything out." Where were they supposed to go? How long would they be stuck outside? She glanced at Gunnar.

"Guess that means you're coming home with me to wait things out."

She yanked in her chin, letting her shock register in her eyes. "But I need to submit this info for the Heartbeat on Heartlandia log. Ack, but my laptop is in my room."

"You can use mine."

There might not be any way around this. Regardless of what she'd told him about her shoes being comfortable, right about now her toes were aching, and the thought of hanging out on the street for God only knew how long, wasn't the least bit appealing. Plus she could upload her newspaper info on Gunnar's computer. He must have been reading her thoughts. Again.

"It's either that or stand around in those high heels on this cold sidewalk until they let you back in."

He made a solid point, and she was a reasonable person. Plus all that comfort food, and not to mention the vodka, had made her very sleepy. "Okay, but don't get any ideas."

He paused, as if some great plans had been dashed. "Okay—no hanky-panky...unless you ask nicely."

Chapter Six

Lilly was beyond impressed with Gunnar's semi-A-frame house. Modern-looking, built of solid wood with loads of windows and a wooden deck to sit and stare out at the river, the house nestled in the center of a tree grove. When he escorted her inside, she glimpsed his Swedish heritage in every room. There were clean white walls and light blond wooden floors, with pale gray club chairs and a white L-shaped couch, the only color contrast being a black throw rug under the glass-and-chrome coffee table. Oh, and the black modern-looking fireplace that hung a foot off the floor, extending like a triangular mushroom at the end of a long black vent pipe anchored high up the wall.

His taste in art seemed to be heavily Asian influenced with the exception of one modern art, pen-and-ink drawing that looked like a Picasso knock-off.

The spotless kitchen matched the white of the rest of the house with the only contrast being stainless-steel appliances and some surprisingly colorful yellow-and-blue curtains. Could a guy get any more Scandinavian?

Truth was, Lilly liked it. It was clean and well kept,

and it said something about this man. He was proud of his heritage, just like she was proud of hers.

"Hey," he said. "While you make your newspaper entry, why don't I open a bottle of wine?"

Even amidst the ultramodern atmosphere, Gunnar had still managed to pull off a homey feel, and when he put logs in the fireplace, she decided a glass of wine in front of a real fire sounded fabulous.

"Sure."

She got right down to business logging into the newspaper before the midnight print deadline and posted her information, then called Bjork who wore many hats in the small twice-a-week paper operation, including final copy editor, layout manager and printer. The jobs Lilly would have to learn and do if she wanted to become a small-town newspaper mogul. By the time Gunnar had opened the bottle of Pinot Noir and placed two glasses on the table in front of the fireplace, she was ready to join him.

As bossy as he seemed at times, she'd discovered over dinner he was also fairly easygoing. He'd bent over backward to make her feel comfortable both at the restaurant and now here at his house, and she couldn't ever remember a guy doing that for her in San Francisco. The vibes back home had always been "show me what you got, impress me," both with her parents and her dates. Except for Sobo. She could always be herself with her grandmother.

Before she would take her first sip of wine, she thought about checking with the Heritage to see if the evacuation had ended. "I'm going to call the hotel for an update."

He didn't say anything, just let her do her task. When she'd finished, keeping the fact to herself that the alarm was now all cleared, she headed for the couch.

"What'd they say?"

"They're still checking things out." Oops, she'd already

broken her promise to be straightforward with him. Did little white lies in her favor count?

Gunnar had taken off his sport coat and unbuttoned the collar on his shirt, even slid out of his loafers, and now gestured for her to join him on the couch. It looked inviting to slide under his shoulder and strong arm, and on a snap decision, she accepted his offer and snuggled into the alluring spot.

"Wouldn't it be crazy if that false alarm was just another decoy for the person who set the brewery fire?" She couldn't help thinking out loud.

"No shop talk on dates."

She sat straight in order to look him in the eyes. "We're dating?"

His head rested on the back of the sofa, eyes closed. He didn't bother to open them. "Yes. We are. Get used to it."

Just like that? She'd asked him out for an apology dinner and the next thing she knew they were dating. She stared at his eyes, which refused to open. Back home she'd take offense at any man making assumptions about her status. For some crazy reason Lilly kind of liked the idea of dating the Swedish-American cop. Just for the sake of being contrary, she could call him a chauvinist for telling her what she was or wasn't doing with him, but for once she decided to just go with the Zen of Gunnar Norling.

She took a quiet breath and went back to snuggling by his side.

"So this is nice," he said, all nonchalant, obviously not realizing what a big deal this was for Lilly.

She sipped her wine. "Yes. Nice place." She toed off the heel of first one pump, then the other, then crossed her ankles and rested her heels on the table next to Gunnar's.

"I meant cuddling, but thanks. I designed and built the house with the help of Leif Andersen."

"My future landlord?" The guy with the house she hoped to rent, who also happened to be on that secret committee. She shouldn't take anything for granted but Daddy had always said, go for your dreams, big or small. Take them. Make them happen.

"Yeah, we designed it with two sets of plans. One for right now, which is what you see, and the next for when I want to expand."

"You mean like adding on?"

"Yeah, with a couple more bedrooms, another bathroom, a rumpus room…"

"What the heck's a rumpus room?"

A lazy smile stretched across his lips, his eyes were still closed. "Like a big family room, or a man cave. I haven't decided which it will be yet."

The more she learned about Gunnar the more she was impressed. Somehow, during the conversation about how long he'd been living here—five years but with plans to expand for what, a family?—and in between more sips of wine, she battled covetousness. She wanted a house of her own and to know exactly where she wanted to be and what she wanted to do with her life, just like Gunnar. To settle for something, instead of always striving for the next big dream. But so far all she had was a sketchy idea about wanting to own her own newspaper in a town she wasn't even sure she liked yet or fit into. A stepping-stone gig. And after that, what? A bigger paper? Another city? More fitting in? Who knew?

She drank the end of her wine and laid her head back on Gunnar's shoulder. Natural as can be he leaned down and kissed her. Not a hungry, crazy kiss like their first one, but a soft and comforting kiss, as if they were a couple who'd been dating awhile. And just like the Swedish comfort food, the kiss made her all warm inside. She relaxed into his now familiar mouth and let her thoughts drift away to a little island in her head known best for sexy slow kisses and expansive chests that welcomed her with strength and amazing pectoral muscles.

If this was what it was like to date Gunnar Norling, which he'd already assured her she was, she wanted to sign up for the whole package.

After they kissed for a while, like a gentleman he offered her another glass of wine, and because she felt so darn good from the first one, she accepted. Except she was really tired and experiencing carb overload from that huge dinner. When he got up to refill her glass he took a little too long, going to the bathroom first, and since she could hardly keep her eyes open...she...closed...them.

She'd been shanghaied to heaven.

Lilly woke up in a bed she'd never been in before—in a clean, midcentury, modern, Scandinavian-style bedroom. It was minimalist in design and decor, just like the rest of Gunnar's house. Pale gray walls with ink-washed Japanese prints in black frames lined the room. The same blond wooden floors as in the living room were covered in intricately patterned and muted-colored throw rugs, a white duvet draped over her on the bed with icy blue sheets. The A-framed bedroom ceiling had two large windows and the bed was positioned to look onto a hillside where pine trees and wild flowers grew. No need for curtains.

Little drills seemed to be working on her temples from all of the rich food, not to mention the vodka topped off with a glass of red wine she'd enjoyed last night. She heard clanking around outside the door, as if maybe Gunnar was opening cupboards and drawers in the kitchen. Something smelled great.

Streaks of daylight cut across her face. She squinted

and turned on her side in the big cozy bed. How had she wound up in Gunnar's bed? Or was this a guest room?

A tapping came from the door. "You decent?" Gunnar's smoky smooth voice said on the other side.

Was she decent? She hadn't a clue. She peeked under the covers, finding she was still completely dressed, thank the stars, but man, with all the wrinkles she'd have to ask Gunnar for the name of a good dry cleaner.

Good to know the guy was a gentleman.

More knocking. "Hello?" he said.

He was going the gentlemanly route this morning, too, knocking before entering. She wanted to pull her hair out in confusion about what exactly had gone on after that first kiss on the sofa last night.

Oh, right, she'd fallen asleep. *He wouldn't take advantage of me while I slept, would he? Completely dressed, remember?*

He tapped again.

She cleared her throat. "Sure. I'm *decent*." *Whatever that means at this point*. "Come in." She tried to sound calm and upbeat, like yeah, sure, she was a modern woman who spent the night with all her dates.

So not true.

With cheeks and ears blazing hot, wondering how to handle things—feeling more like a lady who'd worn out her welcome after the first date—she waited for the godly and obviously well-mannered Gunnar to come into the room.

She sat in the center of his bed like a delicate water lily in a rippling blue-and-white pond, looking bewildered. He smiled at her widened eyes and mussed-up hair. Damn she was cute, even with raccoon-like makeup smudges under her eyes.

"Good morning," he said. Wolverine ran into the room before him and jumped on the bed with a thud.

"Ach!" She pulled the covers over her head again.

"Sorry. That's my cat." Who hadn't bothered to check in last night, but only showed up for food this morning.

She peeked over the top of the blanket. "Big boy."

"Yeah, he's what we call a Maine Coon cat. Weighs over thirty pounds. One false move and he'll lick off your face."

That didn't garner the kind of response he'd hoped for. She hadn't relaxed a bit, but slowly lowered the covers while staring down his big old gray tabby as if he was a bobcat. Looking at Wolverine, could he blame her?

He crossed the room carrying a breakfast tray with scrambled eggs topped with cheese and basil, a toasted and buttered English muffin, sliced tomatoes fresh from his yard and a mug of coffee.

"About last night, uh…" Getting right to the point she insinuated the rest of the question with those kissable pouty lips, as she reached for the coffee.

He placed the tray across her lap. Yeah, not many people knew he had a bed tray, but what the hell—he'd been known to go to great lengths to impress a girl.

She sipped nervously.

"Nope," he said. "Nothing happened."

The answer did what his cat couldn't—it changed her tense expression to one of tremendous relief. But it didn't stop there. Her pretty pointy features registered something along the lines of *Wow, this food looks and smells great, and I'm famished.* She put the mug down and reached for the fork.

"Thanks for breakfast."

"You're welcome."

"Gorgeous tomatoes."

"I grow them myself."

"Seriously?"

"Most definitely."

She dug in. He liked watching her. And he was still smiling.

Stopping midreach for the toast, she narrowed one of her eyes, sneaking a peek at him. "So we didn't get married or anything last night, I take it?" It was nice that she was lightening up.

"No, ma'am, we did not." He scratched the morning stubble on his cheek. "It's not every day a lady falls asleep in the middle of making out with me, though. I guess that's what I get for going to refill your wine." He poked the side of his cheek with his tongue. "Kind of hard on a guy's ego."

Alarm flew back into her gaze and the tips of her ears turned red. "I fell asleep after making out with you?"

"Frankly, judging by your enjoyment at the time, I'm surprised I have to remind you—" He raised his palm. "One moment you were kissing me like you meant it and after I come back with more wine, you're making these little purring sounds. At first I thought it was my cat, then I realized you were out cold."

"Are you serious?"

"I swear. Want me to cross my heart?"

"And that's all we did?"

"Honey, if I made a move on you, you'd remember every detail. I guarantee."

She started to breathe again, shook her head and finally picked up the fork, then played around with the eggs. He sat on the edge of the bed.

"I stayed up really late Thursday night covering the fire, then worked all day yesterday."

"Unlike me who got the day off so I could sleep?"

"You said it, not me."

"Gee, thanks, now I don't feel like such a failure putting you to sleep with my kisses."

"Oh, God. I hope you don't get the wrong impression, but, honestly, I'm not usually like that."

"A narcoleptic kisser?" Her list of titles kept growing—jaywalker, Tipsy Tina, narcoleptic kisser.

Her eyes nearly doubled in size. "How embarrassing." She shoved another bite of eggs into her mouth and chewed quickly. Her cheeks went pink and her ears lit up again.

"How'd I get in here?"

"I carried you."

Now she ate like she'd been doing gymnastics all night. Stuffing food into her mouth and avoiding his gaze.

His face must have given half of his thoughts away because Lilly suddenly looked suspicious as all hell. "The thing is, I don't remember anyone else in the bed…"

"I slept on the couch."

The tiny worry line between her brows softened. "Thank you for not undressing me."

"I have to admit I thought about it, only so you'd be more comfortable, you see, but even then it seemed too cheesy." He stretched out beside her on the bed, crossed his ankles and leaned on one elbow, took half of her toasted muffin and crunched into it. He stared at her making a silent promise that the first time they got undressed together would be something neither of them would ever forget.

Avoiding his gaze, and after a few more deliberate bites of breakfast, Lilly pushed the tray away. "Oh, man, this is embarrassing," she said. With her sudden move, Wolverine scrambled off the bed and headed for the living room.

Gunnar took her delicate hand and kissed the back of it. "No it isn't. You're an amazing woman, and if you were going to conk out anywhere in Heartlandia, I'm glad it happened at my house."

He put out a special unspoken invitation through his gaze, hoping she'd pick up on the meaning. If she felt like sticking around, the morning was young and the bed, which they just happened to be laying on, was ready for the taking. That is, if she was interested, now that she'd had a good night's sleep…

Instead, she hopped out from beneath the covers, suddenly all business, smoothing out her wrinkled clothes, searching for her shoes. "I'm pretty sure the hotel evacuation is all clear by now."

Disappointment hit like a punch to the solar plexus. He wasn't used to a lady being so hard to get. They'd had a nice date last night, called a truce on their argument, he'd brought her home so she didn't have to hang out in the cold on the street for who knew how many hours, and now this sudden need to get out of here.

Now that she was awake he'd had high hopes about his day off, but he was a man of honor, and if she wanted to go home, he'd take her there. Not the place he'd had in mind, but that's how life played out sometimes.

"Do you have to work today?" she asked.

"Not until the evening shift."

"Once I go home and shower and dress, would you mind taking me to see that guesthouse?"

"I'll give Leif a call. If he's around, then sure."

It wasn't the ideal way for his day to go, after seeing the vision of Morning Lilly in the middle of his bed, but he wasn't complaining about the chance to spend part of his day with a lady who'd rolled into town and held his undivided interest for going on two weeks.

Heck, in Gunnar's world, it was almost a new record.

Chapter Seven

Gunnar called Leif Andersen from the cell phone in his car while Lilly ran into the Heritage to shower and change clothes. He explained how Lilly was the new reporter in town and that she was looking for a permanent place to live. Surprisingly, Leif was available and not opposed to renting out his guesthouse, and agreed to meet Lilly and Gunnar at noon.

While he waited he thought how different Lilly was from his usual ladies. She was big city, big university, big cash—from her well-to-do parents—everything about her was big except her. *Chitcha*. She was petite and *sweet* when she let down her facade of urban tough chick. The more he got to know about her childhood disappointments and her tough-as-nails father, he liked her vulnerable side— she was someone he could relate to, someone who could understand him.

He liked helping her get settled in town, too, but most of all, he liked how it'd felt holding her in his arms last night and carrying her to his bed. If he got lucky, and they got to know each other better, if they trusted each other more that is, maybe the next time he carried her to his bed she'd be naked.

Once Lilly came barreling out of the hotel in jeans and yet another bright-colored sweater, this one kelly green, she caught him midgrin. To cover for his naughty thoughts, he scratched the corner of his mouth and suggested they take a drive out to the Ringmuren. The famous wall had been built by the Native Americans and the Scandinavian fishermen over three hundred years ago.

Once there, the photogenic wall gave her a spectacular view of the Columbia River, the Heartlandia basin, and also gave him a chance to spout a little history lesson he'd learned about the Chinook and his Scandinavian forefathers from his bookworm college professor sister, Elke.

"The Chinook people nursed the shipwrecked sailors back to health and taught them the secrets of hunting and fishing these waters. Back then, I guess the Columbia River could get really treacherous. In thanks, the Scandinavians, now calling themselves fisherman instead of sailors and who'd been bringing their families over from the homeland, helped the Chinook build the wall." Since he had her rapt attention he continued. "The purpose was to delineate the sacred Chinook burial ground for thousands of souls from the outer edge of town. And to this day, we still respect their land. The barrier has always been honored."

"This is amazing!" Lilly affirmed with her arms out, twirling around as if starring in her own version of *The Sound of Music*.

"I told you you'd like it up here."

"I'd like to do a column on Ringmuren."

"The city would love it."

Suddenly still and serious, she connected with his gaze. "Thank you for bringing me here. I can almost feel the ancient souls in the air. Look, I'm getting goose bumps." She pushed up one of her sweater sleeves to show proof.

Gunnar loved coming here, but he'd never gotten any woo-woo feelings from it, just a deep sense of tranquility and renewed respect for the beauty of his hometown. Lilly's gooseflesh made him feel like an underachiever.

Truth was she'd gotten him all worked up with her display of feelings, and since he only knew one way to process heady reactions like that, he went the physical route and cupped her face, looked deeply into her eyes, then dropped a simple kiss of appreciation on her lips.

Bam, there it was again, a kiss riding a zip line straight through the electrical grid in his body. What was it about Chitcha that got to him so quickly?

After he ended the kiss, she gazed up at him all dewy-eyed with gratitude, and maybe with a little heat in the depths of those dark brown eyes.

Instead of pushing for more, like he really wanted to, he stepped back, letting her soak in the display of affection, and to trust that he wasn't a single-minded guy. Though, for the record she was certainly doing her part to turn him into a single-minded guy. Only so she wouldn't get the wrong idea, he'd fight off that part at every turn.

Luckily the honorable side of him, the side that set him apart from his father, wanted Lilly to understand that he knew how to take things slow, and how to be a companion and a friend first. A damn good companion, too, especially when it came to showing people around his hometown.

They stood there watching each other for a few more moments, Gunnar admiring her porcelain-like complexion and wanting to touch her more. The lingering morning might have taken a different route if he hadn't glanced at his watch. It was twenty to twelve, and Leif lived on the other side of this mountain at the opposite end of town.

He grabbed Lilly's hand. "We've got to run if we want to make it to the house on time." Like a track star, Lilly, having worn far more sensible shoes today, kept up with his trot back to the car, and Gunnar only wished he'd parked a little farther away so he'd have the excuse to hold her hand longer.

At one minute to noon Gunnar pulled into the circular driveway of the most opulent house in Heartlandia.

The Andersen contracting company had been established by Leif's father fifty years ago. When his father developed debilitating arthritis and his parents moved to Sedona, Arizona, twenty years ago, Leif, a mere twenty-two years old at the time, had taken over the business with the help of his father's trusted foreman, who had since retired. Leif rode the wave of his father's success and doubled it, stepping into the twenty-first century as a competitive construction force to be reckoned with.

A hands-on guy, Leif had also found himself in the middle of the incident that had spawned the secret committee sorting through the contents of a buried trunk from an infamous sea captain, after he'd discovered it while breaking ground for the city college.

Lilly nearly gasped when they drove up the long and winding drive to the main house. "This is unbelievable!"

"Oh, it's real, Chitcha, all four thousand square feet of it."

"I can't wait to see the guesthouse." She clapped like an excited kid.

Gunnar had watched this house being built twelve years ago just before Leif got married. Most people started small and worked up to having their spectacular homes, but being in construction, he built the house of his wife's dreams right off.

A half-room-size bay window pushed out from the front

of the two-story, gray-and-white-painted contemporary house. Matching gables bookended the main house, with large windows everywhere, and balconies for every bedroom, of which there were four or five, Gunnar wasn't sure.

He had only been inside a few times, but was struck by the wide-open floor plan and pristine craftsmanship. The guy knew how to build top-notch homes.

Leif met them at the door dressed more like a contractor than a comfortably rich man. He wore jeans and a blue polo shirt that had seen better days with a misshapen collar half up and half folded at the back of his neck, like he'd just grabbed it out of the dryer and thrown it on. Trim as ever, his tanned arms wore the muscles earned from hard work when he reached for Gunnar's hand for a shake.

Leif's nearly white brows gave him the appearance of being world-weary, and his piercing blue eyes made Gunnar feel the guy was reading him, even the parts he wanted to keep hidden. But that must have been the skills a man picked up who'd lost all of the most precious people in his life—first his father, then his mother and then his beautiful wife.

"This must be Lilly," Leif said, offering his hand and giving a worked-at, dutiful smile.

"Hi." She stepped forward and gave a firm handshake, and to her credit Leif was an imposing figure.

"I hear you're looking for a place to call home?"

"Yes. I want to make Heartlandia home for now, and living in a hotel gets old really fast."

"Well, I don't know if this guesthouse will be convenient enough for you, it's a bit of a drive to downtown, and I'm fairly secluded up here."

She smiled. "I've commuted in San Francisco all my life, a winding drive through the hills is a piece of cake, and I like the idea of peace and quiet."

"Well, let me show you the place, then."

They followed Leif through his entryway and grand room and straight out French doors to a professionally landscaped yard beside a swimming pool complete with a mini waterfall. There was an overgrowth of gorgeous plants and flowers beside the pool, and the interlocking pavement pattern lead to a cozy path and a picture-perfect cottage.

This time, Lilly didn't hold back her gasp. "Oh, this is beautiful."

"It's completely furnished, but if the furniture doesn't suit you and you'd like to use your own, we can store it in the garage."

"I don't have any furniture, so that's great, but I'm afraid I won't be able to afford this cottage. What do you usually charge?"

"I've never rented it before, but money isn't an issue. We can work something out, all I'd ask is that you pay the utilities."

Lilly grabbed Gunnar's forearm and squeezed hard, her excitement radiating through her fingers. "What do you think is a fair price?"

"Just throw in a few extra bucks."

"Why so cheap?"

"You're a friend of Gunnar's. We Swedes stick together." For the first time, Leif gave an honest-to-goodness smile before winking at Gunnar.

Lilly smiled back. "I'll throw in the same amount I'm paying monthly at the Heritage, how's that?"

"Whatever that is, cut it in half." Case closed. Leif had spoken.

Lilly raised her brows, but being on the winning side of the decision like any smart person would do, she didn't argue. She accepted his kindness in stride by keeping her mouth closed and protests to herself, other than saying, "Thank you."

"You're welcome." He'd studied Lilly like he'd looked at Gunnar earlier, sizing her up and most likely deciding she'd passed his character test.

What wasn't to like about Lilly?

"By the way, I enjoyed that piece you wrote about animal services. My dogs have always come from shelters."

She looked flabbergasted that the man had read one of her articles. As she thanked him, Gunnar noticed Leif's comment was about the human interest story, not the headline news about the recent fire.

He was also stunned by the great deal Lilly was getting, and feeling pretty damn good about leading her to it. "Is there a side entrance?" Back to practicality, Gunnar was curious if he'd be able to come and go without Leif always seeing him. That is, if Lilly let him visit, which he seriously hoped would be the case. Often.

"Yes. She'll have her own private entrance and parking spot." Leif pointed to the right. "Over there." He unlocked the door and they entered a homey cottage with top-of-the-line amenities from ten years back—wood floors, granite countertops and upgraded appliances in the kitchen, and a doorless shower in the bathroom alongside a soaking tub. There was an abundance of windows throughout the four rooms with views of foliage, hillsides and even a glimpse of the Columbia River in the distance from over the sink in the kitchen.

"Sold. I'd like to rent this on the spot," Lilly said.

"But you haven't even seen the bedroom." Gunnar couldn't think of anything practical to say, he just wanted to make sure Lilly wasn't making too snap of a decision. Though, as far as he was concerned, he was right there with her on the sold part. The place was perfect for a single lady. Thinking like a cop though, there were things to consider, like would she feel safe here all secluded and alone? And on other fronts, would the winding hillside commute get old? Would she feel out of the pulse of the city, and wasn't that important for a journalist?

Maybe when they were alone she'd want to bounce some of those issues off him. Get his feedback, but unless asked, Gunnar would leave the decision completely up to her.

Leif opened the double doors to the single bedroom and Lilly emitted another gasp.

"How did you know what my dream bedroom was?" There she went again, acting as if the hills were alive with the sound of music.

It wasn't a huge room, but spacious enough for a queen-size bed, a desk, a loveseat and chaise lounge, and French doors out to a private patio complete with a small wrought-iron table and chairs, and a trellis overrun with morning glories.

"This is heaven!"

"You'll have to arrange for cable TV and internet access. We get good cell phone reception out here, though."

"Mr. Andersen, if you are willing to rent this to me, I would love to move in right away."

"Sure. Let me get my cleaning staff in today, and as far as I'm concerned it's yours tomorrow."

"Don't I need to sign anything?"

"Gunnar's vouching for you. That's all I need."

And that was that.

Gunnar had to fight off all of Lilly's hugs and kisses as they drove back down the hill, and he loved every second of it. She squealed like a teenager meeting a rock star, and thanked him over and over again for suggesting the place. He grinned and laughed all the way back to the Heritage, quickly forgetting his concerns. Surely Leif had state-of-the-art surveillance for his home, she'd be safe up there secluded and cut off from the rest of the city.

"I've got to get to work, but how about I meet you around ten tomorrow, and we can load up all of your stuff and move you in?"

Once they were out of the car and on the sidewalk, she rushed him like a contestant on a shopping-contest show. Her arms encircled him and held him tight. "Thank you, thank you, thank you, Gunnar. You're a prince. I've never been more excited about living somewhere in my life."

He laughed, receiving a contact high from her joy mixed with a few typical guy-type reactions stirring inside whenever touched by the pretty lady. "Every once in a while I come up with great ideas. I'm glad I could help."

Her arms moved upward from his middle to around his neck. She pulled him down to connect with her mouth, and without another thought, they both showed how glad they were to know each other with some major lip gymnastics and tongue contortions. She kissed great under normal circumstances, but wow, right now flying high from renting her new place, she made out phenomenally, working his blood from simmering to nearly boiling in record time.

Too bad they were once again in the middle of the sidewalk with Saturday-morning tourists and residents zipping by all around them. Too bad he had to go get ready for work, because he had it in his mind to sweep Lilly up and carry her into the elevator and right up to her room so she could show him exactly how much she appreciated his helping her find her dream cottage. Not that that had been the reason he'd done it.

But she broke up the kiss in the middle of his fantasy, looking as ruffled up and titillated as he felt. Good to know they were on the same page in that department. "I'll see you tomorrow at ten, then, okay?"

He needed a second to get his thoughts together before he could respond. "Sure."

She popped another quick kiss on his overstimulated lips. "Thank you with all of my heart."

The sincerity oozing from her eyes cut through his chest forming a warm pool beneath his breastbone. "You're welcome, Lilly," he said, really meaning it.

It seemed as if she wanted to say a lot more, but now wasn't the time or place, and when she finally did get around to telling him exactly how she felt, he wanted to be alone with her, and in a place where she could take all the time she needed.

"Now I've got shopping to do!"

"See you tomorrow," he said, smiling, and with his feet seeming incredibly light, he walked back to his car.

Careful, Norling. Don't be such a pushover with this lady who might just throw you under the bus for a good news story.

Chapter Eight

Lilly waited eagerly for Gunnar to show up Sunday morning. She'd spent the rest of yesterday afternoon shopping for items she'd need in her new place. Sheets. Towels. Bathroom rugs. A set of ceramic dishes and flatware, service for four. Because her bank account was already feeling the strain, and there was no way she'd ask her parents for a loan, she'd bought the bare minimum of pots and pans. After she moved in she'd hit the grocery store and stock up on food.

At five minutes before ten there was a knock at her door. She'd already discovered that Gunnar was a stickler about being on time, and her type A personality liked that about him. But that wasn't all she liked about him—he was proving to be an all-around great guy. Her hunch that he put a lot of effort into making up for his dad's wrong deeds had panned out. She'd hit a raw and exposed nerve when she'd written about it in the news article. To offset the imbalance, she'd exposed to Gunnar more about her own insecurities and the messed-up relationship she'd had with her father over dinner than she'd shared with most of her good friends the entire time growing up. Understanding his sense of dishonor made her less ashamed about her own situation. In her opinion, they were good for each other.

"Coming!" She swung the door wide and allowed a moment or two to take him all in. He'd come ready for work in old jeans and a nearly threadbare T-shirt that hugged his torso and put all kinds of ideas into her head. If she got lucky, maybe he'd offer himself as a housewarming present.

She'd gotten used to his always-serious eyes, looking as if they drilled right through her, but it knocked her a bit sideways when he came bearing a smile, like this morning— his idea of a smile, anyway. His version was kind of like a grammar-school class picture, a bit forced yet still genuine.

"Do I need to feed you before we get down to business?" he asked, always on task, wanting to do the right thing.

"Nope. I ate some cereal."

He leaned in for a quick cheek buss. "Good morning."

When he pulled back, she followed suit dropping a light kiss on his lips. "Morning."

After the kiss, those intense eyes eased up, taking on a playful glint and maybe something more. "I wish I could help you all day, but my shift begins at three. You'll just have to use me while you can."

She could think of ways to "use" him right now, but that wasn't the plan. "I don't have that much to move." She'd organized her things into a few significant piles: kitchen items, bedroom items, clothes, more clothes, bathroom items. "I lucked out that the place came furnished."

"Absolutely. Okay." He clapped his hands, all business. "I borrowed my buddy Kent's pickup truck so we should be able to get most of this stuff moved in one trip."

"I'll put all the clothes in my car."

"Will you be able to see out the windows?"

She delivered a frisky punch to his arm. He acted as if it hurt. "I'm just being practical here."

And that was another thing, since when had she ever been this playful with a guy before?

After several trips up and down the elevator, sneaking sexy smiles whenever they passed in the hallway, the truck was full and so was her car and amazingly, nothing of hers was left in the extended-stay hotel room.

After the last item was put in place, Lilly tugged the air. "Yes!"

Gunnar slid on his serious-as-hell sunglasses, the kind that made him look like a motorcycle cop holding a grudge. "Let's hit the road."

"I've got to check out first, but I'll meet you up there."

A half hour later, she used the key to her very own cottage and they reversed their duties from the hotel. By one o'clock, not only had they brought every last item inside, but they'd almost had the kitchen and bathrooms set up. What a team.

She tossed her new sheets onto the mattress.

Gunnar's eyes lit up. "Those are nice."

She glanced at the mauve-colored sheets. "I found all this stuff at Helga's Home and Hearth. What a cute little department store."

"Yeah, we pride ourselves on not allowing the big chain stores into Heartlandia, so folks like Helga have a fighting chance to keep their doors open."

"I could have bought a lot more, but I decided to wait and see what else I'll need." She'd run out of money and refused to ask her father to spot her a loan. He'd never let her hear the end of it. *You're thirty years old and still can't manage your finances.*

Before she could make her bed, Gunnar flopped onto the mattress and flapped his arms and legs, sort of like making snow angels without snow. "This feels good. You should try it."

She wasn't sure what came over her, maybe it was the fact that Gunnar had bent over backward to help her find this place and move her in, that he was the most decent guy she'd met in a decade and that, well, he was sexy as hell. Most important, she liked him, she really liked him. But she crawled onto the bed, catlike, until she looked down on his face, then hiked up one leg and slowly moved her hands and knees on both sides of his body.

On reflex, his hands went to her waist as he looked her dead-on in the eyes, communicating they weren't horsing around anymore, that her climbing over him like that was as serious as sex in the afternoon.

The message he sent both scared and excited her, and she didn't want to let this chance pass her by. She made a half pushup pose, lowering her face to his, and kissed him with the intent of exploring every possibility. Her breasts pushed against his solid chest as his hands found her hips and edged her flush to his lap. She'd worn shorts today, and his palms made a pattern over her rump and down the sensitive skin on the backs of her thighs. The gesture made her skin wake up with prickles.

They kissed like that first night, though this time they were fueled completely by each other and not beer. She let all her weight drop onto him, amazed how spectacular he felt. His hands continued an exotic exploration, caressing areas she'd never thought of as erogenous zones before, but under his touch, oh, yeah, every little curve and canyon apparently was.

Slipping under her top, his fingertips kitten walked across her back, making her contort with tingly pleasure. As their kisses deepened, and their breathing grew more ragged, his hands grew rougher, kneading her skin, pulling her tight to him, making her fully aware of his complete reaction to her.

Totally out of character, she broke away from his kiss, straddled his hips and pulled her top up and over her head. That smile returned to his face, looking nothing like a grammar school kid, but more like a man intent on having his way with her. Her excitement kicked up a notch, nerve endings tightened, she was ready for anything as heat pooled between her hips.

Gunnar sat up to do the honors of removing her bra. She was far from busty, but the way he looked at her made her feel like the most perfect woman on earth. She grabbed his cheeks and kissed him hard, enjoying the feel of the tips of her breasts rubbing against his old worn-out and scratchy T-shirt. But she wanted to feel his skin and, like magic, and with excellent teamwork, his shirt disappeared.

Heat radiated from his skin and she rubbed tight against the dusting of hair on his chest as they made out like ravenous lovers. His hands covered every part of her in their never-ending explorations. The warm pool in her center coursed down between her legs, readying her for him. Still straddling him, she moved over his erection beneath his jeans. Strong as steel, his wedge thrilled her, but their clothes were in the way and something needed to be done about that.

An attentive lover, Gunnar read her mind and soon made sure that first her shorts then his jeans both disappeared. She finished by pulling off her thong while watching him release his fully extended self from his briefs. The sight instantaneously became tattooed in her mind. He literally took her breath away with his muscles and sinew and full erection, and she needed to feel him again. It was his turn to crawl onto the bed and she went back on her elbows welcoming him.

She dropped back her head when he found her breasts, kissing and taunting them with his tongue while his fullness prodded her belly. She clung to his back and repositioned herself to capture his erection between her thighs, savoring the smooth steely feel of him.

The kissing never stopped as their bodies heated to near boiling point. He probed with his fingers, gently opening her, making sure she was ready for him. Hell yeah, she was. She bucked underneath him, impatient to feel him inside.

He came up from a particularly exciting kiss, a questioning look on his face. "Do you have condoms?"

"I think you know the answer to that," she said, remembering that glint in his eye when he'd noticed her little naughty box in the cart at the market the other night.

"They'd come in handy right now, right?" He grabbed and kissed her before she could protest.

She pointed, speaking over his lips. "They're in that box labeled Bathroom."

He zipped to the box, ruffled through the items inside until he found the box labeled "ribbed with heating lubrication for extra pleasure."

On the condom went and after another rough and hungry kiss, Gunnar entered her one blissfully consuming inch at a time.

Soon they were completely lost in each other, taunting, teasing, pleasing and generally driving each other crazy. Slowly but steadily over several minutes their lovemaking built to a frenzy and onward to the most unbelievably intense orgasm Lilly had ever experienced.

She gasped and clung to him, the sensations surging inside her and fanning across her entire body in tingling heat waves as he made another powerful thrust accompanied by a groan, then he followed her off the cliff to free-fall into paradise.

After a moment's reprieve, he rolled onto his side, still tucked deeply inside her, and brought her along with him as if she was weightless—which she pretty much was seeing that she'd essentially catapulted out of her body with the thrill he'd just provided. Once he caught his breath, he said the one word that would keep Lilly flying for days to come.

"Wow."

She wanted to jump up and dance around the bed saying yes, yes, yes! Never before in her adult life had she made a man say wow after having sex. Granted she'd only dated a few guys, and her experience was very limited, but still...

As far as her end of the deal went, well, for a journalist she should have been able to come up with something better than "Double wow," but at least it made her point, and Gunnar seemed to like it.

There was that bright grammar-school grin crossing his face again, but this time with the addition of blue-ribbon pride for outstanding athletic performance.

Chapter Nine

Gunnar hated that he'd had to leave Lilly naked in her bed in order to shower and leave for work on time Sunday, but he never missed work unless a hospital or doctor's diagnosis demanded it. Sure, it was part of "making up for the past" but it also was because of his total respect for the job and his fellow officers. His sister had once accused him of being married to his job, and truth be told, he didn't argue with her. For the past ten years, being a cop was as much his identity as being a Norling.

Monday he stopped by Greta's Garden and bought a Kalanchoe indoor flowering plant for Lilly that Greta promised anyone could care for. Though he enjoyed growing his own vegetables, he didn't have a clue whether Lilly had a green or black thumb, so he went with easy care and surefire blooming. Plus the planter was made by a local potter and the flowers on the plant were small but bright pink and reminded him of Lilly.

In his experience with women, he knew they liked to be thought of after the big night, or afternoon in their case. Buying flowers may be general etiquette where Gunnar and dating were concerned, but this plant, designed to last, seemed different. It made him think of Lilly and new possibilities, and that made him smile until he started to squirm at what those possibilities might be. Trusting someone was paramount for being together. At this point, Lilly still had some proving to do, but that didn't stop him from being a gentleman about their first time together.

She wasn't at her desk when he delivered the gift on his way into work that afternoon.

"I sent her out to the college to cover the story about the search for an artist to paint the city college mural," Bjork said.

Gunnar knew the administrative board of the college and the city council had agreed to hire an artist to tell the history of Heartlandia in pictures on the college campus walls. It would be a huge undertaking, and if Leif Andersen hadn't contributed bucket loads of cash, either the project wouldn't have moved forward, or they'd have had to settle for a local artist or the art majors at the college to complete the task. Who knew what quality of art that would have turned out? Last he'd heard they were down to a handful of finalists from all across the nation.

"Then she said something about interviewing a guy who raises free-range chickens after that," Bjork said.

It sounded as if Lilly's day was completely booked up. Gunnar packed away his disappointment at not seeing her, and scribbled out a quick note—"Lunch tomorrow? G."—then headed for his department and signed in for duty.

On Tuesday he took Lilly to his favorite lunch place, the Hartalanda Café. It was right across the street from their building, so they could walk over. She knocked him dead in a smart-looking business dress that he guessed would pass for sophisticated back in San Francisco. It had fine black plaid on the bottom with the top half being cream-colored with lacy trim and black pearl buttons down the front. He dug the schoolmarm-style collar, especially after knowing what a wild kitten Lilly had turned out to be in bed. Plus she wore a thin cardigan in an odd shade of green with pushed up sleeves and a little flare out at the bottom since it was end-of-summer cool and overcast.

When he first saw her, a weird dip deep inside his chest made him pause. Then she gave a bright smile that matched the pink flush on her cheeks, and he forgot about the odd sensation, having become completely wrapped up in her. He leaned in and kissed her, setting off a cascade of memories that they'd made so far, and after that the first-time-seeing-each-other-since-making-love nerves vaporized.

"Did you know they're down to choosing from four famous artists for the city college mural?" she asked as they walked to the diner.

"I haven't been keeping track, but I'll be sure to read your article to stay up-to-date."

She grinned at his subtle message reminding her they'd made a pact not to talk shop with each other. If he let her talk about her stories, she'd expect him to share about his job, and that might be a conflict of interest, plus it could overtake their time together. He wasn't going to let that happen, not if he wanted to get to know Lilly, the real Lilly, even better.

The waitress sat them immediately, since she'd been saving Gunnar's favorite table for him. He didn't need to look at the menu, so he sat back and enjoyed the view of Lilly in decision mode perusing the daily choices. She wound up asking the waitress to recommend something and went with the soup of the day—Scandinavian summer soup, even though early fall was already upon them, and half a turkey sandwich.

After the story on *husmanskost* came out in the newspaper Monday, word was people in town looked forward to having their establishments featured, too. In his opinion, the Hartalanda Café was deserving of a public review, but he'd let Lilly make that decision.

"My sobo sent me some seaweed so I wanted to invite you over for dinner Thursday for sushi, since you're off."

"Remind me who Sobo is again?"

"Oh, sorry. My grandmother."

"Ah, how nice of her to send you seaweed."

"Don't make fun. She wants to make sure I don't forget my roots."

"Can we make that Friday?" He had another special meeting on Thursday night and didn't want her to know. Elke had been visiting Ben Cobawa in the hospital while he recovered from his second-degree burns and smoke inhalation, and had been discussing her findings from the journals. With Ben's help she'd figured out approximately where the buried treasure might be located and she wanted to run it by everyone, so they were having an emergency meeting.

"You have another hot date Thursday?" she asked in a playful, teasing manner.

"Uh, I've got something I have to do."

She lifted one pert brow but didn't say a word. He wished he could tell her why, but knew she'd been asking around about the committee meetings. The last thing he wanted was to leak the story after all their efforts to control the information.

"Okay. Friday," she said, not pursuing the point. Surprising him.

After a great lunch, he found a tree they could stand under to hug, since it had started to drizzle. Lilly smelled like roses and expensive soap, and he inhaled deeply when he snuggled into her neck. He'd missed holding her, and from the way she was hugging back, maybe she'd missed him, too? The thought made him grin.

They glanced into each other's eyes, hers sparking with intent, before sharing a kiss, this one a real kiss, not one of those flimsy hello deals. Nope, this was a "Welcome back, where've you been?" kiss. Man, he'd been waiting ever since Sunday for it, too, and she didn't disappoint.

There was something about Lilly's mouth fitting perfectly with his that sent him on a sexy mental detour every time they kissed. And she nested right into his arms, as if she belonged there. He needed to watch himself or he'd be falling for this one, and…well, while kissing her he couldn't think of any reason why that would be a bad thing. But usually where women were concerned, it always got sticky down the line. They'd start complaining about his job taking up too much of his time, and he'd begin to think they weren't nearly as amusing as he'd thought in the beginning.

"Lunch tomorrow?" he asked.

"Okay. Can I pick the place?"

"Sure."

"Then let's go to Lincoln's Place."

"I love that place."

"I'm thinking about writing an article about how he came to Heartlandia, and why he likes it here."

"That'd be a great idea. Oh, and sometime you should think about interviewing his pianist, Desi Rask, too. She's got an interesting story."

Lilly nodded. "I'll make a note of that."

"Well, I've got to get back. We're working some burglary jobs related to the cruise ships."

"Hmm," she said, sudden interest gleaming in her gaze.

"I wonder why Borjk doesn't keep a police radio scanner in the office. We miss out on all of the interesting stories."

"Probably has to do with the fact we'd arrest him if he did for using information he's heard on it for personal gain—i.e. the newspaper."

"Ah, okay, so I learned something new today."

"You can pop into the department anytime and ask to see the police log, though."

"I can?"

"Sure. Hey." He reached for and held her shoulders to look square into her eyes. "I learned something new today, too." He tugged her close for a hug. "I miss you when you're not around."

Her body language showed she liked that, as she held and hugged him back. "How much longer are you working evenings?"

"Another week, then I'll be back on days."

She kissed him lightly. "Good. I get lonely in that cottage all by myself at night."

"Leif isn't good company?"

"He's more like a ghost. Sometimes I see him standing at his big old bay window staring out toward the river for a really long time."

"He's been through a lot."

"Well, you know me, I want to know the story. And why isn't a man like him married?"

"I told you he was, didn't I? Or I meant to."

"Really?" She wiped the quizzical look off her face when she noticed Gunnar's disapproving gaze. "Yeah, I know that's none of my business."

"It's not like it's a secret. His wife died about two or three years ago from cancer. He built that house for her, now has to live without her. I'm surprised he stays there. Don't know if I could."

"Wow. That's sad."

"Yeah." It was time to lighten things us. "By the way, the whole town already knows that story so don't get any ideas."

She socked his chest halfheartedly. "Can't I find out about my landlord?"

"Sure you can, just don't print it."

"Besides, I've got half a dozen human interest stories lined up for the next few days." She ignored his jab. "I'll be learning how to make cheese with the Svendsen brothers tomorrow morning, and Hilde Pilkvist promised to demonstrate collecting wool from sheep, dyeing, spinning and weaving it at Hannah's Handmade Sweaters." She tossed him a glance showing her frustration. "Not everything's a story for the newspaper, Gunnar. I know that."

Now he'd ticked her off, and he hated ending their lunch on a bad note so he kissed her until she quit squirming and started kissing him back. Then her cell phone rang, and she broke away from the kiss. "That's my father's ringtone. I've got to answer."

He needed to get back on the job anyway, so he kissed her forehead and took off. "Good luck," he said over his shoulder.

Thursday night, Gunnar thought he saw something in the bushes while heading from his meeting at city hall. He shook his head when he added up the probabilities. Lilly. Did she really think she could get answers from hiding in the bushes?

He walked Gerda Rask and his sister to their respective cars, noticing Lilly's red two-door way at the end of the parking lot. Did she really think he wouldn't notice? What kind of a cop did she think he was? Once the ladies had both left the lot, he got an idea.

Feeling perturbed about Lilly's snooping around after he'd specifically asked her not to, he strode to his car, which was near the bushes, and made a fake phone call, talking extra loud. "Yeah, the information we got tonight will blow your mind. I'm heading over there right now." Then he got into his undercover police car and started the engine and drove extra slowly out of the parking lot to give Lilly time to get in her car and follow him. At least that was his cheesy plan, and what do you know, surprisingly, she bit.

He'd been using the undercover unit while working the cruise-line-burglary case, and had been up so late last night he'd driven it home. He'd planned to trade it in for his own car after the emergency meeting tonight, but now that Lilly was trailing him—just like he'd planned—he decided to hold off.

He made a wicked grin, turned onto an isolated road ready for a game of cat and mouse, and headed for his favorite secluded beach. Lilly tailed him all the way along the high cliff roads and turning into the hillside canyons. What could she possibly think she could find out? Was she expecting a secret meeting of the local wizard coven or something?

In his gut, he didn't feel comfortable leading her on a wild-goose chase—in fact he kind of felt like a pompous jerk. Here he was concerned he couldn't trust her, and then he pulls a stunt like this. What if she thought he was mocking her? That wouldn't exactly help them learn to trust each other, but at this point he'd have a lot of explaining to do no matter what he did. This wasn't right. What the hell had he been thinking? He decided to put an end to this little caper and come clean.

Gunnar made a snap decision to take a turnout just around a tight bend and take the consequences. He deserved them. He planned to turn around and stop her, put an end to his little game. He'd confront her on why she insisted on breaking a big story about the secret committee when she had all these really great stories lined up with the locals. *Give it up*, he'd tell her. *You're not going to find out anything from me.*

It seemed like a good enough plan, anyway.

Except when he made his U-turn and got back out onto the road, she'd already passed where he'd turned out and was heading farther up the secluded coastal road.

She sure wasn't very good at trailing people. She'd made a completely wrong turn and would end up on a dark dirt road to nowhere if he didn't stop her. Thinking fast, he put on his police lights and sped up behind her. There wasn't any place to pull over, so she stopped dead in the middle of the narrow road.

He brought his heavy-duty flashlight along and got out of the car. Lilly stayed in her car, using common sense and probably big-city precautions. Good thinking.

Between the flashing undercover police-unit lights and his flashlight, he could tell she was staring straight ahead and was ticked off. His heart sank a little thinking he'd given her a fright. Sometimes he came up with bonehead ideas. Now he'd have to fix the fallout.

He tapped on her window. She cautiously turned her head. "It's Gunnar. Open your door."

"No."

"It's me. Come on. At least open your window."

"No. You lied to me."

Oh yeah, she was pissed, but not about what he thought she'd be angry about—his playing a juvenile game on her. She'd homed in on the fact he'd never been straight with her about his involvement in the secret meetings, even when she'd asked him point-blank at the bar that first night.

Truth was, it wasn't her business. She'd find out when the rest of Heartlandia found out, but now he needed to deal with the situation at hand.

"I hardly knew you then, and you were being too nosy."

Finally she turned on him, and between his flashlight and her facial expression, the picture wasn't pretty. Anger turned her normally lovely features into sharp lines and shadowed angles, reminding him of the Japanese folklore ghosts called *yurei* he'd often read about.

Through the closed car window she sounded muffled, yet he understood every single word. "You lied, and you continue to lie. And now you tried to scare me and trick me, and make me feel foolish. And I especially don't appreciate your taking me on a wild-goose chase."

She put her car in gear and drove off leaving Gunnar standing in the road kicking himself for his insensitivity. He'd really screwed up; now what the hell was he supposed to do to make things better?

One thing was for sure, he knew she was heading to a dead end and didn't have a clue how to find her way home from this location. He also knew this was the only way in and out of this particular canyon and she'd have to retrace her path straight to him. Moonlight dappled the surface of the Columbia River as it lapped the rocky shoreline, and he waited for Lilly to return so he could grovel and beg for her forgiveness.

Less than five minutes later, her headlights came barreling down the bumpy road. He'd turned his car around while he waited, so he jumped inside and with his flashing lights led the way for her out of the canyon. He switched them off when they drove across town straight to her cottage door. Once there, he waited for her to park and get out of her car, then he jumped out of the cruiser when she approached.

Lilly's furious expression clued him that he was still in deep doo-doo.

She socked him in the chest. Unlike usual, this one was meant to hurt but fell far short of the mark. He'd need to teach her some defense techniques for her safety.

"I'm not a game. How dare you humiliate me."

"I'm sorry. I messed up." Admitting his stupid mistake seemed like the only tack to take.

The admission made her pause a half beat but she recouped quickly, anger coloring her disposition.

Gunnar stepped in front of her, and tensed his muscles in preparation for another sock, but she didn't hit him. "I'm not a game, either," he said. "You can't know everything I'm involved in, and you just have to accept that for now."

"That was a dirty trick, Gunnar. You made me feel like an idiot."

Ah, jeez, he'd messed up beyond what he'd thought, made her feel like an idiot, never his intention, and he didn't have a clue what to do. Daring to gaze at her, he had a hunch there was more on her mind than his taking her on a detour for his own amusement. Her usual good-sport attitude had evaporated somewhere back in that dark canyon and maybe she wanted, no, needed, to talk about it.

"You're not an idiot. Couldn't be if you tried."

She folded her arms and huffed, studying the ground as if it was covered with diamonds or something.

He could wait it out. No matter how strong his urge to comfort her was, instinct told him to give her a chance to open up. But, ah jeez, her eyes were welling up and she bit her lower lip to fight off the tears. And since he was the source of her tears of humiliation he wanted to kick his own ass. "I'm the idiot. Not you."

She'd launched off into another time, it seemed, as she

looked over his shoulder and stared at the poolside waterfall.

"No one can make me feel like an idiot like my father. No one." She wiped away the first wave of tears spilling over her lower lids with a shaky hand. "I could never do anything right enough for him. No matter how hard I tried, he'd find the flaw somewhere, someway." She shook her head. "He was big on teaching me lessons. Showing me the error of my ways. Humiliating me. And he didn't give a damn who was around to hear or see it, either." She took a deep breath, held it then blew it out. "When I graduated in the top ten percent in my high school class, he wanted to know why I wasn't in the top three percent. When I got accepted to one of my top two university choices, he wondered why I couldn't get into an Ivy League university, then said it must have been because of my SAT scores. When I landed a job at the *San Francisco Gazette*, he asked why I didn't try for the *Chronicle*." She pressed her palms against her temples. "I have racked my brain and cannot ever once remember him praising me."

Gunnar wanted to hunt down Lilly's father and coldcock him right here and now. But more so, he wanted to rip his own heart out for bringing on this walk down nightmare lane because of his stupid and careless actions.

"I've been so wrapped up in all of these local folks' interviews for the newspaper," she said "I'd forgotten about your stupid meetings. But my dad called yesterday."

Gunnar remembered the cell phone call that interrupted their most excellent kiss after lunch.

"It took him less than ten seconds before he asked when I was going to break my big story. Then I realized I'd gotten off track." For the first time she nailed Gunnar with her tortured gaze. "I tried to tell him about all of these wonderful interviews I've been doing, but he reminded me that nothing should derail my goals. Nothing. Then I remembered you'd said you were busy tonight, and I put two and two together. Followed you. And where did it lead? To you teaching me a lesson."

"That wasn't my plan, Lilly, I swear. I just wanted to mess with you for snooping around. I didn't know how... How could I know?" He stepped closer, wrapped her in his arms in apology. She didn't fight it, and he was grateful. "I really am the idiot."

"My father was the master of teaching by humiliation. I don't need that junk from the man I'm dating."

Oh, man, he'd pegged her so completely wrong. Her tough big-city-woman persona was nothing but a shield for a vulnerable girl, and his desire to protect and serve had never been stronger.

"I'm sorry. I'm so, so sorry." He hugged her tight, wishing he could take back the past hour, trying desperately to make things better. Hell-bent on being the opposite of his father, he'd acted nothing short of a bully tonight, apparently just like Lilly's father. It would never happen again. Ever. "I'm sorry, Chitcha, please forgive me."

The soldier-like tension in her body relaxed. She leaned into his chest and rested her head on his shoulder. "I shouldn't have been following you. I wasn't even that interested."

He kissed the top of her head. "Agreed. You absolutely shouldn't have been following me. So no more games, okay?"

"No more games." She looked up.

"No more snooping?"

"No more secrets?"

"Touché," he said just before capturing her mouth for a long and tender kiss as they stood under the light of the perfect half-moon. He was in a sticky situation being on a committee that Lilly was dying to find out about, and just now promising not to keep secrets. How was he supposed to juggle that double-edged sword and not get injured, or worse yet, injure her?

Soon, the kiss heated up and his body stirred. Lilly must have felt the same way. She broke up their heady outdoor make-out session, took Gunnar by the hand and, without the need for another word, led him to her door.

On the way, he thanked his lucky stars for makeup sex.

Chapter Ten

Things were going great with Gunnar. Even though he'd taunted Lilly like a child that Thursday night—she'd gotten her feelings hurt, gotten furious and in his face, recalling far too many bad memories—he'd apologized like a prince and the next thing she knew she'd invited him in and they were having makeup sex. The next night he'd sung praises over her homemade sushi, even though she knew she'd done a mediocre job compared to her sobo. They'd gone out for breakfast on Saturday before he went to work, and Sunday he'd driven her to interview a fascinating young woman named Desi Rask. Of course that gave Gunnar the excuse to visit with his best friend, Kent, and his son, while she did. He'd spent the next week showing her around the county like she was an out-of-town relative. And she'd loved every minute.

Falling for him would change her focus in town. Her father had warned her about that. She could think of a million reasons why she shouldn't get involved with him while she was at work and out from under his spell, and that's pretty much what she'd decided he did whenever they were together—spin some kind of magic. They'd been dating almost four weeks, the longest relationship she'd ever had.

Sad but true.

Her parents' faces popped into her head, looking tenser and tenser. Gunnar wasn't her goal. He wasn't the reason she'd come to Heartlandia. She needed to stay focused on her plan to own and run her own newspaper. Having a relationship with the police sergeant would only complicate things.

So why was she smiling and going all gooey inside thinking about how he liked to snuggle with her while they slept, and how no man had ever used her nickname from her grandmother before—Chitcha—until Gunnar. It scared her how drawn she was to him, all of him, not just his made-for-work body, and his no-nonsense attitude, but his down-home personality and surprising gentle side, too.

She shook her head, as if that might jiggle some sense into her brain, and stared at the computer screen on her desk.

Over the past couple of weeks Gunnar had taken it upon himself to be her own personal guide around Heartlandia. Through the point of view of someone who'd lived here all his life, she'd developed a new respect and fondness for the place. What worried her the most was how much she genuinely wanted to be friends with the townsfolk, and how easily they accepted her. Which was a very foreign feeling coming from her family background. Some of her greatest ideas for articles came while touring the out-of-the-way spots in town with Gunnar. Yet she remained a little homesick for her sobo.

All mixed up with these mostly good feelings, she stared at her desk computer in the newspaper office, nearly squirming in her chair from the lack of inspiration that Monday morning. How could she make her mark at the

Herald? The most feedback she'd gotten was when she wrote stories about the locals. The townsfolk never seemed to get enough of those kinds of stories. Plus, she'd been told by a couple of the cruise-liner captains that they'd started buying and distributing to their guests her stories as a point of reference while touring Heartlandia.

Emil Ingersson had told her just the other day that his tourist trade had almost doubled since she'd written the article about his bread factory on the outskirts of town. How he'd had to hire a couple of the local housewives to help serve the samples and collect the sales. In fact, his monthly production had increased by a quarter, and he pointed to Lilly as the reason.

Since she'd shared Desdemona Rask's interesting tale of returning home to a family she never knew she had, Lilly'd heard that Lincoln's Place was packed on the weekend when she played piano there. And that Desi's estranged father had become her biggest fan.

She smiled, remembering how she'd choked up hearing about Desi's search for her father and the loss of her Heartlandia-born mother. She wondered what it would be like to have a special relationship with her father, for her father to be her biggest supporter. As if that could ever happen.

But she could pat herself on the back for other reasons. Truth was since she'd become the main reporter, the newspaper subscriptions had definitely increased, and deep in her heart she knew it wasn't because of Borjk's boring op-eds. But her father had always told her to remain humble in personal achievement, to never settle and always strive for more.

She'd wanted to tell him the last time they'd spoken on the phone how excited she was about the newspaper's recent surge, but knew it wouldn't be enough. He wouldn't get it, not something that subtle. Until she purchased the paper, she'd keep her mini steps of success to herself.

Sobo's soft-featured face came to mind, and Lilly had a yearning to make sushi with her. Maybe she'd share a personal profile about her roots and influences with the people of Heartlandia. Suddenly her fingers flew over the computer keyboard: I Dream of Sushi in Storybook Land. An Outsider's Perspective of Heartlandia.

Besides sharing a little about herself in the column, she could think of a dozen people to feature off the top of her head, starting with the mayor. The stories would be as plentiful as the population. And, *bam*, just like that she'd created her new column. Now all she had to do was convince Bjork the idea was a winner.

All the lectures in the world about single-minded goals didn't keep Lilly away from Gunnar that Thursday night. She tapped on his door at nine-thirty, knowing he'd had yet another meeting at city hall. No, she wasn't there to break him down and finally get the lowdown on those darn meetings. She'd promised and they'd called a truce; she was there to tell him her big news about the new weekly column.

Funny how Gunnar's face was the first and only one to come to mind once Bjork had given her the okay to run with the column.

He opened the door, wrapped in a towel, looking surprised. "Hey, I was going to call you in a few minutes. What's up?"

"I've got a great idea and I wanted to run it by you. Have you got a moment?" The guy was wrapped in a towel, maybe it wasn't the best time...

"I was just going to jump in the shower." He opened the door wide to let her enter. "Have a seat. I'll only be a few minutes." He pecked her on the lips and turned to mosey down the hall toward the bathroom. "Unless you want to join me? You can tell me all about it under the shower head.."

"I'm good thanks," she called after him. Girl! Why not take him up on it? She'd come here for one reason, to tell him about her new column, and showering with Gunnar wasn't her goal. Maybe she should reevaluate that.

"Make yourself comfortable," he said, closing the bathroom door.

She sat on the couch and briefly closed her eyes. She was too excited to settle down, so she glanced around the room. Wolverine mewed from his favorite spot on the rug by the elevated fireplace. Her gaze continued on toward the kitchen. Gunnar must have just finished a sandwich, judging by the crust sitting on a plate on the island counter. Leaning against the counter was a mailing tube, the kind that usually held blueprints.

Her mind drifted back to the first night she'd been here, when Gunnar had told her about Leif and him working on the house design together, and how this was just the first phase. What would the rest of Gunnar's house be like? Curiosity got the best of her.

She walked across the room and, seeing that the tube wasn't sealed, opened the lid, turned it upside down and pulled out the contents. Instead of the blueprints, like she'd expected, she found an aerial view of the portion of town that thanks to Gunnar she'd come to know as the Ringmuren, the great wall surrounding the northernmost corner of Heartlandia. The second page seemed like the same area, but it looked like some kind of heat map, like you'd see on those weather maps on TV.

Intrigued by the pictures, and forgetting about the blueprint idea, she sat on a kitchen stool and studied them. A bright red spot stood out in the upper left corner on the far side of the long and ancient wall. What in the world did that represent?

Completely engrossed, she jumped when Gunnar touched her arm. "What are you doing?"

"Oh! I'm looking at your pictures."

He didn't look happy. Nope, the guy looked disturbed and maybe a little angry judging by the creases between his brows. "Who gave you permission to go through my stuff?"

Oh, gosh, he'd taken it all wrong. She wasn't being snoopy, well, maybe she was, but it wasn't for the usual reasons, those secret meetings. "I thought this might be your house-upgrade blueprints."

He took the documents from her, rolled up the aerial photographs and put them back into the tube. "You know, if we're going to have a shot at a serious relationship, you've got to quit this stuff. Give it up. I'm not ever going to tell you about the meetings."

"I had no idea this had anything to do with the meetings."

He flinched. Now he looked ticked off at himself. Had he accidentally given away a big clue? He may have tried to put out a fire, but now he'd only made her more curious.

"Does it?" she asked, his ironman stare looking right through her. She didn't let it intimidate her. "Have to do with the meetings?"

He popped the lid back on the tube and put it on top of the high refrigerator, a place Lilly would need a stepping stool to reach. "None of your business." He turned toward her. "Did you even hear what I just said? About us?"

About having a shot at a serious relationship? Of course she had, and her knees had gone rubbery, but he'd buried the statement deep in his reprimand and then she'd gotten caught up with those special meetings again.

"Being exclusive? Yes, Gunnar, but first I need you to understand that I wasn't trying to go behind your back about anything just now. I made an honest mistake thinking that blueprints were inside that tube. I got curious about your house addition…maybe because I *was* thinking about us…and the future. Can you accept that?"

She'd stepped over the line and insinuated herself into his future. Talk about a turnoff to any guy, especially a contented bachelor like Gunnar.

He inhaled, his broad chest going even wider beneath his tight white T-shirt. "Because of your history of snooping around my meetings, Lilly, you can't fault me for thinking the worst."

She felt upset and huffy—a normally foreign feeling to her—but to add insult to injury the guy just blew off her admitting she was curious about their future. So right now, ticked off and not going to take it anymore, she blew off his willingness to be exclusive with her and decided to tell him how she felt about everything else. "Well, if all you can think is the worst about me, then I guess there's no point in…"

He grabbed her and dropped a quick kiss on her lips to shut her up. "I'm sorry," he said, then took the follow-up kiss to the next level. She wanted to resist, to recite her full-blown speech about her hurt feelings and his riding roughshod over them, but her heart wasn't in this fight, and he felt too damn good to stop kissing. By the time he'd made her go all dreamy-eyed, he ended the kiss. Tease! Why did he always have to take charge of things?

"Let's start over," he said. "I'm sorry I accused you of snooping, even though technically you were."

Why could he make her crack a smile at the craziest

moments, especially when she was upset and didn't want to? He'd given her a mini ultimatum—either forgive or make a big deal out of it. Hot off his superkiss, smelling the sporty soap on his clean skin, having just run her fingertips over his ultrasmooth, fresh-shaven jaw, she'd be nuts to go with door B. "I promise to never snoop around your stuff without your okay, again."

Crap! She'd just become Christine to his Erik in *Phantom of the Opera*. Somehow he'd gotten her to do exactly what he'd wanted.

He watched her for a few moments, those green eyes invading all of her barriers, as if studying her face for the first time and liking what he saw. "You know I'm nuts about you, right?"

He was? Well, sure, they'd been sleeping together about every other night since she'd moved into her place, and they'd been spending just about all of their spare time together, too. But he'd never, ever talked about being exclusive. Besides, that wasn't the way of the modern San Francisco woman whose profession came first. This was all too confusing.

Wait a second, wait a second, did he just say he was nuts about her?

"You are?" Could she sound more lame? Why not be honest and tell him she was crazy about him, too, but suddenly her tongue had knotted up.

"Against my better judgment, I am." He moved one longer lock of hair behind her ear. She knew her ear tips gave her true reaction away, feeling hot and probably being bright red.

"Oh, man. This changes everything." Without giving it a second thought, in a very un–San Francisco sophisticated woman way, she leaped into his arms, straddling his hips with her legs. Catching her didn't even faze him.

It felt like hitting a boulder, he was that rock solid. She kissed him as if she'd never wanted anything more in her life. She might not be able to tell him how she really felt just yet because something about saying the words scared her witless. She sure could show him how she was feeling, though, how she was falling...*gulp*...in love with him.

Gunnar sat in roll call Friday morning a bit stunned. He'd left a sleeping Lilly in his bed, and had taken a few extra moments standing and watching her before he'd left. This wasn't good. If his plan was to become chief of police down the road and move on to mayor once he was in his forties, he needed to show he was a solid Heartlandia citizen. Which meant he should get serious, settle down and quit sleeping around. In his mind he and Lilly were exclusive. He just hadn't gotten around to saying anything about it until last night. When he had, from her reaction, she was very receptive to the idea.

The take-out coffee turned bitter in his mouth. Yeah, he was crazy about Lilly, but he had to face it, Lilly wasn't a "stand behind your man" kind of woman the way his mother had been. Lilly was out for Lilly—and honestly a little of that mind-set sure would have been helpful for his mother. But Gunnar wasn't like his father, and if he wanted to become chief of police then mayor one day he needed a woman who'd support him all the way. A woman he could trust with every single secret. Was she capable of that? Was she capable of saying one thing and doing another, like his father who'd sworn his innocence right up until they'd led him off to jail? Later, the Norling family had learned how involved his father really was, taking hush money and turning his head while the smugglers did their transactions, nearly running the legitimate factory into the ground.

As a type A personality himself, Gunnar recognized an overachiever when he met one. Lilly was single-minded about taking over the newspaper—how proud she'd been to tell him last night amidst crumpled sheets fresh with the scent of their sex, about her new column with the catchy name. I Dream of Sushi in Storybook Land. It was also clear that she treated the *Heartlandia Herald* as a stepping stone to her future—which meant her future might not be around these parts.

Either the coffee or the day's police log had made Gunnar queasy. If he were to bet the feeling had more to do with a pair of perfectly placed dark eyes, and short, crazy-to-run-his-fingers-through hair. Not the ongoing dock mayhem and cruise-line robberies.

Was he ready to let himself completely fall for someone? To completely trust her?

Though making inroads with Heartlandia, Lilly was still an outsider with big plans for her future. Would having a real relationship, like Kent and Desi had, with a lady like Lilly be wise, considering his goals? Or the dumbest venture in his life…

He knew how his body felt about her, but it was time to check in with his mind and figure this out. Maybe Kent could set him straight since he'd been through a lot worse, getting divorced and feeling abandoned, yet he'd still managed to fall in love again. With an outsider. To look at Kent and Desi these days, they were the perfect pair planning their wedding and seemed nothing short of a miracle.

Was it out of the question to think Gunnar and the tiger lady, Lilly, might be right for each other?

"You ready?" Paul, his partner, prodded Gunnar's foot with the tip of his boot.

"Huh? Oh, yeah, sure. Where're we heading?"

"I knew you'd checked out. You were all but drooling."

"I was not." Gunnar stood, ready for the day. They walked in friendly banter out to the car.

Like radar, Gunnar's eyes went right to the red car pulling into a parking space, and the woman who expunged herself from behind the steering wheel. Lilly. He'd never admit it in a court of law, but his pulse did a little blip at the sight of her. Wearing a girlie version of a suit—straight-legged, tight-fitting black pants showing off all the right parts, and a waist-length matching jacket looking more like something Michael Jackson might wear back in the day, with gold epilates and brass buttons down the front, totally San Francisco—she walked with her usual good posture toward the newspaper office.

Warmth spread across his chest as he waved. Her serious face brightened the moment she noticed him and waved back. Damn, she was something.

Who knew what would pan out between them? All he knew for sure was he liked being with Lilly. Loved being with Lilly. And yeah, he was crazy about her on more levels than in his bed. She was a go-getter, just like him, she had goals, just like him, she was confident in her abilities despite her old man, just like him. And nothing would stand in the way of her getting a story. That was the part that got stuck in his throat.

And that's where they were different. His father would always be his point of reference for making a choice or going too far. He hoped Lilly's conscience knew when to stop her, too.

He believed she'd made an honest mistake looking at the latest bombshell from the committee—buried treasure smack in the middle of sacred Chinook burial ground, according to Ben Cobawa.

Leif had funded the special aerial study using something called infrared thermography. The way he'd explained it, the special camera recorded the energy emitted from objects. No one wanted to invade the burial ground, but the next step would be utilizing a high-tech metal detector to gauge whether the dense infrared image was in fact a sea captain's trunk, and if so, precisely how far down in sacred land it was located.

Paul started the police unit and backed out of the parking spot. Gunnar watched Lilly open the door and go inside the building, realizing a broad smile stretched across his face again.

There was just something about Lilly...

"What're you smiling at?" Paul chided, knowing full well the direction Gunnar had been looking.

He didn't bother to answer.

For a guy with a questionable track record as a player, maybe he'd surprise everyone and work something out for the long term with Chitcha.

Chapter Eleven

Lilly thumbed through the Rolodex—yes, Bjork was antiquated enough in his record keeping that he still used a Rolodex—looking for the contact information for Mayor Gerda Rask.

What better way to kick off her new column than with an interview with the mayor pro tem?

To her surprise the mayor, who insisted Lilly call her Gerda, graciously invited her over for tea that very Tuesday afternoon. Lilly parked in front of a huge Victorian-style house painted bright yellow and with soft green trim, reminding her of the colorful painted ladies back home. The house was on a huge lot with plenty of space between it and the next house, unlike San Francisco. As she knocked, she glanced across the yard to Gerda's neighbor, a bland white Victorian house in the early stages of being brightened up with jazzy lavender trim.

The stunning mocha-colored young woman she'd interviewed for the newspaper a couple of weeks ago opened the door. "Hi." Desi hugged Lilly like they were old friends. "Come on in." Desi was Gerda's granddaughter.

The warm welcome fueled the first-meeting excitement Lilly always got at interviews.

They briefly exchanged small talk as Desi showed her down the hall, across creaky ancient wooden floors to the sunroom, where Gerda and a fresh pot of tea awaited.

"Grandma, Lilly's here."

Lilly shook Gerda's bony hand, surprised by her warmth. Her aging blue eyes brightened as they smiled at each other.

"I've been looking forward to interviewing our mayor ever since I came to Heartlandia. Thanks so much for agreeing to see me."

"Oh, I'd much rather talk to you than deal with all the headaches going on at city hall these days," Gerda said, looking resigned and sitting back down in her classic oak rocker, as if she had the weight of the world on her narrow shoulders.

"Well," Desi said, "I've got my first piano student in five minutes. I'd better go get ready."

"Nice to see you again, Desi."

"You, too."

"I'd like to do a follow-up article on you and your dad sometime."

"Hmm, I'll have to think about that," the tall and lovely woman said as she closed the door, somewhat noncommittal.

Glancing at the pale, nearly colorless grandmother compared to the warm-toned granddaughter, Lilly knew there was a lot more to Desi's story to tell.

Gerda poured them both some tea and Lilly got right down to the interview, beginning with the mayor's genealogy going all the way back to the first founders of Heartlandia three hundred years ago.

Her previously bright eyes softened and seemed to drift far away as she told her more recent family history. Pain crossed her face when she spoke about her daughter, Ester,

and how she'd run away as a teenager and had never returned home, and how Gerda hadn't gotten to really know
Desi until after Ester had died from cancer.

If Lilly wasn't sure before, she was positive now about
interviewing Desi from a different angle, not just about
being the new town music teacher and favorite piano bar
player at Lincoln's Place, but the rest of her story, too.

"These days, with Desi being engaged and planning
her wedding to Kent, I should be thrilled. And don't get
me wrong, mostly I am, but being mayor came with a lot
of surprises."

"Like what?" Lilly sipped her tea, trying to keep her
cool while hoping Gerda might tell her more.

"Oh, just a few things about our city that I'd never
known before."

She'd already gotten in trouble with Gunnar for bad-
gering him about the secret meetings, and he'd basically
admitted they were going on. Plus, since she'd stumbled
upon the aerial pictures, she knew they had something to
do with the sacred burial grounds. She decided to go for
it, bait Gerda with the little information she'd already acquired to see where it might lead. Wasn't that what any
journalist worth their salt did?

"Do the things you never knew about city hall have anything to do with the secret meetings going on over there?"

Gerda's thin white brows tented. "You know about those
meetings?"

"Am I not supposed to know about them?"

Gerda's brows dropped low over her eyes. She seemed
in a quandary. "Well, we haven't gone public with any of
our findings yet, but there will come a time when we'll
be forced to, I guess."

"Care to elaborate on what those findings are?"

"No." Gerda put down her teacup and folded her hands in her lap. "Sorry."

"May I quote you on the other part?"

"Which part?" She knotted her hands together.

"On your surprise about some of the 'things about city hall you'd never known before' and the need for a special committee and time-consuming meetings."

Gerda leaned forward. "Just how much do you know about our special committee?"

Lilly sat straighter, not wanting Gunnar to get blamed if Gerda found out they were dating. "Anyone who reads the town website can figure it out."

"Really?" Gerda snatched up a nearby pencil and note-pad, scribbling out a quick sentence. Evidently she hadn't checked out the town website lately.

"Are these meetings about Heartlandia's upcoming birthday? Are you planning a celebration?"

"Our tercentennial, you mean?"

"That's three hundred, right?"

Gerda nodded. "I wish that was the reason. No. We're dealing with a glitch in our history that needs to get ironed out. Once we've worked it out, we'll let the community know everything."

"And may I quote you on that?"

Gerda's thumb flew to her mouth. She chewed her nail while thinking. Her previously serene face was now etched with crisscrossed lines and beetled brows. "I guess that's okay, just maybe only mention we're ironing out some issues regarding our town records. I don't want to get over-run with questions I'm not able to answer at this time."

"That's fine. Any idea when the community will be informed about what's going on?"

"It's too soon to say, but hopefully in the next month or two? Maybe I'm being too optimistic, but I'm hoping this won't be anything too earth-shattering to report. We just have to work out the particulars, present it in the right way and maybe…" Gerda's gaze shot up. "Oh, goodness, I've said too much already. Please disregard everything I just said."

"So I can't mention that you hope to have resolved the issue in the next month or two?"

Gerda shook her head. "I'd rather you didn't, in case we need more time."

"Okay, you have my word on that, but is it okay if I still mention the glitch in the town history being ironed out in the special meetings?"

Lilly could tell she'd talked the poor woman in circles, and by now she wasn't sure what would be okay to say or not, yet she pressed on.

"I guess that part would be okay."

"I must say you've really piqued my interest."

"Oh, goodness, that was the last thing I wanted to do."

Lilly didn't want to leave Gerda in a dither, so she changed tack and asked her what a typical day at city hall as mayor pro tem was like. That seemed to smooth out Gerda's concerned expression as she explained the many duties of a sitting mayor.

Fifteen minutes later, with a boatload of notes, Lilly finished her tea. "Well, thank you for your time, Mayor Rask. I truly appreciate it."

"My pleasure, Ms. Matsuda. By the way, I've really enjoyed your stories about our local entrepreneurs."

Knowing people were reading her little articles never failed to please Lilly, even though they weren't big breaking-news stories. But in her bones, she knew she was on to something with those up-close-and-personal stories.

Gerda showed Lilly out by way of the back deck, and as she trudged around the house, hearing the clunky piano playing of one of the young students through an opened window, she also overheard Gerda call out to Desi. "Do you know where my stomach medicine is?"

Lilly hunched her shoulders, figuring she'd been the cause of the mayor's stomach upset with her pointed questions, and a pang of guilt accompanied her thoughts about pushing the line with the dear lady. Was a breaking story really worth the discomfort it caused those involved? It wasn't as if they were common criminals trying to hide something horrible, not if Mr. By-the-Books Norling was on board.

Gunnar had volunteered to work the evening shift again on Wednesday night due to the continued illegal activities down at the docks. He'd dressed in shabby jeans, a ripped T-shirt and a pea jacket and would drive an undercover car. He'd changed to lead the surveillance task force for the evening. This would be a double shift, since he'd been in uniform all day doing the usual job. Three other undercover units were assigned to the watch. But things weren't set to officially begin for another hour.

He hitched a bun on the corner of another officer's desk in the department, and noticed the *Heartlandia Herald*, so he picked it up and began to peruse. Quickly, he discovered Lilly's lead story in the I Dream of Sushi in Storybook Land column. The subtitle nearly made him choke on his coffee.

What's So Secret about the City Hall Meetings?

She'd interviewed Mayor pro tem Gerda Rask and though the article started off with the usual personal history and charming anecdotes from the interviewee, Lilly had quickly veered off into another direction.

"Word has it around town that there are secret meetings going on with a special panel. Would you like to tell us about them?"

Looking uncomfortable with my line of questioning, the white-haired matriarch of Heartlandia, and acting mayor, commented, "[We're] ironing out some issues regarding our town records."

When asked how soon before the town would find out the reason for these meetings, Mayor Rask declined to answer, but she assured the meetings didn't have anything to do with the upcoming three-hundredth birthday of Heartlandia.

A lightning bolt cut through Gunnar's chest. His fists tightened and released as he used all his will not to wad up the newspaper and throw it in the trash. He counted to ten then strode out of the department, clomped across the black-and-white tile in the building foyer to the newspaper office entrance.

Bjork and three other employees were milling around working, but Lilly was nowhere to be seen. Having caught on to Lilly and Gunnar's relationship over the past few weeks, Bjork intercepted Gunnar's question.

"She's taking a late lunch break at the Hartalanda Café."

Having gotten the information he'd come for, Gunnar left the office without uttering a single syllable.

He counted to ten again before opening the door to the café. She'd really pushed things too far this time, especially after the incident with the aerial photos and promising him she wouldn't blab about those meetings. Evidently his feelings on the matter didn't mean squat to her.

She glanced up from her salad, a smile beginning but ending just as quickly when she noticed his dead-serious stare. He approached her table, and she sat straighter, as if steeling for a fight.

He wouldn't give her the satisfaction of arguing. Nope. She'd taken things too far and needed to hear him out. If he got in her face, she'd tune him out, and it was really important for her to hear what he had to say.

He sat across from her, determined to keep his voice down. "So let me get this straight. First you trick me into admitting I was involved in the meetings, I tell you I need to be able to trust you, you promise me I can, then you print the information for the whole city to read. What gives?"

She blinked. "I printed what Mayor Rask said. I wasn't quoting you."

"And that makes a difference how?"

"Two sources. One verified the other. Plus the mayor said it was okay to quote her."

Still keeping his voice quiet, the intensity went up a notch. "So it doesn't matter to you what I ask?"

She reached across the table and grabbed his fisted hand. He didn't pull away, just stared at their hands, wondering why he'd ever let himself get involved with a girl like Lilly. A single-minded reporter.

"Of course it matters to me what you want. What's the big deal if there's a glitch with the town records and you've all been assigned to a committee to work it out? What's the big deal, Gunnar? The people want to know and this should satisfy them until you make the big announcement."

Her voice wasn't nearly as quiet or controlled as his. She had no idea how big of a deal it was, and still she was determined to report it and risk putting the entire town in a tailspin. Not to mention all the questions poor Gerda would have to stave off. At least Lilly hadn't named the entire committee.

He removed his hand from under hers and gestured for her to keep her voice down. "What about trust?"

"You can trust me. This interview had nothing to do with you and me."

"So you think tricking someone into disclosing private business is okay?"

"I didn't trick her. She brought it up. Look, I'm a reporter. That's my job. I respect our mayor and asked her on two different occasions if I could quote her. One she okayed, the other she didn't. The second comment wasn't in the paper."

He wondered how much more Gerda had told Lilly and it caused his stomach to twist with the possibility she'd exposed everything before they'd ironed out their line of action. But more so, it stung like hell to realize he simply couldn't trust Lilly with everything in his life. "You need to let this go. Just leave this alone. Focus on the human interest stories."

"This *is* a human interest story." She sat back in the booth and folded her arms, her brows tense and her mouth pursed. "You're the bossiest man I've ever met."

He leaned forward. "And you're too nosey for your own good."

"You call it nosey, I call it doing my job."

"If you'd just realize you don't have to be the person your dad tried to make you." Gunnar shook his head, thinking how his own father's actions had shaped his life, making him an overcompensator and a stickler on rules and regulations, and sometimes rigid where his personal life was concerned. How he functioned in black-and-white with Lilly being in the gray area. He thought how Lilly's father had pushed and pushed and pushed her to become a tougher person until her gentle spirit had given in. Her judgment was damaged.

"Our fathers really jacked us up, you know?" he said. "But we're in charge of our lives now, and you don't have to play by your father's rules anymore."

"Old habits" was all she mumbled as she tore off tiny pieces of paper napkin. "And you don't have to be so rigid."

They played out a staring duel. He tried to read behind the steady set of her eyes, hoping she'd see his way of thinking, but he couldn't see past the glare. Yes, making up for his father's actions had made Gunnar inflexible at times but in his mind, trust meant everything.

"On this one point, I can't back down, Lilly. If I can't trust you, there's just no reason for us to be together, you know?" He cleared his throat, sad yet angry as hell to say what he knew he had to next. "I think it's best for both of us if we quit seeing each other."

Her chin shot up. He detected a fleeting flash of sadness in her eyes, perhaps a tinge of moisture gathering making her irises shiny, but she quickly toughened up. "Fine." Faced with his challenge, she put on her armor and turned as angry as he was sad.

Tension simmered between them for the next few moments as he breathed deeply yet had trouble getting air into his lungs, studying her, trying with every brain cell to figure her out. She wouldn't back down from the challenge and neither would he. Stalemate. Everything they'd shared, all the great moments, had been shot down because of a news story. That forced things into perspective for him.

If she was incapable of seeing that, there was nothing left to say, so he stood. "Go ahead and print our breakup on the front page, why don't you?" he said quietly struggling to sound nonchalant, as if his heart wasn't squeezing so hard he thought it might pop. Tucking his lower lip inward and biting on it to keep from saying another word, he turned and left the diner.

"Maybe I will!" she said in a strained whisper that broke at the end.

His step faltered. Chitcha didn't know how to back

down. Her father had seen to that. He briefly closed his eyes and shook his head. Breaking up with her was the last thing in the world he wanted to do...

But he couldn't trust her.

Lilly's stomach seemed to sit on her shoes. Her breathing came in spurts, and a panicky feeling that she'd just blown the best relationship of her life over a stupid snip of a story made her tear up. She was in public, she couldn't melt down here. She pushed away her half-eaten salad and pretended for the sake of the waitress and the couple sitting at the adjacent table that absolutely nothing wrong had just happened. It was always important to save face according to her parents. Never show weakness. Never.

Guilt ate at the edges of her thoughts. *You don't have to be the person your dad tried to make you.* Her stomach went queasy. Was she so success-oriented and hardhearted that she'd betray Gunnar's trust?

She curled her lower lip and tensed every muscle in order to not lose it in public. Slowly, her mind stiffened up, too.

How had she let a small town guy like Gunnar get under her skin in the first place? She'd lost sight of her goal. Why had she let that happen?

She knew exactly why. Gunnar was the truest, most honorable and dependable person she'd ever met. Sure, he'd been trying to make up for what his daddy had done, but in his case, it was a good thing. Everyone trusted and respected him.

It wasn't just Gunnar who made her feel like kitty litter at the moment. Once she'd ventured out and put names and faces on the people of Heartlandia, she'd lost her edge. The entire town had found a way into her heart through trust and innocence.

And she'd blown it all.

Her self-control nearly gone, she picked up the tattered napkin, and with a trembling hand dabbed at the corners of her mouth and, when she knew the couple at the next table wasn't watching, the corners of her eyes. Crying in public, showing weakness, failing in her father's ways, made her mad. She had to brush Gunnar out of her mind in order to survive the moment.

An inkling of fight returned.

She'd concentrate on something else, anything in order to make it out of the café without making a scene. With her napkin thoroughly shredded, she squeezed her brain to think. Something was going on with the town history. The people in power had decided to keep it quiet. It was so big her boyfriend had just broken up with her over it.

Stay focused, Lilly. She heard her father's voice.

As a reporter it was her job to bring the story out into the open. Full disclosure. *Transparency.* Wasn't that the buzzword of the decade?

As she reached for her purse and paid her bill at the counter, the guilty feelings gathered momentum again and invaded her breath. *Do not cry. Do. Not. Cry.* She had trouble inhaling, as if a blockade had been set up in her throat.

She'd just ruined any chance of ever having a relationship with Gunnar. Was the kind of success her father taught her really all about the goal and doing anything to achieve it? Maybe Gunnar was right, she didn't have to be that way.

Maybe it really was as easy as making a conscious decision to back off the story.

In a massive conflict of interest, she'd thrown over her best guy and set the town up for a confrontation with city hall, all for the sake of one stinking, smug, I-know-something-that-you-don't story lead.

She'd hate to look in a mirror right now. An overwhelming sense of failure enveloped her as she left the café.

Her father might be proud of her for breaking a major town story, but a gaping black hole had just opened up in the middle of her self-respect. She owed Gunnar and the entire town her heartfelt apology.

While trolling the dark streets of the docks with his lights off, Gunnar saw the first flames on the far side and drove toward them. It looked like the Maritime Museum had been hit. He parked, followed protocol and alerted his task force, then notified the fire department. He could wait for backup and risk losing his lead or jump out of his car and run for the scene. In his mind he did the right thing, lunging out the door and sprinting toward the fire.

A hundred yards out, a flash in his peripheral vision grabbed his full attention. It was someone dressed all in black running like a speeding shadow. He made a U-turn and hit the asphalt in full pursuit chasing down his target. The suspect dived behind some bushes, and Gunnar flattened himself against a shack, drawing his weapon and listening over his ragged breath for a clue where the suspect was hiding.

He edged to the corner of the wall, readying his heavy-duty flashlight with his left hand like an ice pick in the Harries hold, his gun hand resting on the wrist of the other hand for stability. He counted to three and stepped around the corner, his flashlight scanning the bushes. He saw movement and turned toward it at the exact moment a shot rang out. He rapidly returned fire and heard a loud groan, having hit his mark. Only then did he feel the white-hot pain in his left shoulder.

The police backup was right on his heels and the officers swarmed the bush, finding the guy curled into a ball hugging his right thigh.

Searing pain shot up Gunnar's shoulder and into his neck. His vision doubled and he had to sit down. Unable to hold up the flashlight any longer, he let go of it and lowered his gun, then dropped first to his knees then onto his butt. The jolt of hitting the pavement sent sharp nauseating pain up to his shoulder. His head felt swimmy. He put it between his spread legs and bent knees and concentrated on breathing through the raging sting zinging along the nerve endings in his shoulder.

Sirens sounded from all directions, coming for the fire no doubt, but hopefully an ambulance was on its way for him, too, since the sticky wetness from his gunshot spread quickly across his chest and dripped down onto his stomach.

His peripheral vision going dark, Gunnar shivered and clinched his eyes closed.

Chapter Twelve

Lilly was still in her office peering through the ceiling-to-floor windows into the building's foyer, trying her best to get her mind off the saddest day of her life, when she noticed a couple of officers run out the door and in to their cruisers. Thankful for distraction, she scurried over to the PD's front desk.

"Anything special going on?"

"Another fire at the docks," the older man reported.

Lilly rushed back to her cubicle, grabbed her purse and headed for her car. Ten minutes later she showed up at the scene, which was easy to spot from several blocks away. Flames ate through the Maritime Museum as several fire units fought them back. Just like the last time, the police took over the scene blocking off all entrances to the activities. She looked for Gunnar, not that he'd want to see her or anything, but he was nowhere in sight.

She recognized one of the younger cops named Eric and headed straight to him. "What time did the fire start?"

"About a half hour ago."

She flashed her reporter ID. "Is arson suspected again?"

"Don't know yet." Eric recognized her, probably as Gunnar's new girl, not a journalist. "But Gunnar saw someone running from the scene and chased him. Took a bullet. But we got the suspect in custody."

"Who took a bullet, Gunnar or the suspect?" Worry and fear converged and rushed through her veins at the thought of Gunnar being hurt.

"Both."

The news of his being shot hit her like back draft, nearly knocking her over. "Is Gunnar okay? Where'd they take him?"

"Got shot in the shoulder. Wanted his buddy Kent to take care of it."

Lilly had been dating Gunnar for a month, and though she'd heard all about his best friend, Kent, she'd only briefly met him once when she'd interviewed Desi. Fortunately, she knew where his Urgent Care was, since it was the only medical facility in Heartlandia.

"Thanks," she said, gathering all of her wherewithal to think straight and keep moving, just before she snaked through the gathering crowd and sprinted to her car.

Ten minutes later, she rushed the entrance of the UC and ran to the reception area. "I'm looking for Gunnar Norling," she said, nearly breathless.

"We can't disclose any names of patients. State law," the full-bearded, college-aged receptionist said, looking distracted by whatever he was inputting on his work computer.

"Did a gunshot wound just come here?"

"Sorry. Can't disclose anything."

"I'm his girlfriend, damn it!"

The kid finally looked up. His gaze swept over Lilly head to waist, since she stood at the low reception counter. He thought a few seconds and then picked up the phone. "I have Sergeant Norling's girlfriend at the front desk. Can she come back?"

Oh, God, he'd just broken up with her, now she wanted special privileges to see him. Would he let her?

She folded her arms, fueled by adrenaline, nervous pangs running the length of her body as she tapped her toe.

"Okay." The receptionist put down the phone. "Dr. Larson will be right with you. Wait over there." He pointed to a secluded area by another door.

She did what she was told, fearing that Gunnar was too injured to see her, or worse yet, never wanted to see her again. Oh, God, she could barely take the anxiety zipping around her stomach, making her feel as if she might hurl.

She swallowed, and swallowed, forcing herself to shape up.

"Lilly?" A deep and soothing voice said her name from behind.

She spun around to see the huge guy, at least a foot taller than her, in a white coat, and like so many of the other men in town, a regular Nordic god.

"I'm Kent, Gunnar's best friend, remember me?"

"Yes, of course. Hi. Good to see you again. Well, not under these circumstances…" *Get a grip!* She inhaled. "Is he okay?"

"He is. Got a nasty bullet lodged in his shoulder and I don't have an adequate procedure room here to remove it. We've taken X-rays and now we're cleaning up the wound and getting him ready for transport to Astoria for surgery."

Her hand flew to her mouth, and tears pooled and overflowed onto her cheeks. "May I see him?"

Kent's lips tightened into a straight line. "I'm sorry, but he really isn't up to seeing anyone just now."

Damn, damn, damn, she'd ruined everything and Gunnar had sent his friend out to blow her off. He obviously didn't want anything to do with her. She dropped her head, not wanting Kent to see her cry. How many more people in town could she bear to see her cry?

His huge hand clasped one of her arms and he gave a gentle squeeze. "I gave him a pain shot and he's practically out to the world." He took out his prescription pad and wrote on it. "Here's the address of the hospital we're sending him to. He'll be going to surgery once he gets cleared in the ER there, but you can stick around if you'd like."

"Thank you." She took the paper, wanting to fling her arms around Dr. Larson, for giving her hope. Maybe Gunnar really didn't know she was here. Maybe he really was out cold from a pain shot. Maybe he hadn't said the most despicable words she could think of—I don't want to see her—after all.

Kent nodded, then ducked back behind the private door as an ambulance arrived in the parking lot.

She went outside and hung around in hopes of glimpsing Gunnar.

Five minutes later she got her wish. Out he rolled on the narrow gurney, eyes closed, chin slack. He was shirtless with a large dressing on his left shoulder, getting rolled toward the back of the vehicle.

She rushed to his side and took his hand, squeezed, before the paramedic could stop her. "Gunnar, it's Lilly. I'm here. I'll see you after surgery." It might have been her imagination, but she thought there was a faint squeeze in return.

The EMTs loaded him into the back of the ambulance and she stood and watched until they left the parking lot, hit the road and started the siren.

Fingers crossed, he didn't know she was here, and he hadn't banned her from the procedure room. Maybe she could mend the mess she'd made with him. There had to be some way to win back his trust.

She stood watching as the red light flashed farther and farther in the distance and the piercing sound of the siren faded.

The drive her father and mother had instilled in her since she was a child took over, and instead of following the ambulance to the hospital—since Gunnar would probably be going to surgery ASAP after clearance in the ER—she went to the newspaper to input her report first. She rationalized that she wouldn't be able to see Gunnar until recovery anyway, and the story would only take half an hour to write. This second fire story inside of one month needed to make the front page.

The instant she pressed Send on the story and attached photograph to Bjork, she got back into her car and drove to Astoria to find out about Gunnar.

She'd tell everyone at the hospital she was his girlfriend, and since he'd be unconscious, they'd have to believe her.

Nothing would stop her from being by his side when he came to.

The tall, thin blonde named Elke Norling called all the shots at the small Astoria hospital. A fierce sister, taking charge, she questioned Lilly the newspaper reporter like a prison guard in the surgery waiting room.

"How do I know you're not only here to get a story?" Her features reminded Lilly of a young Meryl Streep with a pointy nose sitting crooked on her face.

"I've been dating Gunnar for a month now."

"He's never mentioned you to me."

That sort of said it all, didn't it? He'd never told his only living family member about her. Her earlier optimism from Kent sank to the pit of her stomach like a bag of sand.

A racket ensued behind her. She turned to find a middle-aged man, dressed all in black including a hoodie, hand-cuffed to a gurney, getting rolled into the ER. His leg was bandaged and it appeared he hadn't been given the pain relief that Gunnar had when she'd seen him.

Two policemen followed the emergency medical technicians pushing him on the gurney to the emergency department.

The wild-eyed man looked right at Lilly. Recognition flashed through his eyes. "Her. I want to talk to her."

One of the policemen accompanying him she'd met at the last fire, and he noticed her. "Why do you want to talk to her? Do you even know who she is?"

True, her picture ran beside all of her stories in the paper, and Heartlandia wasn't exactly running over with Asians, but did anyone really know who she was?

"Sure. She's the lady from the *Herald*." There he went again, staring her down like a wounded feral animal with a plan. "I want to talk to you."

The look creeped her out.

"You're going to see a doctor first," the wise cop said.

A young head nurse met them at the ER entrance. Wearing an unearthly color of green scrubs, she stopped them. "I'm sorry, but we're out of rooms. Put him over there for now." She pointed to a long hallway at the back of the hospital entrance. One other gurney complete with patient was already parked along the wall. "We'll have to do the intake from there."

Lilly turned her attention back to Elke, who hadn't moved, pleading with her eyes. "I'm in love with your brother. He doesn't know it because I haven't told him yet." Elke seemed to stare into her soul, and Lilly stood with her head tall letting her. She made a snap decision to confess. "He broke up with me tonight." She connected with Elke's gaze, hoping with every breath the woman could understand the situation, and that she'd believe her. "You've got to let me see him, though. Please."

Something had softened in Elke's eyes. Maybe she did believe Lilly. She nodded. "Once he's out of recovery and assigned to a room, I'll make sure your name is on the list of visitors."

Without a thought, Lilly dived for Elke and hugged her. "Oh, thank you. Thank you. I've got to straighten things out with him."

Another ER nurse popped her head out the door, apparently searching for Elke. Then she found her. "Your brother's on his way to surgery now. It will be a few hours. Why don't you go get some coffee or something?"

Elke nodded. She looked at Lilly. "Come with?"

"Sure."

The only way to the hospital cafeteria was down the long hallway. Lilly and Elke walked past the man on the gurney. "I need to talk to you. You need to hear my story. I know things!"

She tried to ignore him, but couldn't. She stopped in her tracks. "About what?"

"Heartlandia's all a big lie. I have proof."

Was the guy off his psych meds? What the hell was he talking about? But why did it seem to tie in with the recent secret meetings and the "glitch in the town records" they needed to iron out?

And why was there a startled expression on Elke's face? "I know that man. He's been attending extension classes at the college. He's never been in any trouble or anything that I know of, but we do get our share of kooks at school."

Lilly's hard-earned "better judgment" took over and she ignored the fanatical patient and continued on with Elke for some coffee.

* * *

Two hours later, head slack against the chair in the waiting room, someone tapped Lilly's shoulder. It was that young ER nurse again. She'd come all the way upstairs to the surgical waiting room. "Roald Lindstrom asked to talk to you rather than call a lawyer. He's in the ER. Do you want to come?"

Lilly shook her head to wake up. The man on the gurney with the crazy accusations about Heartlandia? "The guy with the leg wound?"

The nursed tipped her head. "Said he might not get the chance again. Wanted to talk to you instead of a lawyer."

Lilly glanced at Elke sitting quietly and peacefully next to her.

"Go if you want to," Elke said. "I'll text you the instant I get any word."

Lilly gave Elke her cell phone number, then grabbing her bottled water, followed the nurse into the elevator and headed for the ER and the crazy alleged arsonist with a story to tell.

Lilly was officially introduced to Roald Lindstrom while he was under custody with the police, and under the influence of a sedative. He'd calmed down since the last time she'd seen him. His beady blue eyes gave her the willies, so she concentrated on his receding mousy-brown hairline instead.

Evidently the gunshot had hit the side of his thigh and had been a clean in-and-out wound. The nurse said they'd only used a local anesthetic for the wound care, but had given him something to calm him. Now he was all bandaged up and ready for transport back to jail. They were waiting for an available ambulance, since the fire had kept all units tied up most of the night.

A police guard sat just outside the ER cubicle, and seeing that Roald was still handcuffed to the gurney, she felt okay going in alone. The guard checked her purse, made her leave the bottled water with him and did a halfhearted frisking before she could enter. When she entered the cubicle, she kept a safe distance from the prisoner.

"You wanted to talk to me?"

"You need to know some things."

"About?"

"Our bogus town history. Heartlandia, my ass."

"Why don't you tell me a little bit about yourself first?" Lilly wanted to know whether or not this guy was totally nuts or if he might actually have some insight into what was going on at city hall. From the looks of him, she suspected it would be somewhere in between.

"I've lived here all my life. My people go back to the beginning."

"I mean, what do you do? What is your job?"

"I'm currently unemployed. Used to work at the fishery, but they closed up a couple years back, so I took early retirement."

This was a guy with a grudge. She wondered if he was out to sue the city, or was money even what he was after? Then why burn down a building and go to jail? Nothing made sense with this one.

"I heard you're attending classes at the college," she said.

"Yeah. I'm an adult student in the genealogy extension course. That's how I discovered all the right places to look for information." He quirked one shaggy, gray-tinged brow. "Did you know the Maritime Museum was the original immigration holding area for the state?"

She shook her head wondering what that had to do with him burning down the building, and while talking to her, would he also implicate himself in the microbrewery fire? This guy needed representation not a newspaper reporter. "Are you sure you don't want a lawyer?"

"I want you to tell this story. You need to write it. Everyone thinks Heartlandia is the perfect little town, well, it's all a lie. One of my distant relatives got shanghaied from a bar that used to be where the microbrewery was."

Oh, gosh, the guy was as good as confessing he'd pulled that job, too.

Roald kept his voice down, so the guard would have to strain his ears to hear the story. Did she want to be in the middle or have information like this on her shoulders while protecting the confidentiality of her source? And wouldn't everyone know who it was, since they were in a public place, and the guy was arrested? He really should have called a lawyer.

"Do you know what shanghaied means?" He broke into her thoughts.

"Yes." She'd heard that term in regards to Heartlandia before, but more in a fanciful way, more like an urban legend from Mr. Lincoln at his grill. Now this guy was insisting it was true.

"My relative had come through immigration not more than two weeks earlier. See, the pirates who ruled this place, not those peaceful fisherman and Indians like everyone yaps on about, found their marks in the holding area. They all worked for the captain who discovered the inlet here. They controlled everything and looked for young men with muscles. Then they'd crimp them by getting them drunk, so drunk they didn't know they were getting sent out to sea. Work them half to death and not give a damn."

So Roald was exacting revenge for his relative three centuries later? Was the ancient building that housed the microbrewery the place where his relative had been shanghaied? Her head was twirling with the wacky information. Pirates?

Where had this dark past come from? Certainly this wasn't the history she'd read about Heartlandia.

Under different circumstances Lilly would be salivating to research and run with a story like this, but her conscience and newfound fondness for the Heartlandia people, and loving one over-bossy resident in particular, sobered her. Too many things needed to be checked out first. This wild story could be a figment of the arsonist's twisted imagination.

She should have asked the ER nurse if the guy had been given a psych evaluation before agreeing to hear him out. Of course, since Elke confirmed they had genealogy classes at the college, Lilly could ask what the source of their information was. If anyone would know, a historian like Elke would.

Wasn't it interesting that this new information came on top of the secret meetings at city hall, meetings that were important enough for Gunnar to break up with her over?

Snap! Elke had been attending those meetings, too. She'd seen her with her own eyes when she'd spied on Gunnar.

A police officer entered the room with an ambulance technician and broke up her powwow with Roald the avenger. Thank goodness!

"You've got to believe me," he pleaded as the officer asked her to leave when he unlocked the handcuffs.

"I'll look into your story, Mr. Lindstrom." Though unlike her usual self, she felt completely halfhearted about the promise.

Without trying she'd stumbled upon the meatiest information of her career—provided it was true. Could those secret meetings be about pirates? Then where did those aerial views at Gunnar's house come in? They were of the sacred burial ground. How did one have anything to do with the other? That was the question of the day.

This could be the huge story she'd been hoping for! This could seal her reputation as a top-notch journalist. This story, if she could parse it out, and if it was true, could even get national coverage or go viral on the internet.

Sleepy Little Oregon Town Founded by Pirates. Or better yet, Ancient Revenge!

It could be her ticket to stardom. Damn it. Her father had taken over her conscience again.

Her stomach was tied in a knot and she felt a little sick at the thought. *You don't have to be the person your dad tried to make you.* Was she so success-oriented and hardhearted that she'd betray Gunnar while he was injured and in the hospital, and ruin any chance of ever getting back together with him? What about being in love with him? Was success really all about the goal and doing anything to achieve it? Just how big a price was she willing to pay for recognition?

Her parents may have raised her to be this way, but after meeting Gunnar, did she really want to hold on to the tail of a dragon and miss out on the important things in life, like the love of a good man?

She wasn't sure how she'd get to the bottom of this potential news-breaking story, but it was her duty as a journalist, and she knew she'd start by talking to Elke.

Not tonight, though. Nope.

Tonight was all about Gunnar. The man she loved.

After Lilly stepped out of the patient room, she strode back to the elevator. Her head still spun from the crazy story, but her mind immediately compartmentalized the information. Thinking only of Gunnar, his surgery and, more importantly, his recovery, she rushed back to see him. Hopefully, this time he'd want to see her, too.

Chapter Thirteen

Elke was exactly where Lilly had left her in the waiting room. She sat quietly reading a decade-old magazine from a nearby table piled high with them. The blonde woman glanced up and smiled. "Anything interesting?"

Lilly inhaled and raised her brows. "You wouldn't believe what that guy told me."

"Try me." Elke glanced at her watch—it had only been a couple of hours since Gunnar had been taken to surgery. "We've got time."

"You said he went to Heartlandia CC, right?"

"Yes."

"Well, according to him that genealogy extension class your school offers gave him the key to finding out a lot more than he expected." Lilly took out her bottled water and took a sip. "Have you ever heard about people getting shanghaied here in Heartlandia?"

Elke went quiet briefly, as though planning what to say. "Oh, we've got a rich supply of seafaring stories to pass along to tourists, if that's what they're after. They're more like urban legends than truth, though."

"So you think this guy's story is off base."

"Could be."

Lilly wasn't sure if Elke would lie straight-faced to her or if she was the sane person who Lilly should believe, rather than the whack-job arsonist. She'd always prided herself on being a solid judge of character, and her gut told her Elke was the one to trust. But those darn secret meetings stirred up all kinds of doubt about who she could believe or why.

Lilly shuddered and rubbed her arms.

"You okay?" Elke asked.

"I hate hospitals."

"Most people do."

"My dad wanted me to be a surgeon. I was afraid if I ever set foot in one he'd lock me inside and never let me out. Made for quite a struggle when I needed my tonsils out at twelve." Lilly gave a doleful laugh and was surprised when Elke reached over to hug her.

The phone in the surgery waiting room wall rang and Elke jumped to answer it. Her eyes widened and over-flowed with relief as she listened to the person on the other end. She hung up. "He's out of surgery. Everything went great, and I can see him as soon as they get him settled in recovery."

What about me?

Elke must have read the disappointment on Lilly's face. "After I see him, I'll see if you can go in for a quick visit, too. Okay?"

Lilly grabbed her forearm and squeezed. "Thank you so much." Maybe the anesthesia would make him forget they'd broken up just hours earlier. A girl could always hope. "I'm not just his fly-by-night girlfriend, you know."

"You're not." Elke's kind expression and confident words reassured Lilly, even though technically she wasn't

Gunnar's girlfriend *at all* anymore. At least until she could change things.

"He's a great guy, and maybe a little hotheaded when it comes to Heartlandia." Lilly leveled a gaze at Elke. "You may as well know that he thought I was snooping when I wasn't. Not on purpose anyway. I swear on a stack of Bibles I wasn't."

"Didn't you write that article mentioning how he may have become a policeman to make up for our father being a criminal?"

"I did." Lilly winced, now realizing firsthand the implications her story had had, the very ones Gunnar was so upset about.

"And the story about Mayor Rask?"

"Yes, but…"

"He was probably ticked off about that, too," Elke said.

"Tell me about it. He broke up with me over it!" That wasn't the whole reason, but for the sake of conversation, she'd leave trust out of it for now.

But that was only half of her problem. She'd let herself fall in love with him. He could always make her laugh, and he was a great match of wits with her. He'd opened up a whole new world showing her around Heartlandia and introducing her to the inhabitants. He made her feel protected and cherished, and above all accepted for who she was—such a foreign feeling. And their lovemaking was like nothing she'd ever experienced. The list went on and on.

The hole in Lilly's chest widened as she thought about actually losing Gunnar because of her mistakes. It wouldn't be fair. Her first blunder was before she'd completely fallen for him. Then the mix-up about the aerial views of the sacred burial ground was completely unintentional.

If he loved her he'd believe her. She'd thought that mailing tube had held the blueprints for the next phase of his house, that's all. That was the honest-to-God truth, yet she'd never managed to convince him. His natural instinct to mistrust people until proven otherwise had driven a wedge between them. Soon enough she'd pushed everything over the ledge. She'd run the article on Mayor Rask, heavily hinting at town secrets.

She'd ruined everything—broken his trust.

Since the scene in the restaurant, she'd had time to calm down and come to her senses. Gunnar had driven home some very important points. Success at all cost was a loser idea. *Gee, thanks, Mom and Dad.*

The big question was, could Gunnar think things through and decide what they had was worth keeping?

Of course not! He didn't have time! He'd had to rush off to a fire and he'd gotten shot.

Every thought must have played across her face because she snapped out of it and noticed Elke's empathetic expression. Lilly decided to lay it all out there.

"I love your brother, and I kind of thought he'd fallen for me, too. That is until this afternoon when he read me the riot act and walked off."

"He has a way of flying off the handle. Basically, he likes to be in control, has ever since our father left. He's got a lot of pride, too." Elke smiled. "Give him some time. If I know my brother, falling in love would mean he'd lost control of his heart. The last thing he ever wants to be is out of control. He'd be primed for finding ways to avoid it." The smile changed to a sad downward turn of her lips. "You picked a guy who prefers to be married to his job, trusts only himself and insists on testing people all the time, so it won't be easy, but something tells me, with your determination, you'll work this out."

The phone rang again, and in a flash, Elke had answered

it. "Okay. Thanks." She turned. "I can go see him now. Give me a few minutes to make sure he's okay, then I'll ask them to let you in."

"Thanks."

Lilly watched Gunnar's sister disappear behind a door operated by pressing a metal plate on the wall. Elke had decided Lilly was determined enough to make things right again. She only hoped Elke was right. But at the moment, the last thing she felt was determined. Truth was, she felt defeated and hated every second of not being in charge of her life the way her parents had taught her to be. She'd have to throw everything she ever knew out the window in order to regain his trust.

She and Gunnar weren't exactly a match made in heaven, with his lack of trust in her and her old habits tripping her up at every turn, yet she'd finally found a guy to be crazy about. Too bad he'd dropped her on circumstantial evidence.

Fifteen minutes later Elke reappeared looking relieved. "He's doing great. Still pretty out of it from the drugs, but he's coming around. They said you can see him for five minutes." She pointed to the double doors she'd just come through. "Push that plate and once you're inside, he's in recovery bed four."

"Thanks." After a quick squeezing of each other's hands, Lilly set out to see Gunnar, her heart tap-dancing inside her chest. What if he kicked her out? How could she save face after that?

The thought was too painful to consider. She trudged into the recovery room pasting false confidence onto her face.

Gunnar nearly took up the entire hospital bed. His eyes were closed and a huge white dressing covered most of his chest. His left arm was in a black sling. A little round bulb hung from the middle of the bandages. It was some kind of drain, and it was half-full of bright red blood already. His blood. Her heart squeezed.

An IV machine with several plastic bags in varying sizes attached took up one side of the bed, and assorted medical equipment filled most of the rest of the space on the other side. The sight of him looking so vulnerable made her dizzy. She found a wheelchair nearby and pushed it forward to sit on. But she couldn't sit and wait for him to notice her. She only had five minutes. She'd hoped to look into his eyes. To see if he truly hated her or if there was a chance he could forgive her. Since he was under the influence, maybe his true feelings would show.

She ran her hand down his forearm, the side without the IV. His thumb twitched.

He was okay, and the knowledge filled her heart with gladness. She exhaled her relief, not realizing until then she'd been holding her breath. His safety and health were all that mattered right this moment. She studied him with a huge bubble of love welling in her chest.

One of his eyes cracked open. It took a moment for him to focus on her.

"Lilly?"

"Yes. I'm here."

He went silent again for a few moments. "I thought we broke up." His voice was raspy from surgery and whatever they must have shoved down his throat to help him breathe.

She couldn't let on how shook-up she was, so she kept face. "That's your side of the story."

A tiny smile stretched his lips. "Just like Wolverine."

"What do you mean?"

"He won't go away."

She'd seen the way Gunnar adored his huge cat. This hard-ass facade was just an act. "I'm not going to go away, either, until you forgive me." She took and squeezed his hand. He gently squeezed back.

He inhaled deeply as if unable to fight off sleep. "We'll see about that," he mumbled and finally gave in to the sedation.

At least she knew he'd made it through surgery. He was all right. And hopefully he'd remember she'd been here by his side.

"I'll take care of Wolverine. Don't worry," she said, then let go of his hand leaving him to sleep.

She nodded her thanks to the nurse and left the recovery room, finding Elke right where she'd left her.

"I'm going to go to Gunnar's house and feed Wolverine."

"Thanks. I'm staying here until they transfer him to his room. I'll text you the number."

"Great. Thanks."

Lilly approached Elke, she stood, and they hugged, like new friends. Two people who both cared for the same man. One as a blood relative, the other as a crazy mixed-up blabbermouthed lover.

Riding down the elevator, Lilly felt trembly. Her world had been knocked on its head tonight. Though, having Elke put things in perspective on the Gunnar side of the equation gave Lilly a flicker of hope. His being married to the job didn't have nearly the benefits of a living, breathing warm body. Surely he knew that.

It wouldn't be easy to get a guy like him to forgive her, especially if he was looking for ways to avoid getting attached to anything outside of work, but she wouldn't give up. She'd find a way to get back into his good graces no matter what it took. There had to be a way to make Gunnar trust her again.

Right now she'd start by taking care of his cat.

* * *

Gunnar woke to sharp, stabbing pain in his shoulder. It took him a moment to realize he was in the hospital. He nearly knocked over a Styrofoam cup of ice reaching for the bedside call button for the nurse so he could get some relief. He'd had crazy dreams all night. Starting with visions of fire and chasing after someone. He remembered getting shot, stun-gun-level pain and feeling helpless, a feeling he hated more than anything. Then the smell of a hospital, and clattering noise, people talking over him as if he wasn't there.

His sister's face came into view, her voice sounding as if she were under water.

And he'd seen Lilly, or maybe he'd only imagined it. Yeah, it was probably a dream. She'd stood beside him and said something sassy. Wasn't that just like her, too? But having her near had settled him down, seeing her face warming his aching chest.

He shook his head, still trying to fully wake up. Why had Wolverine come into his thoughts? Oh, yeah, someone needed to feed him.

He massaged his temples with his one good hand. Ah, right. Lilly would. Feed Wolverine. Yeah.

But he'd broken up with her. She'd gone over the line printing that information about the meetings, even though Mayor Rask said she could, and he couldn't trust her. Wasn't trust the most basic element for any successful relationship?

So why did he trust her to feed his cat?

The nurse appeared and he was grateful to be distracted from his jumbled-up thoughts. "What day is it?"

"Friday."

He'd lost a day. "I need something for pain."

"Sure. I'll be right back."

Gunnar opened and closed his left hand, tried to bend his elbow just to make sure he could still use it, but the sling prevented him. When he tried to lift his entire arm, sling and all, he let out an involuntary groan.

A doctor who looked like a teenager appeared. "Sergeant Norling? How're you feeling today?"

"I could be a lot better, thanks."

"You're a lucky man. The bullet lodged in the lateral pectoralis major muscle and went through the scapularis."

"Whoa, whoa, Doc, come again?"

"Bottom line, we were able to remove the bullet and all of the fragments in your left outer shoulder. However, the impact of the shot did fracture your clavicle. You'll need to wear a sling for several weeks."

"So my shoulder socket's okay?"

"Amazingly, yes. I'll see about having you released for home by this afternoon."

"I'm in a lot of pain."

"That's to be expected, and we'll send you home with pain relief."

Kent entered the room and Gunnar's spirits immediately lifted. "Hey, man."

"How're you doing?"

"I could be better. Doc, this is my best friend, Dr. Kent Larson."

"Nice to meet you."

"Can you tell him what you just told me?"

He repeated the information for Kent then, all business and no doubt with a long list of patients yet to see, the junior-aged doctor prepared to leave. "I'll need to see you back in a week for a wound check and follow-up X-rays."

"Can I follow up with my friend here? His office is in Heartlandia."

"I run the Urgent Care there."

The kid curled his lower lip, looking at Kent and thinking. "I don't see why not," Dr. Too-young said. "You'll need to do another X-ray to see how the bone is healing, though."

"I can do that, we have radiology equipment at my Urgent Care, too," Kent said with maybe a hint of insult. It wasn't as if he ran a little country clinic in the middle of nowhere. Gunnar knew Kent worked hard at having the best and newest of everything, nearly going into debt to do it on more than one occasion.

"I'll be glad to consult with you over the phone when you're ready," Dr. Kid said.

"Great. Nice to meet you, Doctor." Kent shook the fresh-faced doctor's hand and went immediately to Gunnar's bedside. "So you made it."

"I did. Damn, I don't ever want to be shot again."

Kent smiled. "I don't blame you." Since he'd been dating Desdemona he'd grown a stylish beard, and Gunnar still needed to get used to it.

"What about the turd who shot me?"

"He's in custody. From what I hear, he's a whack-job."

"Attempting to kill an officer of the law, and arson, he'll be put away for the rest of his life."

Kent nodded solemnly.

After a few moments of silence, Gunnar realized how worried his friend had been about him—why else would he show up here on a Friday morning when he probably had a full clinic back home? Gunnar decided to change the topic from near-death experiences. "So, how are the wedding plans coming along?"

Kent's face brightened. "I wanted to talk to you about that. You'll be my best man, right?"

"Damn straight, I will." Gunnar tried to sit up more and tugged on his shoulder wound. "Ouch."

Kent rushed to help him adjust his position. "Hey, take it easy. You're going to need a lot of help when you get home. Maybe you should go to Elke's."

"Yeah, maybe for a few days." Gunnar's mind quickly drifted to Lilly, wondering if it was okay to ask an ex-girlfriend to help out.

"I'm going to need you in tip-top shape to be my best man."

"You name the day and place and I'll be there."

The happiness he read in his friend's eyes sent a sudden pang to his chest. Lately he'd been walking around looking that happy, too, all because of Lilly.

"How come you and Lilly never doubled with Desi and me?"

"Busy schedules. My job. Never had time." Gunnar had to stop for a second and think why Kent would bring up Lilly this morning. Oh, right, she'd shown up at the Urgent Care last night wanting to see him. Truth was he had been keeping Lilly all to himself instead of sharing her with his friends. The timing just never seemed right to make plans, but he really just wanted what little time they had together to be all his. Right now he didn't have the heart or inclination to explain they'd broken up.

"When you get better, we'll all have to go to *husmanskost* for a midnight supper."

"Deal." Gunnar nodded, even though his whirlwind love affair with Lilly might already be over before it had hardly gotten started.

Thinking about Lilly sent him off in all kinds of directions.

Yeah, she was aggravating and contrary and really nosy, but she was also someone he could respect on a professional level. She'd achieved a lot on her own and wasn't waiting around for some man to make her life complete.

She was reaching for her dreams. The only problem was sometimes she needed someone to reel her in when she went overboard. He'd be perfect for the job, too.

Except he couldn't completely trust her. How could he love her if he didn't trust her? Round and round his thoughts went.

"Hey, where'd you go?" Kent said.

"Aw, sorry. I'm still groggy."

The nurse entered the room with a syringe and asked Kent to step aside. Gunnar wanted him to do a favor, and called out from behind the closed bedside curtain. "Will you let Elke know I'll be going home this afternoon?"

"Sure. In fact, I was planning to stick around and drive you to her house."

So, he'd left his own clinic to be by Gunnar's side, but that was the kind of friendship they had. Solid. Always there for each other.

The nurse positioned Gunnar on his right side, opened the back of his hospital gown and rubbed his hip with something cold.

Gunnar stayed deep in his thoughts to avoid what he knew was coming. Why had he kept this love affair mostly to himself?

Was it because he didn't want her thrown in with the list of names, faces and figures he'd serially dated over the past several years? Was it because she was special and he wanted to make sure the feeling was mutual before they spent more time with his best friend?

Was it because he loved her?

"Ouch!" Medicine delivered.

Gunnar clinched his jaw, absorbing the blast of pain, thinking he'd just gotten a kick in the butt.

So if she was so damn special, why had he broken up with the best thing to ever happen to him?

Because someone needed to teach her there was a line, even in journalism, that a person instinctively knew not to cross.

The lady needed some fine-tuning, and now with his gunshot wound, he wouldn't have the time or opportunity to help her out.

But the thought of losing her completely felt as lousy as his aching bum shoulder.

Lilly tapped on Elke's front door after work Friday evening. Elke smiled when she saw her, but the expression changed to disappointment. "Oh, too bad, Gunnar just went to sleep."

Like osmosis, Elke's disappointment shifted to Lilly. "I should have called first, but I was afraid he'd refuse to see me if he knew I was coming."

Elke invited Lilly inside her small but comfortable home. "It's been a rough day for him. I think just about everyone from Heartlandia Police Department stopped by at one point or another. But I think we finally caught up on the pain, so that's a start."

Gunnar had once told Lilly that his sister had lived with his mother in their family home until she'd died a few years back. Being in his childhood home gave Lilly the oddest sensation, as if she could feel his entire history here. Humble beginnings begetting big dreams of being a police officer, of becoming a guardian for his city—and she knew without a doubt that was how he felt about the job.

Married to it. That's what Elke had said.

Wondering if there was any room left for her in his heart, or if she'd never be anything but second place, Lilly followed Elke into the kitchen.

"Let me make some tea."

"You've had a long day, too, so no need. I just basically wanted to know how he was doing."

A mischievous glint flickered in Elke's eyes. "Well, we've had some time to talk, and since he is basically under the influence with the pain meds, he's more talkative than usual."

That got Lilly's attention. She sat on the edge of a kitchen chair, waiting to hear more. "And?"

"My brother isn't simply suffering from a shoulder wound. Apparently he's also got a broken heart."

"What?"

"He'd kill me if he knew I was blabbing my mouth, but the poor guy went on and on about how you were the best thing he'd ever met, how well matched you were for each other. He sounded just like a drunk at a bar moaning over his ex. Then he said the strangest thing, he said he had to break up with you for your own good."

"What?" Wow, even in sickness and on drugs the guy was full of himself. Her usual impulse to play tit for tat stayed at bay. Truth was, he had a point. In his world she'd betrayed him. In hers, she'd done her reporter's duty. Somewhere in between there was the bigger pill to swallow—trust. She'd betrayed his trust.

"Elke!" a raspy and obviously weak voice came from the back room.

"Yes, Gunnar?"

"I need some water."

"May I bring it?" Lilly asked.

"Sure." Elke took a plastic glass from the cupboard and filled it with water from the refrigerator then handed her the chilled glass. The look of assurance in Gunnar's younger sister's eyes gave Lilly the courage she needed to take that glass and walk through that bedroom door.

The room was dark, but a window in the corner was

opened wide enough to keep the air fresh and circulating. Even ill in bed, Gunnar struck an imposing figure.

"Here you go," she said in a hushed voice, handing him the glass.

He shifted his head on the pillow to get a better look. "It's you." He took the water and drank a big gulp.

"Mind if I sit with you for a while?"

"I won't be much company. I'm pretty much doped up."

"We don't need to talk."

After a couple of moments' hesitation he set the cup on the bedside table, almost missing. Lilly rushed to prevent the glass from falling off.

"Oh, yes, we do need to talk," he said. "But not now. My head is spinning."

She took his hand and sat in the cushioned chair beside the bed, a chair that seemed like something his mother may have sat on once upon a time. He let her hold his hand, even ran his thumb over her fingers a few times. They sat like that for several minutes, not uttering a word, just being there, together. Then she felt him relax and his breathing went even. He was asleep.

A most precious feeling curled up inside her. Love. Not just infatuation or sexual chemistry, but real love, the kind she had for her grandmother, deep and abiding. The kind that could grow and weather the rough patches in life. Like the one they were in right now.

Lilly wanted to share everything she had with a man who couldn't trust her. There had to be a way to earn that back.

Thinking of Gunnar and love and how she cared for him in the same way she held a special place for her grandmother, a bright idea popped into her head. Sobo would know how to make things right again, she always did.

Lilly placed Gunnar's limp hand softly on his stomach

and bent to kiss his brow. His nose twitched in response. She took an extra moment to study him while he slept now that her eyes had adjusted to the dark. Strong features, proud jaw, short out-of-control hair that promised to be thick and wavy if he ever let it grow out. Eyelashes thick like a child's. Warmth drizzled through her chest. She loved this guy, and maybe he didn't know it yet, but they *were* going to be together.

All Lilly needed was some advice from her sobo so everything could get sorted out.

Chapter Fourteen

"You must do good, Lilly-chan. Show him," Sobo said

"But I'm afraid I've already ruined his trust in me." Lilly sat curled up on her overstuffed lounger in the small guesthouse living room talking to her grandmother on the phone, gazing out the window onto the night-lighted swimming pool. It had been a week since she'd last seen him, choosing to let him heal in peace at his sister's house, all the while feeding Wolverine for him.

"If you respect yourself, you'll find a way."

Lilly wanted Gunnar's respect, yet all her life her sobo had taught her that self-respect was the most important respect of all. She had a point.

"Remember the way of *chanoyu—wa, kei, sei, jaku*."

Having been schooled in the traditional tea ceremony, Lilly understood when her grandmother suggested the way of tea. *Wa*—harmony, *kei*—respect, *sei*—purity, *jaku*—tranquility. But what was Sobo getting at?

"Show him humility and your imperfection with a tea ceremony. Show him your desire for respect and to be honorable. If he loves you, he will forgive you."

How could her grandmother know this, and how could a traditional Japanese tea ceremony mend her broken relationship with Gunnar?

"I'll think about it," Lilly said.

"Thinking is waste of time. Do."

With that, they said their goodbyes and Lilly made herself some herbal tea, nothing like the tea she'd need for a real tea ceremony. And speaking of tea, where in the world could she find an authentic Japanese tea set or *matcha*, the ground green tea powder, in a Scandinavian town like Heartlandia anyway?

Maybe in Portland? She picked up her cell phone again and used her voice to request information. Within seconds the phone brought up the Portland Japanese Garden, including directions on how to get there. Surely, she'd find what she needed at the gift shop there.

It was a crazy idea, and her heart fluttered even considering it. Could her grandmother be right or would this wind up being the most humiliating moment of her life? She went to bed, unable to sleep realizing she could have lost Gunnar if that gunshot had been just a little lower. The thought sent fear quaking through her. Her eyes stung and soon moisture brimmed, slipping out the corners and coursing toward her ears. He was alive and she still had a chance of getting him back.

They needed to wipe the slate clean, then start over. He'd argued that she should use discretion when publishing her stories. She felt it was her duty to report everything of interest for her paper. He made a good point, not everything belonged in the news, and she didn't know the half of the secret meetings story. There was probably a very good reason why a whole committee of people who loved and lived in Heartlandia wouldn't want their news pasted across the headlines. Maybe it was for the best for now.

Being tenacious wasn't always the answer, and trusting Gunnar about keeping the story quiet didn't diminish her power as a reporter. It just made her levelheaded, willing to compromise, a wiser person, not a news-at-all-cost hothead. Gunnar was right, it was time to mature in both her professional and personal lives. If she didn't she'd lose him. She couldn't lose him.

She rolled onto her side and practiced the movements for the tea ceremony in her mind, remembering every step her grandmother had once taught her, striving to be precise yet simple in every detail. She'd need a scroll to hang with the right thoughts written on it, and she remembered the proper placement and cleaning of the utensils she'd use. Soon, big thoughts of how to prove her love to Gunnar formed in her brain. In fact, this guest cottage was the perfect setting for working the miracles she needed in order to win him back.

The way of tea or *chanoyu* had never been more significant in her life. Now, if she could only shut off her mind so she could get some sleep because she had a big day tomorrow.

The next morning, being Saturday, she was tired but planned her trip to Portland, anyway. First she had another idea up her sleeve.

Lilly drove to Gunnar's house, and Wolverine, being a smart cat, had already figured out what her showing up meant. Food! But she had bigger plans for him today, plans that would hopefully also put a smile on Gunnar's face.

"Here kitty, kitty, kitty..." she cooed, food in one hand, a borrowed dog leash from Leif's collection in the other. All she had to do was click it to the cat's collar and drag him to her car for a field trip to see his owner.

Wrong! That nearly thirty-pound cat wanted nothing

to do with her or the leash, and he was a lot quicker than she'd expected. She lunged and he ran farther away, ignoring the food and distrusting her.

Good thing she had plan B.

Lilly trudged back to the car and found the can of tuna, then depending on his hunger, popped the top open and set it on the passenger seat of her two-door car. No matter how long it took, she'd get Wolverine inside and bring him to Gunnar for a visit. She knew how attached they were to each other, whether the big guy would admit it or not.

Lilly moved to the front bumper and leaned against the hood of the car, the passenger door left open, folded her arms and prepared to wait things out. Wolverine evidently had a weakness for smelly tuna. He ventured closer to her car, and she acted like she didn't notice or care. A couple minutes later, with Lilly pretending to be a statue, the cat got up on his back legs and put one paw on the seat where the opened can rested. She held her breath and slowly slid to a squat, then peeked around the front bumper. He must have jumped inside the car. Yes! She crawled as quietly as she could, praying the cat would remain distracted with the tuna, which he did, then she slammed the door closed. Rushing around to the driver's side she saw her fatal flaw.

Her window was down!

She sprinted to get there before Wolverine could jump out.

His big old face and front paws were halfway out, and though she feared being scratched, she used her best basketball defense pose to stop him. He meowed his thoughts about being trapped in her car, and growled his discontent as she pushed him back toward the passenger seat. His ears were back and he swatted her hand but his claws, in contrast to his given name, weren't out.

He was one scary mass of gray fur with furious eyes, but she held firm.

Lilly sucked in her gut and managed to slide inside a six-inch door opening, figuring he was too fat to make it through. Wolverine looked as if he wanted to eat her face off, but she stared straight ahead, started the engine and closed the window, then drove off with the cat meowing and walking over her as if she was a pile of laundry. Other than a couple times when he perched on the dashboard and completely blocked her view out the windshield, she managed to make it to Elke's house in ten minutes without further incident.

"Nice boy. Good kitty," she repeated over and over as she tried once again to put Wolverine on the dog leash. Since he had nowhere to run, she wrestled with him inside the car for a few minutes, but he was a slippery guy. Then she offered him a tasty morsel of the leftover tuna to distract him. Success!

She opened her door and just before dragging Wolverine out of the car, he backed up and with a quivering tail sprayed her driver's seat, leaving his mark. That would show her for messing with a Maine Coon cat.

She huffed out a breath, spitting more than a few cat hairs out in the process, and dragged the belligerent cat to Elke's front door. Being that it was a lovely late-summer day, she only had to call through the screen door.

"Elke? Can you let me in?"

Surprising her, Gunnar appeared with bed hair, arm in that black sling, shirtless and wearing gray sweatpants. It was probably too hard to tackle putting on a shirt under the circumstances with the sling and all... She dragged her gaze away from his chest. "What's up?" he asked just before noticing his loud protesting cat at the end of the leash.

Not exactly the greeting she'd hoped for, but under the circumstances...

"I thought you might like some company?" Had she done the right thing? Or was she completely out of her mind?

He opened the screen door, his disbelieving expression nailing her, then shifting toward his cat. He shook his head and his features smoothed out until a smile stretched across his face. "You've got to be kidding me." He squatted and petted his cat, who'd recognized his owner and exchanged his griping for walking back and forth so Gunnar could pet him, then rubbing against his legs. "Hey, buddy, I missed you. Were you worried about me?"

So Lilly hadn't been totally off her rocker with this bright idea after all.

Gunnar shifted his gaze up toward her and bowled her over with his grin. "Thanks. This was really thoughtful of you."

She wanted to blurt out, *Does this mean you forgive me?* but checked herself. "No problem."

He stood, she handed him the leash, and the cat followed him inside. "Do you want to come in?"

Yes, of course she did. She wanted to beg him to give her a second chance and spend the day with him, and help him in any way she could. Instinct told her to take it slow, to keep her distance, let him wonder what was going on since he broke up with her.

"Actually, I have to take a trip into Portland today. Is there anything you need before I go?"

"Elke's got everything under control, thanks. I'll text her and tell her to buy some cat food."

"Okay, good. You feeling any better?"

"Still in a lot of pain, but I'm getting by."

Though wanting to throw her arms around him and

take care of him and love him with all of her might, she kept her distance. "Well, don't push yourself. Take it easy for a few days, okay?"

He looked surprised, and maybe a little disappointed that she wasn't sticking around, and that boosted her confidence a little. Without giving it a thought, Lilly went up on her tiptoes and kissed Gunnar's cheek. "May I call you later?"

"Sure." He looked a little bewildered, but she could tell he liked it.

She could have sworn he wanted to reach for her and give her a proper kiss, but she didn't give him a chance. Elated with hope, her mind spinning, she turned and walked away, getting into her tuna-smelly car, and sat. Eew! Right in the stinky urine spot Wolverine had marked on her leather upholstery.

Ugh. Now she'd have to go home and change clothes and clean her car before she drove to Portland.

She pasted a smile on her face, though the cat's sticky gift gave her the heebie-jeebies, waved at Gunnar, who still filled up the door frame, and drove off as if she did this sort of thing—kidnapping cats and delivering them to their owners—every day.

The good news was, he hadn't thrown her out.

Gunnar took the clean shirt Elke handed him and let her help him gingerly put his arm through the sleeve without the sling. Damn it hurt. Then quickly she reapplied the sling for support of his broken clavicle. A week of healing had made a big difference in the pain.

"I've wanted to talk to you about something," Elke said, "but with everything going on, I wasn't sure when it was a good time."

"What's up?" He buttoned the last of his shirt and followed his sister into the kitchen for lunch.

"According to Lilly, the arsonist told her a lot of uncanny information that relates to our committee." Elke handed him a plate with a sandwich.

"And?"

"She's a journalist! She could blow all of our efforts to keep this pirate stuff quiet."

Gunnar sighed and sat, took a long drink of the lemonade she'd already put at his place. He hadn't heard about the arsonist talking to Lilly before now. "When did he talk to her?"

"The night you were in surgery. I played down his claims saying we had plenty of seafaring stories to tell our tourists for entertainment. But combine that with our mayor all but telling her we had some big news to share, and I think a smart reporter like Lilly can run with a big story."

"I haven't seen any stories in the paper other than reporting on the partial burning of the Maritime Museum."

"So far," Elke said.

"Your point is?" Gunnar had quickly lost his appetite.

"I think it's time the committee makes an announcement. Our town deserves to know what we've discovered."

"She saw the aerial views of the Chinook burial ground, too," Gunnar said. "Even the heat images." Elke's eyes widened. He put his one good elbow on the table and leaned on it rather than take a bite of sandwich. "You're right. She could put two and two together and run with it on the front page. That would sell a few extra newspapers."

"It would be better for us to come out first." Elke leaned against the kitchen counter, playing with the ends of her long braid.

"Agreed."

"Should I call a meeting to discuss how best to do it?"

Gunnar nodded, trying to act nonchalant and lifting his sandwich as if his stomach wasn't tied up in a baseball-size knot. Lilly stumbling onto bits and pieces of the evidence was enough for any hungry journalist to dive into a meaty story. The committee definitely needed to beat her to the punch in order to ward off some of the sting.

It was going to be bad enough to tell the town their lovely little history lessons had all been wrong. Heartlandia had been discovered by a pirate who killed the natives and hoodwinked fisherman into working his ships. It was only after the first people, the Chinook, joined forces with the fed-up fisherman and their families that a major uprising occurred. Not to mention the sinking of Captain Prince's ship and his subsequent murder. Then the pirates settled down, got sick and died, or moved on, leaving Heartlandia to the Chinook and the Scandinavian immigrants. Heartlandia's history had only been recorded from that point on, whose idea that had been they'd never know.

Elke made some calls finding Leif and the others. Then making sure Ben's second-degree burns were healed enough for him to go out in public, she discovered his respiratory condition from smoke inhalation was the biggest problem. He wouldn't be able to attend a meeting until okayed by his doctor, which meant the meeting couldn't take place until early the next week. That left the weekend up for grabs at the *Heartlandia Herald*. The tight feeling in Gunnar's chest wasn't from the wound or broken bone. This time it was from the thought of Lilly blowing the whistle before they were ready.

He shouldn't have broken up with her. At least he could have kept better track of what she was doing that way, and picked her brain about what she knew. Like, where had she run off to today?

He couldn't exactly call and ask her to keep the lid on the story because he wasn't sure if she'd connected all the dots and he didn't want to tip her off more.

But if she had put it all together, it was highly unethical to ask a journalist, looking for a way to make a name for herself, to sit on the biggest breaking news in the history of Heartlandia.

Later that afternoon, a beautiful Japanese invitation arrived at Elke's house exclusively for Gunnar, hand delivered by a local middle schooler.

Under the circumstances, Lilly having him over the barrel with information, the fact she'd been incredibly sweet since he'd broken things off with her, and not to mention he still had feelings for her—big feelings—it was an invitation he couldn't refuse.

Gunnar did as he was told, arriving at Leif Andersen's residence around three on Sunday afternoon. He hadn't been cleared to drive yet, but since his left arm was the issue, he felt confident to drive himself over using only his right arm, rather than feel like a teenager with his sister dropping him off.

Leif was out of town, but the lock on the gate to the cottage had been left unlatched. He entered along the side of the guesthouse, overrun with ivy, purple potato vines and grape leaves pressing inward on the narrow pass. As Lilly had instructed in her note, he sat by the pool in a large wingback wicker chair she'd placed dead center on the interlocking pavement tiles. Since no other chair was around, he figured this one was meant for him.

A mild breeze tickled a delicate rice-paper-and-shell wind chime dangling from the roof over the front porch. It made a light tinkling sound that felt calming and intimate. He rested his head against the wicker and, though he hadn't had a pain pill since yesterday, felt as though he'd taken a tranquilizer as the sun warmed his face and tender shoulder. He closed his eyes and thought about what he intended to ask Lilly today. *Are you planning to run with a patchwork story? Wouldn't it be better to get the information straight before shouting it to the world? Would you be willing to wait a few days?*

A shadow quietly crossed before him. He cracked open his eyes. Lilly stood in front of the wicker chair, a soft and beautiful vision outlined by the clear powder-blue sky. Her hair was slicked back and she wore a morning-glory-blue kimono with a white sash making her look like a modern-day geisha. The sight rocked him to the core and nearly knocked him out of the chair. She smiled and Gunnar responded with a dumbfounded grin. Subtle warmth spread from his gut outward to his limbs as he could no longer deny that this crazy big-city sophisticated lady-gone-geisha was the woman he wanted in his life more than anyone.

The vision of loveliness combined with the lazy-afternoon sedation he'd just slipped into caused him to react slowly and dreamily. Overwhelmed by her presence, he struggled to find his voice. "Hi,' he said. It sounded harsh, breaking the peace that had settled between them. Completely out of character, Lilly bowed, her silence beckoning him back toward serenity.

"I'm so happy you're here," she whispered, handing him a pair of white socks with a pocket for the large toe. "These are called *tabi*. Please put them on."

She wore similar "socks" but with wooden sandals and matching morning-glory-blue brocade thong straps. He had a picture hanging in his bedroom of a geisha and he knew the term for the shoes was *zori*. He liked them. A lot. "What's up?"

His mind reeled at the thought of spending an afternoon with a gorgeous geisha who happened to be his ex-girlfriend.

She placed a long and delicate finger over her lips and waited patiently for him to remove his shoes and socks, which was awkward with one hand. When she saw him struggle, she came to his aid and removed the shoes. Her touch sent a flash flood of sensations through his body, wiping out the trance he'd just been in. What was she up to?

"Please remove your watch," she softly continued.

It wasn't like she was bossing him around or anything, but she'd made it known right off who was in charge. Honestly, he liked it, and under the circumstances, a beautiful woman giving all of her attention to him, he'd go along with the program. No problem.

The watch was on his left wrist so he took it off and handed it to her. She directed Gunnar along the garden stepping stones toward the back porch where she had placed a large basin of water to wash his hands. He washed the right one, well, splashed it around in the warm water anyway, and she helped him with the one in the sling then handed him a small towel. He managed to dry both hands on his own.

"What is all this?" he asked.

"Please, no talking. Just follow me."

Gunnar liked the little fantasy his personal geisha was taking him on. He consciously stopped his mind from wandering in the direction it was leaning. But a quick glimpse of him in a huge tub with Lilly washing his back managed to sneak past his guard. With the fantasy pressed firmly in his mind, he smothered a smile and followed her inside to the back room of the cottage, enjoying every trickle of gooseflesh she unknowingly tossed over him just by wearing that getup.

He stepped inside. Lilly had been busy transforming her guest cottage. A simple and unpretentious setting greeted him: a small ceramic fountain sat bubbling in the corner. Large pillows were carefully arranged on each side of a low-lying table with a single, near-perfect red camellia placed in a delicate porcelain vase at the center. Sandalwood incense wafted through the room. Koto music played softly and serenely in the background.

A scroll hung on the wall with a haiku written out in calligraphy. It read: "Tonight I am coming to visit you in your dream, and none will see and question me—be sure to leave your door unlocked! Anonymous."

Gunnar's skin prickled in response to the cryptic and ancient poem. He'd definitely be waiting for her tonight. No woman had ever come close to this display of, well, he wasn't sure what this whole thing was about, but figured it might have something to do with their breaking up.

He needed to stop thinking like a cop, just go with the flow, let Lilly take charge. Like the poem said, leave your door unlocked.

A floodgate opened in his chest and it filled with a new sensation he wasn't prepared to name out loud. How much time had they spent dancing around their feelings for each other the past six weeks? And when things got tough, Gunnar had snapped the budding relationship in two.

Lilly motioned for Gunnar to sit. Once again, he forced his mind back into the moment. She brought him a bowl of tofu in broth, helped him hold it with one hand and drink from the traditional Japanese bowl. Next came a simple meal of fish, stir-fried vegetables and steamed rice. The scene felt surreal, his geisha serving him, no conversation required, any guy's dream. Had all the pain meds he'd taken over the past few days come back to cause a hallucination? He smiled to himself. If so, she was one hell of a beautiful delusion.

Lilly joined him at the table, her fresh lemony scent overtaking the food, and they ate in silence, her helping him whenever he had trouble, since chopsticks weren't his forte. The atmosphere was perfect and he wanted to comment on it to be polite. But he also didn't want to break the magic of the moment by speaking, plus she'd warned him not to, so he went against his impulse for etiquette and respected her desire.

Lilly looked at him, smiled and, appearing far more humble than usual, she blushed. Enjoying her coy geisha persona, he grinned back. Wow, those dark eyes made him a little crazy in the head. He especially liked how the shells of her ears turned pink—her tell—to compliment her beautiful lips.

What would make her go out of her way to do all of this just for him? Was it because he'd been shot? Because they'd broken up? All the nights they'd made love came rushing back into his thoughts. Or that?

When the meal was done, she once again escorted him back outside to sit in the garden.

Disappointment surged. "Is that all?"

"Sit there. Wait for me." She put her finger over those beautiful lips again, turned and left him. He wanted to ask if there was anything he could help out with, but was afraid this pleasant dream of an afternoon might disappear if he did. And she was in charge. For once in his life, he'd step back, let go and let Lilly do her thing. He sat in the waning sun wondering what would be next, excited by the possibilities.

She appeared at the back door looking as beautiful as before, inviting him back inside. Once again, she led him to the table, which was set up for tea. He sat on the comfortable cushion and watched in silence as she placed the tea powder into a fine porcelain bowl, placed a dipper into a kettle of boiling water and filled it. Graceful and perfect in manner, she used a bamboo whisk to carefully whip the tea. Gunnar felt transported back in time, a regular shogun tea ceremony moment. Lilly bowed and presented to Gunnar the tea in a tiny, red-patterned ceramic cup.

He made an amused bow in response and accepted the cup, taking one sip while fighting off the constant stream of chills circulating his skin. The tea tasted tart at first then surprisingly, sweetness lingered.

Lilly reached for the cup and turned it slightly then handed it back for a second sip and, repeating the same ritual, then a third sip. Each movement was repeated exactly as the first. She'd studied her art of serving tea well, and he suspected her sobo'd had a lot to do with the tradition. Seeing this humbler side of Lilly went straight to his heart. What kind of a jerk would break up with her before completely getting to know her?

A guy who'd thought she'd betrayed him, that's who. At least, that was how he'd seen it, always thinking in black and white.

Yet she'd sworn it wasn't true.

When she finished serving his tea, she offered and fed to him a small jellied sweet, which had a distinct apricot flavor.

Lilly then wiped the rim of the cup with a white cloth before repeating the same tea-drinking practice herself. Gunnar watched the ceremony with admiration. It struck him that in this way they partook of their own personal communion and that unnamed feeling flying around in his chest grew stronger. Was this her way of apologizing, or was she trying to tell him that she loved him? Unsure of the particular message, the power of the endeavor was

coming through loud and clear. He was special to her…
as she was to him. But how had he shown it to her? By
breaking up with her over a news article.

The Koto music ended.

They finished sipping their tea in silence. Every time
Gunnar looked at her, her eyes danced away making it
hard to read her game plan. Why was she lavishing all of
this attention on him when he'd been rude and pigheaded
and had broken things off in that coffee shop?

She'd had him so dazed with her beauty and the sensations she'd conjured up, he'd forgotten the obvious reason for all of this. In her own humble way she was trying
to rebuild his respect and trust. She'd shared the cup with
him, wiping their troubles clean. At least that was how
he'd interpreted it. Who knew what the real ceremony was
supposed to represent? Maybe it was just about sharing
tea with someone special.

Wasn't it about time for him to learn to yield graciously?
Lilly's time and effort with the ancient ceremony had
rubbed off on him, making him think about the future.

Lilly cleared her throat, placed her hands on her thighs
and finally broke the solitude. "I want to explain something." Her voice sounded thin and wavering. She sat on
her heels moving her hands to rest in her lap. She paused
and seemed to struggle for composure, fighting back emotion.

He wanted to reach out for her, yet he knew she had
something important to say and didn't want to interfere
or ruin anything.

"In my family, honor means everything. I had a lot of
making up to do just by being born a girl as far as my father was concerned. He taught me the consequences of
dishonoring the family name, browbeat it into me, and

now that I'm independent of him, I still give him power over my life.

"My sobo showed me that being true to myself was honorable. She gave me the courage to claim journalism as my major, no matter how upset my father was about it. But I never completely broke free of my father's hold. And I've made bad choices because of that.

"Whether I think of his form of honor or my grandmother's, I see now that I dishonored you with my duplicity. I wanted that big story. I wanted to make a name for myself, no matter what the cost. And I tricked myself into believing I was just doing my job, that it was expected of me. Now I've lost you and your trust in me and the cost is greater than I can bear. I want more than anything to earn it back."

She reached for his hands, grasped them and squeezed.

"Gunnar, what I've learned these past several weeks from knowing you, and how you've risen above your father's example, is I can do that, too. You've shown me that it isn't about being in the spotlight, it's about doing what's right.

"Please forgive me, Gunnar. I will change. I am changing just from knowing you and being here in Heartlandia."

He couldn't keep quiet another second.

"Lilly. Sweetheart." He tightened his grip of her hands. "I'm a hard-nosed SOB sometimes because of my father, and I've been thinking I've been way too hard on you. I can't dictate what you should or shouldn't report. It wasn't convenient for me if you broke the story, and I was being selfish. I threw around the word *trust* like a pompous jerk, expecting you to do all the changing. The thing is, I can't be in control of everything, and I don't want to control you. Will you forgive me?"

"Forgive you? Of course I will. I love you, Gunnar," she

said with a quivering voice. "I love you so much I don't know how I'd breathe without you."

The words burst into his chest and scattered, forcing his heart open to the root. She loved him, too.

Lilly rose up on her knees, let go of his hands and reached across to hold his face. Her hands trembled as she drew him near and gently kissed him. This one special kiss, knowing she loved him, bonded them like nothing else could. Talk about giving someone a second chance, and by Buddha, this time he'd handle things completely different. He'd learn from his mistakes and do everything right…the way she deserved.

"I've made some mistakes," she said, "but I want to make things right with you."

Her soft, warm lips were eager to take his again. So hungry for her, he was more than willing to oblige. He wrapped his arm around her and drew her close. A flame of passion sparked in every part of his body. She'd taken a huge risk by going first. It seemed only fair to tell her his plans, too.

Breathless, he broke away just long enough to get the words out. "Sweetheart, I've loved you since the day at the hospital when you came to see me even though I'd just broken up with you. I couldn't have been happier to see you." He covered her mouth and kissed her lightly.

This time Lilly broke away. "You love me, too?"

He nodded, smiled. "Oh, yeah." Then he moved to kiss her again.

Lilly pulled back from his embrace and looked directly into his stare. She must have felt his ragged breath against her cheek, saw the raw desire in his eyes since he reeled with longing.

He lifted her hand to his mouth, kissed the palm and squeezed her fingers tightly trying to harness his hunger.

He continued to breathe heavily, yet he never wavered from her stare.

"Let me make love to you," she said. "Trust me."

He swallowed, using every last ounce of power to resist her. "I do." He kissed her quickly again, then looked around the room hoping to find the right words to express these overwhelming feelings.

Lilly backed away and stood quiet, biting her lower lip, seeming to hold back what she wanted to say. He stepped closer and tenderly cupped her face with his good hand. He traced his fingertips across her cheek and ran his thumb along her lower lip then down to her chin, cherishing each centimeter. His gaze followed the path, and he'd never seen a finer face. He'd never felt someone else's pain as easily, or shared in the simple joy they'd found together. He'd never loved anyone like this. "If we're getting back together, I want to make sure we do everything right, but with my bum shoulder it will be tough to make love the way I want."

"Let me take care of everything," she said.

What was she suggesting? "I can't exactly lay back and let you do all the work."

"Do you trust me?"

Ah, gee, she'd used the trust card, and wasn't that what all of this was about—regaining his trust? He couldn't exactly put his foot down and be his usual overbearing self. Hell, he'd just promised to change, too. He wanted to be with her more than ever, but one handed lovemaking… damn. She was waiting for his answer, and he'd probably made her think he had to think about whether he trusted her or not, which wasn't the case at all.

"Of course I trust you," he blurted without further thought. For the first time in his life he was thinking about spending the rest of his life with one special person. Wasn't it about time, like he'd thought just a few moments ago, that he learned to compromise…to bend? And most important, learned true grace.

Lilly didn't say another word. Neither did he. She took his one good hand and led him into the bedroom.

Chapter Fifteen

Lilly had thought up a part to the tea ceremony her grandmother would probably never imagine. She brought Gunnar into her bedroom, the bedspread already folded back, fresh silk sheets scented with roses, and felt his hand tighten in hers—a promise of things to come. Sandalwood-candle aroma filled the room as she'd lit the multiple votives just before she'd served tea. Out with the old. In with the new.

Gunnar stopped her, turned her toward him and kissed her again, his lips firm and hungry, melting through her like one of those candles.

She unbuttoned his shirt and tenderly pulled apart the Velcro sling, loving the sight of his chest and muscles, aching over the bandaged wound on the left shoulder.

She could tell he fought showing the pain that the simple act of lowering his arm brought on, so after removing the shirt, she quickly reapplied the black sling, leaving him otherwise topless. She kissed his right shoulder and the opposite side of the broken clavicle, then the notch at the base of his throat before walking him backward toward her waiting bed. She'd clicked the remote on the dining table and started the Koto music again, its strange ancient plucking sound being somehow perfect for the moment. Using one finger to push his chest, she forced him to sit on the edge of the bed then removed the *tabi* she'd given him earlier for his feet. Next came his jeans. Without being asked, he stood to help her out with a wink, a very cooperative partner.

Down came the jeans, then his briefs, fully exposing him, proving he was already coming to life. "What about you?" he asked.

She resorted to the gesture she'd used several times already this afternoon, placing one finger to her lips, looking deep into his eyes.

She gestured for him to lie down, and he did, smack in the center of her bed, curiously watching her every move. She walked to the right side of the bed and removed her *zoris* and *tabis*. Next she tended to the sash from her kimono, unwinding it over and over until the satin belt hung free, loosening the kimono in the process. She took his right hand, kissed the palm then put a slipknot around his wrist and before he realized what she'd done, tied his one good arm to the bedpost.

He looked amused, not the least bit concerned.

With a demure smile she slid the kimono over her shoulders revealing she'd been completely naked beneath for the entire tea ceremony.

Seeing the desire flaming in his stare, her breasts tightened. She got on the bed and sat primly on her heels as she had throughout the ceremony, exploring the skin on his torso, thighs and chest. He hissed in breath after breath as her explorations deepened, while adding kisses and nips wherever she pleased.

Gritting his teeth throughout, over the next several minutes Gunnar let her do any- and everything she wanted to him, showing complete trust.

He was already fully aroused and tall and she took her time, enjoying the feel of him, the smooth, the rough, the slick. One firm squeeze sent him sucking in more air, and even deeper breaths when she first kissed, then filled her mouth with him.

He moaned and squirmed on the mattress. "I can't take much more of this."

Hearing his plea, she sheathed and straddled him. Even though both were at the height of excitement already, they took their time, her hips gently rolling over him, rising and falling in sweet counter rhythm. It seemed every nerve ending inside worked overtime forwarding thrilling messages to all points north and south, all the way down to her toes and to the top of her head. He dug his heels into the mattress, pumped up the pace, and finding her special spot, she moaned. Then he homed in on it, sending hot jets through her center up and over her hips and back, growing the intensity to nearly unbearable, and soon giving her release.

Her fingers dug into his chest; senses completely overloaded she gasped, and he joined her as they tumbled together in what seemed like slow motion over the brink of paradise.

She collapsed on top of his taut, warm body and for several moments she basked in the afterglow of his love, gathering her breath, feeling her pulse return to normal.

"Are you going to keep me tied up like this or let me hold you now?"

She pecked his lips with a flighty kiss then undid the sash. One strong arm gathered her close making her feel secure and loved. Both exhausted, they cuddled in the bed surrounded by candlelight at dusk.

* * *

Gunnar needed to tell Lilly a few things. They'd forged into a completely new phase of their relationship this afternoon thanks to her taking the risk. Now it was his turn to take a risk and prove beyond all doubt that he trusted her. With everything.

He cleared his throat. "The reason I got so mad at you running the article on Mayor Rask was because you were getting too close to our secret."

Lilly's head bopped up faster than a jack-in-the-box. "Your secret?"

"Heartlandia's secret. At least that's what we've been trying to do with the information, keep it a secret. Until we're ready to tell the whole town everything we've found out, that is."

"Are you sure you want me to know this?"

"More than I've ever been in my life." He refused to throw in the term "off the record."

She gave a tender smile, almost solemn, indicating the significance of what he was about to do. "You're talking about the committee?"

"Yes." He nodded.

"The one I've been spying on."

"So you finally admit you've been spying on me." He softened the tease with a quick smile.

Totally focused on the carrot he dangled before her, she obviously chose to ignore his little dig. "The meetings at city hall?"

"Correct." He took Lilly's face in his hand and looked her square in the eyes. "Only because I trust you with everything I have, I'm going to tell you what's going on." Then he kissed her forehead, but not before noticing her eyes dancing with candlelight and wonder.

Was he making a mistake? If he loved her and she loved him, he couldn't be.

After shifting his position in bed, moving up so his head and shoulders rested on the headboard, he proceeded to tell her the whole story. How Leif Andersen had discovered the trunk filled with a sea captain's journals, small treasures, nautical artifacts, guides, charts, compass and chronometer when breaking ground for the city college. How his sister, Elke, had pored over the journals deciphering the notations, and discovering that Captain Nathaniel Prince, also known as The Prince of Doom, was a pirate who'd stolen men from up and down the Oregon coast, forcing them to work on his ships, until he crashed off the shore of what was to become Heartlandia and settled in. How he had continued his unscrupulous practices from this very spot until the night the Scandinavian fisherman teamed up with the Chinook and overtook their suppressors. They'd pieced together the rest of the information and figured out he was murdered by one of his own men shortly thereafter.

Gunnar explained the unfortunate timing of their mayor dying and Gerda Rask stepping in as mayor pro tem without knowing any of this, only then to be hit with the outlandish news. How the committee had been formed to figure out what they'd discovered in the trunk, and what to do about the information they'd unearthed. How at first they'd thought the whole incident amusing, something to add to the Maritime Museum to draw more visitors. Then how they realized this was a huge part of their history that had been suppressed and left out of the schoolbooks and needed to be addressed.

He watched Lilly, who sat rapt listening to his tale, hoping beyond hope she wouldn't pounce on the story of her lifetime before the time was right.

"To make matters worse, Captain Prince had hinted at buried treasure, and unfortunately, his handmade map and legend points to a spot located in our sacred Chinook burial ground. That's our current problem, and that was the picture you stumbled onto at my house. The infrared thermography shows what might be the trunk smack in the middle of those grounds."

Lilly rolled onto her back holding her head as if it would explode if she let go. "This is crazy!"

"Tell me about it."

"No wonder you didn't want me snooping around."

"In a twisted kind of way you've forced our hand, made us think about bringing this information out in the open. Letting our citizens help decide what to do next."

"It only seems fair." She'd come up on her elbow and pinned him with an earnest gaze. "But then, I'm an outsider, what do I know?"

"You're not an outsider anymore. You've become one of us."

"Then I say, tell the people. See how they feel."

"It does blow our perfect little history right out of the Columbia River, you know?"

She chewed her lower lip and nodded, eyes intense. "But it's the right thing to do, and you always do the right thing."

He put his hand on her forearm and squeezed. "And that's why we need to find the best time to announce the news and have our plans firmly in place for handling the results before we do." He made his pitch to Lilly for holding back on releasing the information. The rest was up to her.

"When's that?"

"We don't know yet."

"Wow, so that arsonist wasn't crazy after all, just criminal."

"Yup. And turns out the fun 'urban legends' that have always floated around, the ones we've used to amuse our tourists, have always been based in truth."

She sat up and stared at him. "Talk about a major cover-up."

"A centuries-old cover-up."

She bobbed her head in agreement. "And ancient revenge." Referring back to the recent fires.

He got lost in her brown depths, wondering what was going on in her mind. He also couldn't help but notice her ears were bright red, which usually meant she was excited or thinking extra hard.

His throat tightened. He loved Lilly, and because of it, he couldn't dictate what he thought she should do, he could only suggest. "That's why I'd like to ask you to write the story...but not until we're ready to tell the town."

"Really?"

"I know you'll be careful, sensitive to detail. Tell it the way it needs to be told."

"You trust me to be the town mouthpiece?"

"With all my heart, but the story isn't quite ready to be heard yet."

"I get it." She took his hand. "It's not always about my timeline. In this case, I understand how important it is to wait until your committee is ready to come out with it."

Trusting her with everything, Gunnar reached out. "Come here, Chitcha."

She obliged, snuggling close to his chest, kissing him sweetly.

Lilly respected the rock and a hard place the committee had been put in. He knew it down to his bones. If she sat on the story for just a while longer, respecting the mayor's wishes, being sensitive to telling the details at the right time, she'd have the major story of her lifetime and he'd have one last and very important question to ask her. And it had something to do with spending the rest of their lives together.

She'd spent the afternoon impressing upon him that she was worthy of his trust. Through her tea ceremony they'd wiped the slate clean. Right now, all he wanted was to get lost in Lilly's love again, to show her how he felt about her, and forget anything and everything that had to do with the town secret.

She must have read his mind, because her expression changed. Those brown depths only focused on him. He couldn't be one-hundred-percent sure if it was him or the story that had suddenly turned her on again, making her ears light up and all, but right this moment with her kissing him crazy, he really didn't care.

Monday morning Gunnar took a deep breath and opened the newspaper. No headline about the committee. Not one word buried in the back of the *Herald* about the story, either. Whew. It was his first day back at work, where he'd be on desk duty for at least a month, and he was glad to be on the job again. Hell, he'd had to twist Kent's arm to sign him off medical leave, but last Friday, after agreeing to only work inside, his buddy had given him the okay. He'd felt lost the whole week at Elke's. Recuperating had been a pain in the…well…shoulder, and had driven the point home how much his job had to do with his identity.

Until yesterday when Lilly had taken him on a surreal trip to ancient Japanese tradition.

He drove and gulped some coffee from his traveler's cup and forced his mind back into the moment, and the day ahead.

It might be boring working the desk, but it was better

than sitting at home feeling sorry for himself. Plus, an emergency meeting for the city hall committee had been called that night, which would surely be interesting. He'd prepared himself to take the fall if Lilly took the story and ran with it, and honestly, he was still holding his breath but choosing to believe in her promises and honorable intentions. She'd changed. Hadn't she proved it to him with the tea ceremony? A woman couldn't very well personify harmony, purity, tranquility and respect one moment then make a play for headline news in the next, could she?

As he parked his car and walked into work, he texted Lilly:

Have I told you lately that I love you?

He entered the building and there stood Lilly at the door to the newspaper, dressed in a pencil skirt, open-collared white blouse with a single, simple string of pearls around her neck, and hair back to its short, springy, fun style, her cell phone in hand.

After Sunday afternoon, they'd stayed away from each other last night. It had been hard, but he needed to move back home from Elke's, and Wolverine needed some extra attention. To be honest, she'd worn him out with her traditional "tea" ceremony, and he realized the gunshot had taken more out of him than he'd thought.

Lilly smiled and waved. Making a snap decision, he strode directly toward her and kissed her as if he hadn't seen her in weeks. After, she had that discombobulated gaze, which he always dug, and her ears pinked up. "Meet for lunch?"

"Sure," she said.

"I'll text you when I know what time."

By the time he walked through the police department door he got her reply text.

Love you, too.

He grinned and walked straighter.

So far, the day had gotten off to a great start.

Later, over yellow pea soup and mixed baby greens in the Hartalanda Café, he told her about that night's meeting. Her eyes widened, but she didn't pursue the subject. This was a welcome change and it forced Gunnar to realize they'd both grown since they'd broken up and he'd gotten shot. He understood her perspective better as a news reporter, and she seemed to appreciate the need for Heartlandia to remain the town with a storybook history.

As they left that topic behind, they alternated between eating and gazing at each other. Things had definitely changed between them for the better. They'd both needed some major attitude adjustments and all of the events of the past couple of weeks had forced that on them. He drank his soda and remembered the first day she'd arrived, all fashion model and attitude, and right now, how especially glad he was that she'd jaywalked.

Seven o'clock at night Monday, Gunnar entered city hall and headed to the conference room. Everyone but Elke and Ben were there, and surprisingly, a few minutes later, they came in together. Ben's second-degree burns from the first arson fire were still noticeable but healing around his neck and jaw. His frequent cough proved his lungs were still in the process of healing. Elke looked happy, and Gunnar wondered what was up with that?

Come to think of it, she'd gotten a few phone calls while he'd stayed at her house, which she always went into the other room to take. He'd assumed it had something to do with the city college, but maybe he'd been wrong.

At 7:05 p.m. Gerda Rask called the meeting to order. "I think we all know why we're here tonight," she began. "Before we get started with our discussion, does anyone have any new business?"

Gunnar smiled inwardly. Did falling in love count?

Elke raised her hand. "I wanted to inform everyone that we've selected the artist to paint the city college mural. Her name is Marta Hoyas and she is the great-great-granddaughter of the sculptor who created our town monument. She comes from Sedona, Arizona, and plans to arrive in Heartlandia next month."

"That's great news," Gerda said, the others joining in with quiet applause. "It's good to hear something positive for a change."

"We'll need to find a place for her to stay, though."

"That's something we can decide when the time grows closer." Gerda's expression quickly changed, growing serious again. "Now I'd like to open up a discussion about our problem and how best to handle it."

"I think we should hold a town meeting and inform our citizens about the error in our town history," Adamine Olsen, the business woman on the committee said.

"I agree, but this should be a two-phase deal," Leif Andersen chimed in. "Tell the first part now, but hold off on the buried treasure part until later. Let them take in the first part before we bowl them over with more crazy news."

"Agreed," Gunnar said.

"Maybe we can distract them with the shipwreck information," said Jarl Madsen, the director of the half-destroyed-by-fire Maritime Museum. "They can concentrate on finding that for a while, then after things calm down, we can bring up the sacred burial ground issue."

This brought on a long and drawn-out discussion about how best to handle the shipwreck along with all of the other information.

When the committee had talked and argued about their sticky situation, and finally come to a consensus, Gerda stepped back in. "Our first order of business is making a public statement about our findings at the college. Then holding a town meeting for those interested telling more about it."

"We could use the *Heartlandia Herald* as a source of information," Gunnar said. "Getting the complete story out there, but holding back on the buried treasure at this point. Lilly Matsuda would be perfect for the job."

"Once the dust has settled on the pirate part, we can reveal the shipwreck, maybe invite teams to search for it," said Jarl. "Make it a fund-raiser to help rebuild our Maritime Museum,"

"Great idea," said Adamine. "That could help our local merchants, too."

"I don't think we should mention the buried treasure." Ben's soft-spoken voice drew everyone's attention to him and squashed the swell of enthusiasm over rebuilding the museum. "It will upset too many people. Just keep the secret."

"We could have a vote whether or not to dig up the treasure or leave it there. What do you think?" Adamine continued.

"I don't think we should," Ben insisted. "It will divide our town."

The room fell silent.

"Let's call a vote on the first part," Gerda said. "We'll deal with the buried treasure at a later time."

Gunnar nodded. Hopefully that vote would come at a much, much later date.

* * *

Wednesday morning, Lilly's bi-weekly column—I Dream of Sushi in Storybook Land—was on the second page as usual, her bright-faced picture right beside it. The good news was, the front-page headline was about Heartlandia choosing the artist for the city college mural, and nothing about the meetings.

They'd decided to unfold the news in three parts. First, announcing a citywide meeting at the community college auditorium, then the mayor's speech and finally Elke discussing the historical authenticity of the journals.

Of course there would also be a question and answer component including all of the committee members, but all had agreed to hold off on disclosing the whereabouts of the potential hidden treasure for now. They all hoped to distract from that with the possible shipwreck.

Gunnar had secured Lilly and the *Heartlandia Herald* as the main source of information for the town. It was a huge responsibility that Gunnar knew without a doubt Lilly could handle. Smiling, he began reading today's column.

Heartlandia has grown on me. Two months ago I arrived in town as an outsider looking for a way in. Today, having had the opportunity to meet and learn about so many of the wonderful citizens in town through this column by telling your stories, I feel like one of you. Yes, I still dream of sushi and hope Cliff Lincoln of Lincoln's Place will add it to his menu one day alongside his soul food, and I miss my roots in San Francisco, but there's one thing I don't miss. Feeling anonymous. It's easy to exist in the shadows of big cities, to get lost in the daily routine, focused on navigating the streets instead of getting to know the inhabitants. Here in Heartlandia, that's impossible. You've invited me into your lives through sharing your jobs, recipes, family stories and rich Scandinavian and Chinook history. You've initiated me into the wealth of Heartlandia with smiling faces, pride for your heritage and a willingness to learn about mine. More importantly, you've taught me honor, honor that is earned by keeping tradition alive, by taking the skills passed down from ancestors and putting a personal touch to them. By carrying out time-tested chores without seeking glory. I finally see that I don't have to blow the top off of Heartlandia with an earth-shattering story to make my name. I can celebrate the people of this community who embrace the simple, everyday joys in life, which is a sure sign of down-home wisdom. Thank you for sharing and showing me that.

Most of all, one person in particular has taught me there is more to life than a great news scoop. Thank you, Sergeant Norling, for teaching me about the hazards of jaywalking, for opening my heart, for teaching me to work with others and for setting me back on the right path.

Today, I salute the people of Heartlandia for helping me find my new home. Thank you for adding me to your roll call.

Grinning, thinking what a great gal he'd fallen for, Gunnar paged through the rest of the newspaper. Something on the next-to-last page snagged his attention: "Maritime Museum Arsonist Rants About Ancient Revenge, by Lilly Matsuda."

With the arrest of Roald Lindstrom, accused arsonist of Olaf's Microbrewery and the Maritime Museum, come claims of justification for starting the two fires. The accused was enrolled in the Heartlandia City College extension program, studying genealogy when he found, what he insists, is evidence of his relatives being shanghaied by pirates three hundred years ago, citing this as his motive for setting the two fires. Mr. Lindstrom will be arraigned on charges of arson and attempted murder of a police officer once he has been found of sound mind and able to face trial. At the time of this publication, the accused unemployed factory worker stands by his story.

Perfect. She'd handled the information like a true journalist, not a writer for a gossip rag flaming the fire of controversy, though in this case she certainly could have. The focus on the man's mental instability was the perfect ending to the brief article, casting doubt on Roald's motives and putting the onus back on him instead of his relatives possibly being shanghaied by pirates.

Gunnar checked his watch. It was only nine-thirty on his midweek day off, since he was scheduled to work that Saturday. But it wasn't too early to take his best gal out for a ride. He'd made a trip to Sven's Jewels on Tuesday and something was burning a hole in his pocket. Maybe if he asked real nice, Bjork would let him borrow Lilly for the rest of the day.

An hour and a half later they drove in silence up the hillside to his favorite lookout spot. He'd stopped at the market and picked up some fruit, cheese, crusty bread, and chocolate, plus some fancy bottled tea to share, something to draw out the moments while they enjoyed the view of the Columbia River off in the distance.

It was a crisp, clear, last-of-summer kind of day with twinges of fall making the sunshine more golden than bright. He parked and grabbed the grocery bag of goodies, wishing he could take Lilly's hand and lead her to the bench, cursing the sling, even though right now it served a perfect and important purpose.

She sighed when she sat and looked out over the pine trees below and outward to the body of water. In the far distance was the superlong bridge connecting Oregon to Washington.

He'd come here throughout his life whenever he'd needed time to think things over. He'd hidden out up here the day his father had left, the day he'd had his first kiss, when he'd finally saved up enough money to buy his first car, the night before he'd graduated from high school, the afternoon he'd applied for the police force and the day before he'd made up his mind to purchase the land and build his house. This weathered old wooden bench had seen him through many deep thinking sessions. Always seeking the wisdom and solitude of Heartlandia, he'd never, in all the years, brought someone with him.

It wasn't as if the place was a secret or anything. Plenty of people knew about the spot. But to him, it was almost sacred ground.

"It's so beautiful here," Lilly said, drawing him out of his memories.

"I knew you'd like it."

"Wow. I could use a place like this to run away to on tough days."

"Or great days. Milestone days. That's why I've always come here." He opened the bag and placed the contents, as best as he could with one hand, between them to share. "Feel free to borrow it anytime." If she picked up on the significance of bringing her here, she didn't let on.

Instead she stared out over the vista nibbling bread and cheese, then popped a grape into her mouth.

They sat in silence, enjoying the weather and view, and each basking in the comfort of the other. They'd come a long way in six and a half weeks, from strangers to lovers to today. A very special day by all standards.

For the sake of not seeming nervous, though he really was, he ate and drank some tea. "I'm planning on taking the lieutenant's exam next month."

"That's great."

"Have I mentioned I also plan to be the chief of police before I turn forty?"

"No, but I think you'd be perfect for the job."

"And mayor after that?"

She paused from eating some bread. "Seriously?"

"I've wanted to be mayor since I was a kid, like my favorite chief of police was. He's my role model."

She studied him, munching on another grape. "You can do it."

The way she'd said it, there was no doubt she believed in him, and it felt damn great.

He gulped another drink of the flavored bottled tea, finally deciding to broach the foremost subject on his mind. "Will you be able to put up with a guy that driven?"

"Oh, that's right, you haven't met my parents yet, have you." She wasn't making it easy on him, playing dumb on the one hand and self-deprecatingly snarky on the other.

Gunnar laughed anyway, her smart-alecky remark helping to take the edge off his nerves. He'd never done this before, had never had the slightest desire to. He looked toward the river to calm his jitters and gather his words.

Lilly must have picked up on his silence. "I'll put up with your being the mayor if you'll put up with me as a newspaper mogul."

Now they were getting somewhere. "Only seems fair."

"Bjork told me he plans to retire next year, and I already told him I want to buy him out when he does. The guy looked so excited that I think he might be revising his plans for earlier."

"That's fantastic, Lilly." So she was definitely sticking around, a really good sign, considering what he wanted to ask. "Did I also mention I've given Leif the okay to start building the next phase of my house?"

"You've been doing a lot of thinking and planning while you recuperated."

"Yeah, so I'm thinking about getting a roommate."

That grabbed her attention. Her head snapped toward him.

"You interested?"

The corner of her mouth twitched, and she scratched it. "Only if you put a ring on that offer."

"Why, Lilly Matsuda, are you asking me to marry you?"

She tossed her gaze at the sky in frustration. "You're the one who brought it—" stopping midsentence she noticed him fish something out from his sling. He'd kept the small, velvet box hidden there in case the perfect moment cropped up, which it just had "—up." She snapped her mouth closed appearing dumbfounded.

When he knew he had her undivided attention, he started the short speech he'd rehearsed all morning after reading the newspaper.

"I don't have a beautiful tea ceremony to show you how much I love you, but I do know one tradition." Gunnar stood then dropped down onto one knee. He opened the box, exposing a simple white-gold band with a solitaire diamond surrounded by tiny emeralds. Taking out the ring, he reached for her hand, then slid the delicate ring onto an equally delicate finger. "Will you marry me, Lilly?"

She'd grown oddly quiet, but from the sudden gushing of tears, followed by her flinging her arms around his neck, almost knocking him off balance and nearly squeezing the life out of him, he figured she'd heard every word.

As if on cue, a Western Meadowlark sang from the shelter of a nearby tree.

Gunnar grinned, feeling all was right with the world, holding the woman he loved and trusted with all his heart, and having a pretty darn solid hunch what her answer to his marriage proposal would be.

* * * * *

Watch for the final installment of
THE SECRET OF HEARTLANDIA *series*
when the town discovers their true history
and must decide what to do about hidden
treasure in the sacred burial ground.

MILLS & BOON®

The Chatsfield Collection!

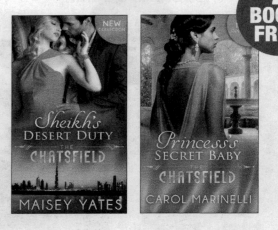

2 BOOKS FREE!

Style, spectacle, scandal...!

With the eight Chatsfield siblings happily married and settling down, it's time for a new generation of Chatsfields to shine, in this brand-new 8-book collection! The prospect of a merger with the Harrington family's boutique hotels will shape the future forever. But who will come out on top?

Find out at
www.millsandboon.co.uk/TheChatsfield2

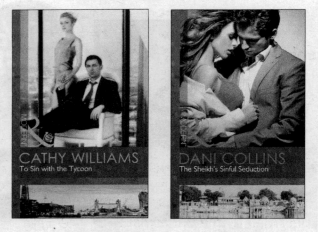

MILLS & BOON®

Cherish™

EXPERIENCE THE ULTIMATE RUSH OF FALLING IN LOVE

A sneak peek at next month's titles...

In stores from 20th March 2015:

- **The Millionaire and the Maid** – Michelle Douglas
  and **The CEO's Baby Surprise** – Helen Lacey

- **Expecting the Earl's Baby** – Jessica Gilmore
  and **The Taming of Delaney Fortune** – Michelle Major

In stores from 3rd April 2015:

- **Best Man for the Bridesmaid** – Jennifer Faye
  and **The Cowboy's Homecoming** – Donna Alward

- **It Started at a Wedding...** – Kate Hardy
  and **A Decent Proposal** – Teresa Southwick

Available at WHSmith, Tesco, Asda, Eason, Amazon and Apple

Just can't wait?
Buy our books online a month before they hit the shops!
visit www.millsandboon.co.uk

These books are also available in eBook format!

0315/23